Eve Chase always wanted to write about families — ones that go wrong but somehow survive; and big old houses, where secrets and untold stories seed in the crumbling stone walls. Growing up with three brothers, she particularly loved creating the four Wilde sisters in this novel, a spirited sisterhood that felt like her own. Eve is married with three children and lives in Oxford.

You can discover more about the author at www.evechase.com

THE VANISHING OF AUDREY WILDE

When fifteen-year-old Margot and her three sisters arrive at Applecote Manor during the heatwave of 1959, they find their aunt and uncle still reeling from the disappearance of their daughter, Audrey, five years before. The sisters are drawn into the mystery of Audrey's vanishing — until the stifling summer takes a shocking, deadly turn. Will one unthinkable choice bind them together, or tear them apart? Fifty years later, Applecote captivates Jessie with its promise of hazy summers in the Cotswolds. She believes it's the perfect escape for her troubled family. But she finds herself increasingly isolated in their new sprawling home, at odds with her teenage stepdaughter, and haunted by the strange rumours that surround the manor . . .

EVE CHASE

◆

THE VANISHING OF AUDREY WILDE

Complete and Unabridged

CHARNWOOD
Leicester

First published in Great Britain in 2017 by
Michael Joseph
an imprint of Penguin Books
London

First Charnwood Edition
published 2018
by arrangement with
Penguin Random House UK
London

A catalogue record for this book is available
from the British Library.

ISBN 978–1–4448–3892–3

Published by
F. A. Thorpe (Publishing)
Anstey, Leicestershire

Set by Words & Graphics Ltd.
Anstey, Leicestershire
Printed and bound in Great Britain by
T. J. International Ltd., Padstow, Cornwall

This book is printed on acid-free paper

For Ben

I know a bank where the wild thyme blows,
Where oxlips and the nodding violet grows
Quite over-canopied with luscious woodbine,
With sweet musk-roses and with eglantine . . .

A Midsummer Night's Dream,
William Shakespeare

Prologue

Applecote Manor, the Cotswolds, England. The last weekend of August, 1959

None of us can bear to touch his belt, so horrifyingly intimate. But as we drag him across the lawn it ploughs into the soil. He's heavier than he looks too, unwieldy. Every few steps we stop and catch our breath, startling at each other's faces in the dawn light, daring each other to look down at the unbelievable fleshy fact of him, the childlike abandon of his outstretched arms.

Daisies are stuck to him now, their pink-white petals opening to the sun that is rising at a worrying speed behind the orchard. There's something very wrong about these daisies, stars in the dark stickiness of his hair. Dot leans forward as if to pluck them out, sit down and thread them into a chain over the hammock of her gingham skirt. If she did, it wouldn't make anything stranger.

Another few stumbling steps, and Dot's spectacles fall off. She starts to scrabble for them. We tell her to stop. There is no time. The birds are starting to sing, all at once, an explosion of noise, a wild loop of fear.

I try to talk myself down from blind panic: we are the same girls we were at the beginning of this long, hot summer. Applecote Manor still stands behind us, gazing sleepily over the valley. And in the meadow beyond the garden gate, our beloved circle of prehistoric stones, unchanged, unchanging. We need to get him much closer to those stones, away from the house and fast — the orangery's glass roof is glinting dangerously in the first rays of sun, even closer than we thought.

A whoosh of nausea folds me in half. I cough, hands on my knees. Flora slips her arm over my shoulders. Feeling her tremble, I look up, try to reassure her, but can't.

Eyes full of fear and light, she blinks repeatedly, as if adjusting to something in my face she hasn't seen before.

Pam, jaw clenched, starts tugging at his shirtsleeve. But the fabric is no match for the dead weight of his arm and it rips, the noise horrible, deafening. Dot smothers a sob with her hand.

'It's all right, Dot — ' I stop short, noticing a splatter of blood across her fingers.

I lower my gaze to check my own hands. Flora's. Pam's. My stomach rolls again. Our summer dresses are butcher's aprons. We all look like we killed him now, not just one of us. Sisters. Bonded by blood.

1

Crime. Crowds. The way a big city forces girls to grow up too fast, strips them of their innocence. It's time for the family to leave London, move somewhere gentler, more benign. They've viewed a number of houses in the last three months — the estate agents' brief, rural, roomy, a doer-upper — but not one that Jessie felt could be called home. Until this moment: standing in Applecote Manor on a late January afternoon, feeling as if she's being filled with sunlight.

It's in a right state, of course. They couldn't hope to afford a house like this otherwise. Evergreens are packed hard against the orangery's windows, threatening to break them and scatter the wooden window-seat with poisonous berries, like beads. The stone flags on the floor undulate, rising in the centre of the room as if a creature might be pushing up from the earth. But Jessie is already imagining oranges dangling, blood-warm and heavy in the hand, the glass doors flung back to the euphoria of summer, the peal of girls' wild laughter.

Her face soft, opening, Jessie tracks the paned glass as it climbs to its geometrical peak, a feat of Victorian engineering that promises tangy Mediterranean fruit in the English climate among the woolly pippins. Something about that

3

optimism — control through enclosure, a sort of forced nurturing — whispers in her ear: isn't she trying to do something similar, only with a family?

Jessie glances at Bella, who is slumped on the window-seat, pecking out a text on her mobile phone. A twist of too-long legs and inky hair, her sixteen-year-old stepdaughter is the striking spit of her dead mother, the first Mrs Tucker. Sensing Jessie's questioning gaze, she lifts her pale, aquiline face, narrows her eyes to glossy pupil-filled cracks, and answers it with a look of fierce refusal.

Jessie's glad Will didn't catch it, that look. Hands stuffed boyishly into his coat pockets, her husband is gazing back into the shadows of the adjoining kitchen with a sweetly furrowed air of recalibration, struggling to square the rural dream — an urban male fantasy of chopping logs, foraging, probably sex outside — with the eerie sound of birds fluttering in cave-like chimneys, the sense of imprisoned pulpy damp, this terrifying, thrilling isolation.

Beneath the shearling of her favourite lambskin jacket, in a 1970s-style that suits these rough-hewn surroundings, Jessie's heart quickens. She tucks her autumn-red hair repeatedly behind her ears, ordering her thoughts. For she knows there's a huge jump between viewing an old country house on a winter afternoon — filmy silver light filtering through skeletal trees, moody and strange, like something dreamed — and the stress of moving hundreds of miles away, shedding their city skins. It would be an act of reckless blind faith, like falling in love with Will had been. But the house simply feels right — as Will did from the start — and, on a level that she can't explain, destined to be theirs.

And, really, the scale of Applecote is perfect. They wouldn't be lost in it. Huge compared to their London semi, it's still a doll's house compared to the real old piles in the area — the name 'manor' is definitely pushing it. Only two rooms deep, the square footage is in the width, and it's rustic rather than grand with gnarled woodwormed beams, walls that bulge as if breathing, no straight edges. A pelt of ivy covers the Cotswold stone exterior, the house not immediately visible from the road. Jessie likes this, the unshowiness, the way Applecote doesn't dominate the surrounding lush countryside but settles into it, like an elegant elderly lady dozing in long grass. Jessie can see Bella finally finding some peace here, and her own daughter, Romy, freed from rubber-matted city playgrounds, climbing trees, those strawberry-blonde curls catkin-fuzzed.

Romy already seems perfectly at home, prodding at the kiss of a snail's fleshy sucker on the other side of the glass with chubby toddler fingers. Jessie is sure her little girl will love the freedom of the countryside, just as she did as a kid, all those secret nooks of childhood, tiny worlds invisible to grown-up eyes. When the snail foams forward, Romy giggles and looks up: Jessie sees her own pixie-pretty features miniaturized, her family's Irish teal-blue, copper-lashed eyes, Will's full mouth. She grins back, Romy's delight her own. Their relationship is still porous, umbilical, the opposite of the one with Bella, which seems to be fortressed by a wall just as thick as Applecote's. Occasionally, she can peer over it, if she pulls herself up, dangling precariously. Not often. Certainly not today.

It's been three years since Jessie crossed the city with her five months pregnant belly, the world's happiest accident, bulking under her coat like a hidden present, and moved into Will's house. Two years after Mandy died. Not wanting to intrude upon his life or his daughter's, she had hung on to her independence and Dalston flat-share as long as possible, resisting the man she'd fallen madly in love with — 'I don't want to waste another minute of my life apart from you. I need you, we need you, Jessie' — until it became ridiculous and impractical. They didn't want to unsettle Bella further by moving then, not with a new baby on the way. And Jessie naively believed that a big heart, an eagerness to love Bella as her own, would eventually win over the fawn-like girl with the haunted eyes, who clung to her father's hand as if he were the last human left on earth. She had no idea that trying to love Bella, let alone parent her as she grew into an angry teen, would be like trying to hug an animal that wanted to sink its teeth into her neck. That she might never be forgiven for invading Bella's private world with her father and bringing forth the joy, noise and disruption that was Romy, a rival for her father's affections, and embarrassing proof of his new sex life. And who could blame poor Bella?

6

Time, everyone says. But time seems to be making things worse for Bella in London, not better, like something fragile left outside in the polluted city air, accruing damage. These last few months have been particularly bad, hormonally explosive with an unsettling crescendo that's forced their hand. Both Jessie and Will are agreed that Bella, whether she wants it or not — not, obviously — needs a fresh start. She must be removed from the skunky parties and the toxic cliques, taken far away from what she did to that girl, everything that happened. There's no point just moving to another London borough. If they're going to do it, they need to be radical, reframe their lives. They will leave the city for somewhere much more innocent and benign. And what could be more innocent than Applecote Manor?

And yet.

The windowpane bisecting the family's reflection seems uncannily symbolic, reminding Jessie that there are other, murkier, reasons Applecote draws them: Will trying to escape the mental imprint of a lorry turning left, the broken body of his beautiful wife churned along a concrete road; Jessie's insecurities, the ones that flare secretly, pettily, in her brain. For how can she tell Will that she's never felt comfortable in his dead wife's smart house, a domestic life that was never hers? That she has to fight terrible childish urges to paint over the chic grey walls with a riot of colour? That this is his second marriage, yes, but it is her first, her only, and she wants it to have its own unique character. And that Mandy,

7

magnificent Mandy Tucker, a subject so huge and heartbreaking that Jessie daren't mention her at all, is inescapable in the London house. Only last week Jessie pulled out one of Mandy's scarves from behind the radiator in the hallway. Sitting down on the stairs, the grey walls pressing in, the scarlet silk limp in her hand, secreting another woman's expensive scent, she wondered what to do with it. In the end, at a loss, she dropped it back behind the radiator and felt terrible. But Jessie knew that bits of Mandy would always be in that house, her marriage, hiding in crannies, waiting, watching.

They wouldn't be at Applecote Manor. No ghosts here.

'I can tell you've already moved in,' says Will, making her start, guiltily pushing away thoughts of Mandy.

She can see her own smile spread in his tawny brown eyes. 'And I can tell you're still on the motorway. Outside London.'

A laugh rumbles up from his thick coat. 'I might turn off.'

So he's losing his nerve. 'Might?'

'We can't afford it, Jessie. Not if you factor in all the work that needs doing. Unless you want to live like a squatter.'

Even this has a romantic appeal. She imagines them all huddled around a roaring fire for warmth, drinking cocoa from tin mugs, telling each other stories.

'The commute to the London office will be like some sort of daily triathlon,' Will says, warming to his theme. 'We don't know a soul here. In fact, there isn't a soul here. We may as well move to Mars.'

Out of the corner of her eye Jessie sees Bella nodding fervently in agreement. She thinks of the journey out of the city earlier in the day through sleepy suburbs, the anonymous banker satellite towns, chocolate-box villages, the cold skies clearing, bluing, until they passed the point at which a daily commute into London was, Will joked blackly, 'completely unfeasible without a mid-life crisis', on and on, a series of country roads, smeared with the bloating carcasses of fox and pheasant, then a narrow lane, squeezed between hedge-rows, a deserted old house, waiting. In a way she doesn't quite understand, it felt like a route deep inside herself. She can't turn back.

'Total madness.' Will's mouth starts to twitch with a smile. '*But* . . . ' He is the only man she's ever met who can seduce only with his eyes. ' . . . it's wild and beautiful, just like you.'

Bella groans, 'Oh, God.'

'And you've got a slightly mad, determined look going on that's making me think you might just move here anyway, whether I come or not.' He grins at her from beneath the mop of floppy dark hair that he likes to wear a little too long, a little rock and roll, a small rebellion against being forty-four, nine years older than Jessie, and the demands of the growing logistics company he set up fifteen years ago with an old college friend, Jackson. A large, loud bachelor, Jackson was the best man at Will's first wedding (huge, white) and absent from his second (a family-only affair in a register office, Jessie in a green dress, scarlet lipstick, a baby on her hip).

'So, yes, there's a chance you might be able to persuade me. A very small chance.' He pulls her towards him, lightly pressing his hand against her bottom.

Jessie wishes they could make love here, right now, mark their territory. She nuzzles against the stubble of his chin.

Appalled by any display of physical affection — and attuned to it — Bella looks up abruptly, and guns her father's right hand. Jessie feels the flinch in the contracting muscles of Will's fingertips. She sidesteps away to make it easier for him. The embroidered hem of her skirt swishes back against her knee-length leather boots. 'What do you think, Bella?' she asks, maybe a bit too brightly.

Bella burrows her eyes into the phone again. 'I'd sooner hang myself from a door by a belt than move here.'

'Don't hold back. Tell us how you really feel,' says Will, gamely trying to humour her. Bella's face remains blank, violently silent.

Romy's large blue eyes look up from the woodlouse scuttling along the floor to her mother, sensing something wrong.

Jessie's fingers reach for her most cherished possession, the gold charm, a tiny gingerbread man, that hangs on the chain around her neck, a necklace Will gave her to mark Romy's birth. The skin-warmed metal calms her, as it always does. She's needed to touch it a lot in the last few months as worries about Bella and the fractures

10

in this rapidly patched-together family roil beneath the surface of her days.

'Bell-Bell.' Romy stomps over to Bella, presents an offering of a woodlouse balled in her cupped hand, and grins, ever hopeful. Bella recoils and shoots one of those chilly looks at Romy that make Jessie shudder. There's something in Bella's gaze that is just not sisterly sometimes, not even particularly human. But she'd never say so to Will.

'Shall we hit the road then, Baby Bear?' Will swings up Romy in his arms, on to his shoulders, where she sits very upright, kicking her feet, like a tiny mahout. He tries to talk to Jessie as Romy covers his eyes with her hands. 'I'm starving, sweetheart.'

'One last look?' Something in Jessie sinks at the thought of returning to London. She fears Applecote might vanish the moment they leave it. 'I'm sure there's a room on the top floor we didn't see earlier. It's probably only a store-room or something, but I'd like to check it out. The agent rushed us past it, didn't he, Bella?'

Bella shrugs. But Jessie remembers how Bella kept glancing back at the top floor as they all clattered downstairs.

'I now have no option at all but to feast on this scrumptious foot then.' Will starts to pretend-gobble Romy's boot. Romy squeals. Jessie turns back into the shadowed old heart of the house, quietly amazed to hear Bella's slouching footsteps behind her.

★ ★ ★

They take the scenic route. Jessie pauses in the old drawing room, where the light is tinged the colour of Guinness and the windows furred with dust. She peers out to the weedy gravel beach of drive, the clumps of unpruned lavender, and watches Will talking to the estate agent, not noticing his little girl stuffing her duffel-coat pockets with stones. She hopes he's sniffing out if there's a deal to be done. He's good at that, surprisingly fierce in business, given what a total softy he is with the girls. But he's always had the two sides to him, a protective outer shell that only the people he loves ever really penetrate.

'Did someone seriously live in this place?' Bella asks, pulling Jessie back from her thoughts. She draws a road in the dust on the wooden floor with her pink Converse. 'Like this. Not done up or anything?'

'They did. A Mrs Wilde. A widow. She was here alone for decades, well into her nineties. Can you imagine? Must have been quite a lady.'

'I bet they discovered her mummified corpse watching telly, eaten by her lapdog. That's the sort of thing that happens in the country, isn't it?' Bella suppresses a smile. 'No one can hear you scream.'

'The truth is a little less exciting, I'm afraid.' Jessie smiles back. Bella's deadpan black humour creates little moments of connection in their otherwise fraught relationship. Jessie's always enjoyed finding little sparkly chinks in Bella's armour. 'The house just got too much. She had a tumble on the stairs, and had to move out to a

12

care home, oh, over nine months ago. Applecote's been on the market ever since. I just can't understand why the place hasn't been snapped up.'

'You can't?' Bella asks, in exaggerated disbelief.

'I just love the way it's stopped in another era, like a pocket watch.' Jessie takes in the wide oak floorboards — really slices of tree, nothing like the reflective laminated wooden floors in their house — the William Morris wallpaper, curling away in fruit-peel strips, dotted with pale squares where pictures once hung. Included in the sale are pieces of brown furniture, bureaus, black-lacquered plant stands, even a crocheted blanket scrunched on a chair, the kind of thing Jessie imagines women once knitted together in the village hall on rainy afternoons. 'Just needs a bit of a tinker, and it'll start ticking again.'

Bella lets out a low moan and leans back against a writing desk, making it wobble, a large glass paperweight sliding along its upper shelf. She picks it up and holds it to the light, where it glints dully like a fairground crystal ball. Jessie half expects to see Applecote's history swirling within it, picnics, croquet on the lawns, girls in gingham.

'Dad will never go for it, Jessie.' Bella sighs, not taking her eye off the glass. 'Way too much work.'

'Oh, it's a paint job,' Jessie says, sensing as she speaks that this might be an optimistic appraisal. Her mother always did up their houses, roping Jessie, protesting, into it: money was tight, and

13

since there was no man about to do these things, her mother simply bought a DIY manual and did it herself, only once nearly electrocuting herself.

'A bank job. Dad says it's a money pit.'

'I'm happy to get my hands dirty.'

'Very dirty?'

'Yes. Definitely.' Jessie realizes just how hungry she is for a challenge, some kind of project, after the warm, sweet drift of being a stay-at-home mum to Romy. She may have overstayed her career in packaging design, frustrated by the prescriptive briefs, locked in by the usual things — habit, rent and saving to buy her own flat, money she never used, invaluable now — but she misses its creativity and focus. And she can't help remodelling this house in her mind, the family, too, seeing them both emerge like a three-dimensional model. 'I hate those overdone country houses anyway. A home should be a bit rough around the edges.'

'But it's never going to be our home,' says Bella, with sudden intensity. 'Dad's not going to risk moving so far from London. Not here.'

Jessie doesn't answer. Yes, there's a risk in moving, she decides, not least for Bella, but there is also a risk in staying where they are. In London Bella could easily float further and further away, like a balloon in the sky, until they lose her completely. She imagines herself and Will looking back at this day, thinking maybe things could have turned out differently if they'd been braver. And who says Jessie can't reinvent a freelance career from the country when Romy's a bit older? She's always been struck by how many smart city women daren't change anything — home, relationship, job — in case it destabilizes the lot, as if all those busy London lives are improbably balanced on the tiniest of points, like ballerinas, and the merest tilt will send everything crashing to the ground. She refuses to become like that.

'Are we going upstairs or what?' Bella puts the paperweight back on the desk a little too hard, jolting the room's stillness. 'I might yet find my corpse up there, you never know.'

'You never know,' agrees Jessie, feeling an unexpected twitch of unease.

* * *

Emerging on the attic-like top floor, it feels instantly colder and smells mustier. Old servants' quarters, Jessie supposes. The doors are in a boarding-house line off a dark, narrow landing.

'That's the room,' Bella says, in a hushed voice, pointing at a scuffed white door at the far end of the landing on the gable wall, almost hidden in shadow.

It takes Jessie a moment to realize that the walls are actually subsiding slightly towards each other, giving the impression that the room is further away than it is.

The doorknob turns reluctantly with a rasp. A soup of dust swirls in front of her, obscuring the room. Jessie feels particles settling in her hair, tastes an odd sweetness on her tongue. As it clears, the room solidifies, still and shadowy as a

Dutch interior painting, its world as self-contained and ripe with meaning.

It is not a storeroom.

The thick black beams on the eaves funnel their eyes to a small porthole window made of purplish stained glass — an ornate pattern of grapes and vines — that bruises the light against the wall. There's another window too, larger, square, with tattered umber silk curtains that drape to the floor, making Jessie think of an antique, disintegrating ballgown. Most curious of all, a sleigh-style bed, still made up: a stack of pillows, a mothy pink blanket, with satin-ribbon trim, folded at its end; a wooden school desk with an inkwell and pen-scarred lid; a mirrored dressing-table, kidney-shaped, similar to one Jessie's late nan owned.

Jessie's footsteps sound far too loud in here: the room feels private, inhabited. It's like coming across a deserted old cabin in the woods, she thinks, and finding ashes still warm in the grate. She glances at Bella, who is hanging back, still standing in the doorway, long arms braced either side of it, countering the force that's pulling her in. Her eyes are enormous, their blackness spreading, wire-tripped awake.

'Well, this is a surprise.' Jessie isn't sure why she whispers. Like you do in a room where a child is sleeping. She encourages Bella forward. The dressing-table's mirror reflects them both as smudges, half-formed future ghosts.

Bella moves cautiously into the room, running her flat palm along the faded floral wallpaper before stopping, staring intensely at the bed,

16

panning it for meaning.

'Do you like it?' Jessie smiles, pleased to see Bella's staple expression of sullen indifference replaced with absorption, as if she's stepped out of herself for a moment. She even looks different in this room, her monochromatic beauty not modern at all.

Bella glances up, surprised, having clearly forgotten Jessie was there. 'What?'

'I think this room might have your name on it, Bella.'

Bella blushes, apparently caught out thinking the same thing. Sometimes, in rare, precious moments like this, Jessie glimpses the girl Bella must have been before her mother died, someone less shut off, more readable. She wishes she'd known that Bella. She'll never give up trying to find her again.

'If we move here, it's yours. We can decorate it together, exactly how you like. And . . . and you can take the room next door as a den or something. You'd have your own bathroom up here too! Imagine that, a bath without Romy's armada of rubber ducks.'

Bella nods absently, seeming not to be listening to Jessie but someone or something else that only she can hear, the wrong pitch for adult ears.

Jessie perseveres, nods at the bed. 'You can have that too. We may have to stretch to new bedding, though.'

And that's when Bella whips around, snaps back to the present, to being Bella Tucker, a teenager who doesn't want to be there, whom

17

the world has royally screwed over. And Jessie knows it's coming, the sudden, unpredictable whiplash of rage that will pull Bella away hard. 'Who are you to say what is *mine*? What we can buy?' Bella's voice trembles. 'It's not your house in London to sell.'

Jessie takes a deep breath. 'Bella, I'm putting all my savings into this too. But it's not about money, it's . . . ' She catches herself. She mustn't mention Bella's behaviour in London: moving here is not a punishment. 'Your dad wants a change.'

'Don't tell me what Dad wants.' Bella stands straighter, broader, a threatening show of strength and unmistakable genetic difference, towering over Jessie's petite five-foot-three frame, her spray of freckles and coppery hair, the softness that has settled on her hips since Romy's birth. 'Like I don't know him better than you.'

Jessie presses the gold of her pendant between her fingers, feeling her heartbeat conducted along the chain. 'He can work most of the week from home. You'll see more of him, we all will.' She tries to steady herself, take a breath. 'He wants a slower pace of life, Bella.'

Bella hisses out the words, 'All Dad wants is Mum back. Don't you get it?'

Jessie recoils, steps back. The oak boards creak, the weight of them — their relationship, the complicated tangle of family ties — too much to bear. She tries to silence the little voice in her head, the one that fears Bella might be right, that she is less loved than Mandy, that she

18

and Will met too soon after Mandy's death for the love to be as real for him as it is for her.

Bella sizes her up. 'You think Dad will come here and forget all about Mum, don't you?'

'Bella . . .' she begins, not knowing how the sentence will end, a guilty heat rising beneath her skin. It is impossible to lie to Bella, even if she wanted to. She is too astute.

'Well, he won't, Jessie. And he won't ever love you like he loved my mother. He never has. Everyone knows he married you because of Romy. And everyone knows this move will end in total disaster.' She looks away, raises her chin.

Jessie blinks furiously, damned if she'll let Bella see her tears. It's not the first time Bella's said these things, but it doesn't hurt any less. 'I only care about what's right for us, for you. Where *we* might be happy.'

'I'm happy where I am!'

'Are you?' Jessie asks quietly. The question rearranges the air. 'Really? Because from where I'm standing, it doesn't look like that.'

Bella's mouth opens, as if to say something, but no words come out. She spins around to the square window, roughly yanking back the curtains. Leaning forward against the sill, her legs coltishly crossed, she looks as young and vulnerable as she did menacing a moment before, and Jessie feels terribly sorry for her.

She waits for the worst of the mood swing to pass — a gritty sandstorm that will obliterate everything for a few moments, choke, then start to clear — before tentatively joining Bella at the window, careful not to touch her hot, angry

19

edges. Sadly, theirs is not a tactile relationship: Bella has made it quite clear that any sort of physical contact with Jessie is so not okay.

Jessie's heart lifts at the view from the window: the wild expanse of garden, the exact opposite of their outlook in London, tiny, Astroturfed (by Mandy), overlooked by neighbours, who see Jessie as a young cuckoo stealing another woman's nest. Their earlier hurried route through Applecote's garden is clearer from here too. She maps it: the orangery's glass roof, the woody area known as the Wilderness, the small walled orchard, the black rectangle of derelict swimming-pool, a bit visually unnerving, like a void. At the end of the garden, although she can't quite see it from here, she pictures the iron gate, where they'd stood staring out at a glorious expanse of meadow with its ancient circle of knee-high stones, like tiny savage people. ('Pretty cool, eh?' the earnest agent had panted, sniffing a deal. 'Hardly fucking Stonehenge,' Bella had replied drily.) At the edge of that meadow, scooped out of it, the distant glitter of the river. Oh, and a bird of prey. A kite, Jessie guesses, with that forked tail. She and Bella track it together, swooping, diving, momentarily united in the act of seeing, the space between them closing a little.

'Is something else bothering you, Bella?' Jessie asks gently. 'I mean, apart from everything, obviously.'

Bella presses her nail-bitten fingers to the cold glass. 'Bad stuff has gone down in this house.' Her voice is thin, sapped by her earlier outburst.

'I came into this room and I could feel it.'

Jessie studies Bella's face, the thoughts rippling beneath the milky translucent skin: she knows it's only Bella's hyper-sensitive teenage mind externalizing its own indefinite fears. 'Can you describe it?' she nudges gently, hoping this might be a way of talking about the emotions Bella bottles up.

Bella frowns. 'A sort of trapped feeling. Like the past is stuck, that's all. Or someone. I don't know, it's weird.'

Jessie feels a sharp pang of sadness: Bella's talking about her own grief, circling it. And Jessie knows better than to try to address it directly. 'The house has been empty a long time, and neglected. But as soon as a new family moves — '

'Even if we move in, this house won't ever belong to us,' Bella interrupts, her voice hard again. Outside, the kite plunges. A flock of birds rises: each one black, tiny, like a handful of nails thrown against the soft blue sky. 'Just like I won't ever belong to you, Jessie.'

2

Chelsea, London, May 1959

Ma's certainly taking her time to die. She's been draped on the chaise-longue beside the window for two days now, barely moving other than to reach for a cigarette and a sticky glass of gin and orange, her heavy-lidded gaze trained on the street below, where wind whips the blossom off the trees in a mocking swirl of confetti. Having declared her heart 'shrivelled to a devilled kidney, barely capable of beating', she's determined to 'fade away gently, surrounded by my four darling daughters'.

This poses a problem. It's Monday. Our home weekend is over and we're meant to be at school. Not only will we get punished for being late, but my classmates, who view my mother as an exotic circus act and stick their faces to the school windows whenever it's rumoured she's not forgotten to pick us up, will think us even more rackety. We get enough of this anyway: 'Ah, yes, *Bunny*'s daughters,' people say, flushing at Ma's name, equally excited and disapproving. I want to tell them we're not so different. That the wonky world of my sisters and mother contains all the passions and squabbles of a hundred normal families just like them, only that without Pa it's been reduced to something more intense and salty, like a sort of gravy.

Ma presses a limp hand to her forehead. Her beautiful face is a study in poetic suffering. I'm not sure dying people look like that. Or wear crimson lipstick. Pam says we should just leave her with a hot glass of honey and lemon and jump on a train. But Ma's purse doesn't contain enough money for our rail tickets — we've checked — and while none of us believes Ma's theatrics, there's still a niggling worry that she'll die anyway, since Ma can do most things when she puts her mind to it.

I glance at the carriage clock eating minutes above the fireplace. My French lesson has just started. Madame Villiot will be calling out my name on the register, powdered chalk on the tips of her fingers, her tiny ruby earrings trembling above her white lace collar. It's hard not to be a little in love with Madame — everyone is — since there are no boys to fall in love with at Squirrels Ladies College, only the head girl with the Botticelli hair. I look back to Ma, feeling my forehead pinch up. 'Are you sure we can't send for the doctor?'

'Don't be hysterical, Margot.'

I stare glumly down at Fang, the moth-eaten tiger-skin rug on the floor, wondering what to do next. Pam tramps into the room, making the glasses on the drinks trolley clink — 'Built like a Boche tank,' Ma always says — and yanks open the window. Blossoms flutter in, to settle like white butterflies on the dark wood floor. Ma winces, pained, and covers her eyes with her hands.

Bunny Wilde is not a fan of fresh air. Her

natural habitat is a smoky, post-six p.m. world, the sodium shadows of West End theatres, Chelsea soirées and Mayfair clubs, lit by guttering candlelight, chandeliers and the gazes of adoring men. Ma loathes the countryside and embraces daylight only in an artist's studio, naked, modelling for Jack Harlow, the painter she's madly in love with, a handsome, dark, crow-like man, who smells of paint and Pernod. He's betrayed her again — taking only my mother by surprise — and is courting a new muse: 'Some Berkeley Dress Show model,' Ma whispered on Friday, too terrible a thing to name out loud, like Russian nuclear weapons or a bladder infection.

Unfairly, the torpedo of blame that should be directed at Jack's house — crashing through the tall glass dome of his artist's studio, a glorious explosion of oil paint — has been directed at us. Last night Ma slurred, in and out of sleep, that Jack would have married her years ago if she hadn't had so many daughters, as if the small fact of her progeny was something that could be reshaped, like her eyebrows. It made me grateful that it isn't just me — 'My dear strange Margot,' she says, as if I have dropped into the parlour from the moon — being an obstacle to her happiness, that there are four of us sisters, so the blame can be divided and dished out into four smaller portions.

Flora, Pam and I were a shoe size apart growing up, an inch of dress hem: seventeen, sixteen and fifteen now. 'Quite impossible not to get pregnant with your father around,' Ma says,

24

mischievously making light of something so terrifying, explained at school with diagrams of mating livestock, investigated by girls in taxis with boys after dances. (I had my left breast caressed at Christmas. It was less exciting than I'd hoped.) Just when Ma thought she was done, her figure safe, along came Dot, three years after me. Dot doesn't look much like the rest of us, dark where we're fair, tiny where we're tall. She doesn't look twelve either. Her spectacles are too big for her face. A late starter as I was, her chest all ribs, like a boy's. She can read well enough — she loves to read, her cocoa-brown eyes widening, living every page — but she can't do arithmetic at all. We think this is because of what happened. How Dot started.

Ma was pregnant with Dot when the engine of Pa's car cut out on the level crossing, seconds before the 14:07 from Edinburgh screamed down the tracks. The policeman took his hat off at the door — I remember that, the icy blast of winter as the door opened, the unseasonal film of sweat on his square forehead. And Ma not believing him, shaking her head, holding the hard balloon of her tummy, shouting no, no, no, not her Clarence, not when he had survived the war, a thumb blown clean off and, after that, the thing that had made him cower under their bed some nights, hands cupped over his ears. Ma went into labour later that day, six weeks too early, and out slid Dot, blue as the Piccadilly Line. After that, Ma was in bed for months, very still, her mind living somewhere else. When Dot cried I would soothe her. Just as other friends had kittens, I had a baby sister, the first thing I remember ferociously loving, wanting to protect. When Dot is sick now — she has lungs that whistle in winter, and needs to be steamed over the bath, like a creased dress — it's me she calls out for, rarely Ma.

For me, embarrassingly, in my sleep, it's Pa. I was his favourite, Ma says. He called me Margot A-go-go because I was so cheerful and busy, always asking questions that made him laugh: 'Where does the sky end and space begin?' 'If God is everywhere is He in the bristles of my hairbrush?'

I like that Pa called me Margot A-go-go: confirmation of a different version of me, the carefree little girl I was, like the photo of me riding on his shoulders, Pa laughing, running across Kensington Gardens in the rain. Also, a great improvement on 'strange Margot', despite Ma and my sisters insisting it was just an affectionate nickname.

Pa's loss still feels epic yet utterly obscure. My memories are tombola random. I remember his face, the strong Wilde jaw jutting out above his medals, the jaw you see repeated in all the portraits hanging from the walls of Applecote Manor, Pa's old family house. But not his voice: it's got muddled with voices on the wireless, voices in my head. Ma says, 'We'd all be destroyed if we could remember everything, Margot.' This is her way of picking over the past, as if it were a box of chocolates, I think, ignoring the nasty coffee creams.

Sometimes I think that part of me is forgotten,

or lost. And I don't know if I'll ever find it, whether it's something you lose and can't replace, like an adult tooth, or if it can re-grow. But, more than this, I'd like to know if my skin will ever be like my sisters', smooth as soap. The red itchy patches at the back of my knees appeared the day of Pa's funeral and never healed. When the sores are oozing and classmates stare in the school showers, I wonder why, out of all of them, I'm the one cursed with it, if my skin is a punishment for a terrible thing I haven't done yet. And what that might be.

My skin is the only thing my sisters won't tease me about, secretly relieved that I got it and not them. It brings out rashes of kindness. Dot lets me sleep in the cooler bed by our bedroom window. Flora rubs ointment into the bits I can't reach. Pam briskly reminds me that at least I'm clever — 'which goes some way to compensate for your missing chunks of common sense' — and that everyone has something they don't like about themselves, apart from Flora, she adds wryly, since Flora is flawless.

That always makes me laugh. I need my sisters more than I do Ma sometimes.

It's not that Ma isn't a good mother. Just that she's different from other mothers, the ones who didn't lose their husbands in odd, terrible accidents, who don't live in tall, narrow, tilt-to-the-left houses on the wrong side of Chelsea, with a sooty stucco exterior, the interior painted the blazing colours of an African parrot — in defiance of English weather and good taste

27

— the rooms strewn with Ma's marabou scarves, curlers and books.

Nothing works here. The fridge is balmy. We can see the picture on the television — Ma bought it with much fanfare to watch the Coronation — only if we hang up the old blackout curtains. The Hoover sulks accusingly in a wooden box beneath the stairs, awaiting a handyman to offer his services for free in exchange for a smile from my mother. Over the years her smile has won over all sorts of handymen.

Ma hates paying for anything if she can help it. Not for Ma dropping her shillings into a shop's cash carrier, waiting for it to ping along the wire to the cashier. Ma's purchases are all on credit. She has complicated bills all over London. She also has the longest legs west of Sloane Square. This helps.

Luckily, the Wildes — Pa's older brother, Perry, and his wife, Sybil, the ones from Applecote Manor — pay for Squirrels, our bracing boarding school in Oxfordshire, where we are meant to be right now. (They chose a grander, far warmer one in Dorset for their daughter, my cousin Audrey, but it wasn't enough to save her.) The Wildes won't give a shilling directly to Ma. It's no secret they don't approve — Pa's parents wanted him to marry a nice steady county girl with a title, and instead they got an outspoken theatre agent's daughter from Bloomsbury, their very own Wallis Simpson, to tempt their second son astray. Also, Ma doesn't care much what people think about her,

28

which makes her quite dangerous.

The summer Grandma Wilde died in a deckchair, happily sunbathing dead for an hour before anyone realized, she told me Ma was 'bringing you up like cats'. I nodded in agreement and sipped my lemonade. It does feel we have as many lives, forced to adjust our manners and allegiances according to the different worlds we inhabit, learning to say the right thing, or not reveal too much, as we move between Ma's bohemian household, the stolid steadiness of Squirrels Ladies College, then our smart London friends' polite parlours for tea, buoyed along by the once-grandish heritage of our surname. Flora and I have learned to slip different selves on and off like socks. I've not decided who I am yet anyway — I feel like a completely different person from one day to the next — and Flora simply moulds herself to the company she's in, always meeting expectation. Dot's strategy is a sweet silence: she observes her surroundings carefully before impinging upon them, pushing her true feelings into her pinafore pockets. Pam can only ever be Pam, always gesturing too hard, saying too much, too loudly, her contours unique and fixed.

Pam's the one who let slip to the Wildes how our drawing room fills with the laughter of Ma's musician friends, men with skin the colour of burnt sugar, their accents strange and rich, fingers flying, like birds, over the frets of their banjos. How Ma prefers the company of artists and actresses from Chelsea to the tightly smiling wives of Kensington, discussing their new (cold)

29

refrigerators on sunny street corners. How she seems to survive on Lucky Strikes and our maid Betty's bewildered attempts — at Ma's insistence — at Elizabeth David's cold tomato soup, gazpacho.

We resent the gazpacho intensely: it makes us different from other girls. Whenever we return from school, we pour the bloody mess down the sink and Flora cooks an old-fashioned English roast. We all love Flora for this. Even Ma forks in the soft flakes of beef, unable to help closing her eyes and purring with pleasure, as if the roast is something lost and found, a taste of an easier, more conventional life. She tells Flora she's going to make a wonderful wife some day — soon, she hopes, to a first-born son, not the impoverished second, like she did, the silly goose. The thought of Flora marrying always makes me stop chewing, my throat closing. I don't know who we sisters will be without each other to differentiate us. Take one of us away and we'd all lose our balance, like removing a leg from a kitchen table.

But I also want Flora to be happy since happiness suits her — I can never quite trust it, I'd rather rely on thinking — and for Flora that means a husband, children and 'a comfortable house where I won't freeze in winter, a housekeeper, a little bit of evolution, that's all'.

Ma also spends a lot of time thinking about our husbands (even though she hasn't got one herself), the as yet unknown cast of four men lurking, waiting in our future, like shadows in a long, narrow London alley. To this end, Ma makes all of us walk across the drawing room in front of Patty, her Royal Ballet dancer friend with the mad lettuce-green eyes, ready to whack us on the back of a leg with a tortoiseshell shoehorn if we slouch. My A grades are viewed as a distraction: 'Unwise to be too clever, Margot.' Pam's ambition to be a nurse (unlikely, given her brute impatience if anyone falls ill) is affectionately dismissed 'I'm sure there are easier ways of annoying your mother, if you put your mind to it, Pam' — and dwarfed by the issue of Pam's athletic 'sturdiness', which refuses to be diminished by the rubber roll-on foundation garments that Ma makes her wear to parties.

'Your faces must be your fortune, girls,' Ma will shrug. 'I won't pretend otherwise.'

The problem is, I don't turn heads like Flora. Neither do I know how to command attention in a room, like Pam, through sheer, unembarrass-able life force. I'm not unpleasant-looking, just not particularly memorable. Given my low position in these rankings, I told Ma it'd be more sensible for me to aspire to a job, teaching, for example, where my face doesn't matter. 'Oh, Margot, have I taught you nothing?' She looked baffled. 'Look at me, forced into independence! You cannot possibly envy it. Far simpler to get married.' She says that being married to Pa was the happiest time of her life. I remember fragments of this, haphazardly sewn together, like the hexagons of different-coloured cloth in my bedroom quilt: my parents embracing in the hall; Ma tenderly kissing the glossy red stump of Pa's thumb. But, really, the truth is, none of us

31

sisters has any idea what a marriage looks like, day to day, or how it must feel to live with men. With such scant evidence to go on, we just have to believe in it, like the Old Testament. But I secretly don't believe in that either.

'Margot.' Flora tugs me into the corridor, out of my thoughts. She shuts the drawing-room door with a supple flick of her hip. 'Ma's not eaten or slept properly in two days now.'

'Ma could survive on gin and air for months, unfortunately. Excuse me.' Pam storms past with a piece of toast and marmalade, in one of those moods when she continually searches us out to make a show of ignoring us.

'I do understand why she's cross, Flora,' I say, after Pam's slammed her bedroom door as loudly as possible.

'Let's not be too harsh.' Flora is kind too, the kindest. Pam points out it must be easy to be kind if you've got a face like Flora's. Even as a young child Flora drew attention, with her violet-blue eyes and *moue* of a mouth. Now she's seventeen, she has something else that makes men stutter stupidly. She frowns, and rather than the frown making her look grumpy, it gives her luminous face complexity and depth. 'It's hardly Ma's fault.'

'Isn't it?'

'No.'

'But she and Jack always get back together and then it happens again.' I become aware of movement at the top of the stairs and look up to see Dot crouched against the banisters, hands wrapping around her spindly legs, looking as

32

though she might dissolve in the watery spring light like a sugar cube, leaving nothing behind but tortoiseshell spectacles. I wonder how long she's been there.

Seeing that she's been spotted, she smiles hopefully. 'Margot, will you play a game of chess with me?' Suggesting chess is a very Dot-ish way of drifting over a crisis. 'I asked Pam. She said she'd rather watch her fingernails grow.'

'Toenails!' Pam bellows, from behind the bedroom door.

'Not now. Sorry. We're trying to work out what to do, Dot,' I say, in the soft voice I reserve for my little sister.

Dot listens as Flora and I prod and poke our predicament into different shapes. After a while, Flora wanders towards the kitchen, muttering about omelettes. Dot slips away.

I check on Ma, who is asleep now, her cigarette a wand of grey ash between her fingers. I stand watching her awhile, my mother in her ice-cube-blue satin dressing-gown on the battered chaise-longue, the faint lines around her eyes and mouth that she battles with cold creams and finger-pinching and don't make her any the less lovely but I know bother her all the same. Her vulnerability touches and irritates me. I shut the door quickly, seek out Flora again.

Flora could almost be Ma from behind, willowy, tall, leggy, except that Ma is far more likely to be melting down an almost-finished lipstick, stretching out its life with cooking fat, than making lunch. 'Get the crockery, Margot.' Flora doesn't turn. We can distinguish each other

33

by the sound of sniffs or footsteps, the particular rustle of a certain leg in a certain skirt.

Pam and Dot join us at the table and we demolish the omelettes in seconds. We're about to fall on Betty's pound cake, fat slices that would horrify our mother, whose waistline owes much to the long ration-book years, when her voice swims towards us: 'Girls?'

To our astonishment and relief, we find Ma sitting upright, bare feet planted on the floor, her fingers tucking under her curls at the nape of her neck. 'I'd murder a strong cup of tea.' Her voice is frogged with cigarettes, her smile sheepish.

'I'll make you one,' says Flora, not taking her eyes off Ma as she backs into the hallway. Without our eldest sister's presence, there's a sense of incompleteness. For something to do until her return, I raise the needle on the gramophone, Ma's American jazz.

Ma starts to tap out the rhythm lightly on her knee. 'Oh, this one just breaks my heart,' she says, with a slow, wistful smile, as if feeling sad is better than feeling nothing at all.

'Tea, Ma.' At Flora's light-footed return, something releases. She slides the tray on to the wobbly bamboo side table: a napkin, a cup of tea, the correct shade of brown, a sugar-dusted sponge finger.

Ma sips, depositing a tea-leaf beauty spot on her lip. She pats the side of the chaise-longue. 'Here. Sit next to me, girls. I want to talk to you. I'm sure we can all fit. Yes, even you, Pam.'

We squeeze up, warm and squished. Ma lifts the sleeve of her dressing-gown, releasing the smell of oranges and cigarette smoke and Elizabeth Arden Blue Grass scent. 'I've had some time to think, these last two days.'

'And drink.' Pam's navy eyes flash beneath her heavy brows.

Ma stares down at her hands in her lap. 'I'm sorry if I worried you all. Really.'

'You didn't,' says Pam, sharply, because Ma doesn't look sorry enough. 'It was perfectly obvious you weren't dying.'

'Please don't be so cross, Pam.' Ma holds her calf, rocking back a little, so that the satin stretches and gleams across her shin. 'Would you like my sponge finger?'

Pam shakes her head but keeps glancing at it.

'You certainly look better,' says Flora, brightly, trying to steer us away from a screaming match. Our rows can be heard in the street. When neighbours whack on the wall, Ma whacks back with the fireside bellows.

'But we're meant to be at school,' I point out. 'It's Monday.'

Ma covers her mouth with her hands. 'What a twit I am. Well, you mustn't let that fractious old rhino of a headmistress punish you. You must blame me entirely.'

'We will,' Pam says tightly. 'And we do.'

Ma waits a moment, lets Pam's words settle, the music rise and fall, then clinks down her teacup and says, 'Well, first, you may as well know that I do intend to live a little while longer. Which is a relief to me at least, although possibly not to Pam.'

Pam scowls but still can't quite hide a minute

35

flicker of a smile. The next moment, she swoops down on the sponge finger, which we all recognize as forgiveness of sorts.

Heartened, Ma wiggles herself straight, her breasts shaking beneath the satin. 'Second, who remembers the Beamishes? Old friends of your father's. Mad Sophie Beamish. Ginger husband, Foreign Office. Enormous ear lobes.' She parts her fingers a couple of inches.

We shrug, wary of the Beamishes intruding into a conversation that still may career off in the wrong direction at any moment, like a bike without brakes, as charged conversations involving Ma and Pam often do.

'Well, they've only invited me to Marrakesh!' Ma lowers her voice conspiratorially, widens her eyes at each of us in turn. 'Imagine. Bunny in the Red City.'

Flora and I exchange an alarmed look. We'd rather not.

Ma inhales before speaking, then the words rush out: 'They've offered me a secretarial job with the consul, girls. A fancy apartment, maids thrown in.'

The sponge finger crumbles as Pam bites into it.

'Secretarial?' I splutter. My mother could start a third world war with her typos. 'Why on earth — '

'Thank you, Margot,' Ma clips. 'They said I'd bring colour, liven the place up a bit. And I speak good French. There's a girl to type and whatnot.'

'So you've said no, obviously?' Flora says.

36

'Well . . . ' Ma's voice wavers, betraying doubt and excitement, like a bride about to marry a man she doesn't know as well as she should.

'Dear God,' groans Pam.

The back of my knees immediately start to itch ferociously.

'I can't stay here in London, bumping into Jack and that — that girl.' Ma's forehead furrows, and I see the lines that are waiting for her turn to get old. It strikes me that she looks, for once, her full thirty-nine years today. 'And I need to earn some proper money. Margot, stop that infernal scratching.'

'But *Marrakesh*.' Flora blinks very fast, trying to absorb the steamy foreignness of the word.

★　★　★

'For how long?' Pam demands sharply.

'Not long enough for you to forget me,' Ma tries to joke. But it falls flat. She picks up her cup and attempts to sip some tea, but it is empty. The rest of us have a shocked conversation with our eyes. 'A few months? A year? I'm not sure. It'll go in a flash.'

But it is suddenly impossible to imagine Ma not on the chaise-longue by the window, sipping tea, Fang's paws outstretched.

'You can't make this sort of decision now. You've been so upset these last two days, Ma, and you've not had lunch,' says Flora, stricken.

'Flora, darling, I'm quite lucid, and think much better on an empty stomach. You see, as well as earning, I could let this house — there's a

37

shortage, lots of country families looking for townhouses. Everyone's talking about it.'

'What? Something old and damp in SW10?' scoffs Pam.

'Pam, listen.' The room trembles on the edge of a row again. 'I have four girls to keep in stockings, hats and food on my own. *Four*. I've already sold my best bits of jewellery.' I feel a fresh flush of shame recalling Ma's and my last furtive trip to the small dark room at the back of the jeweller's in Burlington Arcade, the pained passing over of Grandma's brooches, each one a small glittering scandal, a defeat. 'The theatre work is drying up. Artist-model earnings? Hopeless. I'm running out of options.'

'I won't let you,' says Flora, eyes glistening. 'I won't let you go.'

Ma touches Flora's smooth cheek lightly with the back of her hand. 'Flora, my lovely Flora, you are seventeen, leaving Squirrels this year. I want you in Paris by the autumn.'

The rest of us flinch, hating the reminder that Flora will be bundled off to a finishing school in Paris, where she'll learn to speak fluent French, type, talk about art, things that will help her find a good husband and can then be promptly forgotten, lost in a puff of flour and baby talc.

'You'll be wanting some sort of coming-out party too. It all costs, costs, costs.' She shakes her head despairingly.

'The Season finished for good last year, Ma. And I really never expected to go to Paris,' Flora says unconvincingly. (She's already bought a beret.) 'I don't need Paris.'

Ma lights a cigarette, sighs the smoke out. 'The Queen may have stopped the curtsying, now that anyone with a bit of money can buy their way in. But the debs are still dancing, as you well know, Flora. Their mothers will make damn sure of it. How else will they make a match for their little darlings?' Her eyes glint. Ma relishes her outsider status — she wasn't a deb herself — yet is determined that we fully exploit our Wilde heritage to secure good marriages. 'And every girl needs Paris.'

'Every girl' means Flora. I'm not sure Ma seriously considers the rest of us worth the investment.

'When? When will you go, Ma?' Pam's cheeks are stained a vivid, anxious red.

'Beginning of July, or thereabouts.'

'So we'd live at school always? Even during the summer holidays?' asks Dot, voice high with panic.

'No, Dot. Don't worry.' Ma's face starts to shut. And it is immediately obvious that there's something important she's not telling us.

'Where, then?' Pam and I demand in unison.

Ma's gaze slides away. 'The simplest thing would be for you all . . . ' She stalls. Her voice rises. ' . . . to live at Applecote Manor with Aunt Sybil and Uncle Peregrine.'

None of us speaks. In the shocked hush, I can see Pa's family house, the honeyed stone, the shallow valley spilling beyond, all spinning, whirling, a vortex of dragonflies, birds, grasses, cartwheels, picnics, long-lost summers. But the sky is black.

'You'd have a wonderful address. Not even a

house number,' Ma appeals eagerly to Flora. 'Think of letter headings.'

'I'm not ashamed of where we live or who we are,' declares Pam, raising her chin. Flora reaches for her hand and holds it in a stagey moment of Girl Guide-ish solidarity.

'I'm not suggesting for a moment that you girls should be ashamed. I certainly am not. But I am nonetheless a pragmatist, and rather bloody short of cash.' She brings the cigarette to her mouth quickly, again and again. 'It will be good for you to have a male figure in your lives. And Sybil, I'm sure, will spoil you rotten.'

I see my aunt then, as I last saw her five years ago, all bouncing red curls and bone-china features, laughing, bending down to pat a cloud-grey whippet puppy, Uncle Perry, walking towards her, a huge, handsome swagger of a man, hunting rifle over his shoulder. Then the puppy yaps. There's a patter of small footsteps. A swing of a plait. A flick of yellow ribbon. Something pulls at the edges, a darkness that no one dare name.

'Such an idyllic place to live.' Ma continues talking herself into it. 'I may not be a country girl, but you've all got apples and hay in your blood. Old Father Thames springs not too far from there, doesn't he?' I think of the rush of glassy green that passes close to Applecote. 'Well, you do too.'

To my dismay, I can see my older sisters turning, a light in their eyes that wasn't there a moment ago, won over by Ma's absurd pastoral oratory.

'You remember the bathing-pool, Pam?' Ma continues, conjuring up the Italianate pool buried deep at the bottom of Applecote's garden. 'And there's an orchard, Dot. Perfect for climbing.'

I'm upside down, swinging, skirt tenting my head, the mossy branch velvety in the clamp of my palm. A girl's voice is counting down to ten. And something else is counting down too, but we can't hear it.

'The weather's incomparably better, of course. More daylight, further west. Pretty sunsets and things, you know.'

The sky on fire. A lolly melting, dripping a line of stickiness down the inside of my arm.

'A proper English summer, girls,' Ma breathes out in a curl of cigarette smoke.

Applecote Manor *was* summer: Ma dropped us by the front gates in August, returned two weeks later. Then, five years ago, summer stopped: none of us has seen Sybil or Perry since. We only overhear snatches, Ma telling friends that Sybil hasn't left the house in years, shunning all company, that huntsman Perry is now crippled by a pain in his back that no doctor can diagnose or treat, and rarely moves from his armchair.

'The area is so pretty, never pummelled by bombs, not like dirty old London,' Ma continues, ignoring all this. She presses a finger to her lips. 'Sorry, I forget, a German pilot did crash into Applecote's meadow, didn't he?'

'Aunt Sybil found his head perched on top of one of the Applecote Stones, like a dress-shop

41

dummy,' Pam recounts with relish. 'She said he was actually very handsome.'

Dot pushes herself closer to me. Her eyes are owlish.

Ma squeezes Dot's hand. 'The pilot's head is long gone now, don't you worry, Dotty.'

But I can see that it isn't the pilot who's varnishing Dot's eyes with fear. That it's something worse. And since Flora and Pam are weighing up the advantages of Ma's proposal with a silent exchange of animated, quizzical looks, it's left to me to blurt, '*ButwhataboutCousinAudrey?*'

3

At 6:02 on the first morning of her new life, Jessie is woken by a riot of drunken birdsong. She squints sleepily through her lashes and sees a dead spider as big as a fist, a bloom of damp on unfamiliar floral wallpaper. She wonders where she is. Why she is camping on a mattress in a huge, bare room that smells of soft old fabric. Then she remembers.

It is the second week of August. Eight months and two days since they first saw Applecote Manor. And, unbelievably, it is theirs. She smiles slowly, and turns her head on the pillow towards Will, whose arms are tightly wrapped around her waist, as they always are, as if to stop her vanishing in the night. His rugged good looks slackened in sleep, the strain of yesterday's move is crosshatched in tiny lines across his face, like a woodcut. Jessie tenderly pushes a lock of dark hair off his forehead, revealing a streak of silver. Will's is the kind of face — noble, life-weathered — that could easily have come from an ancestor portrait, such as those that must once have hung on these walls, she decides. He belongs here. They all do.

Jessie likes the idea that there's an unbroken thread, a pulse of energy, running through the lives of the historic owners, the Wilde family, and their own. It feels like they're picking up something precious but broken, putting it back together again. She loves Will deeply for being brave enough to take on this old house, this new, unknowable life. He's been under a lot of pressure to bow out: Will's old loyal friends, not wanting to lose him, tried to persuade him to stay; Bella swore she'd never forgive him if they moved, that there was something 'bad' at Applecote, like a gas you couldn't taste or smell that would poison them all in their sleep.

Jessie's nerve was shaken at times. She didn't like the way two local builders went silent on the phone when she mentioned the name of the house, refusing to explain why they didn't want to work on it. But she made light of it to Will: there had been many times in their relationship when one of them had had to reassure the other. Sometimes it is him — yes, Romy really will sleep through the night soon, of course Bella will grow to love her little sister — sometimes her. This is how they roll.

But the possibility that the move might be stirring up Will's old grief has been niggling. A few days ago, she'd woken in the early hours, discovered his side of the bed empty and got up, wondering where he was. She'd only got as far as the landing and stopped: music was drifting from beneath the closed living-room door, up the stairs, like smoke, songs that had nothing to do with her, old hits from the time of his first marriage, the nineties Brit-pop Bella had once told Jessie that her mother loved. Jessie crept back to bed, the lyrics to the Blur song, 'Country House', whistling ironically in her head. She told herself it was just Will's way of saying a final goodbye to the house, his life with Mandy. Closure.

But the timing of her mother's words the next morning hadn't helped: had Jessie seriously considered what moving to the countryside could do to her marriage? The undertow there, Jessie knew, was that Jessie's father had fled sleepy Somerset in the eighties for an adventurous new life with another woman — christened 'The Hussy from Hampshire' by Jessie's mother — when Jessie was three, only to die in the Hussy's arms in a moped accident on the Costa Brava six months later. So Jessie can't blame her mother for pocketing the belief that a marriage might be broken into at any time, or simply explode, like a faulty gas boiler. Aware that she's not had a father's opinion to counterweight her mother's, Jessie's always made an effort consciously to discard her mother's anxieties. But it can be difficult at times. Like trying to separate a sound from its echo.

Maybe for these reasons she had secretly feared the deal might fall apart right until yesterday morning when the removal lorries turned up. She had watched, stomach knotted, as their London lives were dismantled, bound with tape, memories rolled up like rugs. It struck her both how replaceable things were — throws, food mixers, unread books — and how easy they were to forget once removed from view. And a tiny voice in her head guiltily hoped that Mandy would be too, just a little.

Will wore his darkest sunglasses during the move yesterday, joked blackly about how he never thought he'd get sentimental about logistics. But Jessie didn't cry: she was, she realized, completely ready to go, and had been for a while. Since she'd had Romy, the big booming city she'd loved had shrunk to the same circle of tightly packed Victorian streets: the park she would circuit with Romy, wondering if she could face taking the Tube to the Tate Modern or if she'd get the pram wheels stuck on the escalator again; Greta's, the coffee shop whose sweet staff never complained about her nursing a coffee for hours to give Will and Bella space alone at home; the lovely Lebanese grocer where she'd blindly buy exotic ingredients for supper, hoping to make a meal that Bella might not compare unfavourably to her late foodie mother's or, worse, one of the beleaguered au pairs'.

Jessie suddenly recalls the day Camille — the last au pair in a long, frequently sobbing line — left their household. It was the first day of Jessie's maternity leave: she was determined to embrace her new role and show Will she could manage both girls without any hired help. (How hard could it be?) As they waved Camille off, Bella hissed in Jessie's ear that she'd merely taken Camille's place: 'You'll probably stick around a little bit longer. But I wouldn't count on it.' And Jessie had replied, in the steadiest voice she could manage, that Bella could absolutely count on it, actually. Bella would always be able to count on her. As Jessie lies on the mattress now, staring up at the flaking plaster on the ceiling, she hopes that one day Bella will

46

see Applecote as a physical manifestation of that promise.

Yesterday she and Will ran around madly, trying to make the unlived-in house homely for the girls, Will struggling to put together Romy's cotbed, Jessie scattering their cushions and rugs around the grubby old drawing room so that one place at least felt familiar. Then, after the girls finally fell asleep — Romy in a room adjacent to theirs, Bella in the peculiar little room under the eaves on the top floor, any ghouls or poisonous gases preferable to close proximity to her family — she and Will opened a bottle of warm champagne and walked around, hand in hand, marvelling, giggling like trespassing children in those big draughty rooms lit by bare bulbs, a house they still couldn't quite believe was theirs.

Jessie did puzzle at the charred remains of a log fire in the drawing-room grate — it looked so inky-black, not silvered with dust like everything else, and she was sure it hadn't been there when they'd looked around in January, or their last visit in March. Will joked that someone had clearly broken in to toast marshmallows, and she'd laughed and dismissed it, not wanting to dampen things. They swayed together on the veranda under a fairylight net of stars, and decided that Applecote was tilted more closely to the elements than anywhere they'd ever been, that all the upheaval was worth it. By midnight, Will had conked out, like an overwhelmed child at Christmas, unable to process any more. But Jessie had lain awake, enchanted by the countryside hush, the creak of wood, a tick of a pipe, a faint scurrying, the sense that the house was stirring around her in the darkness, waking again from a dormant state, observing its new inhabitants.

Jessie's first restless night at Applecote had jolted her own recent past vividly to the surface. Pitching on the edge of sleep, she could see her life flickering in the room's shadows, like old film rushes, how it had been so radically rerouted, fast-tracked from one place to another . . .

*　★　★

The bijou East London flat she shared with her girlfriend Lou, pre-Will. Flamingo wallpaper. An orange sixties egg chair bought from a shop on Brick Lane. A tumble-dryer scorching 'hand wash only' knickers. Jessie is in her early thirties: the decade of wedding invitations has begun, the first pregnancies, and dating has started to feel a bit like a game of musical chairs, no one wanting to be the person left standing. Mostly, she thinks, this is nonsense: if it happens, it happens. She'd rather be on her own than with the wrong person. Still, she can't help but wonder why it hasn't happened to her yet.

She's applying red lipstick, leaning into a gilt oval mirror in a flatteringly lit room. Her face is wide, girlish, her complexion still undimmed by motherhood's broken nights, completely unlined since her pale skin has never been able to take the sun. The bedroom reflected in the mirror is tiny, crammed with an old shop rail — smart fifties-style dresses for work, cowboy boots,

48

heels, far too many ankle boots, an ongoing costly quest for the elusive perfect pair — a bookshelf sagging with magazines and second-hand books from her favourite stall beneath Waterloo Bridge, photos she's never had time to organize in an album even though she has no responsibility for anyone but herself.

Through the thin, adjacent bedroom wall she can hear Lou and her boyfriend, Matt, giggling, a prelude to the noisy sex that will soon follow, the sex that she isn't having, and hasn't had in nearly six months. In her hurry to leave before it gets awkward, she forgets her Oyster card. She likes her Oyster card. Her flat-share. Her busy city life. It still gives her a kick because, like all non-native Londoners, Jessie carries around the knowledge of where she started: a cottage in Somerset, the familiar sequence of noises and smells that is her mother, dressed in her nurse's uniform, making an intense breakfast for the two of them, the day Jessie leaves for design college in London; Jessie, clutching a holdall of her least uncool clothes; her mother's eyes wet and needy, making Jessie feel guilty and more desperate to get away. Her judgemental younger self has no idea that she will have a daughter too one day, and that the thought of her little girl ever leaving home will make her feel like weeping. Or that motherhood will make her crave the sort of landscape she is fleeing, the damp soil, the simple worm-turned grassiness of the country childhood her mother worked so incredibly hard to provide.

Jessie's polished single self is arriving at work,

the design 'studio' — a large, beige office — humming with the quiet industry of over-qualified multinational twenty-somethings, the beep of software updates, the hiss of the coffee-maker, like a huge industrial machine. Corporate packaging. She's good at it — she has a reputation for being creative, a little maverick, working on projects late into the night. Sipping a soy latte, she sits in her lime-green ergonomic chair, moving lines about a screen, rotating three-dimensional shapes, considering the typography on a toothpaste tube, but a deeper bit of her brain, the unpredictable irrational bit where desire, dreams and stories live, is wondering if that man will be in the park at lunchtime again.

Same bench in St James's Park, close to Horse Guards Parade, where you can smell peaty horse dung and hear the growl of the diplomatic cars around Downing Street. Older, maybe in his late thirties — she's always liked this, something to do with growing up without a dad around, Lou says — he is not particularly tall but has wide, strong shoulders, like a swimmer, and a mop of dark hair, a crumpled air of Parisian dishevelment. He is easy to imagine sitting up in bed, naked, smoking, a black-and-white photograph. She is intrigued by the way he stretches out his legs, laces his fingers behind his head and glares up at the sky as if challenging it to a fight. Sometimes, as she walks past, their eyes hook — his an unusual speckled brown — and she feels it as a physical tug.

Afterwards, she wonders if she's imagined that connection in order to compete on some silly erotic level with Lou. She cannot imagine this man existing outside St James's Park. But one warm June evening he materializes miraculously on a Bloomsbury roof-terrace at a party thrown by one of Lou's boyfriend's friends. Lit by a halogen beam flickering from a wall of bamboo, he cuts a brooding figure, raking his hand through his hair, smoking fiercely. Like he doesn't want to be there. She watches him until he notices her, and his expression changes: surprise, something else. He stubs out his cigarette and cuts his way through the crowds. 'You're the girl from the park,' he says, his voice soft, low, already private. She nods, suddenly shy. 'Will,' he says, shaking her hand, smiling right inside her.

They kneel on the bench overlooking the roof-terrace wall, the city spreading beneath them, a landscape of light. Behind their backs, the party is now at a great distance. Will doesn't laugh much, but there is a woody warmth in his voice that draws her in, a gentle sense of humour, and unlike most men, he asks her lots of questions and listens carefully to her answers. He tells Jessie he's in 'the deeply unglamorous business of logistics', but can't be trusted to transport his own sunglasses to a party without sitting on them, and pulls out a broken pair from his shirt pocket. She laughs, and wonders why she's never found logistics fascinating before — you order things one day, they arrive the next! — and she can tell by the way his eyes shine that he's enjoying her, this conversation, her unlikely enthusiasm. Jessie feels she could talk about these things all night, that there's a world beneath this world she's never fully appreciated before, that they all take for granted, like electricity or WiFi or air — but their talk moves on, to the show at the National, their loathing of the gym, their love of Woody Allen, Minstrels, the smell of bonfire smoke, mown paths through long grass, her half-baked dreams of being a freelance illustrator one day, having her own little art studio at home, Will's dream of selling the company, living a less frenetic life . . .

Then, without warning, like a man urgently compelled to declare his true identity, he blurts out that his wife died in a cycle accident just over a year before. In the distance, a fluming firework, a splatter of red. 'I'm so sorry,' she says, forgetting herself, having drunk more than she meant to, reaching for his hand. Before she has a chance to feel foolish, his fingers close over hers as if they've been waiting for them. And in the pressure of his fingers she feels his need for contact. They sit in silence, an electric current circuiting their hands, their bodies. It is both the strangest and most intensely natural ten minutes of her life. When she looks up people are leaving, shooting them curious second glances. He doesn't take her number. For some reason, she cries all the way home.

By the following evening Will has got her email. He suggests meeting in the park at lunchtime on Monday. It sounds sweet, chaste. And it feels like an invitation to a dirty weekend in Paris. 'Very, very complicated,' warns Lou, who's asked around about Will and discovered a daughter, 'who sleeps clutching her dead mother's nightie', and a handsome widower known not to be on the market for anything more than no-strings hot sex. 'Damaged goods, Jess,' she says. 'He'll break your heart.'

Jessie agrees. She meets him on Monday anyway. There are wiry dark hairs flattened under his watch. She can't stop looking at them. Will's smile always starts in his eyes, spreading slowly, remaining there even when his mouth has stopped smiling. He has a way of teasing her, a bit like a brother would, someone she's known all her life. She likes it, even though she doesn't feel remotely sisterly to him. He is endearingly intrigued by her creativity, as if she were an artist, not someone who designs soup packets. He makes her see that she's got too used to herself, like a person in a stale marriage ceases to see their spouse for who they are: she's forgotten she can intercept the trajectory of her life, completely redesign it. They meet up every day that week because it feels a mad squandering of happiness not to. They visit galleries, seeing familiar artworks entirely anew. They wander central London's back-streets, the city never looking more beautiful. He does not try to kiss her.

One day, Jessie runs home from work and falls into Lou's arms in despair. Disaster. Code red. She's fallen in love with a man who doesn't fancy her. 'It's fur-coat-and-no-knickers time,' advises Lou, pouring Jessie a glass of white wine while opening a bag of Twiglets with her teeth.

So it is that three weeks after the party, one

53

sunny July lunchtime, she meets him in her success dress — tiny waist, a breathless starlet décolletage, the red a brilliant, unforgettable clash with her gleaming copper hair — and teaches him swing dance steps in the park, the ones she's learned at her Hackney evening class, not caring about the people staring, pressing him close to her, feeling his knotted body soften, something in him give. Afterwards they lie in the grass laughing, and he pins her to the ground by her wrists, lowers his face to hers and they kiss for the first time. She blows him away, he whispers, his eyes full of tears, his lips brushing her ear lobe, a gust of Heaven, a light in a deep, pitch-black mine. Later that day, after work, in her tiny bedroom, he will peel off that red dress (the dress that hasn't fitted since she had Romy), and kiss her singleton's drum-flat belly, her thighs, her neck, over and over until it is impossible to tell where she ends and he begins. The noise of the office, Lou and Matt fucking, the traffic roaring beneath her bedroom window, the pain of a sandal blister on her heel, it is eclipsed that summer by the sheer lust and happiness that turn her into one of those London women who smile and blush to themselves as they swing from a handrail in a hot crowded Tube carriage . . .

★ ★ ★

The memory started to fade: a peachy dawn light nosed its way into their Applecote bedroom, wiping Jessie's old life from the

54

shadows, as if to say, 'Do you see how all those disparate moments were connected, plotted like a line to this old house in this remote Cotswold valley? You are here now. Sleep.' And she did.

★ ★ ★

'Oh, Jessie.' Will opens one eye, takes in his strange surroundings. The corners of his mouth curl with a sleepy smile. 'Where are we? What have you made us do?'

Laughing, she kisses him on the lips. She likes the animal taste of him in the morning. 'Coffee? I'll hunt down the pot.' She grabs the nearest clothes from her suitcase — a yellow tea dress, smelling of the London house. 'Brr. This place needs warming up.'

'I'll chop logs later.' He grins. 'You know, I think I might have been waiting all my life to say that.' Propping himself on his elbows, Will watches his wife brushing the restless night's tangles from her hair.

When she was pregnant, Will would brush it for her, their eyes locked in the mirror, her hair luxuriant with hormones, floating with static, as they seemed to float above ordinary life. There hasn't been much time for that sort of thing since Romy was born or in the last manic few months since they decided to move. This summer, Jessie thinks, these last two weeks of summer, we will find the time and peace to be that couple again. The agony of decision-making is over. They are here. For better, for worse.

55

* ★ ★

Walking into the kitchen, Romy a warm, dense weight on her hip, Jessie can taste the weather in the room. It is draughty, damp, stirred by the smells of the morning garden, even though the windows are all closed and the black range radiates a doggy heat. The oldest part of Applecote, it's easy to imagine a dumpy cook making pies in here, a maid scrubbing mud-clagged potatoes, the beams greasy with lamp smoke. She loves the bath-sized butler's sink, the butcher's block, scarred with knife and scorch marks, the rows of cavernous wall cupboards still stuffed with dented copper pans.

Jessie loves it because it is the opposite of their modern stainless-steel London kitchen, Mandy's kitchen, the site of those indelible awkward dinner parties of the early days: Romy screaming down the baby-monitor, Will's friends, older than her, far more successful and serious, until they got drunk and the husbands would stare at her with an odd mixture of envy and suspicion, and make jokes about Will being thrown back into the nappy years, and the wives would start crying about Mandy, then apologizing, flapping their hands, and saying they're sure Jessie's lovely too, which made it worse. Yes, she's happy to say goodbye to all that. A dishwasher would be nice, though.

Making a mental note to call the plumber, Jessie arranges Romy on a cushion on one of Applecote's spindle-back chairs — Romy's still too small to reach the farmhouse table properly,

56

and her own high chair was broken in the move. Romy sits, not wriggling for once, gazing around the room in wonder, eating dry Cheerios from a plastic bowl.

It's like the first day in a holiday house. Jessie digs the coffee pot from a cardboard box, sets it up on the unfamiliar range and hopes for the best. After a while, a satisfying drip falls from it and beads on the hot plate, rolling, fizzing, until it vanishes entirely with a sizzle, like their London life.

'Bell-Bell,' she hears Romy chunter.

Jessie turns around, smiling, then starts. Bella is wearing a dove-grey silk dressing-gown Jessie's never seen before, her dark hair loose, swirling dramatically over her shoulders. 'Wow, where did you . . .'

'Mum's,' Bella says, defiant yet needy of approval.

The word sucks the air from the room. The dressing-gown ripples. It has fine black lace edging, Jessie notices, a discreet sensuality. And it looks expensive, very expensive. A gift. A Valentine's present, maybe. Jessie is aware of the high risk in saying the wrong thing at this point.

'It was in the boxes of Mum's stuff — the boxes Dad brought down from the attic at home?' Bella watches Jessie's reaction carefully.

Jessie nods, her mouth dry. In the chaos of the last few hours, she'd forgotten about those two boxes, Mandy Boxes. She'd never been sure what they contained — photos maybe, some of Mandy's more poignant things; it felt way too intrusive to ask — only that Will stored them

57

away shortly after she'd moved into the London house, in a way that had seemed sweetly symbolic at the time. 'Well, it's . . . very glamorous,' Jessie says, recovering herself. 'How did you sleep in your new bedroom?'

'Like a bad trip,' Bella retorts sharply, grabbing at the cereal box, leaving Jessie to worry if the reference is serious, based on an authentic druggy experience.

She sighs silently. Silly to expect Bella to embrace the move straight away. These last two weeks of August will be a period of transition. They must bear with it until Bella starts at Squirrels Ladies College, a stable new routine. Squirrels, as it's known, is an independent — unlike Bella's London school, or either Jessie's or Will's old comps — and ruinously expensive. But all the decent local state sixth forms were full and they've decided it's better to forgo expensive building works and foreign holidays than take a risk with Bella's education at such a tender point. It also has an unflappable headmistress who wasn't spooked by Bella's last school report.

'But . . . ' Bella leans back against the warm range, picking at her bowl of cereal with her fingers. 'I did get an excellent view of our stalker from the window.'

★ ★ ★

Now, where might she find their first nosy neighbour? Jessie remembers them clearly from her own childhood, those benign bustling village

58

women who knew your business without ever being told. They'd always turn up on newcomers' doorsteps, clutching Tupperware boxes stuffed with scones. She'd like to say hello. Anyway, it's an excellent excuse to explore the garden.

She blows a stream of kisses to Will and Romy at the kitchen window, then walks away from the stone veranda, her heart quickening. The garden has changed almost beyond recognition since January. No winter windows between bare whiskery branches now, just soaring walls of green. A leafy puzzle of edges, beginnings and endings, it feels like the kind of impenetrable garden that might change shape as you walk through it, lead you out of one century into another.

Roses are everywhere, their stems running amok, like feral teenagers who have taken over in their parents' absence (Jessie knows something about this). Amorphous lumps of yew and box squat in the overgrown lawns. Beyond them, the ground starts to undulate, swelling over the splayed toes of trees, following the inclines of forgotten paths, ponds and beds, tracing the garden's original structure, like a lost ancient settlement. And the Wilderness is so verdant, tangled, it no longer resembles garden at all, the tiny historic well — sealed, thank goodness — just visible beneath a dense hive of brambles, like a chimney to a hobbit's house.

Nothing is quite how Jessie remembers it. The apple store's warped wooden door is ajar, revealing a deserted wasps' nest hanging from the rafters, like an enormous hard cheese. The small dirty shed window has been polished in a circle by a hand from inside, the fingermarks still visible. Peering through it, she notices a scuff of muddy footprints on the shed's wooden floor, and her mind trips back to the charred fire in the drawing-room grate again. Someone has been in there recently. She feels a tiny flicker of disquiet.

But the orchard welcomes her with a cheery clack of jackdaws, the buzz of waspy plums. And it is as she is reaching up, plucking a biblical red apple, that she catches movement on the other side of the sagging perimeter wall, and remembers the purpose of her mission. Jessie climbs on to a tree stump and peers over, just in time to see a woman walking away: a leopard-print headscarf tied, silver hair curling beneath it, two black Labradors. The same woman Bella described earlier. Jessie calls shyly, 'Hello there!'

The dogs glance back, tug on their leads. But the woman quickens her pace and is soon obscured by hedgerows as the lane twists away.

Oh, thinks Jessie. Maybe she's just hard of hearing. Maybe they do things differently in the country now. She stays there a moment, hanging on with her small strong hands, her yellow dress blowing around her legs. It's beautiful, the floury clouds, the wild flowers, the birds, but feels surprisingly lonely.

Not wanting to return to the house on a flat note, Jessie delves deeper into the garden, dwarfed by the trees into something more doe-like, vulnerable, as she searches for the rectangle of liquid darkness she can see from her bedroom window. The pool gate shivers as it opens, kissing a peeling forget-me-not blue paint to her palm. Bordered by the looming yew on one side, rose-scrambled walls on the others, the area feels completely cut off from the rest of the garden, eerily seductive. The rainwater collected in the tank has a cinematic jet-bead glitter, the visible cold of an underground lake. And at each corner of the pool stands a goddess statue, fragile, beautiful, broken, like survivors of some terrible natural disaster.

The otherworldliness holds her there. Jessie sits down on the pool's edge, her feet dangling, the reflection of her sandal soles flashing on the water, like pale fish. And the anxiety she's felt so often these last few months bubbles up again, taking her by surprise. Maybe it's the leaves rotting on the surface, the thought of how they'd close over her head if she fell in. The water's vertigo pull. But Jessie can't stop her mind spiralling back to what Bella did in London, and something of that day returns, that heart-stopping phone call from the school — *Bella Tucker? Yes, it's her stepmother speaking, her father's away, yes, you can definitely talk to me* . . . She has promised to forget about it, like Will, and take Bella at her word. Only she hasn't, not quite.

Seeking escape from the chaff of such thoughts, Jessie looks up at the lime-yellow tree canopy, stirred by gusts undetectable at pool level. She half closes her eyes. She lets the garden wrap itself around her, sounds becoming brushstrokes: the neon chatter of birdsong; the blue of the wind; and something else, sepia, weightless child's footsteps. Jessie starts and glances at the gate, expecting to see Romy and Will. 'Romy?' she calls hesitantly. 'Will? Bella?'

Silence. There is no one, of course, nothing at all, just a magnesium lick across the pool that dazzles momentarily, leaving behind her own wavering reflection, and something else, something that makes Jessie lean forward, heart racing, and part the slurry of leaves with her fingers to check that the submerged smudge is not a body bobbing at the bottom of the pool, just a trick of the light.

4

Ma's not wrong. Applecote Manor is just the same, the iron front gate, the house behind it creamy and solid, like a block of vanilla ice-cream. Clouds of lavender, drowsy bees. Uncle Perry's black Daimler on the drive, powdered with pollen. The high garden walls — although they don't seem quite as high as they once did — are garlanded with fat baby-pink roses, the size of Ma's hats, so unlike the buddleia and ragwort that explode out of London's old bombsites and thread into our terrace garden. Behind the wall, its stone scorched white as teeth in the July sun, the head of a topiary peacock that, as a small child, had made me think of the garden as an animal enclosure at London Zoo, although the animals were made of clipped box hedging, delicately sculpted by gardeners with shears.

The last five years seem to have been snipped away too. Even the sky is as I remember it, huge, blue, warm as a bath, the air transparent, not washing-up-water tinged as it is in London, alive with butterflies and birds, so many birds. So much is the same that it highlights the one crushing, unbelievable thing that is not: Audrey isn't about to come belting out of the house, running down the path, excitedly calling my name.

'Margot, are you okay?' Flora asks, concerned,

63

as the taxi that met us at the railway station rumbles into the distance. 'You look sort of peaky. Don't be sick on your sandals. You'll never scrub the stench out of them.'

I bend over, head spinning, hands on my knees, not knowing how to explain that we're all older, coming of age — I'm wearing black Capri trousers that make me feel like Françoise Sagan — and Audrey is for ever a girl in a blue dress the colour of meadow cornflowers.

'Ah, the curse,' Pam diagnoses briskly. 'It lives up to its name in this heat. You just have to soldier through it, Margot.'

I straighten slowly, wondering how it is possible that my sisters are not feeling it too. Audrey's disappearance has been pressed on to our lives faint as a fingerprint until today — the subject taboo, rarely discussed, too awful to think about, irreconcilable with the gay tug of our everyday lives — but here it is physical, internal, like a snap of bone beneath the skin.

'Better?' asks Dot, sweetly.

I nod. Even though I fear this is just the start.

The sun daggers into our eyes. We lift our hands simultaneously, shielding from its beams. A small stalling action that puts another moment between this one — the familiar taste of London still gritty in our mouths, the tack of our mother's departing kiss — and crunching up the gravel path to Applecote's front door sheltering in the mossy shade of its portico. Dot thumbs her glasses up her nose. The silence twitches in the heat. My trousers stick to the back of my legs.

'So, here we are, abandoned by our dear mother in the middle of God-awful nowhere, a place where young girls have an awkward habit of disappearing off the face of the earth on summer evenings,' Pam observes. 'Never to be seen again.'

Dot sidles closer to me, as if I might protect her from a similar fate, all the more petrifying for being unknown and because Audrey has never been found, alive or dead.

'Don't, Pam.' Flora grimaces.

'Someone has to say it,' Pam sighs.

Pam and Flora never thought this day — a fleetingly amusing idea back in May — would actually happen, that there would be an end to London's dances, gossip and suitors; that Ma, derailed by events of her own making (probably never expecting Sybil to agree to her outlandish idea in the first place), would sail for Africa tomorrow.

'Margot,' Dot whispers. Her spectacles are smudged with greasy fingerprints from the cheese sandwiches we ate on the train. 'It is *very* quiet.'

'As a grave,' says Pam, swinging her heavy suitcase easily in her hand.

'Maybe they've forgotten we're coming,' Dot suggests hopefully.

'No, no. They'll be in the garden on a day like today, that's all,' I say. Above the trees, a flock of birds, dozens of black Ms, like Audrey and I used to draw them. My stomach lurches again.

'The gardens are heaven, Dot,' Flora says, trying to reassure our nervous little sister.

Pam snorts. 'Yes, and when we wake up in the countryside tomorrow morning we may well feel like we've died.'

'Don't make everything worse than it is already, Pam. She's teasing, Dot, don't worry. Come on, we can't stand here for ever.' Flora starts to walk towards the house, her pale blue skirt brushing the lavender, stealing its scent in its folds. The rest of us follow in Flora's shadow, as we always do, the sun beating down on our snowy legs.

As we get closer to Applecote, London further away, like it might not exist at all, I'm hit by the odd sensation that I'm walking back in time, cat's cradling the last five years between my fingers, like elastic, that I might even be able to alter the past somehow, pull Audrey away before anything terrible happens. That if I try hard enough, I can un-vanish her.

★　★　★

It is Aunt Sybil. It's not Aunt Sybil. A woman fiercely squirts a tumble of roses beside the garden gate, her fingers on the trigger of a spray. A shock of straight hair, white as table salt, where the vibrant auburn curls used to be. Far thinner, all bone and shadows, her head large on the vine of her neck, she's not wearing a jaunty yellow dress, the colour of Spanish lemons, the dress I always picture her in, but something heavy, navy and shapeless, as if she's a season out of step, inhabiting her very own winter. Twenty years appear to have marked her face, not five. My mother's age, Sybil now looks like she was never young.

Turning slowly, she seems equally shocked by our appearance. 'Bunny's girls? My goodness.' Her gaze slides cautiously from one of us to the next. Her eyes are small, watery, colourless as puddles. 'How grown-up you all are,' she says, three lines pressing between her eyes, like the impression of a fruit fork, as if she finds it unbearable that we have grown up and Audrey hasn't. 'So grown-up,' she repeats numbly.

We smile awkwardly, not knowing how to bridge the gap between now and the last time we saw her, our childhood and our womanliness, the scabby knees we once had, the bras and girdles we now wear, the fact we are here, while Audrey is not. Sybil makes no attempt to close the distance. She doesn't open her arms to us, like she used to, or kiss our cheeks, but recoils slightly, as if touching us, getting too close, might burn her.

'You are a very beautiful young woman, Flora.' Sybil's thin lips hitch into a smile with obvious effort. Flora modestly bows her head, pretending the compliment is novel, not something people continually remark upon. Sybil turns to Pam, her gaze sweeping over Pam's feet — two sizes bigger than Ma's — to her broad sportswoman's shoulders. 'Gracious. I did read somewhere that girls are getting taller since rationing stopped.' She covers a more natural smile with the nail-bitten tips of her fingers. 'You are very statuesque, my dear. What is Bunny feeding you?'

Pam bristles. She will not forgive Sybil's comment easily. 'You don't want to know, Aunt.'

Sybil cocks her head to one side. 'Oh . . . is that . . . little Dorothy?' Dot is shuffling behind Pam, scraping her sandal on the gravel, trying to camouflage herself in a puff of dust. 'Dorothy, last time I saw you, you were . . . ' She lowers her hand to hip height. There is a hiccup, a holding of breath, at the mention of 'last time'. A small nervous laugh cracks in her throat like glass. ' . . . a little sapling of a girl. How old are you now?'

Dot doesn't want to say it. The age Audrey was. Everything here swings back to Audrey, the house's magnetic north. 'Twelve,' she manages.

Something starts beneath Sybil's skin, a comparison between Audrey and Dot maybe. But thankfully they look so unlike, and are such opposites, Sybil is able to recover quickly. 'You are swarthy for a Wilde, Dorothy, like a little Italian.' The silence stretches into the shape of a question, as it always does when people mention Dot's exotic colouring. 'Now, you probably don't remember Applecote very well, do you?' she says, in the remedial voice grownups stupidly use for Dot. 'The pool? The orchard? The stones in the meadow?'

'I just remember the puppy,' Dot mumbles, curling one foot behind the other, forgetting all Ma's instructions to speak loudly and cheerfully, that we're delighted to be here. 'And the jam.'

I suddenly remember how the housekeeper, Moll, would give us jars of Applecote jam — gooseberry, wild strawberry, plum — to take

68

back to Ma at the end of the holidays. It was always something she did in private, when Sybil and Perry weren't around, so it carried a delicious contraband whiff.

'Well, there's a lot for a little girl to remember, I suppose. It's a big house.' Sybil glances up at her home through sandy lashes, her gaze landing at the porthole window on the top floor. Audrey's window. Audrey's room. It winks back, as if about to let us in on a secret. Sybil sighs, adds, 'Too big really . . . ' The pause swells painfully. Suddenly we all know what is coming.' . . . now.'

Pam lets out one of her inappropriate bark laughs, like the ones that escape during assemblies when the head relays news of a despised old teacher 'passing'. I stare down at my feet.

Sybil's Oxford lace-ups swivel towards me on the gravel. I look up slowly and our eyes meet directly for the first time. There's a violent spasm in hers, a rapid dilation of the pupils. 'Hello, Margot,' she breathes.

'Aunt Sybil.'

She frowns at my legs, the black trousers. 'How's your skin, the back of your knees?' she asks, as if this might explain them.

Embarrassed, I mumble something about it being up and down. I hate it for being the most memorable thing about me.

'Well, girls . . . ' She hesitates, her eyes still roaming over my face, as if something about my unremarkable features traps her there. 'Let's get out of this unbearable heat, shall we? I don't remember a summer like it. London must be like Hades.'

Inside the cool stone-flagged entrance hall, it is still and tense, like the silence following a terrible row. I smell wax polish, vinegar, a domestic order we're unused to. The oak staircase, wide as a London bus, sweeps into the hall with the same dark red stair runner, unworn by young feet these last five years. The furniture has not, as part of me always fancied, disappeared with Audrey, sucked out of the windows to be strewn across the Cotswolds in scraps of horsehair, floral linen and silk. I scan the hall for signs of our uncle, as one might for a bull in a field, but can't see anything except a pair of gigantic battered leather boots.

'Margot?' Flora elbows me, then says, through a forced smile, 'The present?'

'Oh. Oh, yes. Sorry.' I dig into my satchel and pull out the cake that Ma's help, Betty, made a few days ago. It slumps wetly from one side of the tin to the other. 'It's from Ma, Aunt. She hopes you like it.'

Sybil prises off the lid, holding it slightly away from her body. 'Goodness.' She blows out sharply, like a puff from a bicycle pump. 'How kind.'

'A fruit cake,' Dot clarifies, lest it resembles something else after the long train journey.

'Oh. I never knew your mother was a baker.' And there are the old tensions again, snapping in the air, like skipping ropes: we all know that what Sybil really means is, 'Your mother is not interested in homemaking and never has been,'

70

so we all chime in unison, 'Oh, she is!' with such loyal passion that the lie is obvious.

Sybil frowns down at the cake. And it occurs to me that it must hurt that Ma, a woman who wears her motherhood so lightly, has a reckless surplus of daughters whereas Sybil, who took motherhood so seriously, lost her only one.

'Wildlings!' booms a voice from behind a closed door. Even Sybil startles, like a hare.

★ ★ ★

He has his back to us: mountainous shoulders, a thick neck swelling from the constraint of his shirt collar, the potato-sack sag in the armchair's base. Moppet, the cloud-grey whippet puppy, no longer a puppy, nervously scrabbles up from her master's velvet-slippered feet. 'My back has the devil in its discs today.' Stout red fingers piano the air. 'Come here, girls.'

We slowly walk to face him, our eyes rudely widening. While the last five years have left Sybil thinner and paler, sucked of blood, my uncle has ballooned, his once-handsome face bloated: I'm sure if you pricked it clear juices would run out. Even his head has expanded, its planes — the square flat forehead, the jaw thrusting out, like a padded boxer's glove — seeming more crudely carved. A gamey smell rises off him in the heat. 'Wildlings,' he repeats, with a nod of gruff satisfaction.

It's odd hearing it. No one has called us that for five years. After the wildling apple trees, the ones grown from rogue bird-scattered seeds, not carefully planted like those in the orchard, Perry's affectionate nickname for us was always pipped with criticism of my parents. Perry and Pa famously never got on, even as boys. ('Brothers always want to murder each other,' Ma would shrug. 'It's sisters you need to look out for. They're the ones who can break your heart.')

'So the tribe returns.' Perry reaches for his drink, studies us down the shaft of his glass, eyes licking over Flora, as all men's do. Sybil stands stiffly, biting the inside of her cheek.

'We're so pleased to be back at Applecote. It's very kind of you to take us in.' No one can lie as well as Flora. She could get away with murder, Ma always says. 'We're very grateful, Uncle.'

'No need for baroque exaggeration,' Perry says, with a bluntness that makes even Flora colour. 'You're Wildes, after all. Couldn't leave you to get gobbled alive on the streets of London while Bunny goes hopping around the clubs of Cairo, could we?'

'Morocco,' I point out, sounding a little too pedantic. He lifts an eyebrow, noticing me properly for the first time, his left eye squinting.

Sweat slides down the inside of my trousers.

Moppet starts to sniff us nervously, cowering, only accepting a stroke from Dot, whom all animals seem instinctively to trust.

'Ma's got a job, Uncle. At the consulate,' says Pam, sharply, the most protective of our mother, and her own role as Ma's fiercest critic. Perry's gaze rolls off me and on to Pam. 'She needs to earn some money,' she adds.

72

At the unmentionable word, I suck in my breath. The silence tilts, sending everything sliding downwards. Then it starts, like far-off thunder at first, his laughter growing louder and rougher, splitting open the air in the room. Sybil turns to stare at her husband in astonishment, as if he has inexplicably started speaking in a different tongue. 'You never did let manners get in the way of your opinion, did you, Pam? I remember now. Excellent, excellent.' Perry shakes his head, his belly quivering, his laugh still moving about inside it. 'Good God. Applecote Manor isn't going to know what's hit it. I hope you're ready for these Wildlings, Sybil. I hope you realize what Bunny's charmed you into here.'

'I'll get Moll to show the girls to their bedrooms so they can dress for dinner,' Sybil says, her voice vinegary. It's hard to imagine her being charmed by anyone, least of all my mother. It strikes me that she must have her own reasons for letting us stay at Applecote, although I can't think what. 'Moll?'

As if she'd been listening outside the door, Moll steps into the room, smoothing her overall with plump busy hands. Stout, rectangular, with an enormous bosom, Moll has the same crinkled round face, a bit like an old apple. I wait for her to smile.

'You remember my four nieces?' says Sybil, tightly. 'Clarence's girls from London,' she adds, like an apology in advance.

Moll smiles: and there it is, the neat black gap of a missing tooth I used to think of as a tiny

73

door. For some reason I'm very glad it's still there. 'Welcome back, girls.' That voice. That accent. Thick with soft country mud, blackberries picked off a hedge. Other things too. Old songs never written down, only ever sung in this valley. Omens, superstitions, country lore that can't be explained, only understood. 'If you'd like to follow me,' she says, a little bit uncertainly, not used to guests.

We clatter up the staircase behind Moll, scuffing the waxed banisters with our bags, Pam slitting her throat with her finger. Halfway up, Flora grabs my arm. 'Oh! Look, a photo of you, Margot.'

I peer closer. A photograph, taken in sharp sunlight, bleaching out the features of a girl with plaits, a cheeky smile. It does sort of look like me, I suppose, caught in a particularly flattering light.

'That's Audrey,' Moll corrects in a whisper, her fingers touching the crucifix at her neck.

'Eek, sorry,' says Flora, pulling a face. Pam snorts.

We climb the stairs a little quicker then, peering down long landings, with closed doors, windows draped in heavy sepulchral curtains. There are more and more photographs of Audrey, like an accelerating panicked heartbeat, and the house gets darker and stuffier the higher up we go, so that by the time we are on the top floor, Audrey's floor, Applecote seems to be sealed tight, like one of Moll's jam-jars, lest fresh air get in, allow what has been so carefully preserved to blacken and rot.

The top step creaks, just as I remember. The landing is as narrow. The bathroom door is open, revealing the familiar claw-footed bath, the long, dangling chain of the lavatory flush and the damp stain on the wall, in the shape of Ireland, from the drainpipe that always blocks outside. I remember how Audrey would proudly show off the names of East End evacuees — P. L. Trotter, May and Teddy — scrawled under the washbasin, and how she added her own, a neat, carefully perfected autograph, ready for when she grew up and became famous. Like she knew.

'I hope it's not too hot for you up here,' Moll says, not quite meeting our eyes. She pulls a handkerchief from her overall pocket, wipes sweat from her bristly upper lip. We're all playing the game of pretending everything is normal, that a girl of twelve didn't vanish from Applecote's grounds five years ago. 'You're all back in the same guestrooms.'

'Lovely,' says Flora, clearly relieved that no one's going to be shunted into Audrey's old bedroom.

It's hard not to stare at it. At the far end of the landing, the pale door seems to pulse in the gloom, drawing attention to itself like the newest stone in a graveyard. I become aware of Moll frowning at me, as if something in my expression unsettles her. 'I must tell you that Audrey's room is strictly out of bounds,' she says, in a furtive voice.

Pam shudders. 'Like we'd ever want to go in there.'

Waiting for my sisters to collect me for our first dinner, I trace the route of Audrey's last known journey from my bedroom window: under an early evening August sun, she'd have run through the garden with her crayfishing line, obscured as soon as she got into the Wilderness, passed the bathing-pool, slipped through the gate and cut across the meadow to the deserted riverbank, where Moll would later find her paper bag of dried bacon rinds, a lone crayfish scuttling at the end of the line, like a clue.

I press my hands against the glass, angry that Audrey is not there still. The only small comfort is knowing how much she would have enjoyed the mystery, the vanishing bit. Becoming such a sensation. I did too, shamefully, although I think Audrey would have understood. Her disappearance lent me a rare celebrity in the Squirrels playground, the popular pretty girls who always ignored me, huddling around, pressing their bodies against mine, hanging on my every word. I remember the strange new power I felt as they started to sob, one after the other, each louder than the next, grabbing one another, competing for who could feel things more, the explosive emoting spreading like flu, taking out whole classrooms, erupting during the Lord's Prayer, as if it was they who had disappeared, or their sister, not a girl in the newspapers whom they had never known. Not my beloved cousin from Applecote Manor.

Or maybe it was just that we all wanted to be

Audrey a little bit, Audrey with her forget-me-not eyes and milk-blonde plaits, her picture in the papers. We wanted to be noticed. We wanted to be missed. But not to die. Dying was not glamorous. Dying meant TB, complications from measles, drowning in a rough sea at Margate. But vanishing, like Audrey, that was a delicious mystery, a secret holiday. It meant anything was possible, like finding out you were adopted. Also, for me, it meant I didn't have to grieve for Audrey, like I did Pa. I didn't have to think about worms wriggling through eye sockets. And it meant she would come back. Only she hasn't.

These last five years, Audrey's always felt alive but silent, like a pen pal who has discovered boys. Audrey-ish things often flare in my mind: the red heart-shaped buttons on the cornflower-blue dress — which I'd fiercely admired — that she was '*last seen wearing*'; her princessy sleigh bed, the way its woven headboard pressed a constellation of tiny stars on to the skin of our bare girls' shoulders. I envied so much of what she had: a father (alive), a room of her own under the eaves with a porthole window and a boggle of sky, a red mole that sat on her knee like a ladybird, the way she never had to share her bathwater.

Yet I always knew I had the thing Audrey most wanted in the world: sisters. She hated the intensity and solitude of being an only child — she'd ripped apart my aunt's womb by escaping it bottom-first — and grew up craving company, a sister's unconditional shrug of love. 'You've got a brain like a board game, Margot,' she'd say sometimes. 'And you're really good at drawing toes. If only we could marry each other.'

Everyone said we looked very similar: the unspoken bit was that Audrey was prettier, her features more finely wrought, better arranged. She was also blonder. Cleverer. Richer. In fact, Audrey was more of everything — a sweet-sharp cordial undiluted by siblings — and by resembling her, but being almost two years younger, falling short of her, I made her superiority obvious, which she liked.

Pam used to say Audrey bossed me about — pots and kettles — and that I shouldn't stand for it. But I was happy to submit in order to taste the rare sweetness of being favourite: Audrey made me feel chosen, special. For two weeks every summer, that was all that mattered. She treated Pam warily — sensible. She adored Flora but at an awed distance. She grandly declared Dot too young to be truly interesting: 'A little insignificant on her own, without the rest of you, like a full stop at the end of a sentence.' I disloyally agreed with her even though I didn't see Dot like that at all. Audrey always made words sound good enough to eat.

I would secretly debate which of my sisters I'd sacrifice so I could have Audrey as a sister instead. The victim changed weekly, depending on how much attention Flora was attracting that day, or whether Pam had slipped a note under my bedroom door saying, 'Dear Margot, you stole my pen, I hate you, your loving sister, Pam.' Audrey and I were never tested, like sisters are, never with each other long enough to grow

78

disenchanted. There was nothing to weigh us down — no dead father, no running out of coal on a winter evening — so the time we spent together at Applecote was honeymoon light. And, of course, it was always summer, summers in which we were suspended like the strawberries in the glorious jellies that appeared from the bountiful kitchen.

Every childish whim was met at Applecote. It wasn't just the jellies. There was an endless supply of colourful balloons purely for Audrey's amusement, enormous cupboards stuffed with more toys, board games and children's books than I'd ever seen. Audrey's home life seemed to me a never-ending birthday party, albeit without any other guests until we arrived. The moment Audrey and I were reunited, a year older than the last time we'd met, we would lock into the same private world of hide and seek, shadow puppets, handstands against the rough brick of the orchard wall. We'd talk fancifully about how one day, if the wind was strong, when we had enough balloons and hadn't eaten too much tea, we might fly. It didn't matter where we went as long as we flew — or crash-landed — together.

But that last summer Audrey wasn't interested in the balloons, declaring them too childish, along with jelly and *Malory Towers*. Something was changing in my cousin. I had no idea what until the morning Audrey pulled me into the apple store — making Dot stand outside — and unbuttoned her blouse to show me how her breasts had budded, impressive at twelve. She made me feel them, tiny cushiony mounds, hard

79

and hot beneath the nipple. Every couple of days we'd return to the cool dark of the store so we could check how they were growing, like greenhouse tomatoes. She reassured me that by next year I would have breasts too. Secretly I wasn't sure I wanted them.

How terrible now to remember that I enjoyed saying goodbye that summer, as I did every summer, the heightened drama of it, knowing Audrey would miss me. I was also relieved to get away from the confusion of my cousin's new breasts, back to the combative simplicity of life with my sisters. Audrey begged to come back to London with us, as she always did — Audrey worshipped Ma as fiercely as her parents disapproved of her — but Sybil would never let her stay in Chelsea, worried that the disorder of our lives might be catching, that we'd fill her head with improper thoughts and nits.

But it turns out she'd have been safer in London. Five days after we left Applecote, Audrey had gone. 'Simply vanished, the poor darling,' Ma told us, in a shaken voice. For years I wilfully accepted Ma's evasive, elliptical account of events because I didn't want any of it to be true. The lack of detail meant I could salt the story with hope and adventure, mix true memories with false ones, and make the story of Audrey's disappearance no different from, no more substantial than, the ghostly yarns Audrey and I used to whisper to each other in the meadow at dusk. Not seeing my aunt and uncle these last five years has allowed me to do this, I realize, not visiting the Cotswolds, rarely hearing

Audrey mentioned. But now we're back at Applecote? Not knowing what happened to Audrey means that even going down to dinner this evening feels like being sent into dangerous terrain without a map. For the first time since she went missing, I realize I desperately need to know the truth.

★ ★ ★

The dining room is the colour of the inside of a Bramley apple, a very pale dense green, in its centre a long, narrow rectangular mahogany table, polished to a mirror finish, with many legs in awkward places. Sybil sits very straight at one end, rigid as a board, eyes sharp and darting, Perry at the other. We are under-dressed in our summer frocks: Perry's sporting a spotty bow-tie and dinner shirt, Sybil an unfashionable long gown — funereal, high-necked, its skirt meanly cut — that gives out the unmistakable pong of mothballs. I notice a livid web of red veins on her un-made-up cheeks — Ma wouldn't tolerate them for a moment. She'd smother them in Pan Stik.

No gazpacho: pork, potatoes, peas, dumplings, a huge boat of gravy. Moppet, forbidden any titbits, lies mournfully under the table. Sybil picks at her food, seeming not to enjoy a single mouthful, her face reflected in the polished silver of her dessert spoon, warped in a way that seems to unlock something of her inner torment. Perry, though, eats like a man with a hole inside him that he can never fill, his lips slicked with grease,

81

waiting impatiently for Moll as she bustles back and forth from the kitchen, hers a solid, fluttery presence, like a nervous wood pigeon.

The air spins with unspoken things, the conversation stilted. Perry says little, his gaze seeming often to travel, disconcertingly, to our mouths. Sybil asks us politely about our studies, our home weekends in London, then coughs into her napkin when Pam tells her about Flora's friend's fancy birthday do at the Dorchester, the calypso band's drums that felt like they were inside you, had taken the place of your heart. Perry puts down his fork for the first time then, listening carefully to Pam, as if soaking up every last detail of a world he'd completely forgotten existed. When she has finally finished — Flora kicks her shins hard under the table — Sybil says tightly that we won't find anything like that here, the country being a quiet place, not liking foreign music or rowdy parties. 'More's the pity,' Perry mumbles, and Sybil's mouth forms a hard thin line, like a zip. Pudding arrives, just in time, steaming bowls of apple crumble and custard.

Sybil eats one mouthful, savouring the taste of her own orchard fruit, but leaves the rest untouched, as if it might be too much pleasure to eat it. Her gaze is continually pulled towards the window, searching for something, seeing something that we cannot. Even as she talks, her attention seems elsewhere, hovering an inch or two above the conversation, like the tiny black flies over the fruit bowl: in this way she's the opposite of Ma, who has the ability to make you feel, if only for a few seconds, like the only person in the universe who matters.

It is only later as we shuffle upstairs, exhausted by the forcing of polite conversation, longing to be just the four of us again, so we don't have to speak at all, that I realize it must be Audrey for whom Sybil is distractedly searching, Audrey she spots, blurring in the corners of the room, smudged in the trees, just as the picture on our television set in London tunes for a brief moment, before a passing motor-car makes it fuzz.

Pleased with this observation, I expound my theory to my yawning sisters as we huddle together on the landing, reluctant to peel off into our own bedrooms. 'It's almost like two layers of time — Audrey here, Audrey gone — have not separated from one another but have elided, don't you think?'

'No, Margot,' sighs Pam. 'It's like a ghoulish country-house weekend, without any other guests, a place where it's not taken for granted that we will survive until morning.'

*　*　*

I can't sleep. Pam's words seem less fanciful in the dark: I keep thinking I can hear feet padding outside my door, wheezy breathing. I jump out of my skin when Dot bangs on our adjoining wall at about eleven. I find her tearful, sheets pulled up to her chin. She tells me how she parted her curtains to see the sky and it looked far too big, while the earth felt terrifyingly small, hurtling through nothingness in cold space. I

83

hold her in my arms, stroking her silky hair until she falls asleep, then return to my bed alone.

Midnight now, halfway between night and day, as Applecote itself feels caught between the past and the present, life and death, a house gummed shut, waiting for news that never comes. I flip the pillow to its cool side, releasing a lavender-water scent that makes me miss London's impolite smells: bus exhaust, Lucky Strikes in Ma's crisp bottle-blonde curls. The sounds, too, drunken revellers on the street, the rush of scalding water into my mother's thoughtless midnight baths, then the *slap slap slap* of the flannel against her imaginary double chin. Here, just a velvet hush shredded by the hoots of owls and foxes that sound like screaming children. Thoughts of Audrey fall through the swirling dark above my bed. I see her head turned to face me on the pillow, trying to tell me what happened that day, but the words keep faltering, stuck in her throat. That's when I get up.

★ ★ ★

'Margot!' Flora hisses.

Audrey's doorknob feels warm in my hand: I might have been standing there holding it for a while.

'What are you doing? We're not allowed in there.' Moonlight splashes off her nightie, the pearl of her face.

'I — I was just curious,' I stutter, relieved to have been interrupted. What was I thinking?

She walks towards me, whispers, 'Curiosity

84

killed the cat, Margot.'

'I wouldn't actually have gone in.' Although I'm not sure. I forgot myself for a moment there, sucked towards the room on a hidden dangerous current. 'What are you doing out here anyway?'

Flora widens her eyes. 'I heard something.'

My breath catches. 'Oh?'

'I got it into my head it was Uncle Perry. Prowling the landing.'

Perry. Of course. It feels good to put a name to that sense of indefinite threat outside my bedroom door.

'But it was you,' Flora says, sounding almost disappointed.

'No, no. I heard something earlier too.' I stoke the fear again, and we peer down the dark staircase, half expecting to spot Perry hiding, pressed against the wall.

Flora folds her arms over her chest with a shudder. 'Uncle has a bit of a look about him, doesn't he?'

'I'd say.' I feel a small, unexpected thrill, an impatience for some kind of drama.

Flora opens her bedroom door, then hesitates. 'I can't get used to the quiet,' she confides. 'I even miss Pam's awful snoring.'

'Shall I come into your room for a bit?' I don't much like the privacy I'd thought I craved either.

Flora snaps on her bedside lamp and botanical wallpaper surrounds us, like a forest. I lie, belly down, on the bed.

Flora flops beside me, warm and sisterly. 'You must try not to think about Audrey too much, Margot.'

'How can I not?'

'Well, don't pick at it, that's all.' She pauses, and *déjà vu* runs through the moment, like silver metallic thread: a close summer evening, back in London, and I'm trying to talk about Pa's accident and Flora is saying, as she is now, 'If we think about it too much, it'll weigh us down, it'll make life impossible.' As if we're four birds that must keep flying upwards or we'll drop out of the sky.

'Being at Applecote without Audrey feels like borrowing something without asking.' I lower my head to the mattress. 'It's her life. It's her house.'

'She'd happily lend her life to you of all people.'

Something inside me lights. I'd never thought of it like that before. I prop myself up on my elbows, resting my face in my hands, a sense of possibility fizzing. I imagine myself crawling into Audrey's life, under it, like a blanket.

'Although it's not the same, is it? It used to be so free and easy here.' Flora kicks up her legs, her feet brushing against mine mid-air. 'Do you remember how Aunt Sybil would take us moonlight swimming in the river?'

The image of Sybil, her black-red wet curls flat on her head, her starlit bare shoulders emerging from the river water, swims towards us. 'She doesn't look like she would now.'

'No, she really doesn't.' Flora studies the ends of her hair under the circle of lamplight, checking for split ends. She looks up and laughs. 'Jump the well wall! My God. Remember that?'

'Now that *didn't* involve Aunt Sybil.' I laugh,

enjoying having my big sister to myself for once. 'She didn't know about that one. Audrey swore me to secrecy.'

The key, Audrey said, was to imagine the narrow well as a shallow pond. Fear made you falter, nothing else. You can do anything if you're not scared. (She took the same approach to scaling the towering beeches in the Wilderness.) It was the one thing I refused to do, the well. And I wouldn't let Dot go anywhere near it at any time. It wasn't just the blackness. Audrey said it was the entry point to the underworld, a labyrinth of tunnels that burrowed right down to the molten core of the earth. That was why if you threw a stone into it, you couldn't hear the splash. It just kept falling, like a stone in space.

'And stars. All those stars,' Flora says wistfully.

We tug open her window. The night gusts in. We pull out the necklines of our nighties, like nets, to catch it, press the cool dark air against our skin, then settle, our chins on the sill. 'Look.' Flora points, like we used to years ago from this same window. 'The Bear . . . Can you see it?'

I nod, although I can see only Audrey's heart-shaped face, stars for eyes, picked out like sequins.

'She must be dead, Margot,' Flora mutters softly, tuning into my thoughts. 'She drowned. Everyone thinks so.'

Audrey's eyes sparkle before a dark cloud masks them again. 'No body.'

Flora shakes her head, curls stippling my arm. 'They say the river can sweep you all the way down to the London docks some days. All those horrible reed beds too.'

'She could have run away,' I suggest, not really believing it.

'What would be the point of that?'

'Well, quite.'

Flora eyes me warily. 'You got more details from Ma this morning, didn't you? I heard you haranguing her. And I can tell by the expression on your face.'

I smile, superior with knowledge, and think of Ma earlier, wilted against the malachite-green parlour wall, surrounded by her trunks, the back of her hand pressed to her forehead in utter exasperation at my questions. She admitted defeat in the end and told me the little she knew, the gaps between facts.

'Go on, then.'

'Boat people,' I say cryptically.

'Boat people?' Flora wrinkles her nose.

'One theory. They stole her. Sooty-skinned river gypsies who wanted a pretty blonde girl to bring up as their own.' I like this version, Audrey rocking on a narrow river-boat, one of those long barges, gold and green, like something from the circus, full of skinny cats and grubby, happy children, running along the vessel's narrow flat roof with bare feet. Audrey is smiling and barefoot, too, her plaits silted with river mud, wild and free as an otter.

'I think there might be rather worse things gypsies do to pretty blonde girls, Margot,' Flora mutters darkly.

'Oh. Yes, of course,' I say quickly, trying to cover my own naivety. I feel a funny sort of heat imagining what might happen to a blonde girl like Audrey, like me, in the hands of a piratical gypsy man. I squeeze my legs together and change the subject. 'There were reports of a man in the area too.' I pause, enjoying Flora's impatience, the breeze playing around my neck. 'A key suspect. Close to the bridge. In a hat.'

'Ooh.' A bat curls towards the window, away again. Then more and more of them, like question marks.

'The police never found him.'

'Bah. Did they find *anything*?'

I shake my head. 'Hopeless, Ma says. Swung a torch on a rope into the well. Checked the spades in the shed for blood. Oh, yes, and searched the village houses belonging to the funny types . . . you know, the men who had never married, the village idiot — at least, the child-murdering sort. But it was too little, too late. A bit of a scandal afterwards. One police officer lost his job.' I put on my grand, high Ma voice, imitating her, fluttering my lashes. 'Darling, if you're going to vanish and prefer to be found, I'd advise you to vanish in London under the beady eye of Scotland Yard.'

Flora's laugh tails off into sadness. We sit in silence for a moment, our thoughts separating. Then Flora says, 'But what about the obvious?' and the conversation plunges somewhere darker, gathering speed.

'Moll was the last person to see her, that's true,' I acknowledge. 'Sybil and Perry were out that evening but Sybil gave Audrey permission to fish *before* they left, Ma said, so that wasn't

Moll's fault, or idea, Audrey being by the river alone. And Moll was the one who searched and searched for her, walking miles and miles through fields with a stick, who never deserted Sybil and Perry afterwards, not like the rest of the staff. Anyway, don't you remember how Moll adored Audrey?'

Flora drops her voice to a barely audible whisper. 'I don't mean Moll.'

'Oh.' Something unspoken seesaws between us. The hairs on my arms spike.

'The police, however dozy, must surely have considered it, Margot, even if he did have an alibi.'

I feel my heart quicken. I think of his bullish neck. His huge shoulders. The peculiar way Ma mentioned my uncle's name, her lips closing around a cigarette, stopping more details getting out. 'You know, Flora, thinking about it, I did get the sense Ma wasn't telling me everything.'

To my surprise, Flora suddenly reaches up and pulls the window shut. 'Let's stop this. Audrey is long gone.'

'You don't want to talk about it?' I ask, baffled. All these years of not talking about Audrey have built up in my brain and are now pressing hard against it.

She shakes her head. 'Don't start dissecting everything like always.'

'But we must.'

'Oh, Margot. I do love you. But I'm tired. It's late. And we're talking nonsense into our heads that's going to make this summer even more unbearable. We've just got to get through the next few weeks, that's all.' She tugs the top sheet over her knees and lies back on the pillow. 'It's only until the beginning of September. Then you'll be at Squirrels again and everything will go back to normal.' Flora extends one graceful arm towards the lamp. 'Goodnight.'

'Goodnight,' I say, closing her door, struck by an odd, overwhelming sense that nothing will ever be normal again, that this summer is going to change everything.

Whatever is about to happen, I'm ready.

⋆　⋆　⋆

In a bathing-suit there is no escape from the plain fact of myself. My skin is mottled, mauve, a heat rash pinpricking the pudge of my breasts. The unsightly, unkissable backs of my legs itch where they meet the wooden deckchair frame. It's impossible not to stare enviously at Flora lying beside me, those long limbs languidly spread as if for a lover, her firm soft skin, radiating gauzy light, the gentle tip of her conical breasts as she reclines. I wonder if Audrey's body would be like Flora's now, womanly, desirable, a little treacherous. Trying to take my mind somewhere else, I open my novel, but it's impossible to read — sweat drips from my eyebrows — so I cover my face with the book instead, wishing someone would invent a way of reading a story by inhaling it.

'This is intolerable.' Pam's voice. To my left. We've instinctively arranged our deckchairs beside the pool in a protective semicircle, like wagons. 'What day is it?'

I try to work it out. Time is shapeless here, the hours indistinct, sliding into each other in the heat. 'Wednesday?'

'It feels like Sunday. It's going to be a summer of deadly dull Sundays.' Pam groans. 'And we've not even been here half a week.'

I remove the book. Scorching sunlight. A damselfly, long and blue as a pencil.

'We could be at a lido, Margot, the Serpentine. Swimming with friends. And young men. Remember them? Rarer in the Cotswolds than pheasants on the Mall.'

I smile. For distraction we have only Billy Waters, Applecote's new young gardener, tall, blond, tanned walnut-brown; he has a particular way of carrying a spade and a shy smile that transforms his face. Or the ghost of the pilot who crashed into the meadow, the spit, we've decided, of James Dean. We no longer care that he is German, or headless, or dead. He is someone to long for, as we twist in our sheets through the airless night.

Pam sighs theatrically. 'Oh, dear beloved London.'

'London's hotter than Africa now,' says Dot, perching on the edge of her deckchair, throwing crumbs of smuggled bread on to the terrace for the blue tits, the thick nylon of her school bathing-suit bagging around her thin child's figure. 'I read it in Uncle Perry's paper at breakfast. It's an official heatwave. And it shows no sign of stopping.'

'No wonder Ma wanted to emigrate.' Pam

bends over, runs a hand along her muscular calf, checking it for stubble. 'She always did have a finely tuned sense of self-preservation. Swim?'

I stagger into the icy water with my arms above my head, gasping, stepping deeper, seeking the shock of sensation, the floating rose petals sticking to my skin like tiny pink tongues. Pam and Flora dive in confidently, quickly becoming a spinning ball of limbs and hair, trying to outdo each other, hands grappling ankles, trailing bubbles, bobbing up, laughing, cursing. Dot sits on the side of the pool, dreamily swishing her feet, the coldness of total immersion too much for her, her skin just not thick enough. And I think how we all swim like how we are.

Afterwards we flop around on the poolside, eating apples, taking bites out of each other, until Pam says, 'Ssh!' and puts a finger to her lips. 'Someone's coming.'

We fluster, arrange ourselves more glamorously, hopeful it might be Billy the gardener with his kind, river-green eyes.

But it doesn't sound like soft-footed Billy. There's a crashing animal sound, the birds chattering electric warnings. The pool gate flings open and the animal is Perry, panting, fanning his hat in front of his face. 'Ah, Wildlings.'

There is a moment of stunned disbelief. Perry and Sybil never swim in the pool. Sybil said so. We are meant to be safe here. Dot sends me a look of distress as our uncle puffs over to the changing hut, clearly intent on joining us. As soon as its door swings shut, we move fast, muffling our horrified giggles, tugging our dresses over bathing-suits, catching pool-tangled hair in buttonholes. Dot hisses, 'Hurry up, hurry up, oh, Margot, he's — ' She stops short, her lips parting.

Our uncle strides out into the sunlight, legs splayed, hands on his hips, the handsome muscularity of his former shape just visible beneath the rolls of flesh, his knitted blue swimming trunks bulging. The sight of those terrible trunks, my sketchy knowledge of what is beneath them, jumpy as a pumping garden hose, separated from us by just one layer of fabric, makes me feel peculiar. And I'm suddenly aware of the round circles on the bust of our dresses, caused by the wet bathing-suits beneath; how the easy innocence of those old childhood summers has been replaced by something that worries the edges. So I try to look away, but, confusingly, my eyes are drawn to his trunks again, as if my body and my mind are splitting apart, developing different opinions.

'It's splendid to see you girls here, the pool used again.'

We smile politely, glance at each other, trying to agree silently on a rescue plan.

I stare at his hands, squeezing into the flesh of his hips. They are strong, fat-fingered, big as spades. They look capable of anything. The air thickens. And I suddenly remember another summer, Perry throwing Audrey into the pool, Audrey squealing, a glittering splash, the jealousy I felt that she had a large, loud father who could pick her up and swing her about and

94

I didn't. And I can't arrange my thoughts properly, or reconcile the two different Uncle Perrys. There is still that gap between them, a long drop of darkness, where the truth about Audrey's fate might lie.

'Well, we'll leave you to enjoy your peace, Uncle,' says Pam, pushing her swim bag over her shoulder. Water drips crudely from beneath her dress on to the stone paving.

'Peace?' His short laugh bounces across the water. 'You think I can ever find damned peace, Pam?'

Not even Pam knows what to say.

'Swim with me,' he says, raising his chin in the manner of a man challenging another to a duel.

'It would be lovely to swim together another time,' says Flora, rushing to Pam's aid. We all agree insincerely. 'But we're worn out now, I'm afraid.'

'Oh.' His forehead rolls into a frown, his bluster gone, replaced by something a little lost, confused. And we move so fast out of that pool gate, stumbling, running, chased by the monster in our heads. When we reach the meadow we collapse into a gasping fit of stifled, horrified laughter.

★ ★ ★

I peer through the triangle of my bent elbow. Waving wands of yellow grass. Hot blue sky. A lichen-starred chunk of stone. Dot's bare toes wiggling, trying to cool. 'When will it be safe to return to the pool, do you think?'

'An hour,' mumbles Flora, who is sitting on the ancient stone next to me, her dress tented over her head for shade. 'Two, to be safe.'

'I'm going to expire of thirst,' moans Pam.

'You know, you sound just like Ma,' Flora says waspishly, from inside her dress.

'Very funny. Lest we forget, while we roast in this god-forsaken meadow, hiding from the lascivious troll of Applecote — '

'Pam!' Flora says, pretending to be shocked, encouraging her. Dot giggles nervously.

' — Ma is sipping Gin Slings in the shade of some Moroccan palace,' Pam continues blithely. She has a sunburned streak across her nose, like war paint. 'By the way, Billy isn't around, Flora. Your display of underwear is quite wasted.' She shoots an irritated glance at Flora's slim, shapely legs.

'There's always the dead pilot,' Flora jokes, emerging from her dress, smoothing it over her thighs.

'Well, he did leave you flowers,' Pam retorts.

It was Dot's eagle eye that spotted the wilting posy in the gouged dip in the meadow, where the plane crashed all those years ago, a small unlikely bunch, tied with twine. We still can't work out who might have left it or why.

'I think that might be this summer's epitaph, don't you?' continues Pam. ' "There's always the dead pilot." A summer so empty of young men we had to dig up a dead one.'

Flora laughs, and tickles Pam's arm with a blade of feathery grass.

After a while the sun sinks lower, bringing

relief, a new, sleepier heat. We give in to the meadow, sinking back against the stones. Dot starts a daisy chain, her little fingers working fast, pinching, threading, each link locked to the next: my brain tries to move as fast as Dot's fingers, but I can't get Audrey's story to link. I lean back on the warm stone, my eyelids heavy, and I think of how my body is touching something Audrey touched, and someone else before that, back and back, to the dirty digit of an ancient, as I, too, will one day be to another girl, not yet born, lolling, just as hot and tired, eyes slowly closing until all is birdsong and scorched grass and hot pink clouds . . .

'Margot, there is a God.' Pam yanks my big toe.

'Ow. What?' I rub my eyes. Everything feels different immediately. Pam's face is rose-tinged, magically lit. The dusk sky is a flame, volcanic and otherworldly, as if something might actually be about to happen. 'Where?'

'Look, Margot. Over there. Yes, yes, just up from the river.' Flora points to the edge of the meadow at the two tall figures in the distance. They are male. Definitely male. And there is a youthfulness to their energy, the way they are kicking through the long grasses towards us, exuding a louche confidence, a sense of entitlement, as if the meadow, the golden evening, each one of us sisters, were theirs for the taking.

5

After a late lunch Jessie and Will loll back on the orangery steps, making the most of the afternoon sunshine, legs outstretched, their bare feet on the mossy stones, investigated by tiny black ants. The television chatters from inside the house, a cooking show, one of the rare programmes Bella and Romy both enjoy, meaning that Jessie and Will are alone for once.

It's the last day of August, mild, damp, already autumny. Birds are nesting in the ivy that beards the house. Insects everywhere: dragonflies, moths, midges, earwigs, bees, more butterflies than Jessie's ever seen. For a brief moment, a cabbage white poses on Will's shirtless tanned shoulder, then spins away as he lifts his bottle of beer. Jessie watches it vanish into the undergrowth, picks a wild strawberry from the bowl cradled between her knees, in the folds of her red dress, and turns to Will with a smile. 'Open.'

Will swallows it with a wince. 'Christ. That is seriously sharp.'

'How a strawberry's meant to taste.'

He laughs. 'I knew you were going to say that.'

Jessie pops one into her own mouth. She likes its bitter-sweet seediness. She likes that it grew in the cracks of the veranda paving too. Somewhere in the house they can hear Will's mobile ringing again.

'Oh, ignore it.' She smiles, resting her head on

98

his shoulder. 'It's Sunday. It's almost sunny. And we're still officially on holiday.'

'Using the term loosely.'

Jessie's lips brush the underside of his jaw. 'The best thing about this particular holiday is that we're already home,' she murmurs. 'It doesn't end.'

Will looks up at the sky. 'And we're never in danger of sunburn.'

Seconds later the rain starts to fall hard. They leap up, squealing. Jessie won't let Will shut the orangery's glass doors, tussling with him, laughing. She doesn't want to close off the outside, not yet: the sound of rain dripping off branches, the smell of apples and river. He gives up, as she knew he would, stands behind her, one arm wrapped around her waist, and picks out the burrs hooked in her hair.

The wettest summer for twenty years, it's not been quite the heat-hazed August idyll Jessie and Will imagined. Will really has had to start chopping wood — and cut open his thumb with an axe last week. (Six stitches. 'The mark of a real woodsman,' he said, impressed.) The central heating is proving temperamental, so to warm the place up — Applecote seems to have centuries of winters trapped in its walls — Jessie's been stoking smoky fires that don't draw properly, coughing smoke into the house. Country walks have been elemental rather than bucolic: 'Insane hikes into the squall,' Bella groans, even though Jessie suspects she secretly quite enjoys them.

The weather has put off all but the most

determined visitors: Jessie's sprightly mother, Will's aged parents; Lou and Matt, Lou entering the house with her hands clapped over her mouth, laughing, muttering, 'Oh, my God, you're not serious?'; a small group of Will's friends who stayed one night fewer than they'd planned, a relief since Jessie and Will seemed to spend most of the time washing up, cooking and justifying their decision to leave London without offending those who had stayed.

She has much preferred it when it's been just them, hunkering down in their old house in its river valley, like a sort of dysfunctional Swiss Family Robinson. None of them has been back to London yet. They've been living another life altogether, hazy, unreal, the damp days seeping into one another: she and Will making love by the fire long after the girls are in bed; Romy stomping around in the fudgy mud, her baby curls dreadlocking; Bella wandering down to the stones to be alone, wearing her huge silver headphones and, to Will's quiet consternation, her dead mother's summer kaftans, retrieved from the Mandy Boxes that Jessie has started to fear are bottomless, their contents tumbling out like lost treasures from an Egyptian tomb. Occasionally, Jessie's glimpsed a local, necklaced in dog leads, peering through their gate, and more than once she was pretty sure it was that woman again, the one with the dogs. But by the time she's gone to greet her, or any of the others, they've melted back into the mizzle and it was as if they were never there.

'Dad!' Bella shouts from inside the house, over

the drum of rain. 'Phone!'

Hearing her approach, Will and Jessie instinctively edge apart. Jessie goes to close the glass door. She sees the rain has splattered her red dress with dark spots, like blood.

Bella appears, trailed by Romy, who is now dressed inexplicably in knickers and a swimming cap, waggling a fistful of dirty feathers above her head. Bella speaks into Will's phone, 'I'm handing you over now, Jackson.'

Will looks at Bella quizzically. 'He says it's urgent.' Bella shrugs, pushing away Romy's hand with the feathers a little too roughly.

Will takes a breath, clicking his brain out of Applecote mode, and presses the phone to his ear. 'Jackson, old boy, what's going down?' He stops, frowns. 'I'm sorry to — What? Wait a minute . . . '

'What is it?' Jessie whispers, wondering why Will's business partner should be calling on a Sunday, why Will's face is growing suddenly so serious. But Will doesn't hear her. He is already walking away.

★　★　★

Jessie takes a breath and dives into the deepest channel of the river. The current is surprisingly strong after yesterday's heavy rain, tunnelling cloudy, brown-black, like marrow in a bone. As she emerges, her hair caps her skull, the dark rich copper of Applecote's pipes, and her face glows with the river's mineral cold, unexpectedly so. Although she's a strong swimmer, she can

101

suddenly imagine the deadly creep of that coldness, the way it would stiffen the muscles, weaken a stroke. She's never felt this with Will swimming beside her. She misses him — he left for a crisis meeting with Jackson yesterday morning, stayed in a hotel last night. She misses the summer already.

She can sense that something is over. And she doesn't know what comes next.

Neither of them could have anticipated Jackson's bombshell, his sister in Australia's breast cancer diagnosis. Jackson wants to be there. Single, unencumbered, he's long thought about moving to Oz. (News to Will.) A wake-up call, he says. Will's changed his life, scaled back, why not him? The only difference is he can't run a European-based company from Brisbane. He's really sorry to bail but he wants to sell his share.

It couldn't have come at a worse time. However much Will sympathizes, it feels more like a divorce — old university friends, Jackson and Will started the company from a kitchen table years ago — and it leaves him with the problem of either raising a huge amount of money to buy Jackson out, or selling the stake to an outsider, losing control of half the company, which he desperately doesn't want to do. If he's to raise investment himself, Will needs to be in London more than ever, not taking his foot off the accelerator, as planned, but flooring it. How the hell is he going to do it from here?

Jessie pushes the thought away — they will manage somehow — and starts to tread water, waving to the girls on the bank.

Huddled under a hoodie, Bella's watching her carefully, protectively even, while ignoring her vulnerable charge, who is picking her way along the gravelly river beach in her bumble-bee swimsuit, carrying a red bucket rattling with pebbles. When Romy starts wading further out, oblivious to the chill on the chub of her thighs, the sudden shelving of the river floor, Bella does nothing to stop her.

Jessie swims back fast, tugs Romy up the bank. 'What were you waiting for, Bella?' she says, more sharply than she intends, still on edge from the night before. Hearing noises in Romy's room in the small hours, Jessie had investigated and got the fright of her life: a figure in the gloom, standing motionless beside Romy's cot bed; Bella, blank-faced, sleepwalking. Shaken, Jessie had led her back upstairs. Bella didn't remember anything about it this morning, which sort of makes it worse.

'She was fine.' Bella shrugs, hands Jessie a towel. Rain starts to fall in a fine mist, like a collapsing cloud. Bella rolls her eyes upwards. 'There can't seriously be any water left up there.' She unfolds her long heron legs and stands up, digging her hands into the pockets of her denim cut-offs. 'I'm off, then. I've got pictures to put up in my room.'

'Oh, yes, I forgot about that. Perfect rainy-afternoon activity. It'll make that bedroom finally feel like yours, Bella, it really will. Wait for us.' By the time Jessie's grappled Romy out of her swimsuit, the meadow is empty, only the stones huddled like a group of small old men in

103

long grey coats. She doesn't like it much, not with Will in London, the responsibility of the girls suddenly all hers.

The isolation that Jessie's relished these last two weeks feels almost threatening now. All August, it's seemed almost unearthly quiet — 'With a sort of two-centuries-behind lag,' as Bella cannily describes it — and Jessie's loved that too, the way the roads have been empty, apart from the occasional coach full of bemused tourists, usually pulled up in front of Cornton Hall, the grand house on the outskirts of the village, even though it's shrouded in scaffolding and green netting that billows in the wind, like sails. Sometimes it feels that everyone's left but them.

'Dog,' Romy announces, with a grin.

Jessie looks up from the swim bag, and is immediately struck by a sense that something is not quite right. There are two black dogs charging along the riverbank, as if called by their owner, a shadowy figure hidden beneath a huge umbrella, walking smartly away. Is it that woman again? Was she secretly watching her swim? The thought makes Jessie feel strange. She stuffs the towels into the bag quickly, wanting to get home.

She is glad when the meadow gate clicks shut behind them. Gladder still when Romy shouts, 'Bell-Bell!' and points excitedly through the trees to where Bella leans back against a huge beech, inspecting something in her hand. 'Oh, Rom, wait!' Jessie calls, exasperated, chasing after her tiny daughter, who gets faster by the day.

Both girls are in thrall to the detritus Applecote's soil spits up: old teacups, shards of plates, rusted gardening forks, shilling coins, tiny broken things that Bella is piecing together to create a sort of character sketch of the house: 'Since there's nothing else to do,' she explains, in case Jessie thinks she may be enjoying herself.

In the house, Bella's discovered names scrawled beneath the basin in her little bathroom, only a few letters decipherable, a large A with a swirly, exuberant curl to it. Last week, newspapers fell out of a cavity in the kitchen cupboards, yellow and crumbly as filo pastry, dated from the late fifties. The headline — 'It's a Scorcher!' — was about a heatwave in 1959, 'Which shows the house has a sense of irony at least,' remarked Bella, carrying the papery quarry up to her room. And then there's the children's things Will found in the attic — a handy child's high chair, a toy pram, some old wooden bricks, pastel alphabet letters on their faded papered sides.

Jessie can see the previous owner, Mrs Wilde, in her mind now: a sturdy, cheerful country-woman surrounded by mischievous pretty young daughters, rocking a cradle with her foot by the fire. She imagines her pounding dough in the kitchen, snapping out starched sheets on the beds upstairs. But, then, she's always had a terrible habit of imagining life stories, of elderly ladies in particular. (One of her 'things', Will affectionately calls it.) In London, she sees old ladies waiting at bus stops, and transforms them into Blitz survivors, code breakers, once glamorous mink-coated women rendered invisible by stained beige padded jackets. For this reason she will always stand up and offer her seat to them on the Tube or bus, make a point of smiling and chatting about the weather. As Will points out, when her own mother does an old-personish thing, asks what an app is or loses her reading specs in her handbag, Jessie gets irritated. But mothers are different. Everyone gets irritated by their mother. Apart from Bella, whose mother will be for ever perfect.

* * *

Later that afternoon, once the hammering has finally stopped, Jessie knocks on Bella's bedroom door, holding a stack of the just-delivered Squirrels' school uniform under one arm. No answer. It strikes Jessie, not for the first time, that Bella's bedroom door has a funny sort of force field to it, and that even the landing has an odd atmosphere, a sense of compression as you walk down it.

'Button,' Romy mutters, pressing her eye to the keyhole, as if she might spot the button Bella found in the Wilderness earlier, a funny little thing, faded pink plastic that might have been red once, heart-shaped.

She knocks again. Nothing. Deciding that Bella probably has her headphones on, Jessie gingerly pushes open the door with her knee. 'So did you manage to get your pictures . . . ' She gasps.

Bella is nowhere to be seen. But Mandy,

Mandy is everywhere. Dozens of photos that Jessie's never seen before: Mandy pregnant, blooming, Will kissing her belly; Mandy and Will swinging a tiny cute Bella over a jumble of autumn leaves; Mandy lying on a beach, wearing one of her signature kaftans, laughing, Bella's head in her mother's lap. A gallery of private moments from which Jessie will for ever be excluded.

Jessie's always known such moments must have existed — although she and Will rarely discuss them — but actually seeing them, documented on the walls of Applecote, the day after Will's departure, shakes her to the core. She feels as if she's been chased down by them and, for a moment, she cannot breathe.

Romy explores the fascinating, forbidden zone of her big sister's bedroom, while Jessie moves in a sort of trance. The photos pop from the dark walls — Bella insisted on sludge grey, exactly the same shade as their London house — that she and Bella painted together last week to make it more homely. Was Bella always planning this? Did she know that afternoon as they painted side by side, listening to the radio? Was she waiting for Will to be out of the house? Jessie can't help feeling betrayed.

But the worst thing of all — and Bella must have known this — is how bloody amazing Mandy and Will look together. Mandy's face is chiselled, androgynous — the exact opposite of Jessie's girl-next-door prettiness — with a piercingly intelligent gaze beneath an inky Hepburn crop, one of those serious hairstyles

107

adopted only by women confident of their cheekbones. Unlike Jessie's chaotic clash of eras and colours, Mandy's style is faultless, a restrained palette of beige, navy and black, a slash of red. She exudes self-possession, a woman who has bigger things to think about than what ankle boots to wear in the morning, a human-rights lawyer, after all. Jessie gawps at her, painfully aware of her own crumpled jersey dress, the smell of the river on her skin, the grubby old feather Romy's stuck in her pinned-up mess of red hair.

It's just Bella's way of not leaving her mother behind, nothing else, she tells herself. It's not about me. She must shut the door, go downstairs and face Bella calmly, like there is nothing wrong. But she doesn't. Something powerful holds Jessie in that room of her own dark imagining, transfixed by the woman she was hoping to escape.

It looks like Mandy herself might have just got undressed in here — a stylish black felt fedora sits on a bedside chair, the silk dressing-gown swishes from the back of the door, and an indigo kaftan is slung casually across the sleigh bed, the same one, Jessie realizes with an inward jolt, that Mandy wears in the beach photograph.

It's like being immersed in Mandy. It's like diving into her. And maybe that's why Jessie does it. Because the room has a current, a pull to it, something that makes her put down the school uniforms and pick up that kaftan, rub its beautiful crewel embroidery between her fingers, and then, knowing she shouldn't, that she's crossing a line, she holds it up, letting it rustle down over her legs, puddle on the floor. She presses the cool cotton against her breast, the accelerating pump of her heart.

'Pretty, Mummy.'

Jessie starts. Romy is sitting on the bed, holding the heart-shaped button between her fingers, looking a little puzzled by this strange new version of her mother.

Horrified at herself — what if Bella walks in? What would Will think? — Jessie throws the kaftan back on to the bed. Flustered, she wrestles the button out of Romy's closed fist and hurries them both away from that strange little room under the eaves where, for a moment, she had felt she might lose herself completely.

6

The evening sun is huge, gold as a grapefruit, making the silhouetted figures glow at the edges, rays burst out of their heads. We catch the young men's voices, bubbles on the breeze blowing up the hill, popping when the wind changes direction. We don't dare speak, risk ruining the moment, already perfect, that we've somehow willed into being through the sheer force of our collective longing.

They saunter slowly, carelessly, until the anticipation is almost unbearable, their steps synchronizing with the patter of our hearts, the quickening of our breath. We can tell they're not locals: their trousers are cut close, not baggy country-boy breeches. Smart hair, floppy on top, short at the sides. When the breeze blows it flattens summer shirts against sinewy bodies, not the beefy bulk of farmhands.

'I'm not sure about this,' says Dot, suddenly, decapitating a daisy with her thumbnail. 'Shouldn't we go back for dinner?'

'Ssh, Dot.' Pam arranges her dress around her legs, so that only her best calf is revealed, her navy-blue eyes trained on her targets with predatory focus.

As the men's attractiveness becomes more obvious, I feel a wave of self-consciousness about the lack of my own, eased only by the knowledge that I'll be overlooked in favour of Flora anyway.

'Should we stand up?' I whisper.

'Have you grown a beard?' Pam murmurs.

Flora glances at me, laughs. 'Oh, Margot, you've got your nervous grimace on. You look like a murderess. Be natural.'

'Nonchalant,' hisses Pam.

'Smile,' mutters Flora, through the rictus of her own.

I smile so hard my jaw aches. There is a trail of crushed grass behind them, like the tail of a comet. We could be the last two surviving groups of people on the earth, each imagining ourselves to be alone until now. A strange hush falls as they approach, just the whoosh of the grasses moving in the breeze, the fibrous crunch of their footsteps. We discreetly nudge each other — Pam's fingers flicking against my knee, Flora's toes on Dot's arm — in a mark of sisterly solidarity, before holding our siren poses once more.

'Ladies.' He speaks with no trace of a country accent. Since he is far too handsome to look at directly — dark, Roman-featured, he might have tumbled out of a Renaissance painting — I watch tanned, elegant fingers stub out the cigarette against a stone, snapping its spine in half. Sparks shower down, setting light to the tussock of dried grass beneath it. It is the other young man, the shorter, sandy-haired one, with a round freckled face, like a harvest moon, who stamps it out. 'We won't set the summer ablaze just yet.'

How old? Nineteen? Twenty? I don't know enough men to guess accurately. All I know is that the shorter, sandy one is staring right at me with leonine yellowy-hazel eyes, and the point where our glances meet seems to solidify in mid-air, like something I could reach out and touch.

'Sorry, I forget my manners. I'm Harry. Harry Gore.'

The name is vaguely familiar. But I can't place it.

He grins, drops his wicker picnic basket on the ground where it clanks. Brown-glass bottle tops nose out of it. 'And this is my cousin, Tom. Fire starter.'

Tom taps out another cigarette from the packet, clicks his metal lighter under his thumb, a chunky silver lighter, like Pa's from the army.

'Pam.' My sister leaps up, does an extravagant deb's curtsy, one leg behind the other, dropping low, making everyone laugh, breaking the tension. But Harry and Tom's eyes are already sliding to Flora. And I'm reminded of the unfairness of being female, that even if Pam and I were the kindest, most fascinating girls in the entire world, these men would still be staring at our exquisite older sister.

'And you are?' Harry asks gently, his eyes tracking upwards from Flora's bare feet — she must have kicked off her shoes without me or Pam noticing; if we had, we'd have done the same — to the creamy-blonde curl coiled loosely around her finger, like a question only she can answer.

'Flora,' she says slowly, honey off a spoon. She flicks her violet eyes at Tom, looks down again,

112

then back at him. He stares at her with a look of awed wonder.

'Flora,' Harry repeats slowly, beneath his breath, his gaze moving so reluctantly away from her to me that I feel bad for depriving him.

'I'm Margot,' I pre-empt apologetically, before he feels he has to ask. I notice the oppositions of his face, the way his careless, boyish grin seems at odds with the serious knit of his eyebrows. Something crackles around us, like the flame in the grass.

He cocks his head, trying to place me. 'Have we met before?'

'I don't think so.' I don't know how I should sound. How to sit. What I should do with my hands. To shift his attention from my burning cheeks, I say quickly, 'And this is our little sister, Dot.'

'Ah, Dot.' Harry squats beside her. A silver-lidded pen pokes out of his back trouser pocket, like a pet. 'You know, I think that might be the longest daisy chain I've ever seen.'

Dot smiles shyly. I like him for noticing Dot's daisy chain. For the pen in his pocket. For being less obviously handsome than his cousin, the way his features are arranged slightly wrongly on his face, making them right.

'Applecote Manor,' says Pam, artlessly shoving our new social credentials into the conversation. 'We're staying there with our aunt and uncle. The Wildes? With an e. Do you know them?'

At the name Wilde, a million tiny strings seem to be yanked beneath the surface of Tom and Harry's skin at the same time. 'Yes, we do,' says

113

Harry, grabbing the cigarette packet and lighter out of Tom's hand, then sticking a cigarette into his mouth, an excuse not to say anything else.

'Our mother is abroad,' explains Flora, sensing the kink in the air, subtly trying to distance us from Applecote again. 'So we were shipped out here from Chelsea.'

'Like evacuees,' quips Pam.

Harry blows out a puff of smoke, his eyes catching Tom's again. And a fragment of an old summer reassembles: Audrey and I in the meadow, early morning, two older boys across a foggy river, waving at Audrey through the mist, Audrey waving back. 'Did you know our cousin, Audrey?' I ask, the words flying out into the gap in the conversation before I can stop them. 'Audrey Wilde?'

Pam widens her eyes at me, telling me to shut up.

But it's too late. Harry's face has changed again, as all faces change whenever I bring up Audrey: that spasm of recognition followed by something blank and awkward. 'We did know Audrey, a little. When we were young.'

Tom's Adam's apple dips and rises. He offers Flora a sincere, apologetic smile. 'Dreadful business. I'm so sorry.'

Harry's freckled lips are slightly parted, as though he might have more to say on the matter.

But Pam jabs a finger into my ribs so I don't ask any more questions and Audrey is swept away, as she always is, by the clearing of throats, the slide of eyes, and exists only as an omission again.

'Where are you two staying?' asks Pam, brightly, brushing grass off her dress.

'Cornton, my parents' place.' Harry nods at the rooftops in the distance, as if Cornton Hall were a small thatched cottage rather than the most extravagant house for miles, rising on the hill at the edge of the village, like a patriarch at the table. 'Do you know it?'

A secret smile flashes between Pam and Flora.

'But we're not there much.' He tilts his face back and blows smoke rings, one, two, three, like nooses of rope. 'My parents prefer their London house these days.'

'Or that scruffy little dive in the Côte d'Azur,' teases Tom, making me suspect he doesn't come from such wealth himself.

'The Côte d'Azur.' Pam sighs longingly, all nonchalance forgotten. 'Lucky you.'

Harry nods, as if he doesn't quite believe it. 'They've handed us the keys for one last summer here anyway.' The word 'last' hangs in the still air, making everything feel urgent, soon to be lost. 'My last hurrah before I go up to Oxford, Tom here to National Service,' he explains, with an easier smile. 'Doing rather well on the domestic front, aren't we, Tom, darling?' Tom laughs. 'A perfect married couple. We've only flooded one bathroom and smashed two vases so far.'

'We? *You.*' Tom's sharpness suggests this is an argument they've had before.

Tom and Harry stare at each other, each refusing to look away, jockeying for position, an old rivalry that the rest of us can only guess at, until Harry bends down and holds up a beer bottle with a stack of battered metal tumblers that makes me wonder if they knew we were here. 'Shall I be mother?'

We sneak thrilled glances at each other, trying to read the other's reaction. We might sip half a glass of champagne at a party, but beer in a meadow with strange young men? Unthinkable.

'The local brew. Tastes better than it smells, I promise.'

'That's very kind of you . . . ' begins Flora, taking the moral lead.

'Yes, please.' Pam sticks out a hand and tosses her hair. Dot's eyes widen behind her glasses.

Flora, annoyed that Pam has made her look prim, says, 'Since when did you drink beer, Pam?'

Pam shrugs. 'I'm dying of thirst.'

Flora hesitates, laughs. 'Oh, you know what? I'll have one too.'

'Flora,' I mutter in astonishment, wondering where this will all lead, if we've been out too long in the sun. Or whether it's just the stones themselves, the way their shadows are lengthening, lapping at the grass, making the red sky spin. But Harry is already pouring beer into the tumblers, the liquid foaming over the sides, like thick cream. He hands them to Pam and Flora, who sniff it curiously, as if it were some strange elixir.

'You might be a *little* young for beer,' Harry says to Dot sweetly. 'So I bequeath to you my water flask.' He turns to me, yellow eyes glinting. 'But you . . . '

116

'Margot,' I say, disappointed that he's already forgotten my name, hoping he doesn't think me so young he'll offer me water too.

'Margot,' he repeats, unflinching. 'Margot Wilde, with an e.' He grins, and a freckle on his lip flattens. 'Can I tempt you?'

'No, thank you.' I'm not even sure why I say it when I desperately want to say yes and my mouth is so dry my tongue sticks to the roof of my mouth.

'But this beer has your name on it.' He plucks his pen out of his pocket, and carves 'M' in the creamy white foam. 'See?'

I start to laugh, light-headed, as if I might have drunk barrels of beer already. He presses the cup into my hand, folding my fingers one by one around the metal, deliciously cold against my skin. Sticky beer drips down on to my hand. Bats start to loop behind him, black as the night to come. I lift it slowly to my mouth, feeling the world tilt, come loose somehow. The cool rim of metal pushes against my lips and I taste it, bitter and sweet at the same time, hay and honey.

★ ★ ★

Outside the house, we pass Billy, watering-can angled, spilling a silver liquid line. The way he looks at me makes me wonder if he's seen us, knows where we've been. My older sisters flurry past, barely aware of his presence now — eclipsed by the Gores in a moment — as he straightens, politely removing his straw hat. A few moments later, I turn to smile, remembering

117

my manners too late, but he has gone.

The orangery is like a bell jar, Moll and Sybil its butterflies, Moll fanning Sybil with grey wings of newspaper, making Sybil's white hair fly from her pale, high forehead as she slumps, back to us, on a wicker chair. I can see her spine through the cotton of her dress, bones like buttons, the hard, metallic gaze reflected in the dark window — it's far later than we realized — tracking us as we cross the stone flags.

'Aunt?' Flora says gently. 'Did we miss dinner?'

She doesn't turn. 'I've been worried sick.'

'We're very sorry,' says Flora, with a nun-like bow of her head, sneaking a smile at me. We're not sorry at all.

'I thought something had happened, Flora.'

Something did happen, we want to say. Summer just became a lot more interesting.

Sybil hands a little bowl of browning peach slices to Moll, and twists in her chair. 'I thought you were sensible girls.'

Moll starts fanning her again with the newspaper, which flutters in her thick, ink-stained fingers. The sweetness of jasmine trickles through an open window.

'We lost track of time,' says Dot, bravely, looking at Pam for approval. 'It suddenly went faster.' Pam gives her a small nod. Our little sister is learning.

'Oh, the hours do slip about in this sort of heat.' Moll sends Dot a quick, sympathetic smile that reveals the black door of her tooth. 'There's some cold cuts in the kitchen, don't worry.'

118

'And Flora *is* seventeen,' Pam points out. 'Margot and I not far off. Ma lets us — '

'I don't give a damn what Bunny lets you do,' Sybil spits, naming Ma with unexpected acidity. 'You are *my* charges while you're at Applecote Manor.'

We glance at one another in dismay: the perimeters of our summer tighten, just when we thought they might be thrillingly expanded.

Flora tries to save us. She kneels beside Sybil's chair, the evening still glittering in her eyes. 'Aunt, we were only at the meadow. Quite safe, I promise.'

'Nowhere is safe, Flora. Nowhere.'

She holds up her hand to stop Moll fanning. And it is impossible to see in this gaunt nervous woman the aunt with the easy laugh who'd tell us to run off after lunch, enjoy ourselves and try to be back for tea.

'But the men were terribly nice,' says Dot. Pam elbows her but it is too late.

There is a pause, a gash in the humid evening. '*Men?*'

'Young men, really. Boys. Just a bit older than us,' corrects Flora, quickly. 'Summering at Cornton.'

Sybil starts and sits up a little straighter, hand leaping to her throat. 'Cornton? Cornton Hall? Are you sure?'

Flora nods enthusiastically.

'Tom and Harry.' I taste the bitter beer on my tongue. It occurs to me that I will always be able to taste it. 'The Gore cousins.'

'One's about to go to Oxford, I think, the

119

other National Service.' Pam rushes in with these impeccable credentials.

Sybil stands up abruptly, long skirt swishing around her legs. 'Did you know this, Moll?'

Moll, who is plumping cushions on the sofa, pretending she isn't listening, says, 'I beg your pardon, Mrs Wilde?'

'There are Gores at Cornton Hall again. Had you heard anything?'

Moll looks uncomfortable, lowers her eyes. 'There were rumours at the village-hall coffee morning, Mrs Wilde.'

'Rumours?' Sybil says sharply, waiting for Moll to elaborate.

'Old Ma Peat said she'd had to send her Brian over the other day. The bathroom was awash, the moulding on the ceiling below a right mess.' She raises one eyebrow. 'High jinks. The Gore boys had been at the wine cellar apparently.'

'The *Gore* boys?' His voice booms, orbits the room. Perry fills the doorway, nostrils flaring, like a mare's. Moppet sidles up to Dot's legs. 'What about the damned Gores?'

We cautiously explain, unable to read the contradictory emotions flitting over our uncle's face. After a while, he puts a hand over his mouth, some horrible truth dawning on him. 'Why are we always, always the last to know what goes on in the village, Sybil? Nothing damn well changes, does it? We stay locked away in this house like people who have something to hide.'

I watch him carefully, wondering if this might be a clever double bluff.

Sybil starts to wring her hands, making a pistol with her fingers. The exchange has the feeling of an old argument. 'It was that swim this afternoon. What possessed you? You haven't swum in years, Peregrine. It'll do a mischief to your back. And it's put you in a tizz, I can see that.'

'We act guilty of something, Sybil,' Perry continues, his huge face starting to pulse red. 'Holed away here.'

At 'guilty', Flora raises an eyebrow at me.

'I — I will visit the village soon,' Sybil stutters. 'Yes, I must make an effort to get into the swing of things again. Committees and things. It's been far too long.' She looks out of the window at distant hills with a peculiar mix of fear and raw yearning. 'I'll invite Lady Anne over for drinks,' she continues, her words piling up against each other, like they do when you don't believe them. 'I'm sure she'll return to the house this summer, if Harry is there. Yes, I must.'

'Invite them and they'll be oh-so-busy, just like all the others.' Perry stands at the window, hands threaded behind his back, lost in thought. And he suddenly seems to be a man with the weight of the world on his shoulders, crunching his spine. 'Let us turn this to our advantage.'

'I beg your pardon?' says Sybil, tightly.

Perry swings round, eyes shining. 'Why do you think Bunny really sent us the girls, Sybil? It wasn't just to help her out, or fill Applecote with girls' laughter again, I can assure you, whatever she might have said.'

I hear Ma's shameless sing-song voice, calling

121

across the parched expanse of Sybil's maternal emptiness. It makes my cheeks burn.

'They're not here for us to fatten on Moll's jam. Or would you prefer them to marry Billy the gardener? He's a rather dashing fellow.'

Sybil puts her hand to her throat. 'Good God.'

'Actually, Uncle, I'm going to be a nurse,' says Pam, indignantly.

'*Nurse?*' A huge unexpected laugh bolts out of Perry's mouth, like a pheasant from grass. 'Ah, very good, very good. Well, you might have some work to do on your bedside manner first, my little vixen.' He turns to Flora. 'But *you*, Flora, I hope you're not entertaining any excitable ideas about working for a living.'

'Peregrine,' Sybil warns, a grave expression on her face, as if she knows what's about to come.

He glances at her impatiently. 'Well, it would shut the gossips up, wouldn't it? One of our nieces marrying into the glorious Gores. Damn them.'

'Peregrine, this is ridiculous. You're being ridiculous,' snaps Sybil.

He strides closer to Flora, hands on his hips, a spine of sweat on the back of his shirt. 'If you've got half of your mother's wits, I advise you to aim yourself, like a bloody Hun's missile, in the direction of Harry Gore. Do you understand, Flora? Don't be distracted by Tom.' He dismisses him with a flick of his hand. 'Pretty enough, but not worth a penny. Harry is the lad you want. He's on the rise, that boy, mark my words, quite brilliant apparently, tipped for the top, and heir to a sugar fortune. Understood?'

Flora nods, her face inscrutable. 'Understood, Uncle.'

'Well, good,' he says hesitantly, not quite sure if she's being sincere or if we're all in on a joke. 'That's settled. Your mother will thank you. And so will I. The Wilde family's fortunes are in need of a top-up. We haven't made a decent match in this family for a generation. Good luck.' He turns to the rest of us dismissively. 'And you three fight over Tom, eh? Chop him up and split him three ways to avoid arguments. And stop flirting with our handsome young gardener, or I'll sack him immediately.'

A small sob breaks in Sybil's throat then, a cracking sound, like a hazelnut underfoot. She pulls a handkerchief out of her sleeve, dabs her eyes. We stare at the floor, pretend we haven't heard.

'The pollen again, is it, Sybil?' says Perry, a catch in his voice. But the awful sound of my aunt crying is unmistakable. Moll slips out of the door.

'Forgive me, girls.' Sybil sniffs.

'Not now, Sybil,' Perry says wearily.

As she's clearly about to say something that Perry doesn't want her to say, I encourage her. 'What is it, Aunt?' I ask, ignoring Pam who is shaking her head at me, warning me away from the awkward Audrey conversation we can all sense coming, like the pressure drop before heavy rain.

'Just — just thinking of little Harry all grown-up, about to go to Oxford.' Her voice breaks and her raw grief is there in the room

123

with us, clawing at her legs like a small child. 'And . . . Audrey . . . '

'Sybil, darling,' Perry says, more kindly. His hand hovers above her arm, ready to comfort her, then drops back to his side, as if he doesn't quite know how.

'Audrey will be delighted to find Harry close by again when she comes home,' Sybil says, rallying a smile. 'That is something.'

Silence swells under the glass, like a high-pitched noise about to shatter it. And it is suddenly obvious to all of us that Sybil's belief that her daughter will one day return is her life force, her reason for living. And that Perry sees things very differently.

'For Heaven's sake, woman . . . ' Perry's voice quivers on the edge of something terrible. 'Audrey is *not* coming back.'

As he barrels out of the door, leaving his words hanging in the still, jasmine-scented air, I wonder how my uncle can possibly know this for sure.

★ ★ ★

My little alarm clock says 5 a.m. But no time seems to have passed since the previous evening, Harry's beer, the gunshot jolt of the Gores' names spoken aloud in the orangery, Sybil sobbing and Perry shouting, the past ripping through the fabric of the present, revealing it to be as thin and fragile as antique linen. Outside, a cock crows.

I ask myself, What would Audrey do right now

if she were me, and I her, and our fates had been swapped, like straw boaters, as they so easily might have been in the jumble of the last days of summer?

I pull on my dressing-gown. Avoiding the top stair, which squeaks, I creep down into the cool heart of the house until I can no longer hear Perry's geological snores. There's a thrill that comes with being awake when everyone else is lost in sleep. I don't feel rushed. Or watched. Time even passes differently, moulding itself around me, like a kid glove on warm skin.

In the library, I note Perry's menacing collection of guns and swords on the ox-blood walls. But the drawing room reveals only a lock of blonde child's hair in a tiny, pull-out bureau drawer and, worse, a little cloth bag of milk teeth. Unnerved by them, I slip away into the kitchen. I steal two scones from under a wire cloche — one for me, one for a delighted Moppet — and start to investigate the warren of small rooms around the scullery, impossible during the day since this is Moll and Sybil's territory.

The rooms are so familiar the moment I see them that it's like rejoining an old game of childhood hide and seek. A brick-walled room: shelves stacked with preserves, pickles, chutneys, jammy jewels in glass jars. I remember how I loved the glut of this room, its hive-like organization, how Moll would give me and Audrey the job of tying on the gingham jar tops, binding them with string. Then there's the larder, with its mousetraps, baskets of potatoes, cool caves for cheeses. The broom cupboard, where Flora once hid and tripped in the dark, cutting her lip on the edge of a metal mop bucket, bursting out of the door, her mouth dripping with blood, making us all scream. The laundry room, warm, damp, like a freshly bathed baby, its white sheets hanging on wooden poles — there was an art to standing between them, breathing so lightly you didn't make them tremble — the mangle I'd use to wring out my bathing-suit, just for the satisfaction of churning that heavy handle. Its mechanics fascinated me: we always sent our laundry out to be washed in London. And, next to this, a storeroom that makes my breath catch.

The light is greened by the ivy-spangled window, the air stirred by the draught from a large crack forking along the lower pane. Crammed inside, relics of long-lost childhoods — Grandpa's, Perry's, Pa's, Audrey's — awaiting a new generation that can't be born: a wooden child's chair, with long, slanting, insecty legs, a small china bowl, Peter Rabbit running along the rim. Audrey's dolly pram, the mattress still chewed at one corner — the memorable legacy of Audrey's and my overenthusiastic parenting of 'Baby Moppet'. Skipping ropes, tiddly winks, alphabet bricks, and a small wooden box of dominoes that is like finding something of mine that I misplaced long ago. I slide back its stiff lid, remembering the games we played on rainy afternoons, how I'd let Audrey win, not wanting to disturb the natural order of things. Her fingerprints, I think, must still be over each piece, mine too, something of her, us. Impulsively, I pick out a lucky blank, a talisman, and drop it into the pocket of my dressing-gown. I shut the door behind me, impressed by my own audacity.

When I open the kitchen door to the outside, the morning is soft and blessedly cool. I sit on a garden bench and slowly become aware of a sound: hard to identify, rhythmic, metallic, coming from the side of the house. I get up and cautiously peer around the corner.

'Good morning, Margot,' Sybil says, not even glancing in my direction, secateurs slicing into the ivy creeping over a ground-floor window, the one with the crack.

My stomach lurches. She must have seen me. I wait for her to whip around and shout that I must never, ever snoop among Audrey's things again, and return the domino immediately. But there is only the slice of metal against metal, an amputated arm of ivy falling to the ground, a small puzzling smile playing at my aunt's lips.

★   ★   ★

As our first week progresses, Sybil keeps popping up suddenly, silently, marking our movements, twice catching me standing outside Audrey's door, fighting the urge to open it. Perry lumbers around after us too, noisily, Minotaur-like, one hand on his lower back, suggesting swims or games of bridge. 'But really wanting to suck the flesh off our bones,' says Pam. Yet our aunt and uncle step around each other, like awkwardly

127

placed furniture or guests at a party with a long-running feud.

It's odd to witness. All our lives we've been brought up to want what Sybil has: a marriage to a first-born son, a big house, a loyal maid, clawed silver sugar tongs, a gold carriage clock ticking down to the next wedding anniversary. And yet Sybil grinds pepper over her boiled egg in the morning as if she'd like to wring the neck of the chicken who laid it.

Although she always emerges in the morning fully dressed, her face scrubbed almost raw — it is impossible to imagine her idling in a dressing-gown like Ma, purring over a lazy continental coffee and the gossip columns of last week's newspaper — she hasn't gone further than the village church in five years. She's imprisoned herself behind her own floral swagged curtains.

And it's becoming clear that she wants to do the same to us. When Audrey was here, we'd play in the meadow for hours, scramble across fields in the dark, swim in the river, crowned with duckweed. Yesterday, a proposal of a jaunt into the village, no more than half an hour's walk away, sent Sybil's fragile face into a twitching spasm of anxiety. She tried to persuade us to do something else. A dip in the pool? A game of croquet? A picnic in the orchard, perhaps? As our secret mission of bumping into the Gore cousins seemed to be under threat, Flora suggested Sybil come with us, knowing full well she wouldn't. Sybil blinked and paled, torn in half by the question, and I could see there was something in her that desperately wanted to say yes. But she didn't. Or she couldn't.

She didn't miss much. A baby show on the village green by the duck pond, and dozens of staring locals, their mouths open. I'm not sure if it was Flora's skirt, the pale cotton transparent in the bright sun, or just the sight of four sisters so obviously from elsewhere that disturbed the village air as we moved down the narrow cobbled streets, past bowed-glass shop fronts, leaving something uneasy, troubled in our wake. Lace curtains in cottage windows parted slightly, shivered shut again. Women whispered behind cupped hands, children gawped, ran away, and a couple of times I heard our aunt and uncle's names snag the air. Not one person smiled at us. Returning to the house, puzzled and down-hearted, I saw Sybil watching us from an upstairs window, hand on the curtain, face pale as a plate beneath the glass. And I wondered if she knew the reaction we'd receive in the village, if she'd even tried to protect us from it.

*   *   *

Just when we've almost given up on ever hearing from the Gores again, they trot on sweating velvet-black horses past the orchard wall, and throw over an invitation, like a bunch of flowers. Sybil forbids it. Perry overrules her: 'Go and charm Harry silly, Flora.'

Daphne is a tiny rowing boat, blue and scuffed, sinkable-looking. Fits six easily, Harry says, if you squash up. The water is only an inch

129

or two away from the top of the boat, splashing over the sides, making us laugh and shriek every time someone moves. The river drifts lazily ahead, twisting gently, wide as a country lane, willow trees kissing the cloudy green surface.

Harry is sitting next to me, wearing shorts, his thigh banging against mine. There are hairs on his legs like copper wires. The side of me that touches him is unbearably alive.

The boys start to row. I can feel the heat on Harry's leg, the effort it takes to pull the long wooden oars rippling from his arms through his body. Occasionally he gives me a sidelong, slightly puzzled smile. The smile he beams at Flora is more open and less complicated. Like he wants to lick her.

When the boys stop rowing, we drift downstream, faster as the current picks up, ducking beneath overhanging branches, through the columns of midges, trying to keep our feet out of the water that has pooled in the boat's base, while trailing our fingers in the river, like actresses in films. Blue-black house martins dive low over the water, tails forked. Memories of Audrey dart, sprite-like, peeking between bulrushes: Audrey with pigtails at seven years old, trailing her skipping rope like a tail; Audrey at twelve, the summer afternoon it started to bucket down without warning and our blouses got drenched and went transparent and we ran back to the house, laughing, mouths wide open, tongues out to catch the raindrops.

When I revisit that day in my mind now, it's hard not to wonder if someone else was watching us, noticing Audrey's blooming prettiness, our flaunting of girlish carefree joy. Did our happiness make someone else feel the bitter lack of it and want to trap it for themselves? A lonely fisherman maybe, piercing wriggling maggots to his hook. The man in the hat, lurking under the damp shadow of the bridge.

'Land ahoy!' shouts Harry, grabbing a dangling willow branch, like a lock of a girl's hair, and sliding the boat beneath the tree, those troubling thoughts away.

We throw down a picnic rug on the grassy bank, leaving Harry and Flora to bail out the boat. Lying on my belly, chin on my hands, I watch Flora bending from her tiny waist, giggling behind a curtain of blonde hair as she scoops with a bucket, Harry brushing against her, closer than he needs to be. Tom also watches them, with a look of frustrated longing. And Pam watches Tom.

When Flora and Harry finally join us, flushed, glowing, Harry picking something out of Flora's hair, it's obvious to everyone they're closer, those few minutes spent alone enough time to form some kind of alliance, and that the rest of us are cut out of it, spectators. Over a marbled ham, cold chicken legs, Pam tries to grab Tom's attention but it doesn't work particularly well, so she ups the ante, hitching her dress into the sides of her underwear, showing off her taut brown thighs, and striding back to the boat, hands swinging, saying that she's going to row us all back. The boys whoop. 'Me *and* Margot!' Pam shouts over her shoulder. I shake my head.

131

'Margot, Margot,' Harry chants, slapping a hand on his thigh.

It's the first time a boy has ever chanted my name.

Within seconds my palms are stinging. The backs of my knees grate against the bench. But there is something more at stake than proving we're better rowers than the boys, although I'm not sure exactly what. On the last stretch, I feel unstoppable. Stepping out at the meadow again, our legs shaky, dresses wet with sweat, Pam and I grin at each other triumphantly, then glance around, half expecting applause, or at least an admiring male look. But Tom is glaring at Harry, who is whispering something into Flora's ear, making her laugh, and lingering, as if sniffing her — she is not stinking of sweat. And I remember that I am just Margot Wilde, plain Margot with itchy skin, invisible once more.

★ ★ ★

The curtains in Dot's bedroom are drawn, the scorching afternoon a white scissor cut where they meet. I sit next to her on the bed where she is balled up, facing the wall, looking smaller and darker than ever. 'Still woozy from the boat?' I whisper, stroking her shoulder.

Her toes twitch but she says nothing.

I crouch down. 'Oh, Dot, you're crying. What's the matter? Is it because we haven't heard from Ma?'

The mail boats are erratic, Sybil says. Better to push her from our minds altogether, she says. We

132

are Applecote girls now.

Dot smiles weakly. 'I don't mind not having Ma when I've got you, Margot.'

'What is it, then?'

'I'm too babyish. I try not to be. But I hold the rest of you back, I know I do.'

'Back from what?' I smile, her sweetness touching.

She presses her dark red lips together.

'Do you mean with boys and things?' I ask tentatively.

She nods, shoots me a small smile of gratitude that she has been understood.

'Oh, Dot, I'm as out in the cold as you are, honestly. I'm hardly beating them off with a stick, am I?' I pick a hair off her cheek, where it clings to the tears and sweat. 'Two into three won't go either.'

Dot rearranges herself, rests her head on her hand. 'Harry was looking at you, Margot. In the boat. When you were rowing.'

'He only has eyes for Flora.' Something leaps inside me all the same.

Dot sighs. 'No one ever looks at me, Margot.'

'They will,' I say, my heart starting to pound. Harry was looking at me? *Me?* 'You're still a child, Dot. But you're going to be a beautiful woman, I can tell.'

She shakes her head. 'I wear spectacles. It's a complete disaster.'

'Lots of girls wear spectacles. And I have skin on the backs of my knees that looks like dried Spam.'

Dot smiles. 'You can hide knees.'

'Not in a bathing-suit. Not even in a summer skirt very easily, not without half-decent stockings.'

'But I don't *look* like the rest of you.' Her face grows serious. She speaks in a whisper. 'Why am I so dark, Margot? Why aren't I blonde, like the other Wilde girls? Why don't I have blue eyes? Ma has blue eyes. Pa had blue eyes.'

'Oh, Dot, you could be black as ink and you'd still be a Wilde girl. You're not a changeling. Don't be a goose. Budge up.' I clamber into bed beside her, refusing to wonder about Dot's exotic colouring since it doesn't matter and never has. She feels surprisingly wiry and strong, no longer the pale asthmatic city girl she was just over a week ago. It strikes me that Ma is going to miss a significant summer of us growing up. It shouldn't matter — perfectly normal to be away at school for a term, after all, come home taller — but somehow it does here. We might grow up slightly wonky at Applecote Manor, like roses trained the wrong way along a wall. 'It's been such a long, hot day, have a nap, Dot. Everything will feel better afterwards, I promise. It always does.'

'I love you, Margot.' She yawns, eyes starting to close.

★ ★ ★

Stepping on to the landing, I'm met by an astonishing sight: Moll huffing through Audrey's door with a laundry basket, as if the room were of no more significance than the scullery. I

134

smother a gasp, step back into Dot's doorway and wait for something to happen, the world to end, some sort of static crackle. But Moll doesn't smoke or flash. And she leaves the door ajar.

I watch, transfixed, as she starts to peel the linen off Audrey's bed, tucking in new sheets, smoothing them with her palm. She folds a pink blanket, a blanket I remember well: we made lifelong promises huddled under it that we were never able to keep. As she bends down, I see the porthole window, its spill of purple light, like blackcurrant cordial, on the floor. Moll finished, I edge backwards into Dot's room again, until I hear the soft click of a door closing, Moll's footsteps descending the stairs.

No one is around. Dot is asleep. Pam and Flora are playing Monopoly with Sybil and Perry in the drawing room: I can hear Perry bellowing, 'Ha! To jail, Pam!'

Audrey taps me on the shoulder: well, what are you waiting for? My mind arrives before the rest of me.

The doorknob turns shockingly easily in my hand. I hesitate, as I've hesitated many times before, my heart pounding. The fear remains that if I enter this room a part of me will never leave. Come on, Margot. I feel her fingers pressed over my eyes. Find me. Count to ten. *One, two, three . . .*

As I step in, something in me releases, like a sigh: I feel safe, a little girl again. Nothing has changed. Audrey appears to have popped out to fetch an apple: she'll be returning shortly,

135

extracting a pip from her teeth with her tongue. The room smells not of lost things but of lavender water. Fresh sheets. There is a small posy of meadow flowers on her old school desk — the water clear, the flowers fresh, pink and white — and her pencils, all sharp, their tin case open, are ready for my cousin's busy fingers. On her dresser, her ivory-handled hairbrush, some yellow ribbons in a porcelain shell dish. Long-forgotten memories rush to the surface, not just the games, stories, dressing-up, but how Audrey made me feel my own person, not just one of four sisters. More than anything, I remember the sweet pleasure of feeling chosen, a favourite: the exact opposite to standing on the bank of the river, body aching, the backs of my knees itching, watching Harry woo Flora.

I kick off my shoes, take out my hairgrips, and throw myself back on the cloud of Audrey's bed, tracing the familiar bumps of the wicker headboard lightly with my fingers. Tears curl hotly into my ears, not just for Audrey but the way life hurtles forward so, leaving the past standing alone, shrinking, like a forgotten child on a deserted railway platform. I'm not sure how long I stay there, why I doze off, but when I open my eyes, the sky in the round window is gingery, and I feel different, emptied yet peaceful: I've made a space inside me for Audrey to live. I get up slowly, sleepily: reflected in the mirror of the dresser, my face, her face, the edge between us wavy, dissolving, like an outline in the midday heat. And when I go downstairs to join my sisters, I leave behind not just my forgotten hairgrips but a little bit of myself too, just as I knew I would.

★ ★ ★

I've discovered I quite like having secrets from my sisters. There's a thrill in holding something tight to one's heart, cupped in closed hands, like a baby bird. Also, I know that Pam and Flora would be furious if I told them I'd visited Audrey's room, or slept with her domino under my pillow. They have Tom and Harry to lose now, the summer's precarious freedom. We can't afford to upset Sybil.

I know this too. But I'm unable to resist surrendering to the suck of Audrey's room, sometimes only to poke my head around the door, other times lingering too long, risking being caught. Familiar again to the point of feeling like mine, it's become a refuge from all sorts of things: Ma not writing; Harry peeling off Flora's dress with his eyes; the thrilling fear that if Perry did do something awful to Audrey, he might do the same to us; the discovery of another strange posy in the meadow's crater, a dark red flower and a budding twig, twine-tied, like some sort of pagan offering; and the brick-bake of inescapable heat.

Today there is a breeze but it's warm and wet, like a lick. Dot shelters under a huge, gnarled beech tree in the Wilderness with Moppet, preferring her company to ours. The rest of us gravitate to the pool, seeking relief, only to find Perry already there. We get in, watching him

137

warily, the pink roll of his arms stretched along the stone sides, his stomach a barrel beneath the water, rising and falling. And he watches us.

After a while, he heaves himself out and falls asleep in a poolside chair, his legs outstretched, the bulge in his knitted trunks jumping and twitching as he dreams, making us all dissolve into smothered snorts of laughter. It dies down. The heat intensifies. I leave my elder sisters idly gossiping about the Gores behind the shield of their novels, so absorbed in the subject they barely acknowledge my departure.

I stop at the pool gate, feeling a small pang for the long, dreary days before the Gores spangled into our summer when all we had was each other. No chance I'd have been able to sneak away to Audrey's room then, I realize. Pam would have hauled me back by my swimsuit strap. Flora would have looked into my eyes and seen Audrey's room reflected, as in one of those round, gilt-framed convex mirrors in the hall.

★ ★ ★

Audrey's wardrobe door is ajar. It is impossible to resist.

Audrey was always the best dressed. My clothes, originating from Woolworths or Marks & Spencer, came third hand, the hems faded and creased from being turned up and down. Audrey had new dresses, made by a seamstress in Bath, or bought from the gleaming counters of Harrods. She would make me try them on, even though they were too big, and turn slowly, aching for her dresses, her splendid life: I think Audrey could only really appreciate her fine clothes by seeing them on someone else.

Something of that childish acquisitive excitement returns. My hands are already inside, clicking through the padded floral hangers — broderie anglaise, seersucker, crêpe-de-Chine, lawn cotton, pearl buttons, horn buttons, toggles, zips, hooks and eyes — working from left to right, amazed to see little-girl dresses give way to older-girl dresses, then much older girls', enough dresses to clothe Audrey every season since she's been gone. At the very far right of the rail, pressed against the cedar wood, a dress that brings back the past like a burn: blue — the shade of the cornflowers in the meadow, the huge summer sky — with a white Peter Pan collar and scarlet heart-shaped buttons, puffed with a tissue-thin petticoat. And yet. How can I possibly remember a dress of this size, with darts at the bust?

I slide it off its hanger and hold it against my body, imagining we might dance together around the room, and it will tell me its secrets.

'Margot.' Sybil is a thin dark line in the doorway.

My stomach drops. 'I was . . . '

'I can see what you're doing.'

I don't know where to put myself, or the dress, swishing indecently against my legs. I inhale to speak, say nothing, wonder why Sybil isn't shouting yet.

'Audrey will need new clothes when she

comes home.' Sybil speaks in an unsteady voice, as if it is she who feels she must explain herself. 'Clothes that fit.'

I bow my head, deeply uncomfortable. 'Of course.'

'That was her favourite dress. The one she wore that . . . that day.'

'Yes.' I wish I wasn't still holding it.

'So I had it made up again, just the same.'

'How lovely,' I murmur quietly, as if there is nothing odd about this.

Sybil watches me carefully, gauging my reaction, wondering if she can trust me. 'Don't mention it to your uncle, will you? It would only upset him. He won't come in here.'

'I won't,' I assure her.

'Or your sisters.'

I hesitate. It feels like disloyalty to promise such a thing.

'Margot, you really mustn't tell your sisters. They won't understand.'

'Okay,' I say, because they wouldn't.

Sybil exhales, relieved that I'm going along with her. 'It's not the first time you've been in here, is it, Margot?' she asks, her voice soft, softer than I've heard it all summer.

I shake my head. There's suddenly nothing between us, only an understanding that hasn't made its character known yet.

'Why don't you put the dress on?' she whispers, her voice trembling.

I stare back at her blankly, hoping I've misheard.

'I know you want to, Margot. We don't have to

140

pretend with one another. Not any more. Not in here.'

I shake my head.

'I saw you take the domino, Margot. I saw the look on your face. I know you couldn't help yourself then either.'

My cheeks blast with heat. 'It was just . . . just a silly impulsive thing. I — I'll return it.'

She nods at the dress again. 'Slip it on.'

'I'd — I'd rather not,' I say, almost faint with embarrassment. I've never felt more exposed, more *seen* in my life. 'It's Audrey's.'

Sybil's grey eyes start to swim with tears. 'It would make me so happy, Margot. I can't tell you how happy it would make me. Just for a moment. Just a twirl.'

Mortified, unable to refuse, I self-consciously unbutton my shirtdress with fumbling fingers until I'm standing just in my underwear. The porthole window casts a shard of purple on my white pants, where the elastic hits my belly button. I hesitate, imagining my sisters' appalled faces if they could see me now.

Sybil nods at me encouragingly.

★   ★   ★

I nervously step, foot pointed, into the folds of the dress.

'Oh. It fits! Just that top button.' I try not to flinch from Sybil's cold fingers, tugging the bodice shut. It won't go. My back is too broad. 'So almost perfect.'

Sybil's face is very close to mine, inches away,

141

smiling a long-forgotten smile that transforms her into the Sybil I remember as a child. 'Oh, it really picks out the blue of your eyes, Margot. Just like hers.' She starts arranging wisps of hair around my face. 'No, not quite right. A plait would look better. Audrey loved a plait.'

She's making me collude in a game of her devising, just as Audrey used to. I start undoing the dress, fiddling with the buttons. 'My sisters are waiting for me.' I pull my own dress back on too quickly, ripping a seam with my foot.

'No hurry,' says Sybil. 'Here. Let me.' And she's standing too close again. 'Oh, you have a little sunburn here, Margot.' She touches my right shoulder delicately. 'And a heat rash, I think. I'll get Moll to bring up some calamine. How are your knees?' And before I can answer, she's picking up the hem of the dress at the back and is bending down, inspecting them. 'Oh, my darling. Oh, you poor thing.'

'It looks worse than it is, really.' And while it feels wrong on a level I can't quite grasp, a little part of me is seduced by the attentive maternal concern, the slow trail of a cool finger over the raw heat of the itch.

'You have been terribly neglected by your mother, I can see that. But you won't be neglected any longer, not under my care, my dear.' She drops the hem of the dress and smooths it lightly with a quick brush of her hand, a gesture that seems to give me permission to leave.

I pause in the doorway. 'I'm truly sorry, Aunt Sybil.'

'Oh, I always knew you would come in here, Margot, that out of all of the sisters, it would be you. Don't look so surprised.' Her gaze has unexpected warmth. 'You are just like Audrey. She'd have taken that domino. She would have come in here too, of course.'

It is only then that it strikes me: Sybil left the wardrobe door open deliberately. And it was she who found my hair-grips, not Moll. And she had seen my weakness that morning as I poked around the storeroom. Maybe she knew it was only a matter of time.

Sybil cocks her head to one side, her fingers rolling the seed pearls at her throat. 'You see, I was planning to keep this door very much locked.' Her eyes roam my face. 'But, for some reason, I thought of you, Margot, and I didn't want to lock the room after all. Isn't that odd?'

7

An early September morning, the day summer crumbles into autumn. Thick fog presses up at the windows. Romy sits enthroned in the wooden child's chair from the attic that Jessie has restored, nibbling one of the orchard's first almost-ripe apples. The clock ticks on the newly painted calamine-pink kitchen wall. The silence is shouty. Romy nudges the apple off the table to the tiled floor, where it lands with an impressive thump, its red skin splitting, revealing white wet flesh. 'Uh-oh.'

Jessie glances distractedly at the apple, which is rolling into the little tepee she's made for Romy out of sticks and an old sheet in the corner of the kitchen, then at the clock again, then Will, who is by the range, being careful not to lean upon its greasy flank, blue-lipped from his icy shower, since the plumber didn't turn up. Dressed for his second week wooing investors in his slim-cut navy suit, clean white shirt and Italian leather brogues, he seems almost comically at odds with his surroundings now, and in danger of being soiled by them at any moment: the butcher's block scattered with Romy's craft glue and pasta shapes; the fuzzy grey sheepskins that Jessie's laid over the spindle-backed kitchen chairs to make them more comfortable. And Jessie herself, who has been up for hours already — Romy now wakes with the cockerels at dawn, maddeningly in sync with her environment — and is wearing baggy denim dungarees, splattered with the pink kitchen paint, the knees shiny from bending down, yanking up brambles. 'What is Bella doing up there? Shall I go up?' she asks, even though she'd rather not. She'll never get used to that gallery of Mandy.

'Give her one more minute.' Will frowns.

'Apple, Daddy.' Romy points imperiously at the floor.

'You must think I'm dafter than you, ma'am.' But Will picks it up, hands it back to her, putty in Romy's hands, as he is in Bella's. Guilty too. Soon, he will say goodbye.

Romy, oblivious to Daddy's imminent departure, grins, swings the bare tough tiny feet that seem permanently grubby from weeks of scuffing along the house's oak floor-boards, the centuries of dust and God knows what wedged in their cracks. She knocks the apple off the table again. 'Uh-oh.'

Jessie presses the gingerbread man pendant on her necklace between her fingers, feeling stress rise through her body, like prickly heat, her anxious gaze sticking to the clock. Bella has to be at the school bus stop by eight. Although Will woke her with a cup of tea an hour ago, and was instructed to go away, she's not yet emerged. Since Bella got her GCSE exam results a few days ago, she's been sleeping late, increasingly withdrawn, brooding in that bedroom, like a fierce young owl. The grades were a blow, not an unexpected one, and not because they were

145

particularly bad, only because Bella knew she could have done so much better, that she'd not fulfilled the promise of her early school years, the glowing reports that stopped abruptly with her mother's death. Jessie fears that she'll simply give up, or refuse to go to Squirrels, and that one of the main reasons they've moved from London could fall apart. What on earth would they do then? How could they justify being here?

The question tightens like a belt across her chest. Reality has hit hard this morning. Will is in his suit, armed for corporate combat. The air is wet and cidery, the river starting to swell. Yesterday Jessie saw swallows, tiny beautiful birds, wheeling south for winter, For some reason, the sight made her eyes fill with tears.

Hearing the slow clap of footsteps on the stairs, Jessie and Will rush into the hall, their fingers touching, not daring to entwine. And there is Bella, unexpectedly shy, hand gripping the wooden banister, halfway down. Except it is not a Bella they recognize. In a pleated grey skirt, wool blazer and striped burgundy tie, her face scrubbed clean of make-up, hair tied back, she looks like a schoolgirl from long ago, nothing like the precocious alley-cat teen in tiny denim shorts and black tights who used to stalk around London, eyes cast down, in silent sullen communion with her mobile phone. Will beams. He grabs Jessie's hand and holds it tightly behind his back against the wool of his suit. Jessie smiles. 'You look wonderful,' she tells Bella truthfully.

'I feel like a right twat.'

After a hurried breakfast, Bella insists on walking to the bus stop by herself, no embarrassing family send-off. At the front door, Will stands back admiringly, holding Bella's hands and swinging her arms, as if she were a little girl in a new party dress. 'I'm sorry I have to be in London all week again. It's just until I secure the finance, okay? Good. That's my girl. You don't have to pretend to miss me.'

Jessie glances away, feeling like an intruder. When she looks back Bella is walking down the gravel path into the fog, her skirt brushing against the spent silver lavender heads, and the sight makes her heart lurch. 'Bella!' she calls. Bella turns round and there is an awkward pregnant moment, a moment when a mother would naturally run and hug her daughter goodbye. The thought of Bella's recoil stops Jessie even attempting it. 'Good luck,' she says instead.

Bella nods. The moment has gone.

'Bye-bye, Bell-Bell.' Romy waves excitedly. Bella keeps walking. She doesn't wave back.

Will's turn to leave. He pulls Jessie gently towards him by the straps of her dungarees until their foreheads meet, the tips of their noses. Over the tailoring of his shoulder Jessie can see dense black clouds framed in the paned glass, their shadows like huge airships moving slowly over the hills towards them. She's hit by a sense of foreboding.

And yet she knows this is the sensible thing to do. The days he struggled up to London last week proved that a daily commute isn't feasible,

147

not with these back-to-back meetings, cancelled trains, early starts. And it would be stupid to turn down the offer of a nice spare room in a friend's house during the week — churlish even to observe that his host, a divorced attractive GP called Kate, was one of Mandy's best friends. Besides, it's just a temporary measure. He'll secure the finance quickly.

'You sure you'll be okay here on your own?' he asks gently.

Jessie's thoughts turn to the woman with the dogs, the one Bella said was in the lane again yesterday evening, staring up at the house. 'Check out the dungarees, the hoary leather boots.' She smiles. 'Would you really mess with a woman who looks like this?'

'You do look like you might cut your evening cigar with the wood axe.'

Jessie thinks of the photos of stylish, elegant Mandy in Bella's room, and her smile fades. Does Will ever compare his two wives? Is it even possible not to, given that the pictures are so in his face? Jessie remembers her mother's warnings about moving to the country, what it can do to a marriage.

Will's face grows serious again. 'Now Bella's back at school, you'll be able to meet other mothers in the area, all that stuff,' he says, in the hesitant manner of a man who senses he might be fluffing it.

'Civilize myself?' she says quickly.

'I didn't mean that.'

'It's all right. I know what you mean.' Jessie brushes a roll of dust off his shoulder, one of

148

those grey caterpillars that float down from the beams. She's not sure how she'll be spending her hours here alone. But she doubts that coffee mornings are about to become a priority. There's too much to do on the house. 'And I'll be very busy. Don't worry about me.'

His gaze roams over her face, seeking more reassurance. 'Call me if there's any problem with Bella, won't you?'

'Bella will be fine,' she insists, aware, as he is, that it's the first time she and the girls have been alone for more than a night here without him. Also, Bella, anxious about starting a new school, has pitched into one of her darker moods again, her emotions pinballing, looking for places to land. She sleepwalked again a couple of nights ago: Will found her wandering along the top-floor landing like a ghost. 'Me and the girls will have a blast without you. Really.' She kisses him, her nose lingering close to his cheek, trying to store his scent. 'Now go. Or you'll miss your train and we'll go bankrupt trying to buy out Jackson and have to live like thirteenth-century rural peasants for ever.'

'Don't think I don't know that's what you really want, Jessie,' he calls over his shoulder.

She watches him drive away, until his car is lost to the fog.

★　★　★

Jessie's surprised at how much she misses Bella. Applecote feels too quiet without the stomping and door slamming and sideways dry humour.

149

This is it for now, she realizes, just me and Romy in this huge, silent house on our own. In Bella's room, Jessie puts the laundry basket on the rug and walks over to the little round window, peers through its crossed pane: it gives a bird's eye view, or a teenager's, the way it detaches and elevates, shrinks everything else to insignificance. The fog has finally lifted. The stones in the meadow are like dorsal fins in a distant sea. She feels a real yearning to be out there in the long, wet grass, not in this intense airless room with the memory of herself pressing Mandy's kaftan against her body, greedy for a dead woman's allure. 'Come on, Rom,' she says distractedly, then glances back over her shoulder. 'Oh, you fruitloop. What are you doing?'

Romy has Bella's sports bra on her head, furtively rooting through the laundry basket. Jessie laughs, grabs the bra. 'Bella will kill you. No, you can't wear that either. Oh, my goodness, you munchkin. Scoot.' She removes the basket from Romy's reach, and puts it in the middle of Bella's bed, eyeing the two boxes wedged between the bed and the wall, wondering what might be left inside them.

Romy wanders over to the dressing-table, the curios Bella's arranged into an artistic still life: the heart-shaped button, the old newspapers from '59, a very pretty chipped teacup decorated with little gold flowers, and a new discovery from the Wilderness, a rather unnerving long white bone that is too big to be a rabbit's.

'Don't mess it up this time, sweetheart.'

Having been fiercely chastised by Bella for

rummaging through her things in recent days — 'You're disrespecting my privacy, don't you understand?' Bella hissed, and Romy nodded solemnly, not understanding at all — Romy inspects it all at a distance, her little fingers twitching over her adored big sister's objects, not quite daring to touch them. Jessie smiles, then picks up a stack of Bella's underwear, turns, opens the top drawer of Bella's chest of drawers. And there they are. Letters.

Jessie immediately knows she mustn't look at them, which is part of their appeal. But they aren't tucked right at the back, not like something private would be, but at the side of the drawer, propped up against socks, almost as if they've been put there on purpose for her to find this morning.

Jessie glances at Romy, still absorbed by the objects on the dressing-table, and curiously pushes the stack to see the handwriting. Will's. Letters home to his daughter? Oh, and someone else's, a strong, immaculate hand. In that instant, she knows the letters are from the boxes. She starts closing the drawer quickly, then hesitates, the woman who picked up the kaftan that day slipping into her once more, like an oily black shadow, sliding her hand into the gap.

Sent over the years from various locations Jessie knows Will visited for work, Brussels, Copenhagen, Paris, in the days before he scaled back his travel to be around for Bella, the letters are stung with longing and soft with marital tenderness — 'What did we do in our past lives to be so blessed?' he writes — and an erotic

151

intimacy that makes Jessie blush, dispelling any hope that Will's marriage to Mandy might have cooled into something affectionate, habitual. Eyes blazing, she skim-reads the letters written by Mandy: funny, opinionated, so obviously more articulate than anything she could ever write, they hop from global political issues to the sweetly domestic, Bella splitting a lip on a swing, the scandalous appearance of a mistress at a neighbour's barbecue, how she misses them holding hands as they sleep. Nicknames, jokes, shared conundrums, the letters reveal the intricate private world that Jessie and Will never talk about. And then there is the physical fact of them, not texts or emails, but letters, old-fashioned and romantic. Blinking back tears, Jessie feels the words settle inside her, like tiny fragments of swallowed glass. And it is only the sight of Romy, finally succumbing to temptation and deftly picking up the heart-shaped button, that makes Jessie snap back in to the room, realize what she's doing, and hurriedly stuff the letters back into the drawer, trying to leave them exactly where she found them, but unsure where that was.

★ ★ ★

Jessie is flaying off old wallpaper in the room that will be her studio when she hears the front door slam. Romy, who is drawing wiggles in the dust on the floor with the handle of a paintbrush, stops, looks up. 'Bell-Bell home.'

Jessie nods, her arm still above her head, dust

sugaring her hair. She took letters from her stepdaughter's underwear drawer and read them. She is that person. If Bella put them there deliberately to test her, will she know just from looking at her that she's done it?

Jessie isn't sure. There is one tiny moment as they stand in the hall, a nick in the air, when their eyes catch, and Jessie feels they understand each other absolutely, before she breaks it, firing off a round of questions about school meals and teachers — too many, too fast. The next day, after Bella's gone to school, Jessie checks the drawer again and sees the letters are no longer there.

Jessie calls Lou to confide what she's done to another adult, test the water before she tells Will. But Lou has London gossip to unload first — a friend coming out, a power-crazed boss at work, a Tube station shut by a dancing flash mob — which is like a dispatch from another planet. When Lou asks how she is, Jessie hesitates and decides she doesn't want to share the humiliation of the letters. She's not so sure she can tell Will either. She can't unread them. And any conversation will lead back to her prying in Bella's drawers, a damning trail of distrust, like dirty footprints across a clean floor.

The week stretches on, empty of Will, his laugh, his smell, his sleepy morning kiss, and full of unsettling thoughts and noises and autumn spiders. Jessie and Bella capture them together — rare moments of harmony, Bella shouting, 'Left, right, oh, my God, it's a beast, go, go!' Jessie on all fours with one of the jam-jars she'd found at the back of a cupboard.

Jessie packs her days with physical exertion: less room for self-analysis; less time to think about Will and Mandy holding hands in their sleep. She takes Romy for drives, through valleys, villages, folk-tale woods. On one of these trips, she stumbles into a café. Ten miles away — this counts as local, she's learning — it feels like an oasis of culture. Attached to a plant nursery, it hosts jazz nights, poetry readings, things she thought she'd left behind in another life. Housed in a pretty old glasshouse, decorated with the work of local artists, it's run in a cloud of steam and wry humour by a tall, well-spoken woman in her youthful seventies with a dancer's deportment and a penchant for huge beaded necklaces — fists of lapis lazuli and turquoise — that bring out the brilliant painter's blue of her eyes. She has a way of glancing kindly in Jessie's direction as if she senses something of the tumult of Jessie's thoughts. And the very nice man in the nursery, who has Robert Redford's grizzled good looks, patiently answers her naive gardening questions. He sells her a dwarf lemon tree with three tiny lemons the colour of sunshine that she puts in an earthenware pot in the orangery. She photographs Romy standing next to it with a trowel — a pose that took only twenty minutes to stage — and texts it to Will, proof of their happy new life, then posts it on Facebook. Their life is liked forty times. And she feels a little better about it.

A curling postcard advert, stuck to the village shop's window: 'Joe Peat. Building work. Odd

jobs. House 'n' garden. No job too small . . . '
Jessie leaves a voicemail for him. The surname,
Peat, is reassuring. She also scribbles down the
details of local toddler groups. And although she
doesn't go to any, not yet, she feels she's
accomplished something at least.

Friday, the day Will returns: Jessie realizes
she's been holding her breath all week. The
world lightens. The sun comes out, filtering
through saffron leaves. The air smells of
woodsmoke drifting along the river from the
village. Jessie arranges a mental good-news list of
happy family anecdotes to recount to Will on his
return — blackberry foraging with the girls, the
trip to the ancient stones at sunset with a flask of
cocoa. There's another list of things she won't
worry him with — Joe Peat not calling back, the
evening Bella took Romy bat-spotting in the
Wilderness and lost her for ten minutes. After
settling Romy with the alphabet bricks from the
attic, Jessie pulls out her most trusted recipe
book, stained with golden syrup and olive oil and
the sweat of teaching herself how to cook for a
family after years of living happily on salad bags
and microwave falafel. She will cook everything
better, she tells herself. She will cook a meal as
good as anything Mandy might have made, adds
a small insecure voice in her head.

Will's running late. Really late. Jessie hangs on
until the chicken is smoking. It is shrivelled, the
potatoes burned to a crisp. She puts out
crumpled linen napkins anyway, sticks beeswax
candles into old wine bottles and turns out the
kitchen's bright striplight. The candlelight

155

flickers against the bulging walls and beams, making the fireplace look dark and deep as a cave, throwing the whole room back into a different era. Romy clings to her leg. She pours herself a large glass of red wine.

'Not another power cut?' Bella shines her iPhone torch into Jessie's face.

Jessie puts up her hand against the dazzle. 'We're celebrating your first week at Squirrels. Too bright.'

'Er, why?' Bella frowns, clicking the phone off.

'Because it's a big thing and you've done brilliantly.'

Bella looks genuinely surprised. The frown turns into a small smile.

Jessie lifts Romy into the old child's chair, which wobbles slightly. She'll have to tighten those screws again. 'Your dad's late, I'm afraid. He's really sorry.'

'Wasn't the idea that we moved to the arse end of nowhere and he was at home *more*?' Bella takes a green bean from the steamer and bites into it, wincing at its heat.

'Yes, it was. And he will be.' Jessie's voice comes out a little too tight. 'Let's eat while the meal's still faintly digestible.'

Sawing the tough chicken breast into pieces for Romy, Jessie looks up, making an effort to smile. 'You could invite a girl from school over this weekend.'

'I don't have any friends,' Bella replies matter-of-factly.

'But it's only been a week. You will.'

Bella shrugs, making out she doesn't much

156

care anyway. 'I'm not like them. I never will be.' She scoops her hair into a loose bun, securing it with a grip, her neck long, balletic. 'And they wouldn't want to set foot inside this house anyway,' she adds.

Jessie's immediate response is to take a sip of wine. It burns down her throat, and she feels its effects almost instantly. She's noticed this before at Applecote, the way her body seems purer and more sensitive to alcohol, everything more finely tuned. 'Why do you say that?'

It occurs to Jessie that Bella looks rather pleased with herself, sucking on a secret. 'Something happened here. The girls at school told me. It's legend at Squirrels.' Bella times her words carefully, studying Jessie's reaction. 'They reckon the agent should have told us before we bought it.'

Romy cocks her head on one side, alert to the change of tone, her eyes rolling from Jessie to Bella and back again, sensing something worrying nibbling at the edges of the conversation.

'And?'

'A girl used to live here ages ago, a cousin of some girls who went to my school. Her name was Audrey. Audrey *Wilde*.' Bella's voice drops low, thrilled, and the candlelight flickers up her face, her eyes shining as if she were huddled over a table at a séance. 'There's a photo with them in it, her cousins, I mean, also Wildes, four of them — one of them is totally supermodel beautiful — hanging in Squirrels' Great Hall.'

Jessie takes a larger sip of wine. 'Amazing.'

Bella angles her spoon so that the candlelight flickers off its handle and ripples on the ceiling. 'That's not all.' Bella's face is more animated than Jessie's seen in months. 'Audrey disappeared. She disappeared from Applecote Manor.'

Jessie coughs on her mouthful of wine. 'What — like an alien abduction?'

'She went down to the river one day,' Bella says, irritated that Jessie's making light of it. 'Never seen again.'

Something in Jessie seizes tight. She thinks of the river that snakes through the meadow, its smooth verdigris surface, the surprising kick of its current. 'She drowned?' Her voice drops to a hush. Romy glances at her mother for reassurance, rotating a cindered roast potato in her fingers.

'A man was arrested.'

A man. A bad man. Jessie doesn't want to hear this. She doesn't want a girl to have come to harm in this house. Applecote Manor is their safe place. It's where they're going to become a happy family, and Bella will heal. It is not allowed to have a malign, murky history. She stands up and starts stacking plates.

'Audrey's father was arrested.'

Jessie turns. The air fills unpleasantly with the smell of greasy chicken. 'How terrible. And they — they found her?'

'Not yet.'

There's something about the 'yet'. It means she could still be here, the girl, that they could pull up a floorboard — No, she's being as silly as Bella. This is the kind of story schoolgirls

158

fabricate to whip themselves into a hormonal frenzy. Still, she could have done without it, today of all days. She reaches for the pendant on her necklace and feels her heart pumping along the gold.

Without being asked, Bella starts clearing plates. 'The Squirrels girls say that some of them have *seen* her, this Audrey. Seriously. I'm not joking. That she's old now, because she would be, but she comes back to roam around Applecote Manor. A girl in the upper sixth, Tania — she has shocking acne — she drove past this house on a driving lesson, not even six months ago, when the house was meant to be empty, and saw a face in the window, pressed up to the glass. A woman looking *out*! She nearly crashed the car.'

'Uh-oh,' says Romy.

'Well, they've certainly got lush imaginations,' says Jessie, in a clipped voice.

Bella watches Jessie's evident discomfort with interest, and Jessie wonders if the whole thing is a ruse to unsettle her. 'You remember I felt a bad thing had happened here, the first day we saw the house?' The candle flames, stirred by an imperceptible draught, elongate into long red tongues, throwing shadows against the walls. 'Well, I was right, wasn't I? I knew.'

Jessie turns on the stiff brass tap, seeking the distraction of water sputtering into the sink. First the letters, now this story about the girl. Summer is over. Will has gone. And Bella is determined to fill the house with ghosts. 'Okay, pudding.'

'I reckon there are certain places, houses,

159

where bad things just happen and *keep* happening,' Bella says determinedly.

There's a blast of heat as Jessie opens the oven, burns her fingers on the earthenware dish.

'I wonder what the next bad thing will be. When it will happen.'

'Bella, I think I'm done with legends of disappearing girls. And since I roasted the chicken into oblivion and back, I suggest we all fill up on apple crumble,' Jessie says, trying to bury the conversation beneath steaming dollops of pudding, feeling a sudden unexpected rush of dread, less about the girl disappearing than the niggling sense that something about the story speaks directly to Bella, and that Bella wants to recast it.

8

Sybil tugs the brush through my hair like my mother used to, alternately brisk and tender, pausing to pull apart the worst bathing-pool tangles with her fingers. I sit passively on the floral upholstered stool at Audrey's dressing-table, enjoying the relinquishment of control, my mind idly wandering from Harry's thighs to my discovery of another posy in the meadow crater, and my new theory that it is not a local's pagan offering but something left by Perry, a mark of guilt or a dark secret. I play over my mother's explanation of what happened to Audrey, not the words but the gaps between them, the sense I had afterwards of not being told everything, a wrinkle in the air after she mentioned Perry's name. Or am I imagining it, that wrinkle?

Sybil clinks the hairbrush down on the silver dish and my thoughts slip beneath the surface once more. I see my reflection sit straighter in the dressing-table mirror, the stiff pleats of Sybil's blouse splaying slightly over the neat hard mound of her bust. I know what's coming next. I particularly like this bit, the lift of thick, hot hair off my neck, the splitting into three sections, the gentle tugging as Sybil weaves back time with her fingers, the rhythm filling the room with a strange music all of its own.

When the plait is done our eyes meet with a spark in the mirror. And I know that Sybil is not

161

seeing me but Audrey and that this is wrong and queer. And yet.

I thought it would just be the once. After finding me in this room last week, making me try on the dress, Sybil kept asking if she could plait my hair. Secretly, she said. We wouldn't tell anyone. I could take the plait out afterwards. Her fingers were twitching at the sight of so much unruly hair, so in need of a brush, she said. After a while my refusal seemed mean — I was so grateful not to be in enormous trouble at being caught in Audrey's room. Also, there was this bit of me that couldn't help but wonder what it would be like to sit at Audrey's dressing-table, Audrey's mother's fingers in my hair. I thought of Ma's actor friends, who live their characters' quirks off-stage, and decided the more I submerged myself in Audrey the better the chances of discovering her state of mind the day she disappeared.

It was awful at first, the plaiting. I sat rigid, flinching every time Sybil's fingers brushed my scalp, appalled at the sound of her loud, fast breathing, but after a while I forced myself to surrender and the encounter became almost bearable, then comforting, all that being cared for, fussed over, like a little girl. Afterwards, I went into my room, not understanding why I suddenly felt tearful, and found a gift of the wooden box of dominoes on my bed, the one from the storeroom, complete but for the one I'd taken. And I wiped my eyes and smiled.

The next time she did my hair, I didn't want to see myself in the mirror — what on earth was

I doing back here again? What would my sisters say? — I closed my eyes, started slowly to feel the familiar warmth, deep in my abdomen, that I'd experience in Audrey's company, and I recognized it instantly as an echo of the hazily remembered pleasure of being Pa's favourite girl, Margot A-go-go, a connection I'd never made before. And this small understanding was a revelation, not about Audrey, as intended, but about myself, or my selves, the Margots stacked one inside another, like painted Russian dolls. And here I am, back at the dressing-table again.

'Margot?' Pam bellows up the stairs.

I stand up in a fluster, like someone startled out of a deep sleep. Each time I'm in Audrey's room, it takes a little longer to feel like me again afterwards. 'I've got to go,' I whisper.

Sybil nods, but her disappointment is obvious. A yellow ribbon dangles limply from her fingers.

'I've been calling for ages. Where have you been?' Pam is on the landing below, hands on her hips, staring up at me through the banisters, eyes narrowed. It strikes me that none of us look much like London girls now. Ma wouldn't recognize us. We've been at Applecote almost a month and our hair is bleached the colour of the wheat-fields, our shoulders strong from swimming, our bellies soft from Moll's endless apple puddings and homemade toffee brittle.

We're different on the inside too. There's a sharpness in the way that Pam looks at me, a latent unspoken suspicion of one another. If Ma ever does get through on the telephone — Ma is busy, Sybil tells us, the line terrible — I wonder

163

if she'd hear it in our voices. She went away comforted by the knowledge that we'd always look after each other, a tight group — 'What is the collective noun for sisters? A shoal of sisters? A murder?' Ma mused, fanning herself with a martini-stained copy of *Vogue* — who could 'read each other's minds like telegrams'. No longer.

'I was just up here.' It is not quite a lie, but enough of one to give me a sharp guilty thrill, while leaving me feeling cheapened.

'What on earth have you done to your hair?' Pam scoffs. 'You look about twelve years old, Margot.'

Appalled at my carelessness, I yank at the tight bristle of my plait, roughly pulling it apart. 'My hair felt too hot down.'

'Shall we just leave you behind then?' she says eagerly, like someone who wants to do exactly this. 'Since you're not ready.'

'Ready for what?' As my panic subsides I notice that Pam is wearing lipstick — one of Ma's pilfered crimsons.

'Christ, Margot. You really are from a different planet, aren't you? The Gores. They said they'd be swimming in the river after tea. Remember?'

I clamp my hand to my mouth. My fingers smell unsettlingly of Sybil: roses, starch, something soaped and scrubbed. 'Yes, yes, of course. I want to come!'

Pam doesn't pretend to look pleased about this. The less competition for Tom's attention, the better. She already has the exquisite obstacle of Flora: despite declaring herself 'three-quarters

164

in love with Harry already', she's reluctant to cut the rope from which Tom also dangles, thereby selfishly, greedily stealing the hearts of both boys, rather than sharing the spoils with Pam. 'In that case you'd better be quick. Put on your costume under your dress. Grab a towel. And use the lav first. You can't bob down in the grass with boys around.'

★ ★ ★

Submerged beneath the river's surface, their skin is pale green, like the underside of a leaf, their bodies muscularly wrought, making me think of the statues in the Victoria and Albert Museum. I never thought of boys as beautiful until now, that you might want to study their figures as you do girls'. But they are beautiful, frolicking in the water, compellingly, carelessly alive. We stare at them, enchanted, behind a veil of cow parsley, holding back Moppet by the collar. Above the trees, a giant hot-air balloon rises, tomato-red, its basket swinging.

'This is not a good idea,' Dot tells Moppet. 'I'm going back to the house.'

'No, no. Stay here with us,' I say, squeezing her hand, wanting her to feel included. 'Sybil won't mind.' Since the hair-brushing started, Sybil has relaxed a little, if not giving us permission exactly, then turning a blind eye to meetings with the Gores, as long as it's daylight and we don't venture far.

'She said the river was dangerous.'

'Sybil thinks a bath is dangerous, Dot.' Flora

laughs, trying to exchange an amused glance with me. But I quickly look away, feeling oddly treacherous to both Sybil and Flora since I'm honest with neither, caught between both.

'Yoo-hoo!' Harry waves jubilantly from the water, shouting at us to join them. I can think only of the backs of my knees, which I scratched raw in my sleep last night, breaking through the toothpasty calamine crust.

But Pam is already tugging her dress over her head, keen to reveal her strong, athletic body to Tom. Flora follows, slipping from hers in one graceful liquid movement. The boys exchange wolfish looks. Then I do it, awkwardly, holding a towel in my teeth lengthways to hide my legs. The first to dive in, I am desperate for the cover of water. Dot stays on the bank, stubbornly clothed, Moppet on her lap, like a long thin grey baby.

The water is cold, alive with tiny silver fish. I like the fish, the way they swim like thoughts between my fingers, but they make Flora squeal. Midges halo our heads, rise and fall in columns.

Tom wades close to the muddy bank, all tall, snaky sinew, glancing shyly at Flora, who stands in the shallows, skimming smiles at him across the water. They can't quite stop looking at each other. But when Harry emerges from the deeper channel with a whoop, shaking off stringy reeds — compact where Tom is lean, his energy condensed, pushed into a tighter space — Flora deliberately turns her back on Tom, away from temptation, and propels herself towards Harry with a jump and a laugh that makes her breasts shake.

I suddenly wish that my own breasts were as round and pert as Flora's, or that I didn't have any at all: that I either exceeded expectation, like Flora, or sidestepped it completely, like Dot. I hate always to be in the middle of everything. Only in Audrey's room, I realize, do I feel at the centre.

The Gores and my elder sisters start flicking water at each other, giggling and jumping from branches. Too self-conscious to join in, I turn and swim downstream. Relieved to be on my own, I enjoy the rush of water between my legs, sticking to the cold of the deepest channel since I don't like the mud in the shallows, crawling with crayfish, the way it feels fleshy, like it might be full of bodies.

'One, two, three!' I hear Pam shout, arms above her head, ready to dive from a high tree. But the Gores are not looking at her. They are watching Flora wading up the bank: her bathing-suit has risen up, revealing one round buttock, the colour of top-of-the-milk cream. It suddenly feels like the whole afternoon will be about my sister's bottom, held in thrall to it. That there is nothing else left to happen.

I start swimming again, faster now. Only after a bend in the river, the others obscured, do I drift again and seek refuge in noticing things: the water vole's tunnel; the way a pond skater taps ludicrously over the surface, like a man on stilts. It occurs to me that the world of the river reveals itself fully only when you inhabit it, leave the safety of dry land, lower yourself to its level, and maybe this is true of the past too. I am right to

167

spend time in Audrey's room, letting a little of her siphon into me.

'You don't look like a girl who needs help.'

Harry's unexpected proximity makes me splutter. Where did he come from so silently? 'I'm fine,' I manage breathlessly.

He smiles, circling me, treading water. 'Pam said you were the type to swim off on your own and go too far without realizing, so I grabbed the opportunity to be a hero. The river looks peaceful but it does get quite knotty in places.'

'I know the river.'

His eyes dance. 'Ah, you sound like a modern girl who might object to being saved.'

'I'm perfectly capable of saving myself, thank you,' I say primly, sounding like a peculiar new version of myself. I swim away quickly. To my surprise Harry follows — his stroke splashless, the muscles in his arms bunching as they lift — rather than returning to ogle Flora on the bank.

Nothing about the river is tranquil now, and it has nothing to do with the current. Harry's presence heightens everything, the heat of the sun, the pull of water against my skin. Another gentle bend and the river widens. Everything slows here, the current, my heartbeat. The hot-air balloon, directly above, seems barely to move, holding the afternoon perfectly still.

He grabs my arm. 'Look!' In the time it's taken him to say that word, it's already happened: the bomb of blue piercing the water, out again. 'Kingfisher, did you see it?'

His hand is still on my arm. This moment — the balloon, the kingfisher, his hand — already feels like a small disloyalty, and something else, something thrilling I haven't got a word for yet.

'You know, you remind me of someone, Margot.' He stares at me intensely, making me blush.

'People say I look like my cousin. Like Audrey,' I say, breathless again.

He removes his arm and frowns. 'Ah, yes. I've been wondering what it is about you.' His easy charm held in tension with something else now, something darker, deeper, like the pond skater's feet on the filmy surface of the water.

'You were friends, my aunt says.' I tread water a little faster, scattering the tiny fish. I can still feel his warm hand on my arm, the spread of his fingers.

Harry twists on to his back, very still, as if there were a hidden plank under the water, a conjuror's trick. 'We'd knock about, the first couple of weeks of the summer, before my family went to France. I was the poor substitute — she was excitedly waiting for her marvellous cousins to arrive.' He turns to me and grins in a way that makes something inside me tighten. 'Now I get to see what all the fuss was about.'

I smile and swivel on to my back too, gaze up at the sky. It's easier to talk when I'm not looking at him. And when he moves his hands I feel them as ripples up the side of my body. 'Can I ask you something, Harry?'

'Anything.'

'Are my aunt and uncle not liked around here?'

'Liked?' he repeats, with a small laugh, apparently puzzled that anyone should give two hoots if they're liked or not. Or maybe he's just surprised that I've asked such a direct question. I always forget people never expect it, that it's politer not to say what you mean.

'It's just . . . well, they don't have much to do with anyone now. It's odd.' I turn my head to face him, my ear filling with water. 'Sybil is scared of leaving the house. She can't bring herself to do it.'

'Nothing's stopping her, Margot,' Harry says softly. 'You have to force yourself to do the things you're most scared of. You have to face your darkest fears, don't you?'

I try not to look too impressed. But his words ring true, and wise. I make a note to relay their message to Sybil, coax her out of the house one day.

'Only then can you survive yourself,' he adds, with sudden poetical intensity.

I climb into these words in wonder. Harry doesn't talk like other men. I'm hit by the injustice that Flora will not appreciate him for this, yet I would love him for it.

'Anyway, it's like the Stone Age here.' Harry flips on to his front puppyishly, and something about this gesture lightens things again. 'They believe in Little Folk. Spirits in the stones. And, you know, bad luck is contagious. Missing children too. No smoke without fire, all that.'

The water feels colder now. 'So did . . . did people assume . . . '

'That your uncle and aunt had something to do with it?' he says abruptly, surprising me by finishing the question. I start to sink inelegantly and have to kick myself back to the surface. 'Bloody stupid, of course they didn't,' he adds.

Something feels different, like we're in a new level of conversation. I check that the hot-air balloon is still in the sky. That everything is as it was. The taste of river drips down the back of my throat, a cow-dung grassiness. This could have been the last thing Audrey tasted, not apple pie or a pork chop or honey cake but the river. 'What did your parents think? They are . . . educated people.'

'My parents?' He laughs hollowly. 'Educated? Using the term loosely. My parents prefer not to think, Margot. They simply decide on a course and stick to it, like ocean liners.'

I'm not sure if I'm allowed to laugh too, and decide it is safer to say nothing and keep my face solemn.

'All the reporters were crawling everywhere. They hated their names mentioned in the papers. So they left, and didn't want to be around here much, not after that. Then they just got used to sticking in France all summer, I suppose. The sun. The wine. They're simple creatures of habit, my parents.'

'Why did you want to come back?' The moment the words are out of my mouth I feel it might be one question too many. He double-takes, like people do when they realize someone is leading them somewhere they don't want to go.

171

'Because they'll sell Cornton soon, and when I was a boy this was my special place, synonymous with summer.' I nod, understanding this completely. He grins. 'Really, Margot, all that matters is that I have the keys to Cornton. There are four beautiful sisters at Applecote Manor. It's divinely hot. Elvis Presley is on the wireless. There's not much wrong with the world, is there? We're so lucky, aren't we, to live here, now — I mean, at this point in history?'

I consider telling him about Audrey's bedroom, how Sybil keeps it ready for her return, how she lives only for that day, how nothing is history, nothing has gone. Only time passes, stealing years from Audrey. 'We are,' I say instead. I do feel incredibly lucky to be here with him.

'You've got a very pretty smile, Margot. You should smile more. Not be so serious. Come on, I'm not doing a very good job of saving you. At this rate you'll have to save me. Let's get back.' Filling his lungs with air, he lifts his muscle-bunched arm and sluices it into the river.

I follow in his wake, admiring his powerful stroke, studying the cinnamon freckles across his shoulder-blades, thinking about him and Audrey, trying to see a pattern in the chaos of those freckles, as I saw Audrey's face that time in the constellation of stars in the sky. But they stay just as freckles, a random sprinkling of long-lost summers and river swims, distant solar heat.

★ ★ ★

'Well, bravo, buttock.' There is incandescent fury in Pam's smile. 'If Harry was not yours before this afternoon's swim, Flora, he is now. And so, I dare say, are Tom, the bullocks in the field, the pilot of the hot-air balloon and anyone else within appreciative range of your strip show. Ma would be proud.'

'I swear I'll paint your mouth shut,' hisses Flora.

They glare at each other. Then Flora bends her face closer to my foot, which is resting in her lap, and I feel the cold press of the varnish brush against my nail. She's painted Pam's toes too — she stands wiggling, drying them on Flora's bedroom rug — but it isn't enough. Pam is still smarting.

When Harry and I returned from our swim — 'You two took your time,' observed Flora, puzzled rather than annoyed since she'd never see plain old me as a rival for a boy's affections — the rest of them were basking on the sunny river bank, lips bloodied by cherries. Something was off, the discord in the air between Flora and Pam thorny, almost a physical thing. The atmosphere wasn't improved by Harry's obvious air of preoccupation, the way he dared to chew a blade of grass and stare intently into the gliding river, rather than put all his energy into charming Flora. She looked at me quizzically; I shrugged. Interpreting Harry's reflective distance as a slight — Flora has little experience of slights, after all — she moved away to lie down next to Tom, who was spread out tantalizingly on the grass, eyes shut, head resting on his interlaced hands, naked but for his shorts, turning the colour of toast in the sun. When Flora landed beside him, a huge smile spread across his face: so attuned to her presence, her co-ordinates on the bank, he seemed to know it was Flora without opening his eyes. As they laughed and talked in low voices, I noticed how Flora became more natural in Tom's presence, while Tom was magnified in hers, losing his reserve. Pam noticed it too, contemplated the two of them with the merciless eye of an angry swan — it was enough for Flora to have Harry, not Tom too. I understood that. I wanted Harry myself, more than I've ever wanted anybody.

The unravelling continued into the afternoon. Back at the house, Moll brought us lollies from the icebox in the fridge, normally a moment of collective pleasure, but we took them silently and slumped on striped deckchairs in the shade of the beech tree, as if on separate islands, dreaming, sucking, Pam sulking. At one point, reliving Harry's hand on my arm, I sighed, far too longingly and loudly. But neither of my elder sisters noticed or commented upon it, and I wondered if we had lost the ability to read one another — the guilty conscience in a nostril rub, the words sucked back by a sharp inhalation of breath, the dreams behind a dawdling footstep — or if we were all too wrapped up in our own worlds now to care.

'Dot, move a bit to the left. You're in my light.' Flora dabs at my foot again, and my thoughts stream away. 'Your baby toenail is so fiddly. It's the size of a split pea.'

'Flora?' Dot pushes her glasses back up her nose. It's the first time she's spoken for ages, particularly quiet since we got back from the river. I don't think she likes the way our sisterly allegiances keep changing, realigning in minute ways ever since we met the Gores, like the cloud of tiny midges that towered and flattened above the river's surface.

'Hmm?' Flora says distractedly, holding up my foot, surveying her handiwork. 'Perfect, if I say so myself. But careful, Margot, or it'll smudge.'

'What was wrong with Harry earlier? Why did he go silent?' Dot's mind is still raking over the morning.

I feel Flora's start in the varnish brush. 'Maybe you can tell us, Margot.'

I blush. The chemical smell of the varnish catches in the back of my throat. Pam and Flora exchange a look that has a silent nod in it. Pam grabs a large, pretty glass paperweight off Flora's desk and slaps it from one palm to the other.

'You grilled him about Audrey, didn't you?' Pam says, lifting her chin so that I can see the triangle shape of her Wilde jaw.

'Well, yes. Sort of.'

'Oh, for God's sake, Margot.' Flora rejects my foot from the cradle of her lap.

'Do you have to ruin everything?' Pam looks even more furious, blaming me for the imagined slight that had led to Flora's monopolization of Tom. 'Audrey's no more likely to come back than the dodo. I don't even care who did it any more. Perry, Moll, the decapitated German pilot, the kitchen cat. Audrey's dead! We're alive! Can we just be grateful for that?'

'She's right,' says Flora, more softly.

'Someone has to ask questions,' I throw back at them sharply, guilt about my desire for Harry making me hot and defensive.

'Margot, the questions have been *asked*,' Pam says wearily. 'And there are no answers.'

'That's simply not true.' Indignant, my heart racing, I walk to the open window. I think of sitting at Audrey's dressing-table earlier, the tug and weave of Sybil's fingers: I felt more understood then, certainly more appreciated.

'Do you have to infect everyone with your maudlin imagination?' Pam mutters, beneath her breath.

I shake my head in disbelief that she could be so uninterested in Audrey's fate. 'You have a splinter of ice in your heart, Pam.'

'And you, my strange little sister . . . ' She holds the paperweight up to the light and turns it slowly so that the cobalt swirl in its centre seems to move, like a girl twisting, dancing in a blue dress. ' . . . you have a ghost in yours.'

9

Not dead, dormant: Jessie stares at the bulb between her soil-hardened fingertips. A gusty November wind, smelling distinctly of the orchard's rotting windfalls, pushes against her back. And she wonders. She wonders about the other thing lying dormant at Applecote, waiting for the right conditions to come alive.

The problem is she knows now. She wishes she didn't. She wishes she'd let Audrey be.

But these last two and a half months, since Bella started school and Will his disorienting split Applecote-London life, Bella's not stopped muttering about the 'vanishing girl'. She particularly likes talking about it when Will is away during the week, and it's just the three of them alone in the house, surrounded by a darkness so absolute it is like tangible living matter. It started to spook Jessie a bit so a couple of weeks ago she decided to prove the whole thing was nonsense, once and for all.

She was heartened by a quick search online that came up with nothing. But then, just to be sure, she'd gone on to chat with Sheila, the nice lady behind the till in the village shop — Sheila had been proudly saying she'd been born in the village, only visited London once, which was enough. Jessie casually asked if she knew anything about a young girl who had gone missing from Applecote in the fifties. She fully expected Sheila to laugh, ask her what on earth she was talking about.

'Never forgot the day my mammy told me,' Sheila muttered instead, stuffing noodles more vigorously into Jessie's hessian shopper. 'We weren't allowed out to play for months that summer.' She shook her head. 'That poor Mrs Wilde.'

'But not the Mrs Wilde who lived at Applecote before us?' Jessie clarified, with a delayed smile.

She had to sit down on the bench by the village pond afterwards, bury her face in Romy's cloud of biscuity curls. That night she dreamed of the woman with the dogs again, and called, 'Audrey!' and the woman turned around, revealing no face inside the headscarf, just a smudge. She's dreamed it every night since.

Jessie hasn't told Bella what Sheila said, of course. Bella needs no more encouragement. Rather than growing bored with the story, she seems more obsessed than ever, layering the bare 'facts' with her own details and suppositions, like one of those dark internet memes Jessie's read about. Jessie hopes 'the Audrey story' is Bella's way of getting herself noticed, trying to fit in, egged on by the other Squirrels girls. But Bella won't leave the story at school.

Bella's portrait of 'Audrey' — a rather good collage of a girl with a toothpaste smile, a background of rolling newspaper print — is now stuck on their kitchen wall, next to Romy's innocent finger paintings. And on Bella's dressing-table, that eerie *memento mori* keeps growing: the heart-shaped button, the paperweight from the desk in the old drawing room, those disintegrating newspapers from 1959, joined this week by a stubby pencil with the faintest A on its hexagonal side that Bella found wedged under the skirting board. Jessie secretly wishes she could throw the whole lot in the fire. (In hindsight, she also wishes she'd never given Romy those alphabet bricks from the attic, or fixed up the child's chair.) Will sees no harm in Bella's interest — 'a teen thing, like collecting badges' — but, then, Jessie hasn't told Will what Sheila said yet either.

She tried. But the words caught, and she washed them away with a large gulp of red wine. Jessie's overwhelming instinct is to protect Will from further darkness, not to add to his growing troubles. As it is, there are Skype meetings in the small hours with Jackson in Brisbane that leave Will permanently exhausted. Two business deals have been toasted in the last month, then disastrously fallen through at the last minute, Will's hopes dashed, his professional pride dented. The company's staff are unsettled, a couple jumping ship. Last week there was an embarrassing, expensive cock-up, a cargo turning up in the wrong port.

Will takes it all too personally, as if this no-deal limbo is a failure of him as a businessman and, Jessie senses, a husband. However much she assures him it's not his fault — it's the nervous markets, the lack of accessible capital, just crap luck — Will seems increasingly distant, weighted down by critical introspection. (Jessie is struggling not to take this personally and see her inability to lift his sombre mood as a

179

reflection on the shortcomings of their relation-ship. She's sure Mandy would have known how to reach him.) Given all this, she simply cannot bring herself to tell Will about Applecote's grim past and risk him seeing Applecote not as a rural haven but as a house of horrors. She's terrified he may want to leave. So she lets Will dismiss Bella's story as a schoolgirl's tall tale, and desperately hopes it will all gently fade away, like one season turning into another.

And yet. The house's history certainly explains things. The resistance of local builders — thank God for Joe Peat, who has agreed to work at Applecote, albeit in a vague 'few weeks'. The minute flickers in villagers' faces when Jessie mentions where she lives. The way a couple of the mothers at the local church playgroup in the village hall exchanged the sort of uneasy complicit look that wonders if they should mention anything. Jessie felt she had 'Outsider' crayoned on her forehead. She's just grateful that she hasn't mentioned anything to the woman at the plant-nursery café: she still has one sanctuary with good cake, like Greta's in London, where Applecote's history won't follow her. She needs it.

During the week now, whole days can pass when she doesn't see another adult. Her thoughts loosen and slip away then, especially if she has to go into Bella's bedroom, where those love letters still flutter in the eaved shadows like silver moths, and Mandy's beautiful, accom-plished gaze mocks her from the walls. *What did we do in our past lives to be so blessed?* Those words still taunt her. As does the image of them holding hands in their sleep, especially given that she and Will spend most of the week in separate beds, more than seventy miles apart. All the niggles and natural fears Jessie's ever had about Will — the speed of their relationship, the fact he'd loved someone else so deeply, that Bella still doesn't accept her, probably never will — take on a life of their own in the strange lilac light of that room.

Afterwards, seeking reassurance, she'll phone Will, just to hear his voice. Although Jessie can't picture the house, room or chair in which he sits — she hates this — she can hear the police sirens in the background, the murmur of the city, and she will smell the traffic, the surging scented gusts from shop fronts, and she will picture dear Lou on a Tube beneath the city's concrete crust, applying her deep-black MAC mascara, and she will miss it all with a pang that is almost painful, and bring the conversation to a sharp close, in case she gives herself away, or starts to sound like a sitcom stereotype of the needy, emotionally unstable wife at home.

Alone in the house, followed by Mandy's Mona Lisa gaze, these uncorrected thoughts gather plausibility until Friday, D Day, the day Will returns. Friday is always busy. It is the day Jessie primps the house, fuelled by a manic energy that turns her into a woman she doesn't really recognize: flowers arranged, bread baked, roaring fires lit. No longer the start of a lazy slide towards Sunday, as they used to be, Applecote weekends must now justify themselves. She feels under pressure for it all to feel worth it, the exhausting commute, the upheaval, the cold and mud. She'll scrub the garden soil from beneath her fingernails, and — the image of perfectly presented Mandy never far from her mind — rummage around for something faintly chic to wear.

'I wouldn't bother, Jess. I'm sure he'd much rather just get laid,' Lou counsels on the phone. Jessie loyally doesn't tell Lou that that side of things is stalling. How sometimes, when she and Will embrace, they don't seem to fit together as they used to, as if they are physically changing shape in the days they are apart.

Anyway, it's about the girls now, not her, she tells herself. They miss him terribly, the absent hero. (Bella, in particular, takes it out on Jessie, since she is around to receive it.) Romy launches herself at Will in a frenzy of possessive delight the moment he walks through the door. After hugs, tickles, a nonsensical discussion about Boy, the unfortunate woodlouse Romy keeps as a pet in a jam-jar, Will dutifully retreats upstairs to spend time alone with Bella in her bedroom. Jessie encourages it, as she always has. It's only sometimes, after particularly long chats, when Will comes downstairs looking preoccupied, a little troubled, like he did last night, that Jessie feels the hollow pang of exclusion, and starts to wonder exactly what Bella is telling him about the week alone with her stepmother.

But she says nothing. She carries on cooking. She smiles, maybe a little dementedly at times. She reminds herself that her policy is to share nothing that could stress Will. She might lay it on a bit too thick: how Bella's making such nice friends (Jessie pounces on any mention of a fellow classmate being 'kind of all right' as evidence of a blossoming friendship) and Romy loves the playgroup (she wrestles tractors out of the boys' hands, then demands to go home). She makes light of Bella's sleepwalking, not mentioning how she found Bella by Romy's cotbed again a couple of nights ago, staring down at the snuffling lump of her little sister with cold, blank, unseeing eyes. She doesn't talk about her own irrational wake-in-the-night fear that Romy will disappear, like the girl who lived here all those years ago, that old houses, set in such ancient landscapes, create atavistic reflexes, re-circulate the past, and that bad things will always happen at Applecote, just as Bella once promised.

'Dad!' Bella shouts into her thoughts. Jessie looks up, surprised to find herself still standing in the flowerbed, an allium bulb in her hand, the planting hole empty. This keeps happening, this fleeting loss of herself. Like she might have dissolved into the very substance of the house and garden while Will was away.

The light has changed, bronze now.

'Have you seen him, Jessie?' Bella is standing by the orangery, long hair blowing about her face, arms tightly crossed, wearing her Saturday uniform of skinny jeans, sneakers and a sloppy hoodie.

'Sorry, miles away. Yes, he's taken Romy to the village pond to feed the ducks.' Jessie likes how this sentence sounds, normal, domestic, like they're a regular country family enjoying their weekend. 'He won't be long.'

To Jessie's surprise, Bella starts to walk in her direction across the veranda, its stone still black from the morning's downpour. 'What are you doing?' she asks curiously.

'Planting flowers for spring.' Jessie straightens, presses a hand on her aching lower back. 'We may not have a new roof by then. But we will have flowers. Far more important, wouldn't you agree?'

'Is that a shallot?'

'An allium bulb. Close, though. Same family.'

Bella sticks her hands in her jeans' pockets, raises her shoulders into a shrug. 'Doesn't look like it'll do anything,' she says flatly.

'Why don't you plant it and see? It's a bit late in the season. But the man at the nursery said it should be fine if we get them in this weekend. It's a cool little nursery — I wish you'd come with me one day.'

Bella rolls her eyes. 'Nurseries are never cool, Jessie. You've been in the country too long.'

'Yeah, you're probably right.' Jessie laughs. She picks the paper bag of bulbs from the ground and hands it to Bella. 'There's another trowel in that bag.'

Bella hesitates, but then, resignedly deciding she has nothing better to do, she takes the bulbs and the trowel, bends down and flicks at the soil.

Jessie tries not to look too pleased. Nothing scares Bella off faster. 'About ten centimetres deep . . . That's it. That's great. Shove the bulb in. No, other way. Pointy bit facing up. Then just fill it in. Well done.'

It's an incongruous sight, Bella squatting down, carefully digging tiny holes, dropping in bulb after bulb, entirely absorbed, nudging them into place with her fingers. After a while, she stops and frowns up thoughtfully through her streaming dark hair at Jessie. 'Mum never gardened.'

'No, I guess she didn't,' says Jessie, after a pause. It hits her that there is now a heartbreakingly long list of things that Bella will never do with Mandy. She'd like to be able to acknowledge her understanding of this somehow to Bella but deems it too risky.

Bella starts digging once more, stabbing the trowel deep into the earth until it collides with something. 'Oh. Look.' She is wiping a muddy pair of glasses on her jeans. The lenses are long gone, one arm too, the frame tortoise-shell where Bella rubs the mud away. She forces the remaining arm open, holds the spectacles up and peers through them. They have a cat's eye slant, giving her a definite 1950s air. The sun dips. Jessie feels a little breathless: the house is confronting her with its darkest secret, the one she's kept from Will.

She knows what's coming.

'The vanishing girl, the one you hate me talking about. They could be hers, couldn't they?'

'I don't . . . ' Jessie's words trail off at the terrible timing: Will is pushing through the side gate, Romy on his shoulders, Flump, her knitted elephant, bobbing on his head.

'Ladies.' He bends down to shimmy Romy off his shoulders, grinning, pleased at this rare scene of familial harmony. 'Looking like a natural, Bella.'

'Jessie made me do it,' Bella says, fighting a small smile. Will slings his arm around Bella, hugs his daughter to him.

Jessie notices that Will is wearing his life in layers today: a Puffa coat, muddied from carrying his mid-life toddler; the V-neck cashmere sweater her mother gave him last Christmas — she'd never spent so much on a jumper in her life; a faded Glastonbury T-shirt from 1998, a festival he'd gone to with Mandy, and the year Bella was conceived.

'Ah, Jessie can be persuasive,' says Will, wryly, to Bella.

'You're back quick. Weren't the ducks hungry?' Jessie doesn't mean to sound short. She picks at Romy's curls. They're beginning to dreadlock at the back. She looks increasingly feral, like some sort of woodland sprite.

A free spirit — 'A little too free?' Will wondered yesterday, after getting home — Romy is resentful of any constraints: buggies, playpens and warm clothes. She knows her own mind, her favoured routes through the garden, all the better barefoot, the best places to forage in the undergrowth, finding a brain-like walnut revealed in the skull of its broken shell, rabbit bones that she offers to Bella, trying to win her affection. She eyes the glasses in Bella's hand curiously.

186

'Sorry,' Will says distractedly, looking up from his phone. His eyes take a moment to refocus, the pupils contracting, as if he's moving from one place to another in his head. 'An email from Jackson. Says he's sniffed out another potential buyer, some friend of a friend in the City. Maybe this will finally be it, Jess. I need to make a call.'

'On a Saturday?' Jackson's 'potential buyers' have led them a dance so far.

'If there's a small chance, we can't sit on it.' Stuffing his phone back in his coat pocket, he glances at Bella's hand. Jessie's heart sinks: she'd hoped they might go unnoticed. 'What you got there, Bella?'

'Audrey's glasses.' Bella lays them flat on her palm and holds them up for Will's inspection.

Will sends Jessie a quizzical look. She sends a small shrug back, one that says, leave it, it's just Bella's fanciful teenage imagination.

'Ducks?' Romy presses against Bella's leg, smiling the kind of smile that would melt any heart, just not her sister's. 'Bell-Bell take Romy to the ducks?'

'Bella's busy, sweetpea.' Jessie smiles, scooping her up. But Romy is resistant. She wants Bella.

'No, it's all right, I'll take Romy,' says Bella, unexpectedly.

Jessie is so taken aback she can't think of anything to say at first.

'Will you?' Will looks pleasantly surprised.

'Sure. We'll find some ducks on the river.'

The river. Jessie's heart starts to thump. Bella cannot take Romy down to the water alone. She

187

thinks of the cold, threatening way Bella looks at Romy sometimes. Bella's hot temper, her unpredictability. Jessie scrabbles about for legitimate reasons, the ones she can voice out loud. 'Oh, no, she's such a scamp. She keeps running off and hiding, Bella.'

And this is true. A trying new phase, Romy's attempts at hide and seek. Usually Jessie finds her pretty quickly. But she wouldn't want Romy trying it on by the river, not with that swell of water edging up the bulrushes, its surface fingerprinted with swirling eddies, guilty-looking. A bloated dead sheep was bobbing downstream yesterday, like an over-stuffed pillowcase, its eyes pink holes, pecked out by birds. 'The river is very high after all the rain. And look at those clouds. It's going to bucket down.'

'We'll be fine.' Bella speaks directly to Will now. And Jessie is aware of the self-enclosed lock of their gazes, the way they are silently negotiating without her.

'Off we go!' Romy tucks Flump tighter under her arm. 'Romy and Bell-Bell and Flump.'

'Will,' Jessie appeals to him, trying to talk in a grown-up code that Bella won't understand, 'I'm really not sure it's such a good idea.'

'She means she doesn't trust me,' Bella interjects simply, understanding perfectly.

Will frowns. Jessie feels the day lurch, the first afternoon of the weekend, which was going so well. 'I . . . '

'I told you, Dad,' Bella adds.

What has she told him? When? Jessie glances at Will quizzically. Is this what they were talking

188

about last night in Bella's bedroom? Those long phone calls earlier in the week? But Will doesn't quite meet Jessie's eye. And something in Jessie sinks: she cannot tune into Will as she did, she realizes. Is he thinking of what happened in London at the pool? Because she is. She can't not.

The lifeguard saw Bella holding the girl under the water, the girl struggling, flailing. After he pulled her out — Zizzi Miles, cliquey, popular, an old adversary of Bella's — she gasped on the poolside like a dying fish. An ambulance was called. Zizzi emerged from the incident unscathed, Bella far less so. After Zizzi swore that Bella 'had gone psycho' and tried to drown her, and Zizzi's incensed parents called the police, Bella was suspended, her place in the sixth form revoked. Offered the chance to defend herself, she barely bothered, only saying that she wished she'd pushed down harder, and that Zizzi's drowning act was faked: 'I don't expect to be believed.' And the headmistress didn't believe her. But Will did. And Jessie tried to. It's just that there's always been this doubtful voice in Jessie's head. No, Bella shouldn't be in charge of the little sister she doesn't like very much down by that river.

'Bella will be super careful, won't you?' Jessie hears Will say. And before she can object, she sees Will pull a sandwich bag of breadcrumbs from his coat pocket. 'Here. Duck feast. Hold Rom's hand, Bella. Tightly.'

'And Flump's,' instructs Romy, pushing the elephant's knitted grey foot into Bella's fingers.

★ ★ ★

Will is talking in his fast London voice, while Jessie paces by the kitchen window, peering out of the glass at the darkening garden beyond. The yellow tinge has gone. The sky is heavy, metallic, like a lid. She waits for Will to finish his call, turns to him. 'They've been gone a while.'

'Twenty minutes.' He's looking at her in a funny way, holding her at a distance. 'Bella can handle Romy.'

'It's not a London park, Will.' Worry makes her sound too sharp. Besides, he doesn't know the river, or the girls' dynamic, not like she does. He's never here. 'No one's around. If anything happened . . . '

Will rakes back his hair and says wearily, 'I thought we moved here so the girls could roam free.'

His tone takes her by surprise. It almost seems that a criticism of the entire move is seeded in his question. Rain starts to tap at the window, the sound of little fingers. 'Romy hasn't got her waterproof.'

'That's never held her back before.'

Jessie's not sure if there's an accusation in there somewhere too, or if she's imagining it. Maybe he's just tired and scratchy. 'I can feel another storm coming.'

He follows her into the cloakroom, watching as she rifles frantically through the coats on the hooks, her heart starting to jack, her mind flying off to bad places. 'Jessie . . . ' he says more softly.

'Not now, Will.'

He leans his head against the doorframe. 'I was just going to say how sweet you and Bella looked together in the garden just then, that's all.'

'Oh,' she says, momentarily thrown. Normally she'd seize upon this, evidence of how everything's working out just fine. 'Well, I won't be long.'

The wind pushes her through the meadow, as if it wants her to get to the river faster. It's hard to see in the rain: the stones are battered grey shapes, the trees at the meadow's edge sodden slabs of orange.

The river slurps at the bank, breaching in places, blades of grass sticking up surreally under a couple of inches of water. She runs alongside it, peering through the blackened bulrushes. They're not here, she thinks, her stomach flipping. They're bloody well not here. She starts calling their names, skidding on the cattle-hoofed mud. There's no one around, just the eerie desolation of a river in the rain, a red kite circling above. She stands for a moment, hand covering her mouth, not knowing what to do.

Shadows appear just beneath the surface of the water, like they did in the pool that first day. A corner of an old red shopping bag looks, for a moment, like Romy's welly boot, and a choke of fear rushes up her throat. She calls their names again, louder now. Nothing. She'll phone Will. She must phone Will. But her phone is not in her back pocket. Her phone is on the kitchen table, of course, where she left it. She stops, panting, hands on her knees, tries to think rationally. She must return. Maybe they're back at the house now. Yes, that's where they have to be.

Turning back to the meadow, Jessie freezes.

Ahead, her outline smudged by an undulating curtain of rain and wind, is a little girl, tiny, huddled on one of the stones, wearing glasses.

Romy hasn't seen Jessie yet, not until Jessie calls her name, runs up and grabs her tightly as if pulling her back from the edge of a cliff. 'Oh, sweetheart.'

'Flump gone,' sobs Romy, tightening her arms around Jessie's neck. 'Bell-Bell gone.'

'Gone? Where? Why are you wearing those horrible glasses? Oh, you poor little thing. Let's put this on before you get any wetter.'

She whips the glasses off Romy, stuffing them into her pocket, and tries in vain to push Romy's wet arms into her anorak. Out of the corner of her eye, movement. And there is Bella, out of breath, as if she's run back from somewhere far away, hair falling in black blades across her face.

'Bella! Where were you?'

Bella holds up Flump. The knitted elephant's sodden ears flop pathetically. 'I went to find this. Don't look at me like that. She dropped it. I told her to stay there while I went looking. I've only been five minutes or so.'

'Five minutes!'

'Flump was hard to find in the grass,' Bella retorts defensively. She shoots Romy a cold look. 'I knew she'd keep whining if I didn't come back with it.'

'Your dad told you to hold Romy's hand!'

192

'By the river. He said hold her hand by the *river*.'

'The river is just there. It's there! A toddle away. Romy could have gone looking for you and fallen in.' All the times Jessie's swallowed her anger, her fear, her doubts, seem to rise up at once, and she keeps shouting, even though she should stop, she knows she should stop, and Bella is paling, her blazing eyes darting about like something trapped. Then she is stumbling away over the soggy tussocks of grass.

'Wait!' Jessie runs after her, Romy sobbing on her hip. She pulls the glasses out of her pocket. 'And why did you make her wear these? Tell me.'

A guilty-looking flush rises on Bella's cheeks as she stutters, 'She — she wanted to wear them, didn't you, Romy?'

'Don't like.' Romy pushes the glasses away and buries her head in Jessie's shoulder. Jessie cradles her protectively.

'She does. I was just being nice. Is that so hard to imagine?' Bella grabs the glasses back.

Jessie hugs Romy closer. Something doesn't fit. For all Romy's sense of adventure, she wouldn't have wanted to be left alone in the rain like that. And she'd have protested about it. A small suspicious voice in Jessie's head starts to wonder if Bella, consciously or not, deliberately put Romy in danger. 'I don't like the sound of this.'

'No, you don't like *me*.'

'That's simply not true. I . . . I . . . ' Jessie is suddenly shocked by it all, the force of her own reaction, how a Saturday afternoon could have

193

begun so sweetly and slid into this. She presses her hand to her forehead. 'Sorry. I'm sorry for shouting. We need to get you some help, Bella. I — I'll get you what you need, I promise.'

Bella fists the tears off her face. 'I need Mum back, don't you get it? And I need you gone. No more shrinks. No more talking. No more Romy this and Romy fucking that. Just me and Dad again.'

Romy starts to whimper.

'Let's — let's just stop, Bella. Please. Not here. Let's go back to the house. We'll talk it through.'

'There's nothing else to say. I've said the truth. It's out there now. Do what you like with it.' Bella turns, walks off, bent forward in the rain, like something wild, elemental, completely out of Jessie's control.

'Bella . . . ' Jessie calls weakly, blinking back tears. But her voice is sucked away by the wind. She knows she should run after her, persuade her to come back to the house, warm up by the fire, but she can't erase the image of Romy in the spectacles, sitting on the stone, like a sacrificial offering. So she lets Bella vanish into the rain.

★　★　★

Almost two hours now. Where is she? Jessie listens with mounting alarm to the sound of branches breaking, great limbs crashing to the ground outside, static things airborne, benign things gone rogue, a world spun upside down. She prays for Bella's quick return.

The clock ticks faster on the kitchen wall,

stacking up the missing minutes, minutes when anything could be happening. Jessie imagines Bella crushed beneath a lightning-felled tree, her trainers poking out, the neon-yellow soles.

Out of the kitchen window, the cone of Will's torchlight nudges through the shrubs and shadows. Jessie desperately wishes she could run back into the afternoon, refuse to let Bella take Romy anywhere, listen to her gut.

Will throws open the back door. His hair is flat on his head. His eyes bloodshot. Like a man emerging from a rough sea. 'She's most likely to be at a school friend's house, don't you reckon?' he says breathlessly.

'I don't know,' she replies.

He swipes his car keys from a pottery bowl on the kitchen worktop. 'There's not a particular house she hangs out at after school?'

Jessie swallows. Her throat is sore from shouting earlier. 'I — I'm not sure. I don't think so.'

Will stares at her searchingly, longer than is comfortable. 'But I thought you said that . . . ' He looks confused, then something seems to dawn on him. Or maybe he reads the guilt in her face, the way she's staring down at her hands, cursing her eagerness to tell Will only what she thought he wanted to hear about Bella's friendships. 'She normally comes home after school, if there's no school club,' she says quietly.

'Right.' Will is frowning.

She can tell he feels duped, lulled into believing things about their weekday life that are not exactly untrue, just tangentially true, a version of a life that hasn't quite happened yet. 'I'm sorry if I misled you. I — I didn't want you to worry about Bella while you're in London, that's all.'

A moment passes. 'Right,' he says again, only more tersely, and she feels it like a physical thing, the way distrust slips between them. She stands up quickly, the chair rocking back. 'There's a class list somewhere.'

'I'm going to check the pub. Call me, if you hear anything.'

'Yes, yes, of course.' Desolate, Jessie stares out of the window as Will's car roars away. So it wasn't Romy, she thinks, covering her nose and mouth with her hands. It wasn't Romy who was going to vanish — Romy is happily asleep upstairs, bottom balled in the air, like a baby. It was Bella herself, of course, Bella re-enacting the past. She must tell Will this. That it's about the girl, the vanishing girl, the story planted like a pip in Bella's head, a true story, not a Squirrels myth. Full disclosure now. She is picking up her mobile to call him when the doorbell rings. The police, she thinks. Oh, God.

But it is the most wonderful sight: sodden, mud-sprayed, black-eyed, like a girl who lives in the woods. Jessie reaches out to hug her. Bella steps back, leaving Jessie swiping at air.

Out of the shadows, emerging from a dripping umbrella, a tall woman in a mackintosh. 'I'm afraid I kidnapped her.'

The voice. So soft. So well-spoken. So familiar. Jessie is unable to believe her eyes. 'It's you!'

The woman smiles uncertainly, trying to place her. 'I . . . '

'Sorry, I come to your café,' Jessie explains, trying to collect herself. 'With my little girl? I come and eat cake with my little girl.'

'Of course. Sorry.' The look of recognition is swiftly followed by astonishment. 'And it was you . . . You bought Applecote Manor? My goodness. I had no idea.'

Jessie looks from Bella to the woman in confusion. 'But, Bella, how . . . '

Bella moves awkwardly from one foot to the other, her trainers making a squelching sound. 'I was actually completely fine,' she mumbles.

'It's just that she didn't look particularly fine, that's all. I was driving back from a friend's, and there she was, this determined young thing, marching along the lane in the storm. She refused to get into a car with a stranger, sensible girl. But I begged her to make an exception this once. That lane is no place for a young girl at night. I insisted she get in. Absolutely my fault, not hers.' She smiles, firm but kind. 'You mustn't be cross with her.'

Cross? Jessie can only imagine what Bella's said. 'I'm just pleased to have her home. Thank you, thank you so much. I'm immensely grateful.'

The café woman touches Bella lightly on the arm, says softly, in an easy maternal way, like Jessie isn't there, 'You sure you're quite okay now?'

Bella nods, mutters thanks, and pushes past Jessie into the house. A well-timed flick of her

197

wet hair stings Jessie's cheek as Jessie texts Will to tell him the wanderer has returned.

'Pop along to the café sometime,' the lady calls after her. But Bella's gone. Somewhere a door slams.

Jessie sticks out a hand. 'Jessie.'

The woman hesitates, unsure about revealing her name. 'Margot. Margot Waters.'

Margot. The woman looks like a Margot. 'Would you like to come in? Warm up with a cup of tea?'

Jessie sees her hesitation, the familiar twitch: Margot knows about Applecote, Jessie realizes. Her spirits sink.

'I'd better get back. But thank you for the kind offer.' Margot peers curiously over Jessie's shoulder into the hall. 'You've made it very beautiful,' she says, in a tone of quiet appreciation.

'Oh, it's just a lick of paint, really,' says Jessie, wondering what Margot's comparing it to, how well she knows the house. 'It was always beautiful.'

'It was,' Margot says, lighting up.

Jessie has the odd sensation of being in the way, standing between the house and Margot, as you might two ex-lovers in a crowded room.

'Are you sure you won't come in?' she asks again.

'No. No, I won't,' she says, more firmly. 'I must go.' With one hand, Margot pulls up a leopard-print scarf from her hood, settling it over her mink-grey hair.

Jessie starts. Seeing the scarf, she thinks of the

198

woman she saw that day in August, as she hung from the orchard wall, that woman with the two black Labradors, walking away from the house. No, too much of a coincidence. There must be dozens of women in the Cotswolds with leopard-print scarves.

'I hope you're happy here, Jessie. Bella too. She's a very spirited girl.' Margot lowers her voice into something more conspiratorial. 'A good thing in the end, I promise.'

Jessie's throat locks. She fights the urge to throw herself at the older woman and tell her everything about the agonies of trying to mother Bella, stepping into a dead wife's shoes, but she has a funny hunch that somehow Margot has guessed it all anyway.

'Well, good night,' Margot says, more briskly now, withdrawing.

'Thank you again.'

Margot steps out of the shelter of the portico and stops, turns around once more. 'The drain at the back, it's blocked. It always blocks this time of year.'

'Sorry?' says Jessie, bemused.

'If you don't clear it, you'll get damp in the top-floor bathroom.'

'Oh. Okay. Thank you,' Jessie says, with a small puzzled laugh that soon stops. 'But how do you know . . . ' Her voice trails off.

Margot is already walking down the path to her car in the rain. Jessie stares after her, puzzled. As she drives away Jessie sees them, just for a brief second, in the puddle of light thrown by the lamp at the end of the drive: the two noses pressed against the car's rear window, a gleam of black fur, the two dogs' eyes glowing like lamps, then gone.

10

Not even Moppet can understand it. The treat of raw pigs' knuckles mid-morning. The petting from Sybil. The slow collapse of Applecote's house rules, like something rigid buckling in the soaring late-summer heat.

The only thing that seems to dampen Sybil's mood — pause her flow around the house, opening curtains — is a reminder that we are two and a half weeks off returning to school, Flora departing for Paris. And the only thing that truly stops Sybil in her tracks, so that her foot stills above the staircase tread, her hand leaps to her throat, is a mention of my mother, particularly Dot questioning if there are any letters for her from Ma. (The rest of us have given up asking.)

I'm now sure Sybil's managed to convince herself that Ma no longer exists — after all, she's convinced herself that Audrey will knock at the door any day — and that she, Sybil, is our new mother, we her adopted daughters. And because a mention of Ma seems to rattle her so, and threaten the mood that's led to the delicious relaxation of rules — and thereby our access to Harry and Tom — we mention Ma less and less, even to each other.

Or maybe it's just that Ma's hurt us by not writing, more than any of us care to admit. But I don't know for sure since we sisters no longer talk about our feelings honestly. We used to push them, like a kneaded lump of dough, into each other's hands to hold and squeeze so that we could experience them together. Now we take polemical positions. We have secret desires. We lob spiky feelings at one another, like hairbrushes. And Dot takes herself off on long solitary walks with Moppet.

Sybil, in her own subtle way, fuels this friction. Her quiet relish of Ma's reckless parenting makes me uncomfortable. When Pam mused in Sybil's hearing that Ma's probably run off with an Arab prince and is floating around a medina somewhere, nibbling dates, having forgotten her daughters completely, I'm sure I saw a satisfied smile flicker over Sybil's lips. Later that day, she appeared at dinner wearing an unthinkable slash of lipstick, Ma's distinctive crimson. I wanted to wash it off her face, say, 'You are not Ma, my wonderful, maddening, electrical storm of a mother.' But she looked so pretty, shyly pleased with herself. And she waved us off for a sunset swim in the river. So I didn't.

I keep thinking it can't last, Sybil's mood, this transformation. That it must be induced by a pill, like the ones Ma used to take after Pa died. Or the Dubonnet. That she'll clip downstairs in dark grey flannel the next morning, forbidding life-endangering swims. But then she appears freshly at the breakfast table in that yellow dress, the colour of lemons, and delivers me a private look, long as a letter, that binds me to her, making me feel that my dissembling is allowing her to gather a little of her old self again.

It baffles Perry. He blinks at Sybil as if he has noticed a fundamental change in his wife but has no idea what it is, or why. He double-takes when she ankles across the lawn, a floral skirt swishing around calves so slim and pale from being hidden under heavy dresses for years they are like a shop mannequin's, walking with the accelerating rhythm of someone keen for another day to unfold, rather than the slow step of someone determining to endure it.

Confusingly, Perry suddenly looks less guilty. No longer walking with his hand on his lower back, he is more upright, his belly less swollen with gas and secrets. I wonder if his wife's mood is passing into him, some kind of marital osmosis. This morning at lunch, he even suggested tentatively, as if he didn't quite trust this gay interloper masquerading as his wife, that she join him in the pool: Sybil threw back her head and laughed, not unkindly. She said she hadn't swum in it for years and was far too old to do so now and, anyway, the greenfly on the roses need dealing with. Still, he actually asked and she actually laughed, both unimaginable when we first arrived.

We joke that Sybil is having an affair with the gardener, Billy. Why else the smiles, the laxity, the red lipstick? But one afternoon Pam whips around, hard blue gaze prodding at me like a finger in the chest: 'What do you think, Margot? You're Sybil's pet. How do you read the mood of your mistress?' And I felt Audrey's world seal tighter over me then, its birdcage door swing shut.

I cannot confide to my sisters how Sybil's eyes follow me about the house. My anticipation of her tread on the stairs, her knuckles bunched, just outside my door, the moment before she knocks. How I know she will enter my room, closing the door behind her, circling me with smiles, drinking me in, asking the whereabouts of my sisters, until she suggests that we 'sit in Audrey's room together awhile'.

I'm not sure how to say no, and part of me wants to please her, and part of me enjoys it, and part of me wants to supplant Ma, punish her for not being here, for not writing, and letting this happen at all. It's not that I haven't tried to tell Sybil that it's a case of mistaken identity, that she mustn't muddle me with Audrey, but the stuttering words didn't come out very forcefully, and she shot me such a puzzled, disappointed look. She's just enjoying my company, she said. I knew she was lying. She probably knew it too. But I was so relieved at this simple explanation, the whole thing so awkward and odd and beyond navigable, that I grabbed it. But the longer I let it go on, the more culpable I feel, the more daunting the thought of addressing any of it or confiding in my sisters: the tighter the knot.

I imagine the likely scenario if I do say anything to them: the silencing of their conversations as I walk into a room, already something I've tasted in the last week or so: Pam's delighted disgust; Flora's wounded betrayal; Dot's sense of abandonment; and more than any of this, my sisters knowing that I've wilfully hidden a part of myself from them all these weeks in Audrey's room, a place no one but Sybil dare follow. It will cement my reputation as Strange Margot for ever, even though that version of me, the one who walks in Audrey's shoes, is transitory, an experiment, alive only in the confines of Audrey's room. She isn't allowed to escape, or leave her footprints behind.

★ ★ ★

I can smell Harry on Flora straight away.

Carelessly late for lunch, she sits at the dining table with swollen red lips, a flush on her chest, grass whiskering the back of her dress. She radiates soft light, like a candle. She smiles in a way I've never seen her smile, soft, distant. Perry raises his glass: 'My God, I was thinking it was never going to happen.'

And I feel so unbelievably stupid, so foolishly deluded, that I have to bite down hard on my silver fork to stop my eyes filling with tears. After the boat trip, the kingfisher, the hand on my arm, I stupidly allowed myself to imagine it might be me whom Harry liked a little. But, of course, it's not me. It's never me.

Pam is cock-a-hoop: it's only a matter of time before Tom will be hers, now that the annoying distraction of Flora has been removed. But Tom is more sullen and reserved than ever in the days following that first kiss, and stares after Flora with such tortured yearning that it's hard not to feel sorry for him. Pam, refusing to be beaten, flirts harder. Pam will make him love her, I know

205

that. She will not be left behind with the hopeless cases of me and Dot: 'I absolutely refuse to get to the end of the summer with my innocence intact.'

It seems unlikely Flora will either. The romance between her and Harry develops rapidly, frenziedly, after that kiss, climbing like a fever. We are all sucked up in it: the long, private river swims, Dot made to be the lookout on the bank; the rendezvous in the shed that mist up the small window, Pam patrolling outside, then sniffing inside the shed afterwards, once Harry's slunk away, diagnosing the atmosphere as 'salty, sweet, a bit animal'; Flora, sneaking but after dark under cover of a clumsy alibi — 'taking some air'; 'just stretching my legs' — not questioned by Sybil, if he excuse comes from me. Because of this, to my chagrin, I become the logistical facilitator of those heady evening meetings, and am so successful at it that Flora starts to move about Applecote with a slow, languid siren's grace, trailing her hands over the long grass, as if each tip sends shivers of pleasure down her arm. I watch her and ache. I want to feel what she is feeling. I think of us both, me locked away with Sybil, Flora with Harry, our lives dividing.

One afternoon Harry invites Flora to Cornton Hall: Pam is actually struck mute for three and a half hours by the swinging left hook of her own jealousy. Flora finally returns, dishevelled, glowing, breathlessly describing the stuffed grizzly bear, the carved crest above the fireplace, the suits of armour hanging off the wall, the

206

sweeping gardens, like a London park. "'And at that moment she felt that to be mistress of Pemberley might be something!'" mocks Pam.

The worst thing of all is that I still dream of Harry, more intensely than ever, and wake in a twist of sheets, the dreams so vivid it is hard to imagine he is not dreaming them too. I know it's wrong. I've tried to strip Harry of glamour, imagine him with greasy hair ambling down a grimy London street, past old bombsites and dirty pecking pigeons. But it is as if Harry can exist only in the Cotswold hills, among rivers and meadows, in this stifling summer, shirtless, sun-freckled, his substance all desire and dreams. In the city he'd dissolve into the drizzle.

★ ★ ★

A dip in my mattress. A hand stroking the hair from my forehead, carrying the faint scent of Pond's cold cream. Brain blurred by sleep, I'm sure that Ma is beside me, that I'm back under Chelsea's porridge-grey skies, sharing a bedroom with Dot, my elder sisters chattering amiably next door, Betty scrubbing the doorstep, Tube trains rumbling, and happiness flows through me, like the morning's first mouthful of piping hot tea. 'Ma?'

'I'm here,' a voice whispers.

My eyes spring open.

Sybil's face is inches from mine, emerging from a puff of cream blouse, a lace doily of a collar. 'Good morning, my darling girl. It's quite

207

all right. You're in the right bed, exactly the right bed.'

And that's when I feel it, the springy wicker headboard pressing into my shoulder, the luxurious give of the goose-down pillows. As I lie there in a daze, blinking up at Sybil, the previous night slides back to me, how I spasmed awake in the early hours, my head full of Harry, my body not my own, my thighs twitching, like a horse's flank. I snapped on the bedside lamp with clumsy fingers. There was a moth, a huge moth, its wings woven gold, the colour of Harry's eyes. Fearing such traitorous longing, the ache that pulsed somewhere near my abdomen, a bit of my body for which I have no name, that I don't understand, I stumbled down the corridor, trying to escape the confusion of sensation, searching for the childhood peace of Audrey's room.

How could I have been so utterly stupid as to actually fall asleep in her bed?

'You and I are both such early birds, aren't we? Flying while the world sleeps,' Sybil whispers. Her eyes are oddly bright, lambent with love. A shaft of dawn light pours through the long ochre curtains, rinsing Sybil's hair russet, so it looks a little as it did when she was younger, and time seems to have reversed, rolling backwards slowly, so that I am somehow stuck in it, that the bad thing that happened hasn't happened yet, that it is all to come, not to Audrey but to me.

Sybil brushes a lock of hair off my face. 'I'll run you a bath and then you can slip into your favourite blue dress, the one that brings out your eyes, hmm?'

I pull the sheet up to my chest protectively. It has gone too far. It's wrong, all of it. 'No, I — '

'But I'll bring you up some toast first,' Sybil says quickly, stealing my protest away. 'Raspberry jam. You love Moll's raspberry jam. That was always your favourite.'

'I must get back to my room.' I swing one foot out of the bed. 'My sisters will come looking,' I add, although I know they won't. We go down to breakfast separately now, no longer in a pack like before.

'Your cousins are all conked out. It's Moll you can hear, up with the larks.' She smiles.

Nothing about Sybil's expression suggests she realizes she's just called my sisters my cousins, or sees anything wrong with this. I open my mouth to correct her, but she continues to talk, a low, maternal murmur, the sound of a stream bubbling over small rocks. 'Let me plump the pillow. There. Leg back in. That's it. I'll open the window. Fresh air. Can you smell the roses? They're at their best just after dawn.'

I can smell them, their queasy sweetness.

She hesitates, reading my unease, unsure whether to leave me. 'You will stay here, won't you?'

I nod obediently: there is something in the intensity of Sybil right now, the determination of her delusion, that makes me wonder what she might be capable of if I refuse to play along. She walks to the door, glancing over her shoulder twice to check I haven't moved. The door shuts with a click. I wait a couple of minutes, maybe five, to be sure she's gone, then scramble up, just as the bedroom door opens again.

My heart leaps out of my chest: it's Moll, shuffling in, washing basket on the hunk of her hip. She doesn't see me straight away, and I stand very still, like a girl who believes in invisible cloaks.

She claps a hand to her mouth. A sharp intake of breath.

'I — I must have sleepwalked or something,' I blurt.

I can see Moll's mind racing, her puzzled gaze puddling around my bare feet, rising slowly up the crumpled cotton of my nightie, my tightly crossed arms, my blazing cheeks. To my surprise, she simply puts down by the bed the laundry basket — stacked with clean folded linen — and walks stoutly to the open window, her rectangular frame rocking from one foot to the other. She peers out at the scud of clouds, her back to me, the belt of her overall tightening, loosening as she breathes. 'Mrs Wilde found you, did she?'

'Yes,' I admit sheepishly, wondering if she's just bumped into my aunt on her way to make toast in the kitchen. I try to smooth my nightie, desperately wishing I were properly clothed, remembering Ma saying you can get away with anything if you're dressed well.

'She means no harm in it, Margot.' Moll turns to me, her round face pinched.

'I — I'm not sure what you mean.' I glance at the door, worried that Sybil might return at any moment and I'll be trapped here, pinned to the bed with fuss and toast.

Moll smiles kindly. 'I found your hairs in the hairbrush, duck.'

'Oh.' I close my eyes for a moment. So much for a brain like a board game. Even Moll's outmanoeuvred me.

'Not as milky as Flora, but blonder than Pam and little darkling Dot. Similar to Audrey's hair. But curlier, and shorter.' She picks a pillow off the bed, and skins it of its slip, eyeing me a little more sharply. 'And someone has been rifling through her frocks.'

'I . . . I've been an idiot, Moll.'

Moll snaps back the sheet from the bed. 'I'm saying nothing.'

'Aunt Sybil . . . ' I begin, and stop, not sure how much Moll has worked out.

'I guessed, Margot.' The sheet slacks in her hands. 'I've seen the way she looks at you. But your aunt has faith, you see, blind faith, that's all. Like I believe in the Good Lord, she believes in Audrey. And, well, sometimes she gets too wrapped up in it, that's all. She loses herself.'

I stare down at my toenails, the red varnish suddenly incongruous, and feel a roll of guilt. For haven't I encouraged Sybil? Isn't that what we both do in this room, lose ourselves, hold reality at bay?

'You're a kind girl, Margot,' Moll says, more softly, second-guessing my thoughts, rumpling the sheet back, exposing the blue quilting of the mattress. 'I can see that, the way you look after little Dot.'

My guilt intensifies. I've not been looking after

211

Dot these last few weeks. I've left her to grow up on her own this summer. And, being Dot, she hasn't complained, just taken refuge in Moppet, books, the companionship of her own imagination.

'Your aunt's seen some dark times, Margot, darker than you'll ever know.' Moll flutters over a fresh sheet and lifts a mattress corner. 'But I haven't seen her so relaxed, not for many years. Whatever's gone on in here, in this room, it's none of my business. All I know is that you and your sisters have breathed life into this house again.' She cocks her head, eyes me sadly. 'I can't bear the thought of you all flying away at the end of the summer, like swallows.'

I smile back at her. 'I'm glad you're at Applecote too, Moll. You didn't leave like the cook. Or the old gardeners.'

She shrugs, smooths the sheet with her palm. 'My sweetheart, Arnold, was shot down like that poor fella in the meadow. Missing in action. They never found him either. I know a little of the Wildes' heartbreak, that's all.'

'So is it *you* who leaves posies in the crater!'

She colours. 'I know it's daft. But someone loved that pilot, Margot. If it were my Arnold . . . ' She stops, her eyes pouching with tears.

To give Moll a moment, and despairing at my own fantastical theories, I peer out of the window, my hands on the wavering glass, and watch all the lost loved people, wheeling tracks in the sky, disguised as birds. And I think of the pilot, our German James Dean, how he had a

212

Moll back at home, who was tiny-waisted once, who will always miss him, who will never be the person she would have been if he'd lived. Just like I will never be Margot A-go-go again, without Pa. Sybil will never be Sybil again without Audrey. And I wonder if we're only our true selves as children, before life starts to go wrong.

'Spoiled rotten she was. Little madam, I called her — but I'd have done anything for Audrey,' Moll says abruptly, her thoughts seeming to follow mine. 'And she knew it, bless her.'

It strikes me that the answers could all be behind the black door of Moll's missing tooth. 'What happened to Audrey, Moll?'

'All I know . . . ' Moll hesitates, sieving her words like flour, patting them out in puffs ' . . . is that Mrs Wilde will never leave this big old house. Not while Audrey could come knocking on the door any day. And if they ever find her little broken body, it will shatter her mother's heart. Mrs Wilde lives for hope, Margot, you see. And up here,' Moll taps her temple, 'Audrey's as alive as you or me.'

'But it's been five years. Most people think . . . ' I try to say 'that she's dead' but can't.

'Your uncle did it?' Moll swipes at a pillow. 'Well, of course they did. After he was arrested by those buffoons.'

'Arrested?'

'You didn't know?' Moll clutches the pillow to her chest, red-faced. 'But everyone knew.'

I picture Ma the day we left, pressing the back of her hand to her forehead, the small silence after she mentioned my uncle's name. 'My mother never told us.'

'Well, she probably thought it best,' Moll says quickly, trying to backtrack. 'Now what have I done? Me and my big mouth. It's all your questions, Margot,' she adds, more irritably. 'You ask too many. You were the same as a child, like a bumblebee in the room.'

'So what happened?'

'It's not my place,' she says tightly.

'Oh, Moll. No one ever tells the whole story about anything. Our family history is built on layer upon layer of omissions,' I say, suddenly tearful. 'It's like the river, near the mouth of the Thames, you know, where they say you can stab at the ground and the underground water comes spurting out. Our family's like that, just with secrets.'

'All families are like that, duck.' Moll gives me a sympathetic smile. 'Now, she's got a good heart, your mother. I always thought so. It's not been easy. She does her best for you girls.'

'Moll, please. I won't be able to be in the same room as my uncle if you don't.'

Moll sits down heavily on the side of the bed. 'The police arrested your uncle because they had to arrest someone. That's my opinion, Margot. Couldn't find the poor mite in the river. Couldn't find that funny man in the hat. The grand families around here, the Gores and the like, especially those Gores at Cornton, wanted the matter swept away as soon as possible, exerted pressure at the top, like they always do. And the police had to be seen to be doing something.' She shakes her head, her eyes glassy with tears. 'Awful for Mrs Wilde. She stuck by her husband, though. She knew he'd had nothing to do with it.'

'Didn't he?' I ask, preparing for the worst, thinking of Perry's fat fingers.

'No, of course not, Margot!' Moll looks shocked that I should think such a thing. 'They couldn't pin anything on him, nothing but tittle-tattle and rumour, the mutterings of an old mystic in the next valley, and he was released. Although, in many eyes, he'll always be guilty, but that's the valley for you.' She stands up with a sigh, glances at the door. 'And that's Mrs Wilde's footstep on the landing below, if I'm not mistaken.'

Without thinking, I lean towards her, kiss her warm, papery cheek. 'Thank you, Moll.'

Moll presses her fingertips to her cheek with a look of amazement, as if she's not been kissed by anyone in years. Then she flicks me away, flustered and smiling. 'Be off with you.'

★ ★ ★

Summer is almost over. Suddenly some apples in the orchard are ripe. An evening arrives with a sharp nip, requiring the novelty of a cardigan. Flora shows off a love bite on her left breast, just above the nipple. 'A marriage proposal is only a matter of time,' Pam decides, after inspecting it closely. 'But he'd better get his skates on.'

In just over a week — 'That day,' as Sybil now refers to it, eyes closing as she speaks — we must

215

pack our cases and return to Squirrels without Flora for the first time, and Flora is off to be polished, like a precious stone, in Paris.

There suddenly seems a lot to lose — Flora, Harry, Tom, the possibility of ever finding out what happened to Audrey, even Billy's bashful hellos, Sybil brushing my hair, little things I've grown used to and will miss.

But, most of all, it is the loss of our sisterhood, the tribe of Wildlings we were at the start of the summer, that hits hardest. The four of us are no longer solid, but dispersing, scattering in different directions. I try to close the gap between me and my sisters, especially Pam and Flora, but it's like chasing dandelion seed across the meadow. Just marking time until summer's end.

Dot idles off on long walks with Moppet and Perry's binoculars, enchanted by swallows and swifts tracking across the hot blue sky. Flora is preoccupied with Harry — so much so that when I told her about Perry's one-time arrest she merely shrugged, rather than shrieked, 'Nooo!' But she is less love-dazed now, more serious, absorbed, unreachable: the love deeper, more real, I suppose. Pam is frustrated by Tom, who still shows no sign of succumbing to his romantic destiny. And I am useful to my older sisters only in that I can sweet-talk Sybil into allowing them more freedom. They don't see the price of it. I fear they'd shun me completely if they could.

★ ★ ★

Leaving Dot reading, Pam and Flora to squabble upstairs — ostensibly about the division of un-lost hairclips, really about Pam's fear that Tom is in love with Flora, who does nothing to discourage him — I sit at the edge of the Wilderness, my chin resting on my knees, feeling more distant from my sisters than ever, stoking my own misery in the evening sun.

A shadow cools my back, spreads across the ground like a cloud. I brace myself, expecting it to be Sybil again, come to suggest a meeting later, but when I look up it's into the tunnels of two nostrils.

Perry's wearing his dreadful knitted bathing trunks and a crumpled white dinner shirt, open to the waist, a silk handkerchief knotted on his head. 'May I?' Without waiting for an answer, he lands next to me with a puff of sweat and air. In that moment, I know why Ma didn't tell us about his arrest — how easy it is to make monsters out of large, heavy-breathing men, who sit too close and smell of game and salt — but then the understanding slides away, not quite clarifying.

'Siblings are a nuisance, aren't they?' Perry says.

I shrug, wondering what his agenda might be, not wanting to encourage him.

'I hated Clarence for years, Margot. He made me terribly cross.'

Clarence. Pa's name rings out like a bell. It's a shock to hear it. Perry rarely mentions Pa. Not knowing what to say, I pick a blade of grass and chew it.

217

'He was handsome, your father,' Perry continues gruffly. 'Too clever by half. He married a woman so damn pretty that she made men's hair stand on end, not caring what our parents thought, what it would do to the family name. And then he had the gall to have four daughters whereas Sybil and I only ever managed one, and we damn well . . . ' He kicks out one leg, like a mallet. 'Oh, and the medals. How my brother liked to rub my nose in his bloody war medals, his heroic thumb. He shot Germans. I shot pheasant. Then, after achieving all that,' he laughs hollowly, 'he still bloody well got himself killed in the most stupid way possible and broke my mother's heart.' His *tsk* vibrates on his lips. 'I always thought my little brother would outlive me by a country mile, move into Applecote Manor before I was even cold.'

I'm not sure what to say. Or who my uncle is any more, only that he is not the prowling beast with the lascivious eyes right now, but a huge, lonely man.

'You know, after it happened,' he says more gently, 'the awful business on the rail tracks, I started to miss having someone to get cross about, just every once in a while.' He leans back on his elbows, tilting his head to the sky. 'And now I miss him every day. And I look across this garden, and I see us both so clearly — really, I can see us now, two little boys in breeches, fishing rods over our shoulders, one destined for the battlefield, one for the hunt and the house — and I think . . . ' He stops, swallows hard and his voice goes funny. 'What I wouldn't give to

218

have just one more simple summer's day, Margot, like that, me and my maddening swot of a little brother, everything ahead of us, no responsibilities, nothing to lose, everything still to play for, only thinking about trout.' He stumbles up, squeezing my shoulder under the great ham of his hand. I wait until he's safely gone, then I start to cry.

★ ★ ★

A week to go. We try to think of a gift for our uncle and aunt as a thank-you for their hospitality. For me it's more complicated than this: a goodbye, a very sorry for thinking you a murderer, I'll miss you, and good riddance, all at once. But it's difficult since we have no money and can't agree on anything. The day trip is Dot's idea, shot with unexpected Dottish brilliance. Isn't Sybil locked into this house by her own fear? Perry by the anxieties of his wife? What if we could guide Sybil through it, lead her into the outside world again before we go? Wouldn't that be the most perfect parting gift?

'It'll never happen,' Flora says.

Pam, looking for opposition, says, 'Margot can do it.'

Flora bets me the glass paperweight on her desk that I can't coax our aunt out of the house into the local town.

I tell Dot I'll win it for her.

'I'll be right with you, Aunt, right by your side. Just like Audrey was,' I tell Sybil shamelessly, as she brushes out my hair that evening. She shakes

219

her head incredulously, as if I've suggested she jump from the village church tower flapping tea-towels as wings. But when I mention it again the next day she hesitates, and the brush stills in my hair, as if she's suddenly remembered something terribly important. I know the bet is mine.

'I suppose it's now or never, and I do need a new hat,' Sybil repeats anxiously that Wednesday morning. She looks well, her cheeks less hollow, her thread-veins disguised with Pan Stik. She eats toast plastered with butter, two eggs, almost as if she's enjoying them. Perry watches approvingly, only gobbling a mean bowl of salted porridge himself. And it strikes me that the two of them are really one system, redistributing their appetites, that the marriage that once looked dead may actually be alive at the roots.

In the hall, Sybil succumbs to nerves, clasping and unclasping her best crocodile handbag. We link our arms in hers, steer her down the front path, chatting, pretending everything is normal, that it isn't her first trip into town in years, that her hands aren't shaking.

When we get off the bus, Sybil stumbles only once, when a blonde girl leaps out in front of us, rolling a hoop with a stick. And if she notices the heated whispers of the locals, the gawping and staring, she says nothing, keeps her head high, braver than I thought.

After tea and cake — 'The best Victoria sponge I've ever tasted,' Sybil marvels quietly, even though it wasn't nearly as good as Moll's

— we visit the milliner, insisting she buy the most exuberant hat in the shop, the one with colourful silk flowers crammed about its rim, like a May carnival float. Sybil protests. But she's transfixed by her own reflection, seeming to glimpse another woman in that joyous hat, someone she could be again.

★ ★ ★

I think it's a girl at first, hanging from the back of my bedroom door. And I don't like the idea that Sybil's visited my room and hooked it there as I slept. But I still can't quite resist it. To my surprise, the top button does up this time. I realize Sybil has had it altered.

Oh, it is beautiful. I'd forgotten how lovely, light, yet full-bodied it is, the way the cool petticoat rustles against my legs.

'Margot?' Flora stands in the doorway, a pillow mark down the side of her cheek, her violet eyes wide. I still, but the dress keeps moving, already with a life of its own. 'Where on earth did you get that?'

'Sybil gave it to me,' I explain awkwardly.

'Gosh. Well, lucky you.' She narrows her eyes, assessing it, head cocked on one side. 'Have I seen it before?'

My heart stops. If Flora recognizes this dress as a copy of Audrey's, I'll be forced to explain everything. Flora frowns. I brace. The morning pivots.

'Oh, it must have been in a fashion magazine or something. Anyway, Pam will cut it from your back with her nail scissors. It makes you look like a film star, Margot.' She laughs. 'I can't quite believe it's you.'

I exhale a long breath that I didn't know I was holding, and the bodice loosens.

'Oh, before I forget, that fine paperweight, won fair and square.' Flora puts it on the chest of drawers. 'Even if it's not really mine to give away.'

'Or mine to give to Dot.'

'It's the principle that counts. I'll buy you something nice in Paris, I promise. Here.' Flora adjusts the dress's Peter Pan collar with the same light hot fingers that have run up and down Harry's freckled back, twisted into his sandy hair. It's the first time I can remember Flora touching me in ages. It feels nice.

'We're going to have a party tomorrow,' she says companionably. 'At the stones. Just the six of us. A goodbye to the summer and all that.' She raises an eyebrow. 'A wild party, if Harry has his way.'

'I imagine Sybil might have an opinion on that.'

Flora grins, puffs the dress's folds with her fingers. 'Sybil will be out for the night.'

I start swishing the dress around my legs again, looking down, admiring it. 'She only just managed the milliner, Flora.'

'I have a plan.' Flora looks just like Ma lit by one of her mad ideas, and I suddenly miss Ma physically, like a twist inside. 'A *Midsummer Night's Dream*,' Flora says, with a glint of mischief. 'It's on in town, Harry told me. Sybil will love it. Perry won't object to anything that encourages Harry. There's a hotel round the corner, quite fancy, doormen and everything.' She leans into my ear. 'Perry might get his first screw in years.'

The word 'screw' is a shock, so fast, so wanton, not like Flora at all, making me wonder how far Flora and Harry really have gone: a couple of days ago, Flora confided to Pam, who promptly told me, that they did 'everything but *it* in the garden shed'. ('Wild exaggeration, obviously,' said Pam, dismissively. 'How could they? There's not even a bed in there.')

'You're the only one who can persuade Sybil, Margot.' Flora starts to flirt, fluttering her long lashes. I get a sudden unsisterly urge to pick them out one by one, like legs from a spider. 'Please try, Margot. I need to go off to Paris with a bang.'

I'm not sure if this is Flora's code for doing the 'everything but *it*' again, or for a marriage proposal. Maybe both. I don't want to know anyway. The thought of her and Harry smooching at the stones at sunset is torment enough.

'What's the matter? You've got your Strange Margot face on.'

'Don't call me that,' I snap. Sharp fragments of the summer fly at me: the blank domino, the kingfisher, Sybil's fingers in my hair, Harry's hand on my arm. 'I don't want people to call me strange any more, okay?'

She leaps back from me, hands raised. 'Crikey, okay.'

'And I'm not coming to the party.'

Flora's face falls instantly. 'But — but you can wear your beautiful dress. You'll be the belle of the ball. And it's the last weekend of summer. This is it, Margot.'

I sit on the edge of the bed, gathering the dress between my knees. The distracting smell of bacon is seeping under my bedroom door. 'I can't,' I murmur, unable to explain why.

'But I need you there.'

'You don't need anyone, Flora. You're fine. Everything comes easy to you. It always has.'

She looks hurt. 'Is that what you really think?'

A silence stretches. An ivy leaf brushes against the window. And I think of what Perry said about giving anything for one more summer's day with his brother, and something in me softens.

Flora lowers herself beside me, pressing her leg against mine. 'I also need your advice about Harry.'

'Harry?' My voice comes out high, strangled. 'You'd be better off asking Moppet. I don't know anything about love.'

'Well, you think deeply, deeper than me and Pam, which isn't saying much, I know.' She watches me curiously. I hope my face isn't giving too much away. 'Harry respects you.'

I close my eyes for a moment, reeling inside. I don't want to be respected — the village vicar is respected! I want to be grabbed and kissed and eaten alive, like Flora. But still I ask, 'Advice about what?' I can't help myself.

Flora nibbles her bottom lip. She shuffles on

the bed. 'I — I just wish Perry hadn't told me that Harry was such a catch, that's all,' she stutters. 'So that I could trust the authenticity of my own feelings.'

'Authenticity?' I repeat, amazed.

'I know it's a big word for your stupid sister to use.'

'That's not what I meant,' I say, even though we both know it sort of was.

'I don't want to live the life that Ma wishes she'd lived, that's all, Margot,' she says, with surprising intensity. 'The rich husband, the great house . . .'

I've never heard Flora talk like this before. 'Really? What do you want, then?'

'Oh, I don't know. I don't know what I'm thinking. Maybe it's the heat.' Flora pushes sleep-crimped curls off her face. 'I can't remember what cold feels like any more, can you? Or rain. It feels like it's been summer for ever. My brain's stopped working. And it's been invaded with these — these damn questions.'

'God forbid.'

She laughs. We're quiet for a moment, considering each other, the distance between us. 'Tom asked me what I wanted to do with my life.'

'Tom?'

'He's not what he seems, you know, Margot, so stand-offish, monosyllabic. He's really not, not once he gets going. You just have to sort of crack him first, like an egg. Then he's rather wonderful.'

It strikes me that Flora never talks about

Harry like this. I've never seen her smile so open, so unprotected.

'No one's ever asked me that question before anyway,' she says, blanching a little, as if the thought has just struck her. 'Nor has it ever occurred to me to ask myself.'

'So what was your answer?' The wave of affection I suddenly feel for Flora is confusing since it makes my aching for Harry more disloyal. 'To Tom's question.'

She covers her mouth with her hands, laughs. 'America! It just popped out. I said, 'Go to America,' and I couldn't think why exactly. Just somewhere I could be exactly whom I liked, even though I've got no idea who that might be.' She shakes her head, bewildered by this unlikely, inexplicable shuffle of self. 'Completely daft, obviously.'

I try to picture Flora's hand lifting from a ship's shiny rail, waving goodbye to the wedding ring, the lacy pram hood, Cornton Hall. But I can't. Flora's fate has always seemed so set, a story working towards one inevitable ending.

'Promise me you'll come.'

'To America?'

'The party at the stones, stupid.' She grabs my hands, tugs me from the bed and runs her eyes admiringly over my dress once more. 'Just look at you. I tell you what, Margot, if you come to the party in that frock, anything might happen.'

11

Jessie wakes to the ghostly beauty of February's first hard frost. She gets up carefully, not wanting to wake Romy, who is asleep, sprawled horizontally across her bed. Jessie knows it's probably bad practice — Romy should sleep in her own bed — but she's loved having the soft, snuffling lump of her daughter to hug these last few months when Will's not here. Romy sleeps in when she's in their bed too. Also, Jessie knows she's safe.

Jessie still can't forget the creepy sight of Romy on the stones, wearing those glasses, the niggling suspicion that Bella was somehow trying to turn her little sister into the Audrey girl. Or the nights she's found Bella sleepwalking in Romy's room. She avoids leaving the girls alone together now, and has got into a habit of taking Romy into the log shed while she chops wood, the bathroom as she washes, rather than leave her under Bella's care. Jessie knows she's overreacting, probably. She also knows that Bella senses the distrust. And she feels really bad about it. But it's there.

Jessie pulls back the curtains, eyes widening at the sudden pitch into the frozen trough of winter: the garden is furred with ice, sculptural and magnificent, a Narnia landscape. She wishes Will was there to see it, and that the weather didn't just throw its dreariest drizzle at him every weekend when he returns home. The calendar she carries in her heart flips. Only three more sleeps until he's back. She texts him a photo: 'Jack Frost!' She's been doing this a lot. Maybe too much, since Will doesn't always respond. Bella prefers Skype, privately in her room. But as she points out, 'It's not the same.' And it isn't.

They all miss Will terribly when he's away. But Jessie has started to miss him when he's at home too, a bit of the man she loves somehow left behind in his London office or, worse, at his attractive host's warm, comfortable London house. Or maybe it's her. During the long weekday nights Will's absent, it's too easy to dwell on the intimate first marriage described in those letters, and feel irrationally betrayed by it. When Will returns to Applecote on a Friday, she feels something inside her pulling away from him. The sensation takes a day or two to fade. But by then it's time for Will to return to London, so the cycle begins again.

This is not how it was meant to be. Only the carefully curated images Jessie posts on Facebook resemble the life she'd thought they'd be leading by now: the house swagged with ivy, flickering with Christmas candlelight; a family walk in a winter wood; a bubbling apple crumble, steaming shamelessly in a pastel-blue earthenware dish. Jessie spends a lot of time tweaking her own timeline, admiring this fictitious version of their life, envying it.

The photogenic ice melts later that day, the crisp beauty turning into a freezing wet mush that clings to Jessie's heavy brown boots in fleshy clots, works its way beneath her fingernails and creeps into the house. There is no escape from the mud that week, or the heavy, tallow-grey sky that presses down on the valley. The girls' hands are scarlet and itchy with cold, their lips blue. All their outdoor clobber is wrong, designed for temperate city parks, not winter countryside. Jessie orders heavy unflattering coats, earmuffling hats, insulated gloves from a catalogue based in the Highlands. She hopes for snow. Snow will make everyone happy, she thinks. But the white sky falls as charmless sleet, then rain. The earth is sodden. It keeps raining. There is nowhere for the water to go.

Wednesday, the day Will's to return early and work from home, having promised the girls he'd make up for his absence: flooding. A mercury mirror of dirty grey water, spreading west, gushing over piles of sandbags, drowning homes and fields, turning woods into underwater forests, pushing Victorian femurs and finger bones to the surface of one village graveyard not far away. Applecote's land becomes glutinous — there is a pool of viscous boggy mud, like a dirty old mouth, close to the well, that sucks the welly boot off Romy's foot, making her squeal. Bella calls Applecote 'The Ark', and it's funny, really quite funny, for a second or two, but then Jessie hears the shrill edge to her own laughter, and the sound dies quickly. Will's name is flashing urgently on her mobile. Another crisis at work. A client threatening to sue. An important meeting tomorrow now too, something promising. He's not going to make it back tonight.

229

When Jessie tells the girls, Romy bursts into tears. Bella's face simply empties. She runs upstairs and slams her bedroom door in the way only Bella can slam it, like an act of war.

Even the weather has tantrums that night, the wind howling, muscular gusts punching at the house, like fists. Jessie, hit by a sense of foreboding, locks the doors, and a tiny voice in her head wonders if perhaps she's not locking out the threat but locking something in. Firelight shadows flicker against the old drawing room's wavering walls — like someone making puppets with their fingers — and she can hear things outside, sounds she can't quite identify, sticks breaking maybe, the gravel crunch of a footstep. Heart pounding — it can't be Will so who is it? — Jessie turns off the hall lights and scans the drive through the window, half expecting to see Margot fading into the shadows again, walking away from the house with her dogs. But there is no one.

Margot. Jessie hasn't been back to the café since the day Margot had turned up with Bella. She misses it, more than she expected to, just having a friendly bohemian local place to go. But she can't forget the two black Labradors in the back of Margot's car, Margot's leopard-print headscarf and, more puzzlingly, Margot's detailed knowledge of the house: Jessie investigated the drainpipe the next day and discovered Margot was absolutely right — it was blocked, and there was also a bloom of damp on the top-floor bathroom wall that she hadn't noticed before. But how did Margot know about it? She could hardly see it from outside.

Jessie's mind keeps wandering back to the Squirrels girls' theory about Audrey returning, stalking her old home. And although it's the most absurd thing she's ever heard — women don't vanish as children and reappear with a secret set of keys to the family home fifty odd years later — it's got under her skin: the ridiculous idea that Margot is actually Audrey.

A dog might help, Lou suggests distractedly on the phone, hopping around her London apartment, looking for the lost platform heel that goes with her navy sequin dress. 'Everyone in the country has dogs, don't they? It's practically the law that you must be covered in mutt hair and smell like a kennel. It'll keep you company, Jessie, stop you getting spooked. *And* it'll look good on Facebook,' Lou adds wryly, Lou who can see through everything. Jessie laughs, relieved to be understood. Lou finds her shoe with a delighted squeal, and her taxi is outside. 'Gotta go!'

Jessie sighs, wishing she could follow Lou into that taxi, a buzzy gallery opening, her old life, just for one evening. Instead, she clears a space on the messy kitchen table, opens her laptop and surfs videos of puppies so cute that Bella must surely forgive her for existing if she bought one. She runs upstairs and knocks on Bella's door gently, asking if she's okay, if she wants to talk and, hey, what does she think about a puppy? But Bella rebuffs her, 'I want to be alone,' and suddenly the idea that a puppy might heal the rift in the family, like so many

231

other ideas, seems wildly optimistic. She walks back down into the dark, empty house, thinking of Lou in the brilliant city night, laughing, sparkling.

★ ★ ★

The next morning, the February light browns and thickens as Jessie reaches the top floor, making her grey flannel pyjamas look ink-black. It's colder too. She shivers, pausing on the creaking top step, tightening the wriggle of Romy's hand in hers, and wonders if the walls of this upper landing have actually narrowed further, or if it's her imagination. She can't be sure. Applecote is not like other houses, she's learning. Not a stable, fixed thing, it seems to swell and shrink in response to the weather outside, and the emotional climate of its inhabitants.

'Right, washing,' Jessie says aloud to herself. (Narrating her own movements through the house is a worrying new habit, one of her mother's that, as a teen, she'd rolled her eyes at.) She hurriedly piles Bella's clean washing on to the sleigh bed — she doesn't dare open any drawers now — and glances warily at the Mandy Boxes, still wedged between the bed and the wall, while Romy makes a beeline for the dressing-table on soft, silent feet.

'Romy,' Jessie warns, shaking her head, 'leave Bella's things.'

'Romy likes them.'

'You want to see Tractor Joe?' Distraction is

232

proving more effective than discipline with Romy right now. 'Here.'

Standing by the larger window, Romy on her hip, they watch the vehicle — battered, bandaged with gaffer tape — grind into view, Joe Peat resting his forearms on the wheel. Romy waves, the bracelet Jessie made from coloured paper-clips swinging on her tiny wrist.

Joe arrived last Monday, a few weeks late, swaying his huge bulk up the front path, like a human hay bale, a tweed cap pulled low on his head. Jessie's absurdly grateful for him. He has already removed the knotted heart of brambles and rubble from the bottom of the garden, achieving in hours what would have taken her months. He's built raised vegetable beds in the kitchen garden. Later today, he's going to have a look at the pool, so they can make a final call on it, the old well, other bits and pieces.

When he arrived, Jessie asked him if he knew the house at all, searching for that telltale flicker of recognition, the sign he might not last the morning. But he simply nodded, 'Aye, I know the house,' and said his dad, Sid, and his uncle, Brian, used to do some work at Cornton Hall, just down the road, back in the day. Fine old house down the river, did she know it? She did. Encouraged by Jessie's interest, happy to chat, Joe dug into the grubby back pocket of his trousers, pulled out a wallet and, from it, a grainy black-and-white photo of a shy-looking man in country clothes and a smart hat. 'Dapper fella, my old man.'

Very dashing, Jessie agreed, peering at the

picture, the ornate sweep of the wrought-iron gates of Cornton Hall in the background uncannily the same.

That was his pa all over, Joe continued proudly, always wanting to better himself. Never got the chance. Heart attack. Poor bugger. Jessie had looked up. 'Aye,' Joe said, 'right at the end of that cursed summer,' as if answering a question she hadn't voiced.

At this unexpected, lurching nod to Audrey, the past breaching the present once again, Jessie's heart sank. But Joe lasted the morning. And the week. Thank goodness, Jessie thinks, as the tractor vanishes into a huddle of trees, taking her thoughts with it, and Romy opens her hands and cheerfully declares, 'Gone.'

★ ★ ★

Jessie is stabbing rosemary into a leg of lamb later that afternoon when Joe finds it. As part of his investigation into the tree root beneath the orangery floor, he dismantles the boxed-in window-seat that edges the room — and there it is, a brown paper parcel wrapped in garden twine. 'Old houses always throw up a few surprises,' he says, wiping a thread of sweat off his upper lip with his arm. Jessie thinks she's probably had enough surprises at Applecote, thanks all the same.

The front door slams and Bella is beside them, eyes shining, fingers restless at the sides of her school blazer, desperate to snatch the parcel out of Joe's hand. 'Oh, my God. What's that?'

'Love letters probably,' jokes Joe.

Jessie stiffens. She's had quite enough of other people's love letters too.

As Romy stacks the alphabet bricks on the kitchen floor, Bella starts to peel off the brown paper on the table. Joe is right: letters, water-stained, disintegrating, handwritten. Jessie watches, sucks in her breath — she knows exactly what Bella will be hoping for — and is grateful to see the water-blurred ink is almost unreadable.

'Oh, no, wait!' Bella points to a smudged postmark. 'Nineteen fifty-nine,' she says, looking up at Jessie excitedly. 'That's the year of those old newspapers, isn't it?'

'The heatwave, you're right. How funny.'

'I was totally meant to find this,' Bella mutters, sitting down, considering the letters and then slowly, carefully, sliding letter fragments together using the tip of her index finger. 'I reckon I can work them out.'

Jessie gets a glimpse of a different Bella then, the one the art teacher at Squirrels enthused about in her last report, creative, inquisitive, absorbed.

'Some are sent from . . . from Morocco. Others . . . Oh, look, Jessie, the later ones, from London.'

'A traveller, then,' says Jessie, returning to the lamb. She drizzles olive oil over the skin, tucks garlic cloves around its base.

'Oh. Oh, no. They're not addressed to Audrey,' Bella says flatly, disappointed. 'Someone called Pam. And . . . It's hard to make out the other

235

names. Dot? Is Dot actually a name?'

'Short for Dorothy.' Jessie thinks how the names already sound historic, surely due a revival. No one calls girls Pam or Dot any more. Maybe, if they had another, a sibling for Romy — She stops herself sharply. They're way off that right now, way off any kind of stability.

She sighs, glances at the clock. Will should have made the train. She imagines him settling in, the warmth of his body under his suit, the way he holds his book away from him, in denial at needing reading glasses.

'Listen to this. 'Please, please write back soon, your loving . . . '' Bella reads out, squints, trying to work out the words. 'Ma. It's Ma, isn't it?'

'Uh-oh,' shouts Romy, with unfortunate timing. She pokes the tower of bricks and they crash to the floor.

'It is,' says Jessie, quietly, standing behind Bella, wiping her hands on her apron. And, for a moment, she can almost hear a mother's voice, carried across time by the wind.

'A mother,' Bella whispers, her voice trailing such longing that Jessie is overcome by the urge to gather her in her arms. But as she lifts her hand, it stills in space, unable to reach further, and she's struck by the deluded futility of such an idea. Bella can't bear Jessie touching her. She wants her mother, not a poor replacement. So Jessie turns back to the lamb. The ferric smell of fresh wet meat.

★ ★ ★

Will stumbles in as their supper finishes, drained, pale-faced, the freezing night clinging to him, like a heavy damp coat. Romy wraps her body around his legs, brushes her little fingers lovingly over his evening stubble. But Bella hangs back, punishing him for his unreliability. And when Will goes to hug her, apologize for being a day late, she coolly steps away. Jessie sees hurt ripple over Will's face and squeezes his hand, trying to tell him it'll be all right. He turns to kiss her and, for the first time ever, their mouths miss, and his kiss lands awkwardly on her cheek. She puts her hand to the spot where it lands and laughs. He looks at her, bemused, wondering why she's laughing.

In that moment, Jessie feels acutely all the hours they've been apart these last five months, the way separation creates experiences that are no longer shared, parts of each other's lives in which they no longer live. And she wonders how they will ever get themselves back.

That evening Will spends a long time counselling Bella in her bedroom. Afterwards, he eats some leftovers of the lamb, lost in thought at the table, looking straight through the spray of evergreen branches and berries in the vase, the freshly baked bread in its basket, the claret that Jessie drove for an hour to buy. The temperature plummets. They can see their breath in the hall. That night, under a pile of blankets, Romy wriggling beside them, Will tosses and turns, the adrenalin of city life still crackling through his veins. When Jessie rests her head against his chest, even as he sleeps, she can hear his anxiety, his rising blood pressure, like the gush of a swollen river. He talks in his sleep, and she's sure he's muttering Mandy's name, hungering for the past, the comforts of the marriage that was stolen from him, which the love letters show were irreplaceable. She presses her body against him. He rolls away in his sleep.

Lying awake, she listens to the hiss of the wind in the trees, and picks over her marriage, her mind opening doors to rooms she knows she shouldn't enter. Does Will still fancy her? Why hasn't he found a buyer for the company yet? Is it just an excuse to stay in London? At what point do they declare this divided life unworkable? Then Friday morning breaks, Romy wanders back to her bedroom, and Will's longed-for body finally turns towards her. He rests his chin on his hand, hollowed-out eyes serious and searching, and asks, 'Are you happy here, sweetheart?'

'Happy?' Jessie yawns, surprised. Her happiness has never seemed particularly important, resting, as it does, so much on other people's right now, Bella's in particular. 'I'm happy to have you home.'

'It isn't a weakness to admit you're not, you know, that you — we, I mean — that we've made a mistake.' He takes her hand, opens it and circles the inside of her palm lightly with his index finger, like she does to Romy, *round and round the garden*. 'Maybe Applecote is too remote, too much house and land . . .'

She realizes where this is going. What she should say, to make it easy for him. After all, they could sell up and move back, even if not to central London — prices have rocketed, leaving them behind — then closer to it, some more affordable suburb. 'I've never experienced sadness without wanting to escape it before. I don't need to be happy here, Will.'

Will frowns, puzzled. He doesn't understand. He would have once. He would have known exactly what she meant. 'Are you? Happy, I mean,' she asks, and immediately realizes it's a mistake.

His gaze slips away, leaving her feeling instantly, intensely bereft. 'I was a Londoner a long time, longer than maybe I realized.'

He means he was married to Mandy for a long time, of course. Stupid of her to expect him to lie, stupid of her to ask. So she says, too sharply, hiding her hurt, 'I lived in London too, Will. I didn't lose a wife. But I did lose other things, things that mattered, my career, my friends . . . my freedom. It's not the same, I know. And I don't want it back but it meant something to me, and I gave it all up too.'

Will leans back heavily on the pillow, stares up at the ceiling, not at her. They listen to Bella clattering down the stairs in her hard-soled school shoes. 'I never wanted you to give up anything, Jessie,' he says, in a way that fills her eyes with tears. 'That was the last thing I wanted.'

'It came out wrong, I'm sorry,' Jessie says, although she knows it's too late, that the words are circling. And there's a terrible silence that suddenly feels like an ending.

★ ★ ★

Jessie blows into the lattice of kindling in the grate until flames leap and dance. She's got satisfyingly good at making fires. But in the mirror above the fireplace she sees herself more critically: the streak of soot across her cheek-bone, the wild reddish hair frizzed by the woodsmoke. The slinky black dress she's put on for Friday evening jars with the rawness of her face, the animal brightness of her eyes. Hearing Will's tread on the stairs, returning from Bella's room, she frantically smooths her hair with the flat of her palm.

Will slumps to the sheepskin rug on the floor beside her, leans back against an armchair, his left foot tapping anxiously. She catches his eye and they smile at each other, the hesitant unsure smile of lovers who have been apart too long and fear the other might have met someone else in their absence. In that moment Jessie can see a defensive layer forming around Will. He had it when they first met too. She'd never expected it to come back.

They talk. But gaps open in the flow of conversation, like tiny splits in a seam. Jessie can't remember that ever happening before. There's always been too much to say. So she tries to repair it with chatter about Romy's hide-and-seek antics — their little scamp so fast, so inventive — the latest on the flooding, the rising water table, the intriguing letters Joe Peat discovered hidden in the orangery window-seat.

Then Jessie begins to feel something, a

240

tension, like the moments before an electrical storm. 'What's wrong, Jessie?' he asks abruptly.

'Wrong?' There are so many things wrong, so many hidden feelings, stuffed into her pocket, like unexploded fireworks. 'What do you mean?'

His eyes roam her face, trying to work her out. 'I don't know. You don't seem yourself. You haven't for months. I'm worried about you.'

'I'm worried about you!' she says, with a short, surprised laugh, throwing it back at him.

'That's not really an answer.'

'And how would you know how I am anyway? You've hardly been here.'

He frowns more deeply. He suddenly looks very, very tired, a man with the world on his shoulders.

'Bella's said something, hasn't she?'

Will's mouth opens, shuts, caught between loyalties. 'She says you won't let her be alone with Romy.' He waits for Jessie to reassure him and deny it.

But Jessie's cheeks heat. She won't lie to him any more. 'I . . . I'm really sorry she feels that.'

'It's true?' His eyes harden. She feels he's looking at her dispassionately for the first time.

Jessie wraps her arms tightly around her knees. 'Since that day. Romy, on the stones. I know it sounds silly, but I can't forget it, Will,' she explains quietly.

It's the disappointment in his face that breaks her heart, the cool way he says, 'You need to have a bit more faith in my daughter.'

'*Faith?* All I've ever had is faith!' She recoils at the injustice of it. They are spiralling back in

241

time then, two people knocked off their feet by a gale, and Jessie is standing nervously in the hall of Will's London house, Will introducing his stern, unsmiling daughter, Jessie thinking, You are part of the man I love. I will love you too. Then months later at the hospital, Jessie too sore to move, ecstatic, offering Bella the most precious thing in her entire world, the baby's skin still womb-pink, waxy, saying, 'Do you want to hold your new little sister? You can hold her, Bella. She's yours too.'

Bella shaking her head, mumbling, 'She's not.'

★ ★ ★

Jessie storms into the garden, ignoring Will calling her back, the family idyll she simply can't create shattering behind her, Mandy triumphant. The cold is like a slap around the face. Coatless, Jessie keeps walking. Unidentifiable things splatter under her boots. She's unsure where she's going until she gets there, the padlocked gate of the pool, the slab of oily black beyond, the absence of light. As she did that first morning at Applecote, she feels its pull, the refuge of that enclosed still place, where the past feels parcelled tight. Climbing over the gate, her boots land on the slippery paving with a smack. Above, a frantic rush of wings in the dark. Then, nothing.

She bloody well gives up. She's done. She lets the cold coil around her. Tears slip down her cheeks. She listens to the dispassionate silence, the movements of tiny creatures, the scrape of

242

crossed branches in the wind, the adjustment of beechnuts under the slight weight of a hidden paw. And she suddenly knows she's not alone on this freezing winter night, that there is something else out there by the pool in the darkness, just as there was that August day. She waits for it. She wills it forward. And it comes, not at all other, soft, female, rushing through her like a band of warmth: the spirit of all the women who have ever lived at Applecote, daughters, mothers, sisters, voices long dead, strong Applecote women who never gave up. A moment later, it is gone, cold again. But Jessie is no longer crying. And the first snowflakes start to fall, sprinkled over her upturned face, like frozen white freckles.

★ ★ ★

'Will,' Jessie whispers, in wonder, the next morning. She stands beside the bedroom window, her breath misting the frost-laced glass.

'Hey?' Will mumbles sleepily, turning his head on the pillow. Jessie sees the memory of the argument the night before move behind Will's half-opened eyes, like a cloud. They went to bed barely talking.

'It snowed properly in the night. You've got to see.'

'Snow?' Romy's eyes spring open and she crawls out of the nook of Will's armpit. Jessie doesn't remember Romy coming into their bed in the night. 'Snow!'

Will stands behind Jessie. He wraps his arms

around her: the physical relief of his touch is overpowering. She remembers how much she loves Will like this, dozy, unshowered, the edges between their bodies still blurry from tangling in sleep. 'I'm sorry,' he whispers. He holds her a little tighter. She presses her body into his. They stand there for a while, bruised and tender, Romy burrowing between them. 'I want to take you out to lunch,' he breathes into Jessie's ear.

'Lunch?' It's the last thing she imagined he'd say. 'I'd love that,' she whispers back, feeling something inside lighten.

'Just you and me. Can you even remember the last time we went out alone together? I can't.'

'Like on a date?' She laughs, the idea faintly ridiculous.

'Why is that funny?' he asks, looking slightly hurt.

'It's not funny. It's lovely, Will.' She plays with Romy's hair where it's matted into flat lamb's tail curls at the back. She wonders what she will wear. 'I'll find a babysitter.'

Will doesn't miss a beat. 'We have one in the house, don't we?'

Jessie's hand freezes on Romy's head. She feels her marriage teeter once more. Last night's tensions resurface. She knows Will is simply asking for her trust. Implicit in his question, however gently posed, is that without trust, this cannot work.

'Jessie?' Will asks softly, when she doesn't answer.

★ ★ ★

Jessie forces herself not to check her mobile until they've ordered pudding. It's not like Bella would call her anyway, she tells herself. She wiggles inside the silky cocoon of the fitted parrot-print dress she finally settled upon, a dress she hasn't worn since leaving London, and now feels both insubstantial and restrictive, as if it might belong to someone else. Outside the pub's dimpled windows, snow whirls down in flurries. Jessie wonders where the girls are, what they're doing, if Bella is being kind. Then her mind skitters to the narrow, darkening lanes that lie between this thatched country pub and the house containing their girls. She imagines the car getting stuck, the wheels spinning on black ice. Their mobiles running out of power.

'They'll be snuggled in front of the telly,' Will says, reading the skit of her thoughts. He reaches one hand down to the roaring log fire, spreads his fingers to the scorch of seasoned wood and burning pine cones. 'And Joe's working this afternoon, isn't he? They're not completely alone down there.'

'I guess.' Joe's presence doesn't do much to reassure.

'And I've just texted Bella. So you can enjoy your chocolate tart. Please will you enjoy your chocolate tart?'

'Yes.' She laughs.

They share it, like they used to, spoons clinking. Jessie smiles and nods as Will tells her about his long week in London, a lorry drivers' strike in France. But it's surprisingly hard to

245

disentangle her thoughts from Applecote, a little bit of her still inside its stone walls: she wonders if Bella's answered Will's text yet, if it wouldn't look too stressy to ask.

'Jessie, did you hear what I said?' Will's eyes are alive with firelight. His hands spread on the table, leaning back in his chair, he's grinning at her boyishly, anticipating a reaction.

She winces. 'Sorry. Tell me, tell me again.'

'We've had an offer for the whole company, not just a stake. They want the whole ugly beast. Can you believe it?'

Jessie's mouth opens. 'Finally! Why didn't you say earlier?'

He sips his pint, shrugs maddeningly. 'It's no big deal.'

'Hello! It's amazing.'

'It's a very, very cheeky offer.' He frowns into his pint glass. 'We can't accept it. Jackson won't accept it.'

'Jackson? Jackson's gone surfing, Will.' She leans forward, her heart starting to patter. She can see a new life, the life they were meant to live here. It's within their grasp again. 'We don't need to be rich, we really don't. We just want you back. The girls and me, we want to see you. That's all that matters.'

He takes her left hand, worrying her wedding band with his thumb. 'It's not that simple. We get one shot at it. And we've given it everything, Jessie, for so long. For us to sell it so short now . . .'

'Right,' Jessie says flatly, unable to hide her disappointment.

'One day, I promise,' Will says softly. 'Don't give up on me.'

'As if,' she says. But the atmosphere has sobered. They are silent for a moment. 'Maybe we should phone Bella, just to check she's all right.'

He nods, probably to appease her, and presses the phone to his ear. Jessie can hear it ring, then go to voicemail.

She leans forward, the dress digging into her waist. The fire is too hot. The journey home too long. 'Will . . . '

'Bella probably can't hear her phone, that's all,' Will says quickly. He drains his coffee, stands up. 'Shall we shoot?'

Jessie already has her fake fur jacket around her shoulders.

★ ★ ★

'Girls, we're home!' Will calls cheerfully, as they open the door, stepping into the hall. No one answers. But they can hear the television. On the sofa, nestled next to a half-eaten packet of crisps, Bella's phone, Will's number flashing up as a missed call. But they phoned over half an hour ago — the car made such slow progress through the snow — and Bella checks her phone every thirty seconds.

'Something's wrong, Will,' says Jessie.

'They're probably up in her bedroom, messing about with music and clothes.' He squeezes her hand. 'I'll go upstairs, you check down here.'

Jessie spots the snowy footprints through the

kitchen window: Bella's long and narrow, Romy's chunky and small. A small snowman with a crooked twig mouth. But the relief is short-lived. Outside in the freezing air, there is no sign of them, the footprints circling, looping back on themselves, then seeming to multiply, as if there were four girls, not two.

'Jessie! Hey, Jessie.'

She stops, turns around to see the incongruous figure of Joe lumbering towards her. He is red-faced, agitated. 'Can I talk to yer?'

'Have you seen the girls?' Jessie demands breathlessly.

He nods. 'About an hour ago, making a snowman. Happy as anything.' His accent has thickened. She can barely understand it. 'Can I have a quick word about — '

'So you haven't seen the girls *since* then?' Fear curdles in her stomach. Her breath is loud in her ears.

He shakes his head. 'Sorry. They all right? Wait, Jessie . . . '

Leaving Joe calling behind her, she starts running, making strange stifled sounds in her throat, through the skeletal trees, tracking the little footprints, shouting out the girls' names, futilely telling herself not to panic, she'll find them soon, all she has to do is follow their footprints. But then the girls' footprints separate: Bella's, further apart now, as if running too, soon become untraceable on the snowless ground beneath the trees. Romy's stop at the dark block of yew hedge that separates the garden from the pool, opposite a small gap in the hedge's lowest branches, where they are joined by the starfish prints of two tiny hands.

12

Every moment, something changes. The evening is elastic, pulled into new shapes by a stolen look, a flirtatious laugh, a leg emerging from a scalloped dress hem. There is a faint smell of bodies, the way bodies smell when they're close to one another in the late summer heat, sweat-damp cotton.

Harry is leaning back against one of the stones, his guitar like a girl in his lap. He is singing a love song in French for Flora, laughing and cursing as he misses a note, forgets a word. And I can't help but adore him for his imperfect French, his musical clumsiness, and feel jealous of Flora, who is basking in the attention, blonde and barefoot in a white party dress that belongs in Belgravia, one simple rose pinned in her hair, prettier than I've ever seen her.

Occasionally Harry glances at me too, his eyes alive and intense: I can't help but hope he doesn't just see Flora's plainer younger sister, but somebody different, desirable, even. The funny thing is I *am* different tonight, wearing this blue dress, not only because it covers the backs of my knees so well: Audrey is sewn into it, and some of her energy and irrepressible confidence has become mine. Or maybe it's just the wine the boys have brought, and only Dot refuses to touch, sticking to the lemonade. I'm not used to it. But the taste is pleasant enough after a few sips. Unlike the boys' Scotch whisky, which I have to discreetly spit into the grass.

The sun sinks lower. Above it, the inky patch where sky becomes space. Pam squeezes next to Tom as he lights a small fire, belly down in the grass, cigarette in his mouth, his bare feet beating time to Harry's guitar. The wood he's collected is so dry it flares up instantly. The flames dance light over everyone's faces, and the sun becomes a pool of blood at the bottom of the valley, making us all more lovely, and more aware of our loveliness, drunk on it as well as the wine. At one point I find myself touching the buttons on my dress thoughtlessly, as if I want to get beneath them, before I realize what I'm doing.

I don't know how it happens, who suggests the swim first. I think it's Harry, but it may have been Tom, or it may have been suggested by no one, just something we do instinctively. Suddenly they're stripping off: Harry, yanking his shirt above his head; Tom's tummy a smooth cave as he breathes in. And we all scream and laugh, clap our hands over our mouths, pretending to be shocked. Dot whispers fiercely into my ear, 'Aunt Sybil will kill us.'

'Aunt Sybil isn't here.' I laugh, still amazed that I was able to persuade my aunt to go away for the night — it took much cajoling, and a shameless parading of this dress, my hair plaited — and that only Moll is back at the house. It's hard not to feel giddily uncaged.

Pam is the first to strip — she'll do anything to drag Tom's eyes away from the spectacle of Flora

251

— and eagerly rips off her dress to reveal an oyster satin slip. The boys clap and howl. 'Take 'em off, girls,' they shout. Flora and I look at each other and laugh, tempted, while Dot just sits there and shakes her head, like a shocked little old lady.

Flora shoots me a mischievous secret smile that says: I will soon depart for Paris, the life Ma wants for me. The summer is almost over. Let us live for this one night. Her slip is plain white cotton, unlike Pam's, yet this simplicity only seems to make her more exquisite. Harry grabs at her, pulls her against his belly with a deep growl of pleasure. She throws back her arms against the sky and whoops, and it echoes back against the hills, that whoop, a spinning loose from Ma, Pa, Audrey, all of the people who have died or left, all the forces that pull us down, tether us to the ground. And my fingers find a scarlet button on my dress.

Dot tugs on my arm. 'You don't need to join in, Margot.'

'I do, Dotty. I actually do. Sorry.' I suddenly don't care about my knees or that I won't look as pretty as Flora, as statuesque as Pam. The stretch of smocking, the skirt over my head, the froth of petticoat, then the realization that I'm not even wearing a slip, just pants and a bra, and it being too late to hide and Harry is shouting, 'Bravo, Margot! Come on, come on.' And the grass-crushing rushing sound of a crowd of feet running through the dry meadow towards the bank, geese scattering, white as ghosts, the grass stubby against my soles, the smell of river water the second before the first shock of coldness, the violent joy of it all, the sharp cry.

The water is depthless. Legs brush mine. Hands flit across my waist then vanish, cool, smooth and fast as the sides of fish, and I have no idea if the contact is from my sisters or the boys, and it doesn't seem to matter, for we are a writhing mass of happiness, swimming up and down on the moon-lit water. I don't know how long we swim for, only that when I get out on the skid of the bank everyone seems to have dissolved into the darkness, the vertical reedy shadows. Someone places a jacket over my shoulders. I turn and he is there, as I somehow knew he would be, as if our exchange of glances earlier was pulling us together, the way hands inch along a rope during a playful tug of war.

'You're shivering,' Harry says. I'm not shivering, not even that cold, but I lean against him anyway. 'Sit by the fire?'

I think of Flora, hesitate, but thinking doesn't work.

The fire pulses, a beating red heart. I hand him back his jacket, reach into the grass for my discarded dress and pull it on, safe in its folds again. 'Where is everyone?' I ask, meaning Flora.

'Not sure it matters.' He lights a cigarette from a glowing ember. His shorts are stuck to his body, outlining everything.

I try not to stare. But I catch him smiling. After that, I daren't move my gaze from the fire. I love the sound of it, its hiss and spit, the way it makes me feel connected as I never have before to the stones, the valley, the earth itself, connected to something bigger and greater and older than any of us.

'You're the intellectual in the litter, Flora tells me. What do you think these stones mean?' Harry asks after a while, his words slurring slightly. His elbow brushes against my arm as he lifts his cigarette to his lips. He suddenly feels both familiar and unknowable, like an old friend with secrets.

'Moll, my aunt's housekeeper, she says the Applecote stones honour ancient dead. That they have special powers. But she's a bit superstitious, likes to talk about omens and things,' I say quickly, in case he mistakes Moll's views for mine.

'Ah.' His laugh is warm, gravelly. 'Yes, she would. The people round here might look like church-going people but don't be fooled, Margot.' He leans right up to me, so close I feel I might get drunk on his breath. 'Pagan souls. It's like the last few thousand years never happened. We're only missing the sabre-toothed tiger and the mammoth.'

I reach out my hands towards the fire. 'What do you think the stones mean, then?'

'Me? I only know that from now on whenever I see them I'll think of you, Margot, sitting there in the firelight. In that dress.'

My cheeks burn with pleasure. I can't stop smiling.

'It's just like hers, isn't it?' he says abruptly, an edge to his voice.

My smile vanishes.

'Your cousin Audrey's. The blue dress. The colour of her eyes.'

I'm saved from having to answer by Pam charging out of the darkness, teeth chattering, searching for her clothes, yelping, 'Cold, cold, cold.'

Flora and Tom follow a moment later, breathless, laughing, then, seeing the rest of us, quietening, like children quickly adjusting their behaviour to adult company. I notice how they stand close together, hands brushing. How they make each other look more beautiful, more alive. Perhaps realizing this herself, Flora quickly moves away, bends over to plant a kiss on Harry's mouth.

'Pam thought it a grand idea to get out of the river on the opposite bank,' explains Tom to Harry, a little sheepishly. 'Bit of a detour.'

Harry shrugs. I wonder if he's hiding his hurt pride. Rivalry wrestles the air between them. Suddenly they both seem dangerously drunk.

Pam yanks her dress over her head, asking, as she emerges, 'Where's Dot?'

'Dot?' It quickly dawns that while I've been here, enjoying what is not mine, Dot's been alone in the dark. 'Oh dear.'

'One of us should go and check she's got back to the house okay.' Flora eyeballs me. 'Don't you think, Margot?'

'Yes, you go, Margot,' instructs Pam.

'Oh. Oh, right, okay.' On the way back to the house, tipsier than I thought, indignant that I've been shooed off by my elder sisters, surplus to the party, I linger by the bathing-pool gate, resting my arms along the flaky wood. Reasoning that Dot will be asleep in her bed now anyway, and not feeling in any great hurry for the evening to end, I enter and sit down on the pool's edge, hitching my dress above my knees, bare feet paddling the water. After the coldness of the river it is warm as blood. I like it.

Memories ripple across the water's surface, layered like leaves: me and Audrey diving, Pam racing Flora to the edge, Dot, on a deckchair, watching us over the book in her hands, Perry in his horrifying knitted trunks. All the summers we've spent here, the furthest we've ever been from real life yet the closest to our real selves.

'Margot.'

I peer into the inky shadows, unsure if the voice comes out of them or my head, eyes slowly adjusting to Harry's face in the moonlight, the bone-white flash of his smile. He leans back against the gatepost, louche, dishevelled, his shirt buttons undone. 'Wasn't very gentleman-like of me to let you walk back alone this late.' His voice is slurred, soft. He makes the night feel closer, less full of air.

'I'm not scared of the dark.' I turn back to the water, sonically mapping him from the creak of the gate, the shifting of a foot on stone. Somewhere above me, a fierce rush of wings in the trees, a swift, silent hunt to the death. I look up but see nothing. It is already over.

Harry squats beside me, swaying slightly, muttering something about a storm brewing and how he misses the rain on his skin. Splashing his feet clumsily into the pool he leans back,

256

crossing his arms behind his head. I sneak a glance at his prostrate body, his tummy where his shirt bunches up, the intriguing dip and hair beneath the pin-glint of his belt buckle.

'I'd sit here with Audrey sometimes.'

'Me too.' I like that he mentions her so naturally.

He regards me with amused, heavy-lidded eyes. 'She'd talk about running away to London when she was older, going to live with a particularly beautiful, scandalous aunt . . . '

'My mother, I'm afraid.'

He laughs, sploshes his feet.

'You were fourteen? When she . . . ' I trail off.

'A young fourteen. A late starter. Tom was about two foot taller than me. Practically had a beard.'

I understand then why Harry might have found some equality in the companionship of a lively younger girl.

'Did she ever talk about me?' he asks, his voice carrying the neediness of a formative boyhood crush.

'A little,' I fib kindly. Audrey tended to make a bigger impression on other people than they made on her.

He broods on this awhile. He kicks his feet, sprinkling the hem of my dress with water. I wonder how late it is — or how early. The night is slipping through our fingers like sand, and I don't want it to end.

'Flora . . . ' He hurls my sister's name into the summer air, changing everything. 'Your sister is very beautiful.'

I close my eyes for a moment, feeling so, so stupid for not realizing that Harry's only come here to talk about Flora, not to be with me or talk about Audrey, that we've been having two parallel conversations, not connecting at all.

'Paris is going to love her,' he adds.

The pressure drops. For the first time in weeks, I can actually smell rain, a swirling cold front boring through the valley towards us. 'You know Paris well?' I ask weakly, looking for the right gap in the conversation to get up and leave.

'My parents have a house in the south, so I make damn sure Paris is on the way.' He lolls back, careless of his worldly glamour.

'Easy to see Flora again, then.' My voice sounds squeaky and odd.

'Yes,' he says, after a reflective pause. 'Yes, it will be easy to see Flora again, Margot.'

And I don't know whom I envy more: Harry for being able to see Flora in Paris, my sister for being able to see him. The silence tautens. The wind blows a skim of pale rose petals across the water. 'Well, I'd better go.' I scramble up, inelegant now, the magic I felt earlier in my dress gone. 'I need to check on Dot.'

His hand shoots out, coils around my ankle, making me start. 'Will I see you before you leave?'

'I — I don't think so,' I stutter, baffled by his hand, the urgency of his question. 'We go back to school on Sunday night.'

His fingers tighten. 'I have to see you again, Margot.'

I wonder if I've misheard him. Nothing makes sense.

'I can't stop thinking of you.'

A dangerous, excitable heat starts to spread through me. For the first time in my life, I get a taste of the power that Flora must take for granted, and it feels like a weapon, one of Perry's hunting guns, heavy, unwieldy in my hands. I don't trust myself with it. 'I — I should go back.'

'Sit. Sit with me a little longer, Margot. You have to.' His fingers release my leg, one by one, and I think back to the beginning of the summer, the way he put my fingers around the cool metal cup of beer that evening, the way it all started. 'Please?' he says more softly, remembering his manners.

I sit down gingerly beside him again, careful not to be too close, an unprepared understudy shoved into the lead role, torn between a giddy joy and a sense of foreboding. The rules have all been broken. 'Don't you love my sister?' I ask cautiously, concerned for Flora.

'I suppose.' His voice is distant, as if Flora lives in a different part of his mind altogether, has nothing to do with any of this. 'But I dream of you as I dream of her, Margot.'

He dreams of Flora. He dreams of me. He dreams of hundreds of girls. He will not remember this in the morning. He is drunk. He is a rogue. Maddeningly, this does not make me like him less.

'And now you are in here.' He taps his temple, as if he blames me for climbing inside it. The mood pitches: I wonder what I've done wrong.

He slams one fist into his palm, the slap resounding across the water. 'Damn. What was in that whisky?'

'I'm a little tipsy too, Harry,' I bluster, embarrassed on his behalf. 'Really, it's okay. We can forget . . . ' I watch his hand rising in slow motion through the night air. When it touches my cheek, the curve of his warm palm fits perfectly, and I cannot help but lean into it, just for a moment, just to see what it feels like, closing my eyes, smelling the cigarettes on his fingers and feeling bits of me slip loose.

A distant rumble. Another. The sound of a storm splitting the sky.

'Look what you've done, you sorceress.' He throws an arm around my shoulders, heaves me closer.

I laugh as rain starts to fall, small drops at first, as unimaginable, until a few seconds ago, as his arm about my shoulders. Lightning flashes over the trees, turning the garden silver and black. If this is all that will ever happen, it is enough. Just this. The thunder, the rain, the weight of Harry's arm against my neck.

'Come on.' He grabs my hand, leads me into the garden, bristling, snapping, dripping, alive in the wind and rain, nothing like the gentle English garden we've grown used to this summer. We start walking away from the river, the meadow, the irreconcilability of Flora. But it's hard to see where we're going, walking at a slant into a tilted universe, the garden changing character with every step. Paths don't fork where I remember. Hulks of topiary rise unexpectedly, megaliths on the lawn. I try to tune my ears to the sound of my sisters' footsteps, ready to pull my hand from Harry's. And I'm sure I can hear something, a twig snapping, a shuffle in the shadows. But the sounds stop when we do, and I wonder if they're nothing so much as the sounds of my own conscience.

We run beneath a huge tree, enchanted, a private tent full of forgotten sounds: water funnelling along leaves, dripping through branches. Harry is behind me, his arms tightening around my waist. I suck in my breath sharply, don't pull away as I should, the warmth of his body spreading through the wet cloth of my dress. I'll stand here for a while, I tell myself, then I'll go. Nothing else will happen.

'May I have this dance?' Without waiting for my answer, he starts to turn me slowly, then faster, until I'm spinning round and round, my dress kicking up, the rain flying off, the world too, faster and faster until we skid and fall on to the blanket of leaves and beechnuts beneath the tree. As we lie there, laughing, I think of how Flora and I would play that game when we were little, spinning each other like tops. And how I've gone from that sister to this, and I feel a wash of shame, try to get up. But he rolls on top of me, presses a knee between mine.

There is a thrill at his surprising drilling weight, a need for it, the way it takes away my responsibility. 'I must get back . . . ' I start to say but the distance between our mouths closes. I taste river on his tongue, whisky, wine and honey. His hand is running up my legs, along the backs of my thighs, towards my knees. I tense, wriggle, trying to get his hand away, to save him from recoiling.

Harry is stronger than me, more insistent. He lifts my skirt, holds my legs at the ankles, and, as if he's noticed the patches, knows exactly where they are, he starts to kiss behind my knees. I cannot breathe, paralysed with horror, waiting for his inevitable disgust. But it doesn't come. He continues to kiss, his mouth soft and wet and forgiving, kissing away all the years of scratching and discomfort, the names in the playground, the shame of school showers. I open my eyes, cry out, the sky spins. It is the most physically profound thing ever to happen to me.

I lift my head, peer down my body to look at him, the sight of us together, his eyes half closed, unreachable, glazed with lust. He grabs my hand and places it on the stiffness in his trousers. I fumble at his belt, reach for the sex beneath it, shocked by how gristly, springy and alive it is. Freed, it slaps against my legs, trying to find a way in. His mouth is everywhere, biting my lips, my breasts, and the rain is escaping through the trees, and then I hear it, his whispered voice, rasping, 'Audrey.'

I push him back, panting, 'Did you just call me Audrey?'

'Isn't that what you wanted?' he mumbles, kissing my neck.

'No!'

'But you wore this dress. You've got her eyes, her gestures. And you're not a girl now, you're all womanly and you want me.' He pulls at my

262

dress. Something rips, and I feel a release as a button flies off. Lightning flashes: something has disrupted his face, something ugly rising to the surface. 'You deny it?' He grins.

My answer is a knee in his groin. Still not quite believing what is happening, I try to twist out of his reach but he holds me tight, pinning me down by my wrists. Above me now, his face inches from mine, he is blinking, rain dripping into his eyes, the moment of connection cut, like a wire.

'I am Margot,' I scream, hysteria rising, all the afternoons I spent in her room, pretending it was mine, trying on her clothes, Sybil plaiting my hair, they all fly away, reveal themselves as stupid fantasy, girlish make-believe. It wasn't me he wanted. It wasn't me. It was my cousin but grown-up, some stalled childhood fantasy. 'I am Margot Wilde!'

We lie there in shocked, damaged silence, the rain finding its way through the canopy now, falling, *pock, pock, pock.* Every outline seems changed, nothing what it was.

Very slowly, he lowers his face until the tip of his nose touches mine. It feels more intimate than his kiss, that he is trying to make me understand something. 'Sorry,' he murmurs. 'I don't know what happened. I — I got confused, for a moment. I'm truly sorry, Margot.'

I blink back tears. Questions creep over my skin. I think about the way he recognized the dress — did he remember it from the newspaper? But not even my sisters have remembered it from the newspaper. And I think of us in the river, Harry saying, 'You have to face your darkest fears, don't you? Only then can you survive yourself.' And it strikes me that Applecote *is* that fear, the meadow, the river, the true reason he's returned to Cornton Hall. Oh, God.

'Harry, what happened to her? Please tell me.' I force the words out, heart starting to slam.

I'm sure he's going to hit me, the way he clenches, rears up. Instead, he pulls himself away, buttons up his trousers. '*I* don't damn well know.'

'You're not covering for anyone?' I sit up too, tug down my dress, try to pull my body and mind into some kind of order, sensing this might be my chance.

'Very good, Margot,' he says sarcastically. 'Are you?'

'What?'

'Was it Perry? Sybil? Moll? Oh, sorry, you've guessed,' he slurs. 'It was Tom.'

'Oh, no.' I clap my hands to my mouth, thinking of Flora and Pam, with him now, oblivious, in danger.

'Of course, it wasn't bloody Tom.' He laughs hollowly. 'I wish it were.'

'You wish . . . ' I know the comment reveals something. But it's all too much, my thoughts mashed, my body aching, and I desperately want to find my sisters, be safe among them again. But then I hear it, Audrey's voice in my head, clear as a bell, 'You have a brain like a board game, Margot, don't give up . . . ' and I pull it from deep inside me, that spark, one last attempt at

264

slotting the jigsaw together, a risky, desperate tactic. 'I know you didn't mean to, Harry.'

A silence, a rip in the night. Harry's shoulders seem to drop with something that looks like relief, and it is this tiny gesture that gives me the courage to continue. 'You were only a boy. A child yourself,' I whisper. Out of the corner of my eye, movements in the shadows, but I don't want to turn my head, in case I break the spell. It feels like Audrey is talking through me. 'You held it inside all this time,' I say, my heart pounding in my ears. 'That must be so hard. But you did it, Harry.'

Harry is silent, his breathing heavy, fast. And I get this tangible sense of something swelling inside him, pushing at the edges, vying for release.

'Everyone has secrets.' I lift my hand to touch his face. His skin feels clammy, febrile. 'Everyone has done something they regret.'

His voice is weak, climbing high as a boy's. 'I . . . I didn't know what to do.'

'You met Audrey fishing?' I say carefully, as if I were talking Dot back from a nightmare, trying to keep the tremor from my voice.

'I wasn't meant to be there. I'd argued with Pa again.' Something in his features twists. 'I was never good enough.'

'Nobody was good enough,' I murmur, as Audrey nods eagerly at my shoulder.

'Stupid, stupid boy, get that book out of your hands and do something bloody useful for once. Muck out the horses!' Harry booms, making me flinch. 'I went to the river instead, just to defy

265

him. And I saw Audrey . . . I . . . ' He stops. Even in the gloom I can see that his eyes are bright with fear, back on the riverbank that August afternoon. 'We were playing a game.' He stops again.

'A game?'

'A stupid game. I — I tried to kiss her.'

My breath catches.

'She slipped.' He starts to shiver uncontrollably. 'Her dress. Her hair. Her hands. She was sinking. She was reaching for me. Two hands. Fingertips.'

'You didn't pull her out?' I recoil, feeling the splash of cold water as I speak, the bubbles up my nostrils, my mouth full of grassy river.

'I thought she was pretending — she was always pretending things, hiding so I could never find her, teasing, playing with me like a cat does with a mouse but then . . . ' His voice knots. 'I realized and I — I froze. I just froze.' The beechnuts closest to me move as he shudders again, his fear nudging from one little shell to another.

'You stayed there? With her?' I say quietly. Audrey is shrinking away from me, like a figure pulled back on a rope, smaller and smaller, reaching out for my hand.

'I ran into the stables, and I lay down with the horses. I just curled up next to the horses.' He closes his hands over his face.

'Why did you not get help?' My voice comes out as a croak.

'She was gone, just gone.' And his voice is colder, more certain. 'I told myself I would tell, I would, I really would, in a day or two, the day after that. When they found her, I would explain.' His eyes fill with tears. 'But they didn't find her. They never bloody found her. And I lied and lied. To the police, my parents, everyone. And the lie grew and grew until I believed it and it walked around with me. And it's only now, talking to you . . . ' His voice breaks. He looks wretched, tears pouring down his face in the rain.

I can't stop my own, gulping dismantling sobs. Audrey's never going to come skipping in from the orchard now, a catkin in her hair. She'll never write me another letter, using words I have to look up. She'll never run away to London to live with Ma. But beneath the sadness, white-hot anger. 'Uncle Perry was arrested.'

'I know, I know. It was awful. I couldn't live with it, not that as well. But I turned up at the station to confess, and Perry was walking out, just released, and . . . and it felt like someone was giving me another chance. So I turned around and I bumped into Pa. And there was this moment, this diabolical moment with Pa, when he shoved me into the alley by the baker's and asked what I'd done in the stables that afternoon, and I stuttered something about saddles, I can't remember what, and the next day he moved us all back to London, shut up Cornton. And people continued to talk about boat gypsies and the man in the hat and . . . I lived my life, the life I was *meant* to live. I found I could, Margot. That it was actually possible.'

'Oh.' Harry in his golden life, Audrey swept

267

along the muddy channel of the river.

'She's always there, in my head. I can't sleep. I can never sleep,' he sobs, no longer the beautiful boy who kissed my knees, spun me by the hands in the rain. 'That's why I came back. To prove I could. To prove I could do anything. That it was over.'

'And to lie some more?' I don't mean to shout but the words barrel out as raging red things.

He grabs me by the shoulders, making me gasp, speaking urgently. 'And I met you, and it was like Audrey all over again, the way you filled my head, Audrey, how she would be.'

I try to wriggle free of his hands. 'Let go.'

He shakes me harder. 'What have you done? What have you made me say?'

'The truth!' I shout. 'For once in your life you've told the truth, Harry.' Something in his eyes makes me feel the vulnerability of my position, an animal in a trap.

'A girl who cheats on her sister, who can't keep her drawers up?' he snarls. 'Who'll believe you, the daughter of a rackety model and a mad old soldier, yes, yes, I know all about them both. Chelsea's a small place, Margot. Who will believe you over a peer's son?'

I bite his hand, twist from him, but he pushes me right back down with terrifying ease. 'You made me tell you, Margot. A big mistake.'

Fear bolts through my body. I cry out, struggling to see over his shoulder, but there is no one, just the hammering rain, a bulb flash of lightning. His fingertips press on my collarbone, the softness of my neck, and I think of Ma and my sisters and how I don't want to leave them. But my head is filling with sky, where Audrey is waiting, her arms stretching towards me, like beams of torchlight, and Harry's mouth is grazing mine. I don't know whether he'll kill me or kiss me, or do both at once, and my body detaches, comes away, floats off so it cannot be hurt. Only my brain still chatters. *Find the word that will make him stop.* But no sound comes out of my mouth. I see Harry glance to his left, a look of surprise, then hear a crack. I wait for the pain, knowing it's the end, that darkness will scrub everything out, like it did for Audrey, for Pa. But it's Harry's head that slams against mine, and above the slump of his shoulder, I see the lenses of spectacles glinting like stars.

★ ★ ★

I'm not sure how long Dot and I stand there, watching over Harry in numb disbelief, waiting for him to come back to life, only that Dot is still holding the paperweight in her left hand, transfigured — taller, stronger, fully realized, thrown out of girlhood at last. And the rain has stopped and the sky is pink, dawn-edged, and the birds are singing wildly and the candy-striped deckchairs we sat on yesterday afternoon are a few feet away and we can hear Pam and Flora talking in heated voices, laughing through the trees, incongruous sights and sounds of a life already out of our reach. No Tom, thank goodness. They don't see us beneath the tree at first, about to walk straight past. I call out,

269

mixing their fates with ours, the sound that comes from my throat a funny sort of bark, more fox than human.

Flora and Pam giggle and peer down at Harry, thinking him blind drunk. Then Pam sees the bloodied paperweight in Dot's hand, and nudges Flora, and their mouths part. I am overcome by a yearning to be curled up on Fang, our moth-eaten tiger-skin rug, sucking the hard sugar crystals off the top of sweet sponge fingers.

'Oh, no.' Pam kneels down next to Harry, presses her ear to his chest, then looks up at Flora, shaking her head. Flora whimpers. I try to explain in gabbles — what he told me, what he did, what Dot did, what I've been doing with Sybil in Audrey's room, how it all led to this — then hear myself repeating over and over, like a needle stuck on a gramophone, 'He watched Audrey drown, he watched Audrey drown.'

Pam takes my hand. 'Shush,' she says firmly, kindly, frowning at the bodice of my dress where a button has ripped off, exposing a bulge of breast, a red scratch. 'It's going to be all right, Margot.'

But it's not, clearly. Flora is swaying like she's about to collapse. Harry is dead. And it is all my fault for inhabiting Audrey, pushing things too far as always, treating it all as a game, and the result is that Dotty is in awful trouble, dear Dot who won't even whack a wasp, my baby sister, whom I was meant to protect, protecting me, guilty of the worst crime. What will happen to her?

'Quick. Give it to me.' To our astonishment,

Flora snatches the paperweight out of Dot's hand and lobs it with all her strength into the undergrowth. It leaves a smear of blood on Flora's fingers that she wipes on her dress, briskly, as if it were juice from a sticky red plum, transferring the guilt, violating the very idea of who she is, who we were brought up to be, who we will grow into, well-behaved wives, doting mothers, changing everything. 'The river,' she says, white-faced, glancing at Harry. 'Can we get him that far?'

Pam shakes her head, speaks through the grille of her fingers. 'We can't risk being seen. Not if Tom is walking back to Cornton Hall.'

'The pool?' Dot suggests quietly and, without her saying anything else, we all know exactly what she means, what must be done, our thoughts rallying, collective again, just as they used to be. The decision has made itself.

We drag him out from under the tree, across the lawn. Harry is heavy, almost immovable, determined to stay there and damn us, a meaty lump on the lawn. Worse, he leaves a trail in the wet grass, his belt buckle catching, so we wordlessly agree to heave him up, his shirtsleeve ripping, making a terrible sound. A girl on each limb, we stagger through the trees, our faces stiff with shock. Dot loses her spectacles. There is no time to find them. I envy her inability to see the details — the way blood has started to curl around Harry's ear, bead on its lobe like a gruesome jewel — that I know will be imprinted on my mind for ever.

We let him sag to the paving beside the pool's

271

edge. Can we really do it? Who will do it? Which of us has the stomach? But the sun is rising higher. There's no time to think. A stone goddess waits, her hand protruding just so, ready to crack a drunken falling head, something that might explain his injury. The water is strewn with rose petals, plucked off by the rain, that will tuck over his body like a thick pink blanket. We wait, hanging on to our old selves a little longer. Then Flora nods, and the nod travels between us, like a parcel of light, a binding acknowledgement of a sisterhood that is bigger than Harry, lust, love or marriage, a loyalty that rides above all others.

In the end, it doesn't matter who does it — Flora first, a firm hand in the small of his back, then Pam, a second later, harder, with her foot — since we all watch him sink beneath the surface, the back of his shirt bulging with air, like a lung holding on to its last breath. We lean forward, peering through a gap in the petals, to see him roll hideously, a necklace of bubbles stringing from his mouth. Time cat-cradles back, stretched between our fingers, Harry sinking as Audrey did, the blue shirt, the blue dress, the margins all blurred. There's a heart-stopping moment when I think I see Harry's hand move, grapple for the edge. But then it slips under the roof of petals. The pool stills. And I start to run, tripping, stumbling into the garden, fleeing from who we are, the terrible creatures we've become.

13

A black hole in the ice. On the edge of the pool, huddled, sodden, very still, Romy and Bella. Jessie hears herself scream and scream. A sequence of events, incomprehensible, unendurable: Joe thundering across the stone, Will grabbing Romy. Blue lights flashing over the yew hedge, an awful noise, wind, a helicopter landing on the lawn. Paramedics. Jessie's tongue so thick she cannot talk at all, a silver foil blanket put over her shoulders, hands pulling her up, this way, that's it, the kindness of strangers, the whirr of the blades, a nauseous rise and lift, engine juddering, Romy's little face covered by the oxygen mask, her tiny cold hand in Jessie's. Bella, foil-wrapped too, like a Sunday roast, saying, over and over, 'It was my fault, my fault.' She looks out of the window, sees Will running towards his car in the drive, the earth shrinking beneath them.

In Accident and Emergency, they take both girls away. Jessie tries not to unravel in the waiting room. Her mind flings itself into pitch-black corners. Seconds drag like days. Her parrot-print dress, so shockingly out of place, tightens like a corset. Where is Will? When will he arrive? She can't do this on her own. She is not the person she thought she'd be in a crisis. She is scared. At last, a harried-looking doctor is leading her somewhere. Something is happening.

The doctor is telling her things, important medical things, that Bella is fine, just shaken. But then the doctor's voice changes and she says that they are concerned about Romy. Since they don't know if she swallowed any water, they have to consider the risk of secondary drowning, water on the lungs, something that might not declare itself until hours after the incident, although most likely much sooner. Jessie's stomach lurches. Her entire life constricts to this moment, the bright lights, the sharp inhalation of chemical-scented hospital air. At the observation ward's nurses' station, there is Bella, asking to see her little sister. From the end of another corridor, still a world away, the sound of Will's voice.

★ ★ ★

Bella stares down at Romy sleeping, a pitifully small mound under white hospital sheets, one foot poking out, tubes and suckers attached to her body. The monitor beeps. 'You were right not to trust me.'

Jessie doesn't know how to answer. She was. She wasn't. She can't make any sense of it. A tear slides down her cheek. Wiping it away, she smells the woodsmoke of the pub's fire on her fingers, a lifetime ago already. What she would give for a chance to live this day again, or just the afternoon, to unpick the small decisions, the ordering of the chocolate tart, the musing over what dress to wear, all things that might have inched the timeline minutely, catastrophically forward and left the girls alone too long.

'Bella,' Will says softly. Jessie hears his voice as if under water. She looks up at him, the moist red rim of his eyes. He looks like he's aged ten years. 'Can you try and tell us what happened again?' he asks Bella gently. 'You weren't making much sense earlier. Why did you say it was your fault?'

Jessie's throat tightens.

'I took her outside to play in the snow,' Bella says quietly, gripping the bed's metal rail.

Will nods, clearly trying to be encouraging. But she sees his hand tremble as he rakes it through his hair. The air feels full of tiny electric shocks, like the stings of jellyfish.

'I put on Romy's gloves, her coat, everything. I made sure she was warm, I really did. We made a snowman. It was fun but then . . . then . . . ' She glances at Jessie, away again, as if she can't bear to see the expression on Jessie's face.

There's an irregularity in the monitor's beeps. Jessie cannot breathe. The wait for the next beep, a fraction of time, is far too long. Will puts a hand on Jessie's back, trying to comfort her. But she cannot be comforted. She can barely be reached, nor he. Somehow they are both locked within the same nightmare, yet must suffer it on their own. *Beep*. Jessie exhales. Will nods to Bella to continue.

'My programme was on, the baking one. I guess I didn't — I didn't think to lock the scullery door, Dad. I didn't think at all.' Bella covers her face with her hands. 'So it was my fault.'

275

'That doesn't make it your fault,' says Will.

'I went to the bathroom, leaving her there on the sofa, Dad.' Bella's voice breaks. 'And . . . when I came back, she wasn't there. Romy had gone.'

Jessie screws up her eyes, like someone preparing for a punch. She can see it exactly, like a movie in her read.

Bella bites down on her lip. 'I couldn't find her.'

'So you ran outside,' prompts Will, his voice less steady now. 'You followed her footprints?'

'She didn't make a sound, Dad. She didn't make a splash.'

Jessie pictures Romy's perfect pink lungs, an inhaling choke of dirty icy water.

'I . . . I just jumped in,' Bella says.

Will draws Bella against him. She looks tiny in his arms, a slip of a thing, too young to have managed any of this. Jessie stands beside them, not knowing what to say, at the edge of their embrace.

The nurse returns, checks Romy's pulse, records it, then smiles kindly at Jessie. 'You must be dead proud of your daughter for saving her wee sister like that.'

Jessie waits for Bella to sharply correct the nurse, as Bella always does if anyone insults her by imagining Jessie is her real mother, but Bella just stares down at her feet, like someone who knows if they dare say anything they will cry.

'Yes, I — I am,' Jessie manages.

Bella scuffs her foot along the floor. Then she stands very still, very stern, pressed against the edge of Romy's bed, eyes blankly pinned to Romy. And Jessie is thrown back to Romy's bedroom in the midnight dark, Bella sleepwalking, that tall dark column looming over the cot-bed. She'd always found it so menacing — only now does it occur to her that it was protective, that Bella might have been watching over her little sister.

The nurse reassures Will that he can pop out for coffee and sandwiches, an excellent idea, since they'll be here some hours yet. Reluctantly, Will leaves for the hospital café. The nurse is called away, leaving Jessie and Bella sealed behind the pale-green cubicle curtain watching Romy in anxious silence.

Bella's mouth starts to contort and twitch. She lets out a stifled sob. Jessie is unable to stand it any longer, and gathers Bella tight in her arms. Bella doesn't push her away. Something in her seems to go quite limp, and she buries her face against Jessie's shoulder.

Jessie doesn't want to let go. It's the closest she's ever physically been to her stepdaughter. She finds Bella's scent — a sort of hormonal sweetness mixed with shampoo — and the feel of her flexible, lean body, the softness of her long hair, almost unbearably moving, and deeply comforting. It stirs up a confusing rush of maternal feelings.

With no warning, Bella pulls away hard, as if catching herself falling for a trick. 'You were thinking of what happened in London, weren't you? When you saw me and Romy by the pool?'

'Just for a moment.' Nothing can be hidden

now, everything levelled by the terrible events of the day, the precariousness of Romy's situation.

Bella sinks to the edge of the bed, something draining out of her. They listen to the beeping, Romy's soft, shallow breathing, the wails of the children's ward. Then Bella says, 'Just before it happened, that thing with Zizzi, we were in the changing rooms . . . '

It takes Jessie a moment to realize that Bella is talking about the incident at the pool in London, and she feels a sudden wave of trepidation about what she is about to be told.

' . . . and the other girls were chatting about the mothers' and daughters' school disco that night, this fundraising evening that Zizzi was organizing. And Zizzi said to me — she said it in front of everyone, Jessie — that . . . that I'd have to borrow someone else's mother if I wanted to get in.' Her cheeks blaze. 'I know it sounds like a small thing to get upset about.'

'Oh, Bella. It doesn't. It really doesn't. I'm so sorry. Why haven't you ever told your dad this?'

Bella is silent a moment, cooling her cheeks with her palms. 'I'm not sure. I just couldn't for some reason. Maybe I didn't want to make him sad about Mum again. Or think I wasn't coping. I don't know.'

'I'm glad you've told me.' She feels honoured.

'I wanted to scare Zizzi.' To Jessie's surprise, Bella opens up further. 'I wanted to punish her. I was mad. So I held her down.'

'You did?' Jessie's heart sinks.

'Yeah, I held her down really hard. And it felt good. It felt like I could punish Zizzi for

278

everything that had happened to me.'

'Oh,' Jessie says weakly, refusing to judge her for it.

'But only for a second or two, then I came to my senses and I stopped. I swear. I let go. I waited for Zizzi to pop up and call me a bitch. But she stayed under, flapping her arms about, gasping, dramming it up for the lifeguard.' Her eyes fill with tears. 'I didn't try to drown her, Jessie. I'd have liked to, for a moment. But I didn't. I dunked her, that's all.'

Jessie doesn't know what to say, her emotions scattered in all directions.

Her silence makes Bella's eyes narrow, untrusting again. 'Do you still not believe me?'

Jessie knows she cannot lie, or sidestep this question, that to Bella it's fundamental. After all, if Romy offered such an account, even if it was at odds with the lifeguard's and the victim's, wouldn't Jessie believe her? And hasn't she always said that she will treat the girls the same, or is the shameful, unsayable truth that she doesn't, that Romy is hers and Bella is Mandy's, that blood is blood? Is that it?

'I believe you, Bella,' Jessie says simply, but with all her heart.

★　★　★

It is very late when Romy is given an all-clear by the doctor. Jessie and Will thank her profusely, tearfully. They ache for home. Outside, it is very cold, the sky a powdery starless grey. Bella tucks a blanket over Romy in her car seat. Romy smiles

279

sleepily at this unexpected fussing by her big sister, then nods back to sleep.

Too shattered to talk, they drive silently out of the gritted town streets into the skiddy, treacherous country lanes. Hedgerows crouch against the car's windows. Through the black slats of farm gates, Jessie glimpses snowy fields, desolate and strange. Falling flakes catch in the cones of the car's lights, almost phosphorescent in the icy night air, like something from the ocean's sunless depths. Jessie does feel submerged, still sealed off in the trauma of the last few hours, no longer having anything in common with the busy, casual lives that exist on the surface. She twists in her seat, holds the warm loaf of Romy's socked foot. Even though Romy is safe the anxiety is still within her. Perhaps it always will be, that heightened sense of danger: life can change in an instant, as it must have done for poor Mrs Wilde in the 1950s, the fear as primal, the stakes the same. This comes as a shock, a deadly blow to Jessie's belief that bad things happen to other people. Will and Bella already know this, of course. She feels humbled by that now, foolish too. And still, really, she has no idea of what they must have gone through. Because Romy survived, and Mandy didn't. Romy was lucky, Mandy wasn't.

So many things could have altered the fateful timing of the lorry's approach on the roundabout, Mandy's spinning wheels — a delivery needing a signature on the doorstep, a punctured bicycle tyre that Mandy would have cursed, unaware it had saved her life. Jessie wonders how

Bella, so young, bears those what-ifs, and finds herself filled with a newfound respect for the exhausted pale girl resting her head on the window, eyes half closed, as if still not feeling safe enough to sleep.

★　★　★

After taking the girls up to bed, Jessie and Will huddle in front of the fire, Jessie still in her dress, Will his shirt, like the two surviving guests from a party that has gone horribly wrong. Jessie recounts her conversation with Bella about Zizzi, and he nods numbly, his reactions delayed. Jessie knows he is elsewhere, that something about the hospital, the trauma of the last few hours, has taken him back to the accident.

'You're not okay, are you?' she asks gently.

He says nothing at first then speaks flatly, sincerely: 'If something happened to one of the girls that would be it for me.'

Jessie watches the smoke rise from the logs in fabric twists, and thinks of Mandy's scarf, the one she found behind the radiator in London, and, not knowing what to do with it, stuffed back behind the radiator's dusty grille. It occurs to her that, in different ways, she's kept doing that ever since. And it hasn't worked. The past rises out of corners, gaps, keeps moving to the centre of the room. She wonders what would happen if, rather than pushing it back, she pulled it towards her. 'Did it feel like that when Mandy died?' she says uncertainly, not quite sure of the ground beneath her feet.

Will looks surprised. The question stretches over the silence as he considers it. 'Well, I had Bella. I always had Bella. And my heart had . . . reserves. Mandy filled it up when we were together. And she didn't take it back when she died,' he replies thoughtfully. 'If that makes any sense?'

Jessie nods, moved by his honesty. She can't remember when they last spoke like this, without agenda or rush. And something of the intimacy reminds her of their early days, lying in the grass of St James's Park, revealing bits of themselves, feeling their way around each other's hearts as the city surged behind the plane trees.

'Mandy left me the capacity to love.' Will pauses, catching up with his own thoughts. He flashes a smile at her. The distance between them starts to shrink. 'But I only realized that when I met you.'

Jessie blinks back tears. For the first time, Will is holding his marriage to Mandy on the open palm of his hand, saying simply, *This is it, Jessie. This is the beautiful thing I had. This is what I lost.*

And his words ring true. She thinks back to the handsome man she first noticed during lunchtimes in the park, how he was angry, hurt, grieving, but not broken, not a man who needed total rebuilding — she wouldn't have been attracted to that. He was still Will. He was always Will. The idea that she has Mandy to thank for this is both unsettling and humbling.

'Mandy would have hated me to be alone. She'd have thought it a waste of life.' He shoots her a small smile. 'She had a great *joie de vivre*. Like you.'

'Like me?' Jessie flinches, feeling too many things at once then — flattered, stripped of her own uniqueness, sad that she never met Mandy, that she can't befriend her, yes, all of those things.

'She'd be immensely grateful for all you've done for Bella.' Will's voice falls to a husky whisper.

'Don't say that. I haven't been a good stepmother, you don't have to pretend.' Tears strangle her voice. 'I haven't done anything for Bella, I'm afraid.'

'You don't need to do anything, Jessie. Don't you see? She just needs to know you're there for her, whatever crap she throws at you.' He pokes the fire with the iron. The logs move, settle into new places. Jessie feels something moving inside her too. 'And she's thrown lots and lots of crap at you, I do know that, Jessie. And you're still there.'

'Hanging on by my bloody fingernails.'

They catch each other's eyes and laugh, the past sitting next to them easily, relaxing, warming by the fire. A branch scratches at the iced window, the truth at the edges of their conversation. It is time. 'Will, I need to tell you something.' She takes a breath. 'Bella has your old love letters, the ones you sent to Mandy over the years, when you were abroad, that were stored in the loft in London.'

'My letters?' He looks puzzled, then seems to remember, rubs the back of his neck. 'Shit. I haven't even thought about where those might be.'

'In Bella's sock drawer.'

He raises an eyebrow. 'Right.'

'I found them when I was putting away washing. I think Bella left them there purposefully for me to find. But that's no excuse.' The flames flare blue and orange. 'Will, I did an awful thing. I read them.'

'You *read* them?' he says, with an astonished laugh.

Jessie nods, braced for his anger. 'Back in September.'

'Ah,' he says, with a slowly dawning smile, as if this might explain a few things about her mood these last few months.

'I'm sorry. I shouldn't have done it.'

'No, you shouldn't. I'd hate to read so much as a text you sent to an old lover. I'd want to chop his balls off.'

For a moment, Jessie almost feels cheated by Will's response, the way it sucks the power from those letters, makes a mockery of months of jealousy. 'You've never written me a letter,' she says, unable to let go of it easily.

'Haven't I?' He sounds genuinely surprised.

'No. You definitely haven't.'

'Well, I will, then.'

'You can't *now*. It wouldn't be the same.'

His eyes soften. He leans closer, until the tip of his nose touches hers. 'It was a different life. You are my life now, you and the girls. And I know it's not perfect. But there's nothing else. Nothing else that matters. No woman I love

284

more than you, Jessie.' His hands skate along her tights, brushing the hem of her dress. 'Although I miss your dungarees.'

She smiles, her body starting to heat, tighten. 'You were doing so well. Don't over-egg it.'

'I'm actually not joking.'

'There's something else I haven't told you, Will.' Jessie pulls away. Complete disclosure. It must all come out now. A new wariness settles over Will's shattered features. 'The story about the vanishing girl, the one Bella's obsessing about?'

He shakes his head. 'So you found out too. That poor kid.'

'You *know*?' she stutters, baffled.

Will nods sheepishly. 'I've known for a while. Bella kept talking about it, so I did a search at the library by the station one day when the train was massively delayed.'

Jessie stares at him in astonishment. 'Why didn't you *say*?'

'I didn't want to taint Applecote for you, or freak you out. I just couldn't bear to pop your balloon.' He grabs her more playfully, breathes into her ear, 'And what's your excuse, Missus? Why didn't you say?'

'I knew there was a reason I loved you . . . '

Will kisses the rest of the words away, and, right there, on the sheepskin rug, in front of the flickering fire, he peels off her dress, her tights, takes her apart, puts her together again, and the passion that Jessie thought was gone returns, electric, alive, all-consuming.

★ ★ ★

Jessie sleeps deeper than she has in months. At some point, Romy climbs into bed beside them, snuggling against her breast, like a baby. Jessie drifts back to sleep, dreaming she's floating down a river on her back, an electric-blue kingfisher bombing into the water. She wakes to the second ring of the doorbell.

'I'll go.' She throws on an old dressing gown. Not very glamorous but she smells of Will again.

'Hi!' She's surprised to find the enormous mass of Joe on the doorstep.

'For Romy.' He pulls a white toy rabbit from one of his coat's cavernous pockets. 'I heard she was back safe last night.'

'That's very kind. She'll love it, thank you, Joe.' Jessie takes it, amazed that, while they barely know anybody in the valley, her family's news has travelled. She will make more effort, she decides. She will invite people to tea. She will stop cutting herself off, telling herself she's an outsider. Then she waits for him to leave.

He stamps his feet in the cold. He isn't going anywhere. 'How is the poor mite?'

'Better. We've been incredibly lucky.'

He glances over his shoulder, as if worried about someone overhearing him. 'Would you mind if I came in, Jessie?' he whispers, his breath foggy in the cold air.

'Can it wait until tomorrow morning?' She gestures smilingly at her dressing-gown, trying to draw his attention politely to the fact that they're not yet up, that it's nine o'clock on a freezing Sunday morning.

'Not really. I didn't want to disturb you, not

when you've been through the mill like you have, but — but the wife said I should.' Joe starts tripping over his words. 'What with the police having to get involved and the like. Jessie, I'm out of my depth here.'

'The police? Whoa, Joe, slow down. I don't understand.'

Jessie frowns, uneasy now. 'You'd better come in. Hang on, I'll grab Will.' She runs upstairs, returns with a sleepy Will.

'So, what's the problem, Joe?' Will asks, stifling a yawn, closing the kitchen door so the girls can't hear.

'I found something in the garden.' Joe takes off his cap, revealing a domed forehead skimmed with sweat. He glances at Jessie. 'You might want to sit down first.'

14

We run over the dewy grass, hand in hand, Dot stumbling, the garden seeming to stretch, lengthen, giving us time to adjust from the dead to the living, the law of the wild and the rule of law. I lunge for the safety of the scullery door, and glance over my shoulder, expecting Pam and Flora to be right behind us. They're not. I can see only Flora, some way back, under the trees, gesturing for us to go inside, they'll follow. Somewhere, a jackdaw calls.

The house seems too small. Like we've outgrown it overnight. The clock on the wall says ten past four. In the kitchen Moll, our hopeless guardian, is fast asleep on a chair beside the range, her mouth slightly open, air whistling through the open door of her missing tooth. There are four large pans of cooling jam on the stove, empty jars waiting on the wooden table. Moppet runs up to Dot, her tail beating. Dot holds the dog's delicate head between her hands, and the two look at each other, exchanging something that bypasses my understanding. Then she buries her face in Moppet's flat grey fur, eyes closed, like a girl reunited with the wolves that brought her up. Moppet starts licking Harry's blood off Dot's fingers, excited by the smell, and I have to push her away.

Shutting Moppet in the kitchen, we start up the stairs, adrenalin finally giving way to exhaustion. I feel an ache with each photograph of Audrey we pass, my dead drowned cousin, my lodestar. I pause in front of the one that Flora, the day we first arrived, mistook as a photo of me. But I can no longer see myself in her bleached-out features. I cannot see me at all.

We hover on the top-floor landing, neither of us wanting to peel off into the solitariness of our own little bedrooms, scared of the images that might fly at us like bats. Dot starts to shiver. We hug. We smell bad.

'We need to wash. You have the first bath, Dot.' I rub her goose-bumped sapling arms, marvelling at their deceptive brute strength. 'I'll search for your spectacles later.'

I sit on the edge of her steamy bath, worried that exhaustion and shock might make Dot sink silently beneath the suds. We don't say much, focusing instead on the reassurance of passing the flannel, me washing her back in small soapy circles, the familiar damp mark on the wall shaped like Ireland. If we can wash behind her ears, a corpse cannot roll in the bathing-pool. If her nails are clean, she is innocent.

Dark thoughts still scratch against the back of my eyes: how old must you be to hang? How dozy really are country policemen? But I tell Dot that everything's going to be fine — everyone will presume Harry was drunk and drowned, sort of the truth — and we will always protect her and she must get some sleep. She dries herself silently, numbly, then pads naked into her room, leaving small footprints on the floor.

I take on the duty of dealing with our soiled

dresses. After stamping an exit from mine, noticing the missing button, the smears of mud, grass and blood, I ball it with Dot's inside a pillow slip and stuff it at the bottom of my half-packed suitcase: it is destined for one of the school's vast canteen trash bins in a couple of days' time and will quickly be buried under potato sacking, porridge and rice pudding, then carted away. I won't miss the dress: I came too close to ending up like Audrey last night. I don't want to be her ever again. For once the pure inescapable fact of myself, my naked body with all its inelegant pudges and mauve mottles, is a huge relief.

Lowering myself into Dot's bathwater, I turn on the hot tap with my toes, letting the heat gush in until my legs scald red. I scrub my skin raw but I don't feel clean. I'm not sure how long I lie there, dazed, thinking of poor Audrey's last moments, my head full of rushing river and reeds. After a while, I hear Flora and Pam's hushed voices. Only Flora briefly pops her head around the bathroom door: her eyes are oddly bright, the colour of Parma violets. I tell her what I did with the stained dresses and that she should give hers to Pam to dispose of in the same way. Flora's mouth parts to say something, but no words come out and she pulls the door gently to again. It occurs to me then that Flora, numbed by the violence, her own role in it, is too shocked to speak.

Emerging, wrapped in a towel on the landing, there are no sounds coming from my sisters' rooms. I decide to leave them alone: we must get

290

our story straight but I also want them to sleep, an hour at least, so that they're less likely to make damning mistakes later. I will keep myself awake, slumped on my bedroom chair in my dressing-gown, like a person on watch around a fire. Occasionally I drift off but my body always spasms awake again. I think of Harry kissing me behind my knees, the traitorous pleasure of it, how that hot, soft mouth is now submerged, stiff and cold. I walk to the window for air. Outside, the moon still hangs in the morning sky, faint as a watermark. The garden is engorged, a vivid green after last night's rain, sugar-dipped with dew. I have time, just.

I slip out of the house through the front door — careful not to wake Moll, praying that Moppet won't bark — and into the garden through the side gate, telling myself I'm searching for damning marks of blood, the drag of his body on the grass. But the truth is I want to see Harry one last time. I want to check last night was real. I want to say sorry. I want to say goodbye.

A sprinkle of blood droplets in the grass by the pool gate, balancing on the blades' tips, like the remains of a fox's nocturnal kill. Using the edge of my bare foot, I smear them away — what would have disgusted me yesterday, easy now. The pool area feels knowing and dark, a few hours behind the rest of the garden, something of last night for ever printed upon it. There's a large puddle of water on the stone paving, reflecting the lightening sky, and the pool itself is thickly carpeted with petals and storm-torn leaves, water winking in the gaps, like fragments of a half-told story. Crouching beside the stone goddess on the corner where we pushed him in, I part the petals with my fingers, gently at first, then more vigorously, panicking, prodding at the pool with a stick, desperate for a glimpse of him. I search and search.

Harry is not there.

★ ★ ★

More blood, a path of it, like breadcrumbs through a wood, leading from the pool to the meadow gate — open, a body's width. I almost don't go through it, scared of what I might find.

James Dean. Fallen from the sky.

He is slumped in the crater of the meadow, his forehead resting on his arms, arms crossed over drawn-up knees, like a bloodied soldier on a battlefield.

I rub my eyes, sure I'm hallucinating with tiredness, readier to believe it is the ghost of the dead pilot than him. But Harry remains, a crumpled, solitary figure in a ripped shirt, head lolling. Not dead in the pool. The blood in his hair looks dry and black. And his shirt steams in the early-morning sunshine: he has been out of the water for a while.

Harry has somehow survived: Dot is no murderer. Yet I feel no relief, only rapidly escalating unease. Not daring to breathe, my instinct is to back away slowly and return to the safety of the house so I can tell my sisters about this Lazarus, back from the dead.

But, sensing my presence, Harry stirs. He raises one arm, sheltering his eyes from the light in its nook. 'Margot? Is that you?' he calls out hoarsely.

'Yes,' I manage, trying to hide my shock. For his head injury seems to have circuited his skull and found another way out: his right eye is bloodshot with a milky glaze over a frozen iris, not moving in tandem with the other, damaged in a way I can't bear to think about.

Harry swipes at the air, reaching for my hand. I fight my recoil, knowing that I must appear as normal as possible now, and wade through the long grass towards him. His grip is weak and cold. I heave him up, recognizing that dense dead weight. Once he is shakily vertical, I pull my hand away quickly, the feel of him too strange. 'Shall I go and find Tom? A doctor?'

'No . . . no fuss.' He is disoriented, swaying a little. 'I . . . I'll walk back to Cornton.' He winces at something that hurts, adds gamely, 'I'm fine.'

I don't dare tell Harry he's not.

I watch, breath held, as he cautiously touches that awful eye, as if checking it's still there. 'It's just . . . I can't see too well. And my head . . . ' His fingertips investigate the crusted blood in his hair. And I can almost see his mind grasping into the fog, trying to pull down the events of last night. 'What happened, Margot?'

My mouth opens and closes: I have no idea. Only that Pam must have missed his heartbeat when she checked him in the garden, easy enough, given the late hour and the wine. And that twitch of his hand in the pool? No, I didn't imagine it. But how did Harry pull himself out of the water? Regain consciousness just in time? Someone must have helped him. But who?

'Margot?' he persists, breaking my thoughts. 'Please . . . '

I nod at the scorch on the grass, the ashy remains of last night's fire. Wine bottles on their sides. An empty whisky bottle. Harry's silent guitar. 'You were very, very drunk.'

A moment passes. When I meet his gaze again something in his left eye is sharper, hardened. The other remains like that of a fish on ice. He clamps his hand over his mouth, disbelieving, something dawning. 'I told you, didn't I?'

Fear flutters in my ears, an insect's beating wings, and I feel his fingers at my throat again.

'We . . . we were under the tree. The rain,' he mumbles, slowly moving all the bits together like the shreds of a torn-up letter. 'Dot. Christ. I looked up and saw her, fist raised . . . '

'No, no. Dot was in bed,' I say quickly, betraying too much.

He stares at me, silent for a moment. Then he says coldly, 'You're lying.'

I feel the hairs all over my body prick, a surge of heat.

'I woke by the side of the pool. Wet. Why? Why was I by the pool? Answer me,' he growls, when I don't answer.

'I — I don't know,' I say weakly, truthfully. I cannot tell Harry that the last time I saw him he was sinking beneath the water's surface, a dead man.

He bends down and rests his hands on his

knees, breathing heavily, as if about to be sick. But he doesn't take his eyes off me, looking up through his matted hair. And I see his expression changing as the night starts to solidify. 'Did you and Dot try to *drown* me? My God. You did,' he says, as if something in my expression confirms it. 'You damn well tried to drown me.'

'No.' I start slowly walking backwards, realizing I've stupidly made myself vulnerable again. 'Of course not.'

'You wanted revenge for Audrey. You wanted . . . ' He straightens, covers his face with his hands. And for a moment I think he's going to burst into tears. But when he looks up his face is blazing, dangerous. He starts walking towards me, staggering over tussocks of grass. 'I remember, Margot,' he calls, his voice stronger now. 'I remember everything.'

I pick up my pace, not daring to turn my back to him.

'I know you,' he pants the words out. 'We're the same, you and I. We understand each other completely.' His laugh comes out as a cough. 'You think I can't play your games? You think you'll pull the wool over my eyes? That I'll let your little baby Dot get away with attempted murder? I hope she's got a bloody good alibi, Margot. Because Pa's got some very, very good lawyers.'

'Don't threaten Dot,' I flame.

'That's rich. But don't worry, it won't just be her. I'll take you all down, you and your murderous sisters. I bet Pam was there too. And Flora,' he spits out Flora's name acidly.

'I'll tear you all apart.'

'You've got it wrong,' I insist, retreating faster now.

Just when I think he might run and chase me, he slumps, hands on his knees again, his pallor faintly green. 'Margot, wait . . . A pact,' he croaks. 'My silence for yours? And your sisters', since you act as one,' he adds, correctly guessing that I've already told them.

I stand very still in the grass, mind spinning, trying to work it out: Harry's survival saves Dot, all of us, from having committed the ultimate crime; Audrey, by drowning, surely damns him — but it's his word against mine, a story against facts. Will Sybil believe me? Anyone? And isn't Harry's injury far more persuasive than my report of a drunk man's words?

'Both summer nights . . . scrubbed out. Never happened at all.' I hear a tremor of desperation in Harry's voice then, his fear of the terrible secret that has boiled within him these last five years. 'Margot?'

'I — I need to talk to my sisters first.' I turn, start to run.

Harry shouts something unintelligible behind me. And when I glance over my shoulder he has sunk to his knees again, covered his face with his hands.

★ ★ ★

I find my sisters in Flora's room, awake, ashen-faced, wearing nighties and an air of anxious complicity. Dot and Flora are squeezed

296

up together on the bed, nervously curling and uncurling their toes on the rug, Dot hugging a pillow to her stomach. Pam stands by the half-open window, as if she has been tracking my journey through the garden. She has a strange, intense set to her jaw: I can read her like a telegram again. 'How is he?' she asks, confirming my suspicions.

'So it was you.' I catch the shock of my reflection in a wall mirror, my eyes darting wild flashes in shadowed sockets. 'He's . . . ' I can't bring myself to say 'okay'. Neither can I bear to reveal the gruesome extent of his injury to Dot. ' . . . in the meadow.'

'Oh, walking, then? Good.' Pam blows out with relief.

'Can you please explain why he's not lying dead at the bottom of the bathing-pool?' The words come out too forcefully. Dot startles. I try to sound calmer. 'Why the hell didn't you tell me?'

'We — we weren't sure how you'd take it,' Pam stutters apologetically, realizing she should have. 'You seemed almost on the verge of . . . ' She pauses, stealing a surreptitious glance at Flora. 'We thought it better to tell you after you'd rested, that's all.'

'Tell me *what?*'

'Just after you and Dot ran off, Harry started grappling about, Margot,' Flora says, shuddering at the memory. 'We couldn't believe it.'

My mind returns to those twitching fingers. My refusal to believe what my eyes saw.

'I couldn't just stand there, Margot.' Pam's

voice is unusually quiet. She sits down on the bed, drops her head into her hands. 'It was . . . unethical. We had a choice.'

I can't help thinking bitterly how Harry had had a choice too, to save Audrey, or at least tell her broken parents what had happened, save them years of dreading and hoping. He chose himself, his family's reputation. Until he met me, a pale imitation of Audrey, not his chance at atonement but his nemesis.

'Pam was quite something, Margot,' says Flora, trying to smile. 'Gave him the kiss of life and everything.'

Pam pulls a face. 'He coughed up whisky.'

I collapse on the bed beside her, my body leaden. 'Harry doesn't remember anyone pulling him out of the pool, just waking wet on the stone paving.'

'Well, we left him there, breathing, lying on his side,' Pam explains. 'We thought it best to spirit away after that, rather than make ourselves known. Bearing in mind . . . well, what had happened earlier.' She starts to look worried. 'What? Why are you frowning like that, Margot? What did he say?'

'He's convinced we tried to drown him, not save him. He thinks us murderesses.'

'Gratitude for you,' says Pam, trying to clear the air. But the silence that follows is heavy.

I rub my raw eyes with the heels of my hands: colours bloom and splatter on the inside of my eyelids, like paint. I wonder if this is what Harry sees in his right eye, if he sees anything at all.

'Well, Harry can't stay in the meadow,' Flora

says after a while, her concern about her lover still oddly subdued. I wonder again if her reaction to the night is stalled by shock.

'I doubt he's there now.' I lean back against the reassuring solidity of Pam. 'He said he was going to walk home. Yes, I know. I did offer to get a doctor. He didn't want it.' Spoken aloud, the conversation with Harry seems so preposterous, so unreal, I suddenly wonder if I've dreamed the whole thing.

'I'll find Tom. I'll get Tom to search for him, just to be sure. Tom must have got back to Cornton hours ago, wondering where Harry is.' Flora grabs her dressing-gown off the back of the bedroom chair.

'Flora, you can't,' instructs Pam, sharply, making me think it's not the first time she's had to say it. 'What if someone sees you? We've got to look like nothing out of the ordinary happened last night. We have no idea what Harry's going to do now. He could call the police, anything.'

I rally myself to tell them about his eye, the proposed pact. 'And the thing is — '

'But I have to see Tom!' Flora interrupts tearfully.

'Flora . . .' Pam warns. She turns to me, says matter-of-factly, 'To put you in the picture, Margot, Tom and Flora combusted into high feeling when Harry wandered off looking for you last night.'

'What?' I turn to Flora, aghast. But her face makes sense of it: a funny light in her eyes, that almost-smile. And it's perfectly obvious.

'I couldn't fight it any more,' Flora says simply.

'And before you try to say anything sympathetic, Margot, I'd gone off Tom by midnight anyway,' Pam points out tersely. 'And there are much bigger things to think about right now. Can we please think about them?'

Dot lets out a sob. I turn to her, so quiet beside me, the still point of this storm, and put my arms around her. Up close, I notice the ghost of her lost spectacles in tan lines, the ghost of the fragile little girl she was yesterday, and is no longer. 'You okay?'

She nods, unconvincingly.

'What were you doing in the garden last night?' I ask.

Dot rolls the lacy edge of Flora's pillow between her fingers. It's a moment or two before she can speak. 'I felt lonely in the house on my own,' she says eventually, distressed by recalling it. 'Moll was already asleep in the kitchen chair. And the rain looked so enticing after the heat. I could see two people running under a tree. I thought it was Flora and Harry. But when I got there . . . it was you, Margot.' She lowers her gaze. 'You and Harry.'

So it was Dot following us, not my conscience. I shift uncomfortably on the bed, unable to look at Flora.

'I thought he was going to kill you, Margot. I thought — ' Dot's voice cracks. I take her trembling hand. Tears start to roll down her face. 'And I saw the paperweight on the deckchair with my book, you know, where I'd forgotten it

300

earlier, the deckchairs on the lawn. And . . . ' She can't go on, her shoulders heaving silently.

'It's all right,' I say.

'You're a warrior, Dot. Never forget it.' Pam is unable to keep the respect out of her voice: our little sister has proved herself at last. I feel something in Dot's hand release then: her sisters' opinion is the only thing that really matters.

'Was he, Margot?' asks Flora, urgently. 'Was Harry trying to kill you?'

'I don't know,' I admit.

A bleach of sunlight moves ominously across the rug, warming the tips of our bare toes, a reminder that the day is coming.

Flora covers her face with her hands. 'I just had no idea all that time . . . all that stuff we did . . . It makes my skin crawl.'

I brush my hands over the backs of my knees, thinking how Harry found the most hated, horrible part of my body and kissed it. I wait for it to make my skin crawl too. But it doesn't.

'Did he force himself on you, Margot?' Flora stifles a sob, reaches out to touch a small scratch beneath my collarbone.

I shake my head, knowing that I must tell Flora what really happened, how I kissed Harry, lost myself in his arms. But there is something more pressing, something they need to know, a decision to be made. And I'm ordering the difficult words on my tongue when Pam sighs out, 'Oh, Margot,' and pulls me to her chest so that I can feel her heart's gallop. Then Dot and Flora join us and we are all entangled together on the bed, a scrum of nighties, frenzied heartbeat and hair. And it feels so good, so safe, the place I've missed so much, and I realize in that moment how far I've drifted from them all, lost in Audrey's world, desires, secrets within secrets. I want never to leave the sisterly fold again.

'Nothing can hold us back now, can it?' murmurs Flora, articulating something that I'm feeling too, struggling to accept, that the realization we could actually kill a man if we had to — and share responsibility for that killing — brings with it a new sense of possibility, an awareness of a ruthless female power we didn't know we had. Surely if we can do that, we can do anything, change shape, pull down our destinies from the skies. We are not English girls waiting to be married any more. Not alone, like poor Audrey either. Sisters. Survivors. Like cats. Nine lives. Maybe we always were, just didn't know it.

'Nothing,' Pam sighs.

'Thank God it's all over,' says Flora.

'Not quite,' I say.

★ ★ ★

The world starts to announce itself loudly through the open window — the rattle of a cart down the lane, a farm dog barking, the squeak of Billy's bicycle brakes — shattering the sense that we are somehow suspended over events, can remain untouchable for much longer. Time is running out. Fighting sleep, we try to resolve the

302

irresolvable in rambling, unfinished sentences. My sisters make me describe his eye in detail again; how Harry remembers seeing Dot, the moment before she cracked the paperweight on his head, and thinks we tried to drown him; our moral obligation to expose him against the need to protect ourselves.

We talk in muddled circles, slowly moving towards a centre, like an old tractor in a field. Pam lies down on her belly, ripping at her nails with her teeth. Dot lays her head in my lap, fighting sleep. Flora sits up on the pillows, biting a hank of her hair.

'Okay, listen,' Pam says, after a while, rubbing her eyes so hard they squeak. 'The fact is if we do tell Aunt Sybil and Uncle Perry, we're dealing them torturous knowledge that can't be proved, since Audrey's body was swept away years ago and Harry will deny it.'

'Just when they're recovering their old selves, and Aunt Sybil so much happier,' Flora murmurs quietly, her eyelids heavy, almost shut. 'She'll simply die of grief.'

'Uncle Perry will hunt Harry down with his shotgun,' adds Pam. 'And if he doesn't, we've all had it because Harry will be out for our blood.'

'But it is the truth,' I say.

'No. It's what Harry told you, drunk,' corrects Pam, glancing at Dot in my lap. 'Oh, look, our warrior's asleep.'

I gently lift Dot's head on to a pillow, cover her with a sheet. She stretches out one leg, dangling the foot off the edge of the bed, just like she always did in our bedroom in London.

'But the pact will never end,' I whisper. 'We will be connected to him for ever. And we don't know what effect it — '

'Margot,' says Pam, wearily. 'How can any of us predict our future years from now? I can't even predict how today's going to turn out.'

'My brain aches. I just can't think any more.' Flora collapses back on the pillow next to Dot, closing her eyes. 'I'm so, so tired.'

Pam lowers her head to her arms, her voice slurring. 'I think we'll know for certain what to do, Margot, when we see Aunt Sybil. Then it will all become clear.' Her words trail off into a snore.

I have no recollection of dozing off myself but when I awake Pam's elbow is in my nostril, my sisters still asleep. I hear the deep rumble of Perry's voice downstairs. Everything is almost normal, for two or three seconds. Then I remember.

★ ★ ★

I stumble to the window and peer out at the garden. It's unsettling, the way it looks so peaceful, like a river must after a person has sunk. Bright sunshine now. A morning in full swing. Billy is crouched in one of the flowerbeds, planting. And on the other side of the garden wall, the nose of Perry's black Daimler in the drive gleams, like a bullet.

Returning to my room to dress, I glance at Audrey's door, noticing that for the first time this summer I don't feel its pull. I have no desire to sit on her sleigh bed and pretend it's mine. I want to wear my Chelsea-black trousers, the ones I haven't worn since the day we arrived. They're at the very back of my drawer. I have to suck in my tummy to do up the last button, my figure filled out by Moll's cooking. The trousers feel hot and clingy after weeks of loose dresses but good. I'm a London girl. Myself again.

'Morning, young lady.' Perry winks at me. He's bent over, touching his toes in the drawing room. It occurs to me that I really could turn my uncle's world upside down with just a few words about last night. 'Look, I can almost do it.'

'Like an acrobat, Uncle.'

'Never say never, Margot.' He straightens with a low groan, and rubs his back. 'You look ghastly. Just as well we let you all sleep in. I take it last night was a success then?'

I nod, and try to keep my face free of inflection. 'I hope you had a nice time too.'

He pulls on his ear lobe and grins. 'Yes, it was — fun in fact. And a fine play, a very fine play.' There is a moment of embarrassment, as if I've stumbled into his bedroom without asking and found him in his underwear.

'I was looking for Aunt Sybil.'

'Oh, the garden somewhere.' He scratches the back of his neck. 'You know your aunt.'

'Yes,' I say, because I do.

Outside, the air is like water, the hazy bake of dust and seeds gone, washed away by last night's rain. I weave through the lushness, still not knowing for sure what we should do, if the moral duty to tell Sybil the truth overrides everything

305

else. It will become clear when I see her, I tell myself, just as Pam says. But I still can't see Sybil.

At the edge of the Wilderness, I'm about to turn back, investigate the kitchen garden, when I hear the distinct sound of splashing from behind the yew hedge. Not quite believing my ears I peer around the gate, hiding in a cloud of clematis.

A green dress, thrown over a deckchair with un-Sybil-like abandon. A beige elastic girdle. A bra, like something Grandma wore. Brown sandals kicked off in different directions. Then, rising from the water in a sinuous curve, a rainbow of fine droplets, the unbelievable sight of Sybil herself, flipping her hair off her face, her shoulders, revealing the white shock of bare breasts, stubby red nipples. I suck in my breath, not daring to move, and watch, transfixed, as my aunt rests her head back against the pool's edge and closes her eyes, face dappled by the sun reflecting off the water. The decision makes itself then. Retreating slowly, silently, I leave my aunt in her fragile newfound peace.

★   ★   ★

'Miss Wilde?' As I cross the terrace, Billy approaches, rubbing his hands clean on dirty trousers. He pulls something out of the leather tool pocket slung around his waist and smiles, his teeth very white in his tanned face. 'I found this. I think it might belong to you.'

My whole body jolts. There is no blood on the

paperweight now — washed away by the rain, or buffed by Billy's leather pocket — yet it seems to me like a crystal ball, something that anyone might peer into and, in the right light, at the right angle, see exactly what happened, four sisters dragging a body across the grass, tipping it into the pool.

'It's pretty,' he says, and something about the simple way he says it, the way he's looking at my mouth as he speaks, makes me feel very strange. 'Here.'

I take it, the hard, cold heart of the night before. 'Dot's lost her specs too, if you happen to see them.' I sound almost normal.

'I'll look, Miss Wilde.'

There is an honesty and sweetness about Billy that is like a balm this morning. I hover. For some reason, I don't want to leave his side.

We stand there in silence, smiling shyly up at one another, and I wonder if Billy understands far more than he's letting on. Something, a feeling, a word I don't have, flows between us. But it's shattered by a motor-car roaring down the lane, screeching into the drive behind the wall, the slam of a door.

I don't so much panic as drain of blood, rooted to the spot, my reactions too slow, too late, to be of any use at all. There are no moves left in me, no strategies. All I know for certain is that it is the police, coming to take us away, that I have failed to protect my little sister and, yes, there was a black spot, like a hole, waiting in the corner of the summer sky, and we are all about to fall into it.

'You quite all right, Miss Wilde?' Billy puts a hand on my arm. It seems to me to be my last anchor to the earth. I take hold of it tightly. 'Miss Wilde?'

I can barely breathe, every cell of my body braced for the sound of a heavy boot on the gravel, a heavy-knuckled knock. Billy moves protectively closer, picking up on my sense of threat, my apprehension now his. We listen together. But suddenly the sounds don't quite make sense, the light sharp footsteps, less a boot than a heel picking its way along the gravel. The brisk rat-a-tat-tat at the door. A woman's voice, a yearned-for long-lost voice. 'Peregrine, you old rascal, where have you hidden my darling girls?'

15

Shadows move inside the tent — lit up like a lantern in the trees — as the police complete their grim work. Jessie shivers, thinking of all the times she and Romy have innocently rambled past the little stone well the tent now hides, never realizing they were brushing up against a tomb, that the rising water table was pulling something terrible to the surface.

Jessie didn't look down into that hole for long. But she knows she'll see it for ever, the greenish bone sticking up from the lens of ice. She's glad of the barrier of the police tape now, the way it makes everything more unreal, like a TV show, all those serious figures in white-paper suits, plain-clothes police taking photographs, mumbling into radios, churning the pristine snow into slush with their heavy feet.

It is a bitterly cold Monday afternoon when the first reporters start to ring the doorbell. On Will's advice Jessie politely says nothing, tells them to talk to the police directly. She confides in her mother and Lou, then makes the mistake of letting it slip to a garrulous London friend. Soon her mobile is flashing with incoming messages, people they haven't heard from in months digging for gossip, marvelling quietly at the irony of moving out of the crime-ridden capital for the safety of the sticks.

Will doesn't head for London, refusing to

leave Jessie marooned. Romy waves to the police, tries to pet sniffer dogs, the subdued mood that followed her fall into the pool replaced by a confused excitement. But Bella merely grows quieter and quieter, harder to reach, absorbed in thoughts that she refuses to share. Will and Jessie worry at this self-containment. They worry about everything. With the lack of information, everything feels suspended. Not even the snow will melt.

When Bella returns from school, batting her way through the reporters with dismissive aplomb, Jessie makes the girls creamy hot chocolate, pillowy with marshmallows, trying to provide comfort in the sugar and warm milk. Bella eyes the treat suspiciously. Will and Jessie hover around her, feeling out of their depth. Does the discovery make her feel threatened? they ask. Bella shakes her head. Scared? Of course not. Would she like to board in the dorms at school this week? No, thanks. No, really. After that Bella avoids both of them, the adult questions that come loaded with instructions for how she should feel and react, and retreats — regresses — into building a Lego farm with Romy. Outside the window, the snow still falls.

At any other time such a sight — the sisters playing! Snow falling at the window! — would have made Jessie giddy with happiness. Instead, she feels a crush of guilt that the girls have been brought together by a near drowning, and now this. Mandy would be justifiably horrified, she decides, after all Bella's been through already, all she's lost. Jessie remembers their first viewing, standing in the orangery on that January afternoon, imagining she could force her family to ripen with happiness, like a fruit. She was naive then. She isn't now. She knows what they must do.

When Will returns from talking to the inspector in the garden, conveying the lack of further enlightenment with a shrug, she pulls him to the side of the kitchen dresser and whispers that they must put Applecote on the market. To her surprise, he doesn't immediately agree with her. 'Let's see,' he says, holding her face in his cold hands, snow melting off his boots on to the kitchen floor.

Jessie knows he's clinging to the hope that the bones will turn out to belong to some kind of animal, not human at all. Or, if not, then some unfortunate farmhand who lived hundreds of years ago, picked clean of meaning by time, something archaeological.

★ ★ ★

Later that evening, Jessie is stacking plates in the cupboard, trying to occupy her unsettled mind with the domestic, when she hears a gentle knock at the front door.

'Hello, Jessie.'

And there she is, taller than Jessie remembers, wearing a long deep-black coat, a scattering of snow on its fur collar. Red lipstick. It takes Jessie a moment to collect herself. There is so much she wants to ask Margot, but this is not the time. This is the worst time. 'Excuse me. It's madness

311

here. I — ' She stops. 'You've heard the news?'

'Do you know any more yet?' Margot asks, looking past Jessie into the house.

Jessie shakes her head. 'No one tells us anything. Although the police did say it looks historic. They've been at it for hours. Sorry, I've forgotten my manners,' she says, flustered. 'Do — do you want to come in?'

Margot pauses only for a moment, as if crossing Applecote's threshold requires a mental rallying of some kind. 'Thank you.'

Jessie pushes her hair off her face with the back of her wrist, overwhelmed by the sight of Margot in her messy pink kitchen. 'Here, let me take your coat. Do sit down.'

Margot double-takes at Romy's child's chair — Jessie has the unsettling sense she recognizes it — then sits rather elegantly on a sheepskin-covered chair, just missing a Cheerio, in a pair of slim indigo trousers and a pale powder blue cashmere sweater, set off by a turquoise necklace. She sits very still, too still, someone trying hard to keep control, clasping her hands slowly, purposefully in front of her on the wooden table. Pale hands, long fingers. Jessie notices her wedding ring for the first time, a band of gold.

'Billy,' Margot says, intercepting Jessie's gaze. She smiles, one of those genuine, quick smiles that can't be forced. 'My husband, Billy. He talked you into buying a lemon tree, I believe?'

'Oh, oh, right. Yes, he did. I love my lemon tree.' Jessie puts the pair together for the first time, the weather-gnarled countryman with the

312

glint in his eye, stylish Margot, who sounds like she could be one of the Queen's more bohemian cousins. Unlikely, but she can see how it might work.

'He'll sell you an entire citrus orchard if you're not careful,' Margot adds wryly.

Jessie laughs. And then the laugh stops and she hears her own voice cutting through the kitchen air like a knife. 'Margot, how did you know about the blocked drain, the damp patch in the top-floor bathroom?'

The clasp of Margot's hands tightens. 'I kicked myself for saying that afterwards.' She shakes her head at herself. 'What a goose.'

'So you know Applecote Manor well?' Jessie asks, when no further explanation is offered.

Margot nods resignedly. 'Like my own heart.'

Jessie stares at her baffled, wondering if the woman might be slightly unhinged, or merely eccentric. 'I think I've seen you peering at the house a few times,' she says hesitantly, wondering how far she should push this. 'You walked away once when I called you. In the summer. You were behind the orchard wall with your dogs?'

Margot dips her head and looks up guiltily, a slightly coy, childish gesture that in any other circumstance would make Jessie smile. 'I've always imagined myself rather good at subterfuge, Jessie, but I always, always prove myself utterly useless. I'm sorry.'

'Oh. Well . . . Would you like a cup of tea?' Tea seems a way of making things vaguely normal. Somewhere in the house, Jessie can hear the clatter of a falling tower of alphabet bricks.

'I would like a cup of tea very much. It's been quite a day.'

Jessie stands at the range, watching the kettle, ready to grab it before it starts howling. She takes a sideways view of Margot, the unremarkable, quiet features, the firm jaw, the discreet diamonds blinking in her ears. She's always admired women like Margot, all the more interesting for not being great beauties, women who have had to make their mark on a room in other ways. The question is, though, what other ways? And what room?

Still wondering, Jessie fills her brown teapot, wishing their mugs weren't chipped. 'How do you . . .'

'No milk, no sugar, parsimonious, please.'

Jessie can't help but warm to Margot again. She sits down beside her. No perfume, she notices. No smell at all, like someone who doesn't want to leave her trace behind. She glances down at Margot's feet on the tiles, simple black flat boots, like riding boots, the prints from the melted snow, largish.

When she looks up, Margot is watching her. 'Another question?' she asks. 'Feel free.'

'Okay, and I do realize this might sound very silly, but were they your footprints in the shed? I found footprints in there when we moved in last summer. And someone seemed to have been in the pool changing room. I always wondered . . .'

'I'm sorry. It's maddening, isn't it, always wondering?' Margot bends down and roots around in her large handbag. Jessie glimpses the spines of two battered books. A hairbrush. A dog

314

lead. 'Here. I should have given it back to you months ago.'

The key is dull with age, hanging from an enamel dog keyring. '*Ours?*' Jessie gasps.

Margot sits up straighter, which, moments ago, wouldn't have seemed possible. She turns the turquoise beads at her neck with her fingers. 'I owe you an explanation, Jessie.'

'Yes, you do!' Jessie exclaims hotly. 'Please.'

'It was my aunt, Mrs Sybil Wilde, who sold you the house.'

'Your *aunt?*' Jessie is reeling. So Margot was Audrey's cousin.

Margot nods, almost impatiently, waiting for Jessie to catch up. 'I helped her move, not that she wanted to go. My aunt is very old, and very stubborn. She managed — just — living here, with daily help. But then she had a fall. So it was all a bit of a rush in the end. I'm afraid we left rather a mess. I do apologize for that. But we had nowhere to put anything. My cottage is stuffed to the rafters as it is. My sisters' houses too. And the agent said, 'Leave everything. Any new owner will gut the place before they move in, trash everything, or give it to charity.' So I left . . . ' something catches ' . . . I left things as they were, Jessie, like a ship about to sink beneath the waves.'

'And we kept them.'

'I can see.' Margot glances at the child's chair again, then the walls, stuck with the girls' flapping pictures, the tester paint pots on the kitchen dresser, the clutter of Romy's craft paraphernalia. 'You've brought everything to life

315

again,' she adds, and Jessie can't tell from her tone whether this is a good thing or not.

'Sorry. But why didn't you say all this when you dropped Bella off that night?'

Margot glances down at the key on the table and sighs. 'The honest answer, Jessie, is that it threw me, seeing a new family here. Those lovely girls of yours. I didn't want the conversation.' She looks up and smiles kindly. 'I didn't want to fill your young heads with old ghosts, I suppose.'

Jessie inhales, everything beginning to make sense at last. 'Hang on. You had a key. So someone might have seen you at a window after Mrs Wilde had moved out?'

'Quite possible.'

'You lit a fire in the old drawing-room grate?'

'Oh, it was so dreadfully cold. I felt sorry for the house. I kept coming here to check on it and it felt so abandoned, unwelcoming and empty. Exactly what my aunt had sought hard to avoid all those years. So I brought in flowers, lit a fire sometimes. I wanted to keep its homely spirit ticking over.' Her voice drifts, and Jessie senses her mind going somewhere she can't follow. She frowns, brightens again. 'You know those brilliant memories, memories of being young, that get stronger as the years pass?'

Jessie nods, feeling herself slipping under Margot's spell.

'They're the things that settle in the very soul of a girl. The idea of a memory being something that is over, in the past only, is quite wrong, just another grown-up delusion, isn't it?' Jessie thinks of how Bella would understand Margot's words

316

completely, and what a wonderful confidante Margot would make for her. She leans forward, rapt. 'A memory is a living thing. It breathes beside you, Jessie, it sits on your shoulder, replays itself over and over. And then — '

A thunder of feet interrupts Margot: Bella, Romy on her hip, waggling a wooden puppet spoon with yellow wool hair, a dishevelled Will, in socks, a pair of old jeans and a baggy blue jumper, recently attacked by moths. Jessie fears they must all look like a load of hillbillies. 'Has something happened, Jessie?' Bella asks urgently. 'Do we know who it is?'

Jessie stands up, widens her eyes. 'Bella, this is Margot. Margot who picked you up in the lane that night, remember?'

Bella blushes, taken by surprise. 'Oh, sorry. I thought you were a detective or something. Hi.'

Margot smiles. 'I've heard all about your bravery, Bella. The very best of big sisters, I'd say.'

Bella blushes more deeply, can't quite hide her pleasure.

'And this is my husband Will,' Jessie says shyly, proudly, feeling rather like a girl introducing her boyfriend to her mother for the first time.

'I believe I owe you a big thank-you for returning Bella safely that night,' Will says warmly.

'Hello!' Romy interrupts, with a waggle of her spoon puppet.

'Well, hello there, Miss Spoon.' Margot twinkles. 'What beautiful blonde hair you have.'

Bella shoves Romy into Jessie's arms and sits

on a kitchen chair, settling in for the conversation, gaze pinned hungrily on Margot. '*It's Audrey, isn't it?*'

'Whoa, Bella — ' begins Will.

'Ah. Okay. You do know.' Margot turns to Jessie. 'Audrey's name is spreading on the tom-tom drums through the valley. But I wasn't at all sure if anyone would have told you about her. It takes at least three generations before you're deemed a local.'

Will grins. 'Ah.'

'I thought you should prepare yourselves. And that I had a responsibility to tell you about Audrey, given my relationship with the house,' she adds apologetically.

Will kicks Jessie's foot under the table — a discreet, what-the-? — then stands up, rubbing his hands together. 'Okay, girls, Bella, Romy, let's see what's on telly, shall we? Let's leave Jessie and Margot to it.'

Bundled in Will's arms, Romy taps the wooden spoon against her father's stubbled cheek. Will nods at Bella to move.

'Obviously I'm not going anywhere, Dad,' Bella says, keeping her gaze on Margot.

Jessie squeezes Will's hand. 'It's all right. Let Bella stay.'

★ ★ ★

'Tell us everything,' Bella begs, emptying a packet of sponge fingers on to a yellow plate and sliding it distractedly to the middle of the table.

'Oh. May I? How did you guess I had a soft

spot for a sponge finger, Bella? Goodness, I haven't had one of these in years.' Margot takes a bite and closes her eyes, seemingly transported by the old-fashioned biscuit that Jessie had bought in the village shop only because they'd run out of everything else.

Jessie and Bella wait. It feels like Margot has a ball of string in her hand and is about to tug it, unwind the whole story.

Margot swallows, puts the biscuit down. 'I should have guessed,' she says, her vivid blue eyes darkening. 'But my mother told me the police swung a lamp on a rope down the well after Audrey went missing. I accepted it, even though that hapless lot probably wouldn't have found my cousin if she were lying in the middle of the lawn. Or maybe she was just miles down. I don't know.'

Jessie shudders. Again she sees it.

'After my uncle Perry died, back in the seventies,' Margot continues, her voice a little unsteady, 'I worried about Aunt Sybil pottering about here on her own, so I got that lid fitted over the well. I never thought . . . ' Margot shakes her head, visibly pained. 'I can't bear to think.'

'It's okay, Margot,' Jessie says, touching her arm lightly. Memories seem to be surfacing in the lines of Margot's face, and a certain vulnerability. 'We don't want to upset you with our questions, do we, Bella?'

'No,' says Bella, unconvincingly, drumming an impatient tattoo on her lap with her fingers. Again, they wait.

'There was a game Audrey always tried to get me to play in the garden, you see.' Margot winces. 'Jump the well wall.'

'Christ,' mutters Jessie, spluttering into her tea.

'Audrey was fearless. No one else was daring enough to do it, not even me. She was always looking for someone to play that game.' Margot's fingers roll the turquoise rope of beads at her neck.

Jessie finds herself mirroring her, reaching for her own gold pendant.

'You see, Jessie,' Margot says, and Jessie nods even though she doesn't see at all, 'in hindsight, that game was the jigsaw piece, the bit in the corner you can never find, that makes sense of all the rest but at the time, that summer of 'fifty-nine, I just heard the word 'water' and I joined all the right dots to make entirely the wrong picture.' Jessie notices a tremble on the surface of the tea as Margot lifts her cup. 'And he didn't contradict me. He let me believe that.'

'What was the wrong picture? Who is 'he'?' asks Bella, eagerly, leaning so far forward she's almost sitting in Margot's lap.

'I won't say his name, if you don't mind, Bella. He . . . he was the only person who knew the truth. Let's leave it at that.' Margot seems to consider this a moment, her forehead furrowing. 'He just didn't tell the truth,' she adds, with a hiss of unmistakable fury, clearly unable to leave it at all. 'I was sure he had, many years ago, but he damn well hadn't. He told me they played a game. I assumed he meant a fishing game or something. But — '

'Jump the well wall!' blurts Bella.

'Well, yes, very good,' says Margot. 'You're right, Bella. I think it must have been, that stupid game of Audrey's. And, of course, it would have revealed her whereabouts, if he had let that little detail out, wouldn't it?'

Bella nods. 'So he pushed Audrey in?'

Margot flinches. The question swells in the kitchen. Jessie is suddenly not at all certain they should be listening to this. Surely a police matter. If any of it is true.

'No, I don't think he did, not purposely,' Margot says, after a while, her voice more reflective and distant, as if she's in conversation with herself. 'He told me he tried to kiss Audrey. So he must have grabbed at her or something and . . . ' she draws a breath ' . . . and she fell. That much is certain.'

'He didn't save her?' Bella rises from her chair indignantly. Jessie touches her arm, a gentle warning to tread carefully. Bella lowers herself again.

'No, he didn't. Not everyone is as brave as you, Bella,' Margot says, with a small smile.

Bella sits a little straighter.

'Although the truth is he couldn't have reached down into that well and pulled her out, I realize. It was already over for poor Audrey. Just not for him.'

'But why didn't he reveal where she was?' Jessie asks, puzzled.

'Guilt. Denial. Immaturity. Fear of his father.

321

I'm guessing, Jessie. And I might be being far too kind. But I do know that time has a way of compacting youth's dark secrets, making them harder and more solid,' Margot says, with a steely precision that makes Jessie wonder what youthful secrets Margot might be keeping. 'And he'd convinced himself that admitting knowledge of Audrey's fate would make him look guilty of murder. And maybe it would have.'

'He sounds like a total *arse*.' Bella lurches back in her chair.

Margot laughs, nods. But her eyes are wet. She tries to sniff back the tears. 'Forgive me. It's just a bit of a shock. To believe Audrey had died in the river all these years and . . . and . . . '

Bella rips off a piece of kitchen roll and hands it to Margot.

'Thank you.' Margot wipes her eyes. 'It's not the dead that suffer. It's the living, you see.' She shakes her head. 'All those lives' trajectories changed. Weighed down.'

Bella nods, as if Margot's making perfect sense. But Jessie feels lost in Margot's story, the nameless 'he', the secrets, lies and shifting truths of the 1950s. All she can truly understand is the primal horror of a deep well, a mother's grief. Her throat locks. A child is never a collection of historic bones: a child is always human, loved, missed, their loss incomprehensible. It is just too sad.

'I still can't believe no one saw them that day,' says Margot, after a while, her voice strong again, almost angry. 'Someone must have. This bloody valley, Jessie, it doesn't change. Everyone protects their own. They always have done and they always will.'

'You reckon there were witnesses?' Bella gulps.

'Oh, yes. Yes, I do. A fisherman. And some man in a hat by the bridge who never came forward. My aunt always hoped he would one day. But he didn't, of course.'

Jessie grabs Margot's arm, making Margot jump. 'I know who it might have been!'

Margot and Bella both look at Jessie as if she's gone mad.

'Jessie!' Bella laughs awkwardly, embarrassed on her behalf.

'Joe!' exclaims Jessie, thinking of the photo he pulled out of his wallet the first day.

'Joe?' repeats Margot, blankly.

'Joe Peat. He's doing a bit of work for us. And he showed me a photo of his dad, Sid or something, and he wore a hat, always wore a hat. He used to do work at Cornton Hall in the fifties.'

Jessie can almost see Margot's mind rummaging through the past, like Romy's fingers in Bella's things. 'Loyal to Cornton,' she murmurs, under her breath. 'Yes, he would be.'

'You know what? I'm sure Joe said something about him dying of a heart attack, which would explain why he never came forward. Shall I call Joe? Get him over?'

'No. I'm not sure I can take in anything else today, Jessie.' Margot picks up her handbag from the floor, stands up. 'And I've invaded your kitchen long enough.'

'Oh, don't go. Not yet. You haven't told us

what Audrey was like,' Bella says, crestfallen. 'I really want to know what she was like. I've wondered all this time.'

'You have?' Margot seems genuinely touched by this. She slowly sits back down. 'Well, Bella, Audrey . . . ' she searches for the right word ' . . . Audrey was a gas. You'd have loved her.'

Bella nods encouragingly.

Margot smiles, her face changing in front of their eyes, brightening, animating as she starts to talk, conjuring up Audrey as if she had seen her only yesterday, pulling her out of the distant past and into the kitchen, long-lost summers out of the winter air, the clever, bossy girl with the swinging plait and the bright blue eyes and the fancy dresses, who looked like Margot, only much prettier, who hated being an only child, yearned for sisters, spent her time inventing games, adventures, running across the meadow with fistfuls of balloons in the wind, determined to lift off and fly. Margot is inhaling, about to launch into another stream of anecdotes when Will walks in, and she stops and colours.

Will looks in bemusement at the women around the table, knitted together like old friends. 'I won't ask if I'm interrupting anything.'

'No, no. You're absolutely not.' Margot stands up, pulling herself back together. Jessie feels Audrey's spirit scroll away from them. 'I fear I've quite outstayed my welcome. I was only going to be five minutes.'

'No, no. I have something for you!' says Bella, excitedly. 'I've finally worked it out. You have sisters?'

'Three.' Margot raises one eyebrow. 'Imagine.'

'A Dot?'

Margot nods, puzzled.

'Don't move, don't go anywhere,' Bella shouts, rushing off. They listen to the quickening clatter of feet up the stairs, down again.

'Here you are. Joe found them in the window-seat in the orangery.' She hands Margot the stack of letters. 'From Ma,' Bella adds, when Margot says nothing, her face paling, her lips parting in astonishment as she peels back pages, scans the water-blurred words. She checks the date on an envelope. She turns to Bella. 'Thank you, thank you so much. You have no idea how much we longed for these letters. Oh, my goodness.' She shakes her head, struggling to take it in. 'We never believed Ma when she said she'd sent them. Under the window-seat? All this time? My aunt has some serious explaining to do.'

'I hope we've not got anyone into trouble,' says Jessie, exchanging a concerned look with Will.

'Trouble? My God, Aunt Sybil's never been *anything* but trouble,' says Margot, with a mixture of exasperation and fondness. 'Once again today, I stand corrected.' She looks down at the letters again, obviously stunned, then back at Jessie. 'I'll see the police now.'

'The police?' Will repeats, taken aback.

'I'd like a quick word, if you don't mind. I want to tell them what I know.'

'Well . . . sure.' Will smiles resignedly. 'I'll show you the way.'

'No need. I know exactly where I am going,' Margot says quickly, winking at Jessie.

Twenty minutes later Margot slips out of the garden by the side gate. Jessie hears the *put-put-put* of a car and runs to the hall window. She watches the car's headlights illuminate fragments — a gatepost, a snowy hedgerow, the iced sinew of the lane — then slide back into the darkness, just like Margot herself.

★ ★ ★

Two days later, the police call Will to confirm that the remains are those of the missing girl, Audrey Wilde; relatives have been informed; there will be a press conference in the morning. Jessie and Will say nothing to Bella and curl up by the fire, holding each other tightly, discussing in muted voices how they should break the news to the girls in the morning. They don't know what it might trigger in Bella. Jessie sleeps badly — a nightmare about a dark tunnel, a head torch like a car headlight bouncing off wet, slippery stone walls, no way out — and wakes early. Wanting to ensure they get to Bella before schoolgirls start texting for gossip, or Romy wakes up, she makes her a cup of tea, shakes Will awake, and they rush nervously upstairs.

Bella is already awake, resplendent in Mandy's grey silk dressing-gown, sitting up in the sleigh bed, the bed Jessie's very glad no one mentioned to Margot, just in case it was Audrey's. Despite the early hour, Bella looks rested, radiant even, her hair coiled, twisted over one shoulder. Seeing their solemn faces, she rolls her eyes. 'I'm not about to have a breakdown or anything.'

Will sits gingerly on the side of the bed. Jessie hands Bella the tea and perches, a little further away, eyes soberly lowered. 'Very sad news, I'm afraid, Bella,' Will says gently. A shaft of winter sunlight crackles through the round porthole window, smudging lilac across the wall. 'The police have confirmed that the remains are Audrey's.'

Bella blows out, relieved. 'Thank God. She'd want to be found.'

'That's one way of looking at it, I guess,' says Will, cautiously, exchanging a puzzled glance with Jessie.

'Audrey can have a funeral now. Her mother can finally say goodbye,' Jessie says, then immediately kicks herself for reviving the subject of mothers and goodbyes. She waits for Bella to pounce on her clumsy comment, as she normally would.

But Bella only nods and mutters, 'Yeah.'

Although the exchange is minimal, opaque to anyone who didn't know them, maybe even to Will, it feels significant to Jessie. She relaxes a little, lets her weight rest on the mattress, not just on the tips of her toes.

'It is okay to feel upset about this, Bella,' Will says softly.

'Dad,' Bella groans.

'We realize Applecote Manor is . . . tainted now, not the fresh start we'd hoped,' Jessie says. 'And we want you to have much more say in where we go next.'

Bella bolts upright. 'Next? What do you mean *next?*'

'We'll put Applecote on the market.' Jessie waits for Bella to smile, or at least look triumphant. That is what Bella always wanted after all. 'Remember what you said the first time we saw this room? 'Even if we move in, this house won't ever belong to us,' I think it was. Well, you were right, Bella. You were right about many things. To borrow Margot's words, I stand corrected.'

'We,' says Will, smiling at Jessie. 'We stand corrected.'

'What *are* you two banging on about?' Bella looks appalled by both of them, then starts to laugh, as if they can't be taken seriously. 'You want to move house because of a body from the dawn of time in the garden? Oh, my God. What are you trying to protect me from? Death? Hello? Bolting horses and stable doors.' She shakes her head at their immaturity, then smiles at them both with a look of weary affection. 'I'm not moving anywhere. You can if you like.'

★   ★   ★

A shrine grows steadily beside Applecote Manor's gate: flowers from elderly villagers and old school friends of Audrey; teddy bears from young village children who can't comprehend death but understand the terror of being alone and lost; an exuberant floral wreath from Joe Peat and his family. Among the cellophane and ribbons, cutouts of the photograph that's been splashed across the papers, grainy black-and-white, the tragedy somehow sealed in her innocent prettiness. Jessie studies Audrey's face, tracks traces of Margot in those lively bright eyes, the curl at the corners of her smile.

But it's hard not to see everything through the prism of Audrey now. Even Bella's bedroom feels different, airier, rinsed clean somehow, and the top-floor landing less narrow and dim, as if the house is not caving in but opening up.

Obviously, this change in atmosphere — perception, of course — comes from Bella's lifting spirits, rather than any release of Audrey's. But Jessie senses the two things are deeply connected: as a seismic tremor deep in the earth can nudge something on the surface, the discovery of Audrey has shifted things for Bella. She has no idea how Bella — connecting disparate things as the young do naturally, like artists — has turned another girl's terrible fate into a catalyst for her own change. But she has. Bella is still Bella, of course, complex, contradictory, stubborn. But the high wall that surrounds her is cracking, small gaps Jessie can peer through and see, for the first time, Bella as she really is, the girl she was, moving behind it, like a streak of brilliant light.

The explanation, Will believes, is more straightforward. Bella saved Romy's life, a heroic act that made her realize not only did she love her little sister but that she has a vital role to play in this family, *her* family. Something, resisted for so long, clicked.

One morning, Bella walks downstairs with the

two empty Mandy Boxes, asking if she should put them out with the recycling. The bouquets at the gate start to fade. The news agenda moves on without any mention of the mysterious 'he' whom Margot had made sound so culpable. Jessie decides there's something unknowable about Margot and her story, a fluidity in which solid facts dissolve, and it's best to leave it to the police. She collects up the soft toys for charity (only three quietly 'adopted' by Romy), sends on the notes and messages to Margot at the nursery. She keeps expecting, hoping, to find Margot on the doorstep. But Margot doesn't appear. And Jessie doesn't want to disturb her, or intrude by turning up at the cafe, assuming she has her hands full with the police and dealing with Audrey's poor mother.

Life takes over again. The floods recede. The daylight gets longer. Will leaves for London with a quiet positivity, nothing that Jessie can quite put her finger on but just as if he's resolved a matter that's been privately troubling him. She puts this down to Bella continuing to prove to her father that she is not a girl to be flattened by life's blows, and in this and many other ways, Jessie now suspects she is probably like her mother, a woman Jessie finds herself no longer wanting to push away quite so hard. Her old jealousy seems increasingly absurd — she is alive, Mandy is not, she is Will's wife, a mother to his child too — and the curiosity she's suppressed for so long floats more freely to the surface. Jessie starts to ask Bella questions. What films did Mandy love? What books did she read to Bella when Bella was Romy's age? Did Mandy send Bella to playgroup? At first Jessie's questions are met with a puzzled shrug or a breath of monosyllables, but Bella reveals a little more each time. And it is through Bella that Jessie slowly gets to know Mandy — and the daughter who still misses her so much — and, inch by inch, allows Mandy space to live freely alongside them. One day Jessie catches herself having a conversation with Mandy in her head, like two neighbours gossiping either side of a garden fence. Mandy tells her to love fiercely what is precious, what is not yet lost. Oh, yes, and Bella would adore a dog.

'If not now, *when*?' Jessie says afterwards to Will. 'Bella deserves it, after all the upheaval of the last few weeks.' She calls the local Golden Retriever breeder that evening. They are lucky. There is one bitch left in a litter, smaller than its siblings, blonde with bear-like paws, ready to go. Bella names her Marilyn, and smothers her with love. Marilyn pees all over the house, eats their shoes, digs up the carefully planted bulbs in the garden. One terrible afternoon, she chews off Flump the elephant's trunk. Romy sobs. Bella carefully sews it back on with grey cotton, nicked especially from the school craft cupboard. Jessie forgives Marilyn everything.

Joe Peat works hard, sweating more profusely under his cap as the temperatures slowly rise. By late March, the well and the pool have both been made safe, their structures removed. The statues of the stone goddesses that once guarded the pool's corners now emerge, like wood nymphs, from behind clumps of daffodils. One Saturday afternoon, Lou arrives unannounced, newly single, eyes mascara-streaked, saying she needs to lick her wounds. Bella says, 'Marilyn is good at licking wounds,' and Jessie ropes Lou into helping seed the new topsoil that covers the ghost of the pool's rectangular expanse with wildflowers and grasses.

Lou pulls Jessie to one side, whispers, 'Why is Bella smiling so much? What the hell happened?'

And Jessie says, 'Bella happened.'

★ ★ ★

An unexpectedly warm early spring knocks out winter. Her mother comes to stay, warns Jessie that disasters always come in threes, and not to let her guard down for a minute, then wonders if she could take some cuttings from the garden, and stay on another few days. Jessie enrols Romy in a playgroup in the village hall two mornings a week. It is during these hours, the furry heap of Marilyn at her feet, that she sits in her studio. Studying her reflection in a mirror, she sketches a self-portrait, the woman she is now, wiser, older, scruffier and, yes, happier. Bella, on returning from school, agrees it's terrible but says it's a start at least, and sticks it on the kitchen wall next to Romy's finger paintings and the portrait of Audrey.

One afternoon Bella pulls Jessie aside on the front step and warns her in a furious whisper 'not to act like it's the first time I've brought anyone back or ask stupid questions'. Liv, also a daygirl, is a tall gobby blonde with three brothers whose parents have just completely ruined her life by moving from Camden to Cornton Hall, the spookily big house on the outskirts of the world's dullest village. Over the following days, she and Bella spend hours in Bella's bedroom, listening to music, screeching with laughter (abruptly silent the moment Jessie enters) and hanging out at the stones, leaving a badly hidden trail of cigarette butts in the grass.

★   ★   ★

Will surprises them all by arriving home on a Wednesday, not a Friday. He is grinning like a loon. Jessie fears he's been drinking on the train. He starts raking his hand through his hair, speaking too fast, and tells her he's accepted an offer on the entire company, not just Jackson's stake, that he's been negotiating a half-decent price these last couple of weeks. No, they won't be flash rich, more's the pity, but comfortable enough to take stock, for both of them to set up something here and have more babies. 'If not now, *when*?' he teases. And Jessie kisses him, tastes the mints he sucked on the train on his tongue. 'Wait,' he says, pulling away. 'I got you this.' He slips something small and hard into her hand, folds her fingers over it.

She looks down, opens her palm. A gold pendant figure, an exact match to the one on her necklace, the one Will bought after Romy's birth. 'I can't,' she whispers, covering her mouth with her hand. 'Bella will hang me by it.'

'Bella chose it,' Will says. Standing behind her, he lifts Jessie's hair and threads the pendant on to the chain at her neck. At first it feels odd, two figures swinging in the dip of her clavicle. Then it feels right. She has two daughters, not one. When she touches it, her skin has already warmed the gold.

16

I get up very early, leaving my beloved Billy buried in sleep — no one sleeps as deeply as a plantsman. After feeding our dogs, emptying the car of our young grandsons' carelessly discarded, festering football boots, I drive away, relishing the silence, inhaling the dawn-damp spring air. The cottage, our nest in the woods, shrinks in the mirror. Ahead, the open, empty lane. The hedgerows are foliated with tiny tits, sparkling with dew. Cow parsley is starting to foam now. Sap rising. At the crossroads, I take the road into the valley, the one I normally avoid, to Cornton Hall.

Where will I find Harry Gore, if not there?

As I pull up outside, my pulse thickens. The scaffolding that has caged Cornton for months has gone, revealing stone buffed to the colour of clotted cream, decades of ivy skinned away. CCTV cameras. Two expensive cars in the drive. It is a different house, a different age, most of the old county families like the Gores long gone. But Cornton's windows still wink at me in the watery sunshine, and I fancy I can feel a little of the presence of the beautiful young man with the leonine eyes who swam along the river with me one stifling summer afternoon many years ago. I think of the kingfisher, that bomb of blue, the hot-air balloon dangling over our heads, like a planet. I see the life Harry was destined to inherit, quite how far he fell. Time compresses. My eyes fill with tears.

Houses are never just houses, I'm quite sure of this now. We leave particles behind, dust and dreams, fingerprints on buried wallpapers, our tread in the wear of the stairs. And we take bits of the houses with us. In my case, a love of the smell of wax polish on sun-warmed oak, late-summer sunlight filtering through stained glass. We grow up. We stay the same. We move away but we live for ever where we were most alive.

For Harry, I think, that was Cornton Hall. For me it was Applecote Manor, during that delirious heatwave of 1959. Moll, Perry and Moppet are all just bones now, but while Sybil remained stubbornly hanging on at Applecote, something of those heady summer days was preserved, like the fruit of old harvests in one of Moll's jams. After Applecote finally sold and the Tuckers moved in, I saw that the house deserved a new family, a new chance at happiness. And I started to pray that the past would stay buried. This seemed entirely possible. So much time had passed, the world of the fifties a nostalgic memory, a Sunday-night TV show. But it turns out that the past — and, bizarrely, Dot's spectacles, Bella tells me — was never far beneath the surface of the soil here, rising and falling with the water table itself. And, like the stones, the crater in the meadow, the past somehow holds its form. Only its meaning changes.

★　★　★

We didn't dare tell Ma when she reclaimed us that morning, lured back to London by Jack. Only Tom knew: Flora refused to keep it from the man she still calls her soulmate. He tried to reassure us that Harry would find it very difficult to prove we had anything to do with his eye — let alone a charge of attempted murder — since there were no witnesses but we four nicely spoken girls. Rationally, this made sense. But reason has little to do with fear: the power Harry wielded over us, me in particular, hard to comprehend now, an incantation forged in the mythic heat.

Harry was dangerous, damaged. I was petrified that he'd wreak revenge on Dot if I broke our pact of silence. I dreamed of him most nights, jolting up in bed in a grease of sweat. And he moved, deliberately, I think, in overlapping London circles afterwards, staying close, unable to cut loose either — easy enough since Flora absconded from finishing school in Paris, declaring herself 'already perfectly finished', and wed Tom on a snowy morning in early 1961 while he was on leave. Harry even came to Flora's wedding, sitting sullenly with his aloof rich parents in Chelsea Register Office, as handsome as ever from one side, before turning to shoot us down with that frozen bloodshot eye.

It wasn't just his eye. It was the bloat of his face, the news that he'd dropped out of Oxford, spent his time pushing cards across the baize tables of Mayfair clubs and sleazy Cannes casinos, his nostrils crusted with cocaine, a different woman on his arm every night. It was the loss of early promise, his freckled boyish beauty. Worse, far worse, I discovered that, despite all he'd done, I still secretly longed for him. I couldn't forget the tenderness with which he'd kissed the backs of my raw knees, those sticky summer nights in my sixteenth year when I'd lain in my bed, twisted in sheets and desire, the woman in me awakening.

I'd seek out experiences with other men that echoed my first sexually meaningful encounter. They rarely ended well. While my sisters built upon the confidence, that violent widening of our own expectations, that that terrible summer's night bestowed upon us, and moved on — Pam to medical school, Dot to study English at Cambridge, Flora and Tom to California with flowers in their hair and armfuls of babies — I, like Harry, struggled to find a direction, or a steady partner, scraping by on a series of jobs in auction houses, bars and galleries, unable to settle, living and fighting with Ma in Chelsea, or sharing dreary rooms in Earls Court with other drifting sixties single girls like me: I was always circling around the summer of 1959 in my mind, round and round, like a falcon over the meadow, trying to make sense of it.

Then, the day Harry died in 1966, that bird fell out of the sky. A winding coastal road outside Cannes. A sharp bend. Harry, drunk, driving too fast. A twist of hot metal.

Something in me, taut for so long, stretched to capacity, just snapped.

Pam discovered me shaking in the dark of my bedsit. Ma refused to let her call a doctor, terrified of the electric shocks they'd jolted through Pa's skull all those years before. She wanted me home even though, scandalously, Jack was living there then, his infidelities brought to heel. So I was installed in my old bedroom, like a mad woman in the attic, far above the now fashionable Chelsea streets that teemed with optimistic youth, glorious girls in mini-skirts up to their hips.

I did not recognize myself. But Ma never once told me to pull myself together. She simply sat with my sadness, stroking my hair as I laid my head in her lap. My sisters rarely left my side. But I felt like a burden, a leftover from another — bleak post-war — decade, nothing to do with the fulfilment they were experiencing, the excitement bubbling up on London's streets. I wanted to disappear. But my sisters wouldn't let me. And then Dot wrote to Sybil.

My aunt braved the swinging metropolis alone — the last time she'd done it rationing had just ended. I knew exactly how hard that journey must have been for her, and I never forgot it. My most vivid memory of that time is of stumbling downstairs to find her — wearing her outdated church 'best', clutching her crocodile handbag — rigid on Ma's chaise-longue, open-mouthed at the sight of Jack, who was striding around the house bare-chested with a paintbrush between his teeth. It was on that first visit that I decided to tell Sybil the truth, my pact with Harry now finally over. My sisters agreed, and waited outside the door, ready to stick her together again.

Of course, Sybil didn't believe a word of it: everyone knew Harry had grown from a sweet boy into a rogue and a druggy liar, she said. Audrey was going to come home one day and that was the end of it. And she didn't want me upsetting her husband, or myself, with this gossip, or for me ever to mention it again. She visited London a couple of times after that, accompanied by Perry, who, to Ma's great annoyance, got on like a house on fire with Jack — they'd get roaring drunk and sing Nancy Sinatra's 'These Boots Are Made For Walkin''. But Sybil never mentioned what I'd told her about Harry. And neither did I.

If Harry's death shattered me, it was finally telling Sybil the truth — even though she refused to believe it, and I'd got it wrong — that put me together again. The moment the words were out, Harry's pact broken, I no longer felt that my brain was bursting out of my skull. Slowly, I began to think about the hour after that one, the next day, the next week. The skin at the backs of my knees started to heal, the rashes never to return.

Yearning to feel grass between my toes, smell rain falling on a fresh clean river, I took up Sybil's offer of a restorative stay at Applecote, a house I hadn't bothered to visit for years, wrapped up in my own crashing affairs. As I drove apprehensively through its gates, wondering if I was making yet another mistake, there was Billy standing on tiptoe, tying the baby-pink roses to trellis. A man I'd returned to in my thoughts many times during those intervening years, something between us left unfinished. The front of his T-shirt had ridden up, revealing the hard ridges of his stomach, like sand on a beach as the tide goes out. And I knew.

* * *

Ma didn't live for ever, as we all thought she would, although she outlived Jack by twenty years. We gathered around as her body failed, firing questions before it was too late. Was Pa's accident really an accident? 'Oh, yes, darling,' she wheezed, and I realized that, like Sybil with Audrey, Ma would always stick doggedly to her own version of events and curate our family history. Why has Dot grown to look so uncannily like Jack? 'I suppose it is just possible he was her father,' Ma finally conceded. She squeezed Dot's hand. 'I'm tired, darling. Let's talk when I'm better.' But she didn't get better. We laid her to rest in an emerald-green gown next to Pa. We miss her still. But as I pull away from Cornton Hall, leaving the last traces of Harry behind, the Margot who once loved him, and head out of the valley on the road home, I think how much easier this afternoon will be without her.

Ma always loathed goodbyes.

* * *

Billy meets me with a cup of tea. He guesses where I've been. We stand there, holding each other, his large, rough hands delicately cupping my face, and I think how my younger self would

341

have been incredulous that you can be grey and wrinkled and still in love.

After a pasta lunch I'm far too nervous to eat, I scout around our spring garden for just the right posy — a greeny-white tulip, fern leaves — and bind it in kitchen twine. I pull on an elegant dress — if one is born plain one must compensate by dressing well (Ma imprinted that on me) — but flat shoes. I stack the cakes carefully in the boot.

As Billy drives away, I glance anxiously out of the window at the trees bending, their leaves rattling. We could have done without the gusting wind.

Paul, Sybil's favourite nurse, meets us at the entrance of the care home — 'The dispatch centre,' Pam wickedly calls it — a modern, ugly building that we chose for its kind staff and well-tended gardens. He runs me quickly through Sybil's state of health, which changes hourly, suspended precariously in the twilight zone of her great age: she's well this afternoon, had a reasonable night and, yes, a little lunch. She's been very quiet but seems to grasp what it all means. (Unlike the letters: 'What letters, dear?' I remain wholly unconvinced by her amnesia about those, even knowing the way her memory loops and weaves.) Paul pats my arm. 'It's the right thing, Margot,' he reassures me.

God, I hope he's right.

Sybil seems quite cheerful. She is already in her wheelchair, organized for an outing, a crocheted blanket tucked over her knees and, on top of the blanket, her trusty crocodile handbag, just in case. Her hair — what remains of it — has been specially set into wispy spun-sugar curls by one of the nurses. Seeing me and Billy, she lights up and presses her twisted hands on the arms of the wheelchair, forgetting that she can no longer lift her own feather weight. Since the news broke, the transparent parchment of her skin has shrunk even tighter over her skeleton, so her body looks mummified, every vein and bone visible. She is much closer to the end. The fight — the maternal force that kept her going all these years — has completely gone. She sleeps a lot now, asleep far more than awake, like the time between ticks lengthening as an old pocket watch runs down.

'All ready, Sybil?' Billy manoeuvres the wheelchair forward.

She clutches her handbag, bunching the bulbs of her knuckles. 'I've been ready a long time, Billy dear.'

★　★　★

Billy tucks the sapling into the Applecote soil, a crab apple that sings out each spring with ballerina-pink blossom. I picture its roots sucking up the rich water that rises here in the Wilderness, where the old well once tunnelled deep into the earth; Audrey and I dangling from a branch, the clamp of skin and moss; Ma on a chaise-longue in Chelsea, blossom drifting across the drawing-room floor. So many things. All connected. Still connecting. Not quite finished.

My sisters and I daren't look at one another.

343

We cry at everything, these days. Laugh at the wrong moments too, a particular risk this afternoon since the five red helium balloons — one for Audrey and each of us, eager for the flight Audrey once dreamed of — are snapping madly on their strings in the high wind, Pam struggling to control them. While Romy, our sweet uninvited guest, escaped from the house, is standing by the wheelchair, peering at Sybil with grave fascination, as if my aunt were a museum exhibit she's forbidden to touch.

'What does this little girl think of the tree?' Sybil asks, as the wind cracks the blanket on her lap.

Romy considers this surprising question from the relic, fiddles with the pocket of her blue pinafore. 'Not big.'

'Little is nice too,' Sybil says. 'Like you.'

'Romy not little.'

'No. I'd say you're just right.' Sybil smiles. She is reaching out to touch Romy's cheek when Jessie runs up, flustered.

'I'm so, so sorry. You gatecrasher, Romy! Come here.' She scoops up her adorable little girl and carries her through the budding green trees back to the house. Sybil stares after them longingly, her smile fading. The wind blows harder. The balloon strings tangle in Pam's excitable grey hair.

'Bloody things,' Pam mutters, clicking her tongue like Ma.

Flora laughs. 'Just give them to me, Pam.'

'No, no, I can manage.' Pam sniffs. 'I'm hardly going to lift off the ground.' She grips the strings in her fist and yanks them hard, like the leads of her unruly terriers. 'Let's get on with it, shall we, Margot?'

'Good idea. I can no longer feel my toes.' Flora stepped off the plane an hour late, still dressed for California in white linen and gold sandals.

'I did warn you, Flora.' Pam glances down approvingly at her own navy wool coat and sensible boots. 'You do have a short memory.'

'Not that short,' Flora replies softly. And we all nod, silent for a moment, knowing exactly what she means. It still feels like yesterday. It still lives inside us.

Billy pushes the wheelchair through the gate and across the meadow grass where it jams on tussocks, careers into dips. After a few blustery minutes, we pause on a plateau, not venturing as far as the stones in case Sybil's wheelchair gets truly stuck, a permanent addition to their circle. The others wait solemnly as Dot and I walk over to the grassy crater and lay the posy of flowers for Moll. When we return Sybil's eyes are shut.

'Asleep,' mouths Pam, unnecessarily.

'Look. The buttercups are out, Sybil!' I yell into her hearing aid.

Sybil's milky eyes open slowly, taking in, probably for the last time, the blur of windswept meadow that Audrey so loved, that meeting of grass and a sky filled with swallows, returning for another summer.

My sisters and I edge closer together, just touching. Squinting into the sunshine, I can still see us exactly as we were, unknowingly lovely and lithe-limbed, shedding our summer dresses, our English modesty, whooping, running bare-foot into the moon-cut river, that wild night, the rest of our lives, unaware of the moment's preciousness, its glittering fragility. And I am overwhelmed by tenderness for us all. So too, I think, is Pam, who wriggles out of her warm coat and slides it over Flora's shoulders.

'Where's the little girl gone, Margot?' Sybil says suddenly.

We look down to see our aunt, peaceful a moment ago now agitated, glancing around as if she's misplaced something terribly important. 'My little girl was here, I'm quite sure of it.'

I exchange alarmed glances with my sisters. Don't let Sybil muddle Audrey with the little blonde Tucker girl. Not today.

'I want to see her again.' Sybil's eyes start to swim with tears.

'Oh, Sybil, you will,' Flora says kindly, smoothing the blanket over our aunt's lolly-stick legs. But it is no good.

'Where's she gone, Margot?' Sybil sobs through the claw of her hand. 'Where's my little girl gone?'

'Help,' I whisper to Billy, starting to panic.

Billy — the person Sybil trusts most in the world, who battled the dreaded black spot on her beloved roses — bends down and mutters something to Sybil, which we cannot catch. Sybil stills. Dot squeezes my hand. We hold our breath.

Billy runs back to the house and, a few minutes later, reappears at the meadow gate with the young family, their pup. I start to get an inkling of his idea. But Romy is reluctant, belting an arm around Bella's leg. Her parents can't seem to persuade her. I feel time ticking by, Sybil's distress, the afternoon falling apart. It is Bella who saves it, taking Romy's hand and leading her out to us. Pam bends down — knees cracking — and offers the balloons. Romy hesitates.

'Go on,' Bella smiles. And I see it pipe silently between them, that secret language of sisters. Not taking her eyes off Bella, Romy slowly lifts her right hand and closes it around the tangle of strings.

Sybil watches all this intently, the little girl centred in her shadow-edged circular field of vision as if through a monocle. I'm not sure whether she sees Audrey or Romy now. Only that it doesn't matter any more.

At a nod from Bella, Romy starts to run, wind at her back, a streak of blue dress, surging red balloons. A girl, unvanished. Like she just might fly. In the centre of the stone circle, she spins — once, twice — then stars open her hand, laughing, setting us free.

Acknowledgements

I'm incredibly grateful to everyone who cheered on *The Vanishing of Audrey Wilde* — from the first seed of an idea to The End — especially my brilliant editor Maxine Hitchcock at Michael Joseph and my wonderful agent Lizzy Kremer at David Higham Associates. Also Harriet Moore, Alice Howe, Emma Jamison, Claire Bush, Gaby Young, Eve Hall and Hazel Orme — I feel very lucky to work with you all. A special thank you to Deirdre Bryan-Brown — a treasured friend of my late grandmother — who had me rapt with her tales of upper-class girls in the fifties, and demonstrated a very impressive deb's curtsy in the pub; to my three children, for putting up with me writing all the time and reminding me simply that 'the best books are the ones you can't stop reading'. And Ben: I couldn't have done it without you.

We do hope that you have enjoyed reading this large print book.

Did you know that all of our titles are available for purchase?

We publish a wide range of high quality large print books including:
Romances, Mysteries, Classics
General Fiction
Non Fiction and Westerns

Special interest titles available in large print are:
The Little Oxford Dictionary
Music Book
Song Book
Hymn Book
Service Book

Also available from us courtesy of Oxford University Press:
Young Readers' Dictionary
(large print edition)
Young Readers' Thesaurus
(large print edition)

For further information or a free brochure, please contact us at:
Ulverscroft Large Print Books Ltd.,
The Green, Bradgate Road, Anstey,
Leicester, LE7 7FU, England.
Tel: (00 44) 0116 236 4325
Fax: (00 44) 0116 234 0205

Other titles published by Ulverscroft:

THE WELL OF ICE

Andrea Carter

December in Glendara, Inishowen, and solicitor Benedicta 'Ben' O'Keeffe is working flat out; the one bright spot on her horizon is spending her first Christmas with Sergeant Tom Molloy. But on a trip to Dublin, she runs into Luke Kirby — the man who killed her sister — freshly released from jail. He appears remorseful; but as he walks away, he whispers something that chills her to the bone. Back in Glendara, there is chaos. The Oak pub has burned down and Carole Kearney, the Oak's barmaid, has gone missing. Then on Christmas morning, while out walking, Ben and Tom make a gruesome discovery: a body lying face down in the snow. Who is behind this vicious attack on Glendara and its residents? Ben tries to find answers, but is she the one in danger?